THE
SAINT
PATRICK'S
DAY
HERO

THE
SAINT
PATRICK'S
DAY
HERO

A Novel

DOUG MAYFIELD

GRENDEL'S FEN PRESS

GRENDEL'S FEN PRESS

Published in the United States in 2021
by Grendel's Fen Press and distributed by
Itasca Books
5120 Cedar Lake Road
Minneapolis, Minnesota 55416
Phone: (952) 345-4488 / (800) 901-3480 x118
Fax: (952) 920-0541

"Separation" by W. S. Merwin from *The Second Four Books of Poems*.
Copyright © 1993 by W. S. Merwin. Reprinted with the permission of
Copper Canyon Press (Port Townsend, Washington) and
The Wylie Agency, Inc. (New York and London).

Library of Congress Publication Data
Name: Mayfield, Doug, author
Title: *The Saint Patrick's Day Hero*
Publisher: Grendel's Fen Press, 2021

Identifiers
LCCN: 2020910272
ISBN: 9781733316903 (paperback)
ISBN: 9781733316910 (ebook)

Subject
BISAC - FIC000000 FICTION / General; FIC019000 FICTION / Literary;
FIC027020 FICTION / Romance / Contemporary

Published in the United States of America
1 3 5 7 9 8 6 4 2

Book cover and layout design by *the*BookDesigners
www.bookdesigners.com

For Sally

All things are atoned for, all things are saved by love. Love is such a priceless treasure that you can redeem the whole world by it.

—Fyodor Dostoevsky, *The Brothers Karamazov*

Acknowledgments

The adage tells us that it takes a village to raise a child. But it also takes a village—or at least a sizable support staff—to write a novel. Among those indispensable to the process are trusted readers, like my friends Mike and Peggi Beseres, Liz Hassler, Linda Bird, and my beta reader, Mary Bird. These are people with remarkable instincts, people on whom I could inflict various drafts of this novel with confidence, knowing that I would receive honest, high-quality feedback.

The Saint Patrick's Day Hero, while hardly a courtroom drama, turns on a number of legal issues, and I want to thank my friend and former student, David Harrington, for helping me navigate what was often difficult and unfamiliar terrain.

I would also like to thank Jim and DeAnna Baratto—Jim for his help and suggestions regarding the novel's assorted construction projects and DeAnna for her willingness to wade through the interminable first draft of what would, years later, become *The Saint Patrick's Day Hero*.

Once again, I want to thank my editor, Marna Poole, for performing what might be described as a literary exorcism on my work. Marna and I were paired by a publisher in 2011, and we've been working together ever since.

I want to give a very special thank-you to my wife, Sally, who has as much time into this project as I do, perhaps even more. Without her love, guidance and support, *The Saint Patrick's Day Hero* would still be languishing on the hard drive of my computer.

Finally, I would be remiss if I did not acknowledge Gail and Steve Bauer, owners of Royale Shepherds in Fort Gratiot, Michigan. I cannot thank them enough for breeding such wonderful dogs.

CHAPTER 1

Amongst the Lakes and Pines

WILLIAM PARKS HIS OLD WAGONEER in the same place he's parked for years—in the lot across the commons from his office in Dewhurst Hall, otherwise known as the English building. Most of the buildings at Lothrup College bear the names of eponymous donors, but even so, they are almost always referred to by discipline—*math* building, *science* building, *psych* building. William attributes this to unabashed Midwestern practicality, the benchmark by which all things at Lothrup are measured.

According to its website, Lothrup College is "an outstanding four-year liberal arts college nestled amongst the lakes and pines in Chambliss, Minnesota." Before he went crazy, William thought that they/Lothrup/somebody ought to replace *amongst* with *among*, the former being both archaic and British, but he couldn't find anyone to speak to about it. The Chancellor's Office suggested he contact PR, who referred him to HR, who sent him to IT, who didn't give a shit. Finally, William emailed the putative author herself, a lady over in Admissions named Marlene, who had served on the now-defunct website committee. The subject of his message was "Amongst," and it read, "Prithee, it behooves us, methinks, to replace that antiquated word anon, lest we like tomfools look."

Marlene's reply was the epitome of concision: "William, don't be an ass." Because there is so much William doesn't remember, he wonders why he remembers that. But that's how it works—bits and pieces. There's no sense to it.

William is ten paces from his car, about to check his pockets for the keys, when he finds them still in his hand. Since he was placed on suspension, he no longer has a current window sticker for faculty parking, but the campus police know his car, and so far, they haven't hassled him about it. It's funny, he thinks. He doesn't have a parking sticker, but he still has an active key card to Dewhurst and an office—even office hours. That was Chancellor Gardner's doing, and although it seems like the hearing was a million years ago, it's only been four months.

William had been impressed that all the big shots showed up: Chancellor Gardner, of course, but also the vice chancellor, the provost, the academic dean, the president of Student Affairs (along with the vice president of Student Affairs) and some apparatchik from the teachers' union, supposedly on his side, who opened his mouth only once to suggest that the hearing was in possible violation of Section 13D.01, Subdivision 1(b) of Minnesota's Open Meeting Law. Everyone else had plenty to say, and there was a good deal of gaseous harrumphing. But in the end it was all up to Gardner, and he didn't pull any punches.

"To say that I'm disappointed in you, Dr. Kessler, understates the case considerably. And to be honest, were it not for your heroism during Lothrup's ... darkest hours, I would not hesitate to ask for your resignation." Gardner had almost slipped up and said *campus shooting*, but he caught himself in time to come up with a serviceable euphemism. "But as it is, and in light of your personal tragedy, I'm not sure *what* to do with you." He had then paused for effect and looked around the room. "So I am recommending that we continue to monitor your situation and defer the final disposition of this matter until the end of the year. At that time, we will meet again and review your suspension. Suffice it to say, in the interim we expect your conduct to be exemplary."

Gardner looked at William, who, not knowing if he was supposed to speak, made a noncommittal nod, as though he were listening to a neighbor's plans for the weekend.

Then Gardner surprised him. "Although you will not be teaching,

Kessler, we want you to resume seeing students in an advisory capacity, which means you are to maintain regular office hours and continue to assist those students currently assigned to you."

William still doesn't understand that little codicil—they dump his teaching assignment on his colleagues while insisting that he retain his advisees. But he knows it's a test. Everything is a test.

After that, the hearing wrapped up quickly, and Gardner, clearly believing he had handed down a judicial remedy worthy of Solomon, closed his briefcase and again turned to William. "Is this arrangement acceptable, Dr. Kessler?"

"Yes, sir." William, now halfway across the parking lot, looks around to see who may have heard him. In some ways, he's surprised that Lothrup would even allow him to set foot on campus. Then again, it isn't as though he killed somebody or, God forbid, slept with a student. He just had a breakdown. William realizes this is a huge oversimplification, but it doesn't matter because he's much better now. In fact, he could have taught this semester if they'd let him, but they're scared shitless, afraid he'll go over the hoorah ridge again and ... well, who knows? William worries about that too, so he can sympathize with Lothrup up to a point. But enough already—he may have a flashback now and then, but he can definitely do the job.

As he heads across the commons to his office, William can't help thinking how much he enjoys it, even in times like these. He could park behind Dewhurst Hall, like the rest of the English Department faculty, but no matter what the season, he loves to walk across Lothrup's commons, a three-acre greensward ringed with red maples and bound by a cobblestone promenade that is often featured on the cover of *Lothrup College Magazine*. On one side of the commons are academic buildings and on the other, the student union and four dorms.

Spring has come early, and the air, already redolent of lilac, is filled with the liquid contralto of red-winged blackbirds and the rich whistles of orioles that ordinarily wouldn't show up for another month. And in the commons, where students were making snowmen a few short weeks ago and practicing kick turns on their skis, there are now lovers holding hands, sunbathers on blankets and Frisbees everywhere.

Minnesota has the best springs because it has the worst winters, William thinks. "It's all relative."

When he reaches Dewhurst, William waves his key card at the little box next to the door, and once it determines he's legit, it says so with a buzzing thunk and lets him in. From the outside, Dewhurst isn't much to look at. In fact, its ho-hum facade is the very essence of Lothrup's let's-not-get-carried-away-here philosophy. But inside, Dewhurst is quite lovely and so new it still smells of fresh paint. Its ambience is modernist—lots of glass and steel—and like most new millennium academic buildings, it has surprising amplitude, as well as a large atrium, like a shopping mall. But what William enjoys most about Dewhurst are the murals, the colorful die-cut scenes that adorn the walls, each one illustrating an aspect of Minnesota life or history: the 1980 Miracle on Ice, Mary Tyler Moore throwing her tam in the air, the open-pit iron mine in Hibbing, a loon, a deer, a bear, the 1987 Twins, a walleye about to gobble some minnows.

William picks up his mail, climbs a flight of stairs without seeing anyone and heads down the hallway to his office. When he gets to Paul Bunyan, he has arrived. He lets himself in, hangs his jacket in the closet and sits down at his desk. It's good to be here, he thinks, but he feels like a kid who's just sneaked into a ball game or otherwise put one over on somebody. A lot of this is because he sees only one or two students a day, tops. If he had classes, students would be lined up at his door. But as it is, not so much.

The first thing William does is go through his mail, which today takes less than a minute. There is a notice from *The Atlantic* that his subscription is about to expire; a professional copy of *Daisy Miller*, which William hasn't taught for years; a brochure about an annuity that supposedly puts the competition to shame; and, because it's Thursday, a copy of the *Beacon*, Lothrup's weekly newspaper, which William sets aside to read later.

After the mail, William settles in and looks at the two photographs on his desk. The one on the right is a candid shot of him and Kate, his firstborn. William has no idea who took the picture, but it was taken in the church narthex moments before he walked Kate down the aisle at her wedding. Kate looks happy and beautiful, and she is saying something to William like, "Remember to say it loud, Daddy—*Her mother and I do.*"

The other photo is a black-and-white portrait of William's son, Jon, sitting on a flight of stairs, his elbows on his knees. Jon's hands are clasped together near his face, and he's smiling, though not directly into the camera. William's ex-wife, Marcia, had taken that picture the week before Jon reported to San Diego for basic training. It is a good picture for a lot of reasons, and William thinks it's the perfect illustration of Aristotle's concept of Universal Truth, inasmuch as someone who had never met Jon would know, just by looking at the photo, that he possessed such universal qualities as honesty, kindness and a sense of humor. Few photographs could do that. Not even a painting could guarantee it. Jon had been killed two years ago during the campus shooting, and William misses him terribly.

William holds his hands out in front of him, palms down, and there is a slight tremor in the fingers. But he knows what to do. He turns on his computer and after spending a couple of minutes in CNN's archives, begins to type. He bangs away on his keyboard as though he is punishing it for something; then he leans back and reads what he has written.

19 April 2012

Dear President Obama:

Since June 22, 2011, you have stated repeatedly that the United States will withdraw its forces from Afghanistan by the end of 2014, at which time, you say, "[T]he Afghan people will be responsible for their own security."[1]

I respectfully submit that nothing will be achieved by the end of 2014 that has not been achieved already, and for that reason, logic compels us to withdraw our troops immediately. I understand that you campaigned on this war and profess to believe in it, but by my count, twenty-four empires, including ours, have attempted to conquer Afghanistan, but only Alexander the Great succeeded—and he did so in 335 BC. So the odds are not in our favor, Mr. President, as the horrifying increase in green-on-blue attacks attests.

Please bring our troops home now.

Respectfully yours,

William Kessler

---

[1] https://obamawhitehouse.archives.gov/the-press-office/2011/06/22/remarks-president-way-forward-afghanistan/stay-the-course

William isn't sure about the footnote. It seems a bit much, but he's spent a professional lifetime preaching the virtues of documentation, so he leaves it in. "Looks good," he says. He holds his hands out in front of him again. *Much better.* He then places the letter in a folder on his computer desktop that contains 186 letters, which, like his Obama letter, will never be mailed to anyone.

When he had asked Dr. Spurling if all this letter writing was a good thing or a bad thing, the doctor had stroked his goatee thoughtfully and said it was excellent therapy to write letters—even to people like the president—provided he didn't mail them. "We don't want the Secret Service showing up at your door, William, ha ha ha." Back then, William was writing two and sometimes three letters a day. But he doesn't write nearly that many now, which he takes as a sign that he's better.

William checks his email. There are half a dozen messages but only three that interest him. One is from his buddy Marvin Kreitzer. "Looking forward to the fishing opener. Please call me. Marv." Another is from Kate. The subject is "Reminder." It reads, "Happy birthday, Daddy! You've turned off your phone again. Don't forget you're coming for dinner tonight. BTW, Todd and I have a BIG SURPRISE for you! Love, Kate." Below Kate's name is the Bible verse that she has affixed to her signature for the month: *I can do all things through Him who strengthens me.*

April 19 … William wonders how the hell you forget your own birthday. Leave it to Kate to remind him, though—bless her born-again soul. William dislikes surprises of any sort, so he is naturally apprehensive about the *big* one that Kate referred to. He worries that she's invited one of her female coworkers tonight for his doubtful benefit. Oh, well—whatever it is, he'll find out soon enough. He turns on his phone and types a five-word response to Kate: "Thanks. Looking forward to it."

The third email is from his friend Sam Richter, who rose from the ranks of the English Department to become Lothrup's academic dean. "Please come see me" is all it says. William types a three-word email to Sam: "How about now?" He hits SEND and waits. Not fifteen seconds later, a response arrives: "Now is god." William smiles at the typo. *First Kate and now you.*

William puts his jacket on and is heading for the door when his phone rings. It's Todd, Kate's husband. Todd and William are genuinely fond of each other, but William has never met anyone as decent and high-minded as Todd, and that makes him uneasy at times. Todd is a counselor at LiveRight Health Center, a nonprofit tri-county operation that, among other things, helps people deal with a wide variety of chemical and mental health issues. As a clinical psychologist, Todd could make a lot of money in the private sector, but he's more interested in helping people, so that's what he does.

"I would've bet your phone would be off," Todd says. "Happy birthday!"

"Thanks. I just turned it on. Is anything wrong?"

"No, not at all. Kate just wanted me to call and remind you about tonight."

"She already did. Please tell her I'm not *that* addlepated." William switches to his warm-and-friendly voice. "So … Todd … what's the big surprise you and Kate have planned for me?"

Todd makes a clucking sound of disapproval. "Not a chance, William. I don't even want to *think* about what Kate would do to me if I let that slip. See you tonight. Bye."

William turns off his phone. He has his jacket on, so he knows he was going somewhere. Right! He was on his way over to see Sam about … Sam never said, did he?

CHAPTER 2

The Asshole of the Universe

WILLIAM DECIDES TO WALK to Wellstone Hall, otherwise known as the administrative building. It's a long way from Dewhurst, but on a morning like this, walking is a pleasure. On the day of the shooting, a young SWAT officer was killed on the sidewalk in front of Wellstone, and William has trained himself not to look at the place where he lay, covered with a coroner's yellow sheet. He was the last victim, and he had been shot by the second shooter, who was killed trying to gain access to the building. At the time of the shooting, the media had been reluctant to use the names of the gunmen, referring to them instead as "first shooter" and "second shooter." These designations, which denoted the order in which the shooters had been killed, caught on, and most people, including William, still referred to them in this way.

The second shooter had emptied two magazines at Wellstone Hall, and a number of bullets had struck the big columns on either side of the main entrance. The columns had been repainted and the holes filled with something, but you could still see them. Bullets had also struck the brickwork behind the columns, and although the spalled brick had been replaced, the new ones had a slightly different texture that made them easy to spot if you knew where to look.

When William gets there, Sam's new secretary is on the phone, but she waves him right in. The moment Sam sees him, he jumps up from behind his desk and makes for William like a hungry grizzly. "There he is," Sam roars, "the Saint Patrick's Day hero! Jesus, it's good to see you. Get over here."

"Please don't call me that—you're going to hug me now, aren't you?" William is less than thrilled at the prospect.

"I haven't seen you since the Christmas party, you outlaw." And sure enough, Sam throws his arms around William and gives him a big double-fist back tap. "It's been way too long, William. What can I get you?" He points to a half-eaten Danish roll on his desk. "How about one of these?"

"No, thank you. I just—"

"Have a seat. How have you been?"

There are two oxblood leather chairs in front of Sam's desk. William puts his jacket on one and sits in the other. "I'm doing fine, Sam—couldn't be better." William trusts Sam as much as he trusts anyone, but that isn't saying much, not these days. Sam is his friend, but he is also a hotline to Chancellor Gardner, and William knows it. There are a number of people like Sam who, William suspects, are keeping a watchful eye on him for the higher-ups. But as long as he remembers that, there won't be any problems.

"So what's on your mind, Sam?"

"Nothing. I just wondered how things are going. Are your advisees showing up?"

William nods. "A few. I wasn't sure they would since I'm not teaching this semester, but business is definitely improving." William gestures to a window, which Sam has propped open with a three-hole punch. "Spring is early this year, which means our students have already begun thinking about summer school, changing their majors, running off to Tibet to join a Buddhist monastery—the usual stuff."

"How's Marcia? Are you still separated?"

William looks at Sam closely. "Divorced. I thought I told you."

Sam shakes his head. "I would have remembered."

William is still hopelessly in love with his wife and dislikes all questions about the status of his marriage, but he feels this one is fair. Sam has known both of them a long time. In fact, William learned, through the friend of a friend, that Sam, who is also divorced, had asked Marcia out during their separation, but she wasn't interested. She had other irons in the fire, but William isn't sure how much Sam knows.

"Marcia moved to Phoenix with her dentist over a year ago—with *our* dentist, actually. Do you know Walter Burke?"

Sam looks disappointed. "No, I ... I don't think so. Is he a good guy?"

William shrugs. "He isn't terribly high on *my* list, Sam, but to be fair, our contact is limited—I just look up his nose when he cleans my teeth. I can report that Walter has rather large pores and passable breath. Beyond that, I really couldn't—"

"How about Kate? Is she doing all right?"

"As right as rain. She's getting a little carried away with the God thing, but other than that, she's fine. Have you heard anything about ... my status?"

"You mean about your suspension being lifted? Not a helluva lot. You really screwed the pooch this time, buddy." Sam shakes his head. "Look, I know what you and Marcia went through, and if Jon had been my kid ... well, it would have ruined me. But you can't just decide you're not coming to work anymore, William. You violated your contract and abused the terms and conditions of your leave. Hell, you went so far off the reservation that your own union couldn't defend you. And then, well ... there's that business on the boat." Sam is willing to mention it, but he clearly doesn't want to talk about it.

"It was a ship."

"What?"

"I came unglued on a *ship*."

Sam's eyes open wide. "I don't give a fuck *what* it was. That was some seriously bad publicity for the school, not to mention for you. If it hadn't been for that pissant reporter—what was his name?"

"Bouchard—Paul Bouchard."

"Yeah, if it hadn't been for him and the *Saint Paul Herald*, the whole thing might have stayed on the down-low, but his articles turned you into ..."

"A household name?"

"I was going to say a raving lunatic, but have it your way."

William laughs. "Bouchard actually calls me once in a while."

"I hope you tell him to go fuck himself."

"I do, but he's very persistent. The last time he called he wanted me to comment on that professor in South Carolina, the one who drove his car through the main entrance of the field house after he was suspended for flunking a football player."

"I remember that," Sam says. "The kid was their star running back, and he was ineligible for the playoffs."

"I think it was just one game."

"Yeah, but it was a *bowl* game." Sam steeples his fingers and tries to refocus the conversation. "Look, William, when push comes to shove, you've got my vote, and you probably have the vice chancellor's. As for the rest of them, it's anybody's guess." Sam taps hard on the desk with one finger. "And if the Board of Regents gets involved, there's no telling *what* could happen. Everything depends on your health, William—your *mental* health. So ... how is it?"

"I generally know a hawk from a handsaw, Guildenstern, if that's what you mean."

Sam laughs, but almost immediately his expression becomes serious again. "Have you given any thought to what we talked about on the phone last week? Gardner as much as told me that a little time in *Norge* would go a long way toward expiating your sins."

William rolls his eyes. "Is *that* what you wanted to see me about?"

"Not really, I just—"

"It's like I told you, Sam—I don't care for Oslo, and I have no interest in teaching at Sølberg College. I refuse to live in a country where every building looks like the post office, it's darker than the inside of a goat, and they eat fish 300 days a year." He glowers across the desk. "Jesus Christ! A beer costs fifteen dollars there."

"William, I think you're exaggerating just a—"

"The hell I am. A Big Mac is twelve bucks!"

Lothrup, like most colleges, has a number of foreign study programs that provide its students with opportunities to attend colleges and universities all over the world. The most popular of these programs is the Sister Campus Exchange, a consortium of eighteen colleges, mostly European, that have very close ties with each other, as well as with Lothrup. In practical terms, this means the participating colleges can exchange both students and faculty with a minimum of red tape.

Lothrup's students like the Sister Campus Exchange because it's cheap and because it affords them the opportunity to study abroad without delaying their graduation. The faculty like it—especially the younger professors—because it looks good on a résumé, nobody cares what they teach, and they can migrate from one sister campus to another pretty much as they please. But as far as William is concerned, Sølberg College—more precisely, Oslo—is the asshole of the universe. It's Virgil's underworld, Shakespeare's Mantua and Dante's ninth circle of hell all rolled into one. And Sølberg always needs English-speaking teachers, mostly because Norway is in the middle of nowhere, and a lot of professors don't want to teach there.

William doesn't have anything against the program itself, and there are plenty of places he'd be willing to go, but Sølberg College isn't one of them. That's because he's already been there. In fact, he's the one who got the program up and running in the first place. He hadn't been at Lothrup long and didn't know any better when he was asked if he would be willing to "put the finishing touches on the 'Sølberg Project.'" *I'd be honored*, he'd said, like the ambitious young suck-up that he was.

When William had done everything he could from Minnesota, he went to Oslo for a month to create language labs, establish student and faculty housing, and work out the thorny issues of accreditation. There were also meetings with everyone under the sun, including UNESCO and the Organization for Economic Co-operation and Development. William performed his office with alacrity, crossing every *t* and dotting every *i*. He did a good job— everybody said so—but when he returned from Oslo, he made it clear that he had no desire to participate in the program he had labored so tirelessly to create. He'd had enough of the Land of the Midnight Sun. He told them he might consider Paris or Madrid, some place like that. But Oslo? No fucking way.

"Look, I know how you feel about it," Sam says. "I'm just saying a little sojourn in Norway would smooth a lot of ruffled feathers around here." Sam leans forward, his voice confidential. "We're talking about your career, William—or what's left of it."

William bristles. "I don't give a shit. If Gardner wants me gone, let him fire me. Is Oslo really the best he's got?"

Sam puts his hands in the air. "Goddammit, we happen to need teachers over there, especially good ones like you. Just think about it—that's all I ask." He takes a bite of his Danish and chews thoughtfully. "Are you sure you don't want—"

"I already had breakfast. Thanks."

Sam sweeps some crumbs from his desk with the edge of his hand. "You know, looking back on it, you probably should have accepted the Bloomquist Chair."

William shakes his head. "It wouldn't have been right to accept a reward for what I did, Sam. Besides, how could it matter now?"

The Bloomquist Chair in American Literature was an endowment from Hubert Bloomquist, an alumnus who had graduated back in the early '60s and gone on to become one of the top honchos at Crystal Sugar in Moorhead or Crookston—William could never remember which.

Sam removes his glasses and stares at William. "How could it matter? Are you kidding? The Bloomquist Chair has serious cachet. Gardner could never fire you after you'd received an honor like that."

"Maybe not," William says, "but like you say, an academic endowment is an honor, and it should be awarded for outstanding work—*period.*"

"Jesus Christ, William! If saving students' lives isn't 'outstanding work,' I don't know what is."

"I didn't deserve an award. I didn't deserve *anything.* Can we please drop it?"

The Bloomquist Chair was one of many accolades that William had declined during the heyday of his hero period, the four months following the shooting when he was being lionized by the college, fawned over by the press and acclaimed by TV anchors from coast to coast.

It had been a terribly difficult time for William because he was the only one who knew what really happened that day at Dewhurst—not even Marcia knew the whole story. Not surprisingly, this was the beginning of a great many problems for them as a couple because Marcia recognized that William wasn't telling her everything, but she didn't know what to do about it. She begged William to talk, to let her in, but he had little to say, and it wasn't long before his reticence began to strain what was already a fraught relationship. And by May, William's flashbacks had begun—eidetic hallucinations, accompanied by sounds and smells that were not only horrifying but also indistinguishable from reality. So things were rough back then. But fortunately for William, his hero period came to an abrupt end when he went crazy, which proved something William had long suspected: that crazy trumps just about everything.

"Sure. Take it easy, buddy," Sam says. "Consider the matter dropped." His face suddenly brightens. "Hey, how's the new book coming?"

The question catches William off guard. "How do you know about that?"

"Oh ... I hear things. It's about Tolstoy, right?"

"Dostoevsky. But I haven't even—"

"What drew you to that old Cossack?"

William doesn't know what to say. He would like to answer honestly and tell Sam he was fascinated by Dostoevsky's obsession with guilt, the kind of corrosive, all-consuming guilt that makes even Hawthorne's characters seem happy-go-lucky by comparison. But what he says is, "I'm not sure, Sam. I think it's Dostoevsky's polyphonic narration that really put the hook in me."

Sam laughs. "And I was so sure you'd say it was his Menippean satire."

"That was the other thing." William hesitates, knowing he will appear rude if he doesn't ask. "By the way, Sam ... how are *you* doing?"

Sam takes a deep breath. "Not very well. I've gained thirty-five pounds since the shooting, and after two years, I still sleep with a light on. I also want to marry every woman I meet." Sam tries to smile. "I have no idea what *that's* all about."

"It's been hard on all of us," William says, unable to think of anything meaningful.

The second shooter had fired over twenty rounds through Sam's office windows, and he and his previous secretary had lain prostrate on the floor, certain the shooter would gain access to the building and kill everyone inside. A month later, after working together for ten years, she and Sam had begun an affair that ended both their marriages. William thought their story would have made Freud proud—it was the very essence of Thanatos/Eros duality.

"Yeah, it's been a sonofabitch," Sam says, shuffling some papers on his desk. "And everyone from Gardner on down is still reeling over our loss in appellate court. Jesus, we're now O and 2. If the Minnesota Supreme Court won't hear the case, we're fucked." He looks up at William. "I mean, what if we actually have to pay twelve million dollars?"

William shakes his head. "I don't know, Sam, but we'll need one helluva bake sale."

Fifty-seven people had been killed that day—fifty-three students and four nonstudents, including Jon. Forty-nine of the students' families had accepted the settlement offered by Lothrup's attorneys, but four of the families rejected the offer and brought a wrongful death suit against the college. It was their position that on March 17, 2010, Lothrup's initial active shooter alert was received too late for their children to take the requisite measures that might have saved them. All four of the families had kids who were killed in Dewhurst Hall, and their cell phones, along with dozens of others, indicated that Lothrup's active shooter alert was received on Dewhurst's first floor three minutes later than anywhere else on campus.

The college argued that it sent out active shooter alerts in twenty-seven platforms, including text, Twitter and Instagram, and they were able to prove that they had issued the first alert 182 seconds before the majority of students in Dewhurst Hall had received it. So it was Lothrup's position that if some students, for whatever reason, had failed to receive the first alert at the same time as everyone else, it certainly wasn't the fault of the college.

But in the end, the jury in the Ninth District Court didn't see it that way and found for the families, setting aside a liability cap and awarding them three million dollars each. Lothrup had appealed, but the court of appeals upheld the decision of the lower court, and at that point, Lothrup had no choice but to petition the state supreme court for a hearing. That was nearly three months ago, and the supreme court had not yet indicated whether it was willing to review the case. Understandably, the waiting and uncertainty, along with the two losses in court, had frayed Lothrup's collective nerves.

William tries to be positive. "We'll be okay, Sam. The conventional wisdom is that if the supreme court hears the case, they'll overturn the verdict."

"That's a pretty big *if.* They only take one case in ten. And remember something—just because Virginia Tech got lucky with their supreme court doesn't mean we will."

"When do you think we'll hear something?"

Sam shrugs. "I wish I knew. We filed our certiorari petition the end of January, so we should get word pretty soon."

They talk for a few more minutes about the lawsuit, the unseasonable weather and the Twins' new pitching prospects. Then William stands up and grabs his jacket. "I'm supposed to be in my office, Sam. I'd better get back before Gardner calls to see if I'm there."

Sam accompanies William to the outer office, where he throws an arm around his shoulders. "I'm already looking forward to your book. What does Ruth say?" Ruth Berman is William's agent, and Sam knows her because William introduced the two of them years ago at a book launch party.

"She's okay with a book about Dostoevsky, but she said, 'If you must write about a Russian, why not Pasternak, Ehrenburg or Brodsky?'"

"Russian Jews?"

"Yes, and all great writers."

"I don't know much about Ehrenburg, other than *The Thaw* … Hey, thanks for coming over."

"You asked me to."

"That's because you've become a fucking hermit, and you wouldn't have come otherwise. Am I right?"

"Probably."

"Oh, I almost forgot—Happy birthday!"

William cocks his head. "How did you ... let me guess—you hear things."

"I do. All kinds of things. Stop by once in a while."

William leaves and begins the trek back to Dewhurst. Earlier, it had been clear, but now the sky is dappled with small cumulous clouds, all of them scudding eastward at the same altitude. There's a name for that sky, that particular look, but William can't remember what it is. "It'll come to me," he says. "That's how it works."

William thinks about Sam and smiles. When Sam left the classroom to become an administrator, William had been reasonably sure he wouldn't make it, that he didn't have the right stuff. Sam was clever but rarely brilliant, tough but never ruthless, and he was better at arrogating power than at wielding it. Plus, successful administrators, at least in William's experience, possessed two faculties that Sam didn't have: a highly developed instinct for self-preservation and the ability to see around corners. But Sam was eager, a real go-getter, and the compensatory value of ambition is impossible to calculate.

On the return trip to Dewhurst, William notices the cedar tree that someone had tried to hide behind—a student, a policeman, one of the shooters, perhaps. It had been struck by a bullet that gouged a cigar-sized piece from its trunk. Buildings & Grounds had filled the wound with black tree dressing, but that scar, like so many others, would remain for years.

There was another tree, a little mountain ash, that had to be cut down because a police car that took several bullets to the windshield had jumped the curb and crashed into it. But after Lothrup had buried its dead, the Grounds Committee had a little ceremony and planted a new tree in the same spot, saying that it was a proud symbol of something or other, but William couldn't remember what. Much the same thing had happened to Dewhurst Hall, which had been the epicenter of the carnage—the college simply tore it down and built another Dewhurst Hall in the old footprint. But hardly anyone could bring themselves to call the new building Dewhurst Hall. For a while, they referred to it as Dewey Two, and then, in an inevitable concession to linguistic economy, Dewhurst became *New*hurst—at least to those who felt compelled to call it something other than the English building.

What are the odds? William wonders. What are the odds that Jon would be at Dewhurst that day? Marcia was at work, and Jon, who was home on leave from the Marines, had dropped William off on campus so he could use the Jeep that morning. It was Saint Patrick's Day, and at noon Jon was going to pick William up and take him to lunch at the Chambliss Tap House, where they planned to drink a little green beer. Maybe *a lot* of green beer. Jon was enjoying his new, adult relationship with his father, and that went double for William, who could hardly believe this self-possessed young man, this soldier full of *yes sirs* and *no sirs*, was actually his son.

William looks up suddenly. *A Dutch sky ... that's what it's called.*

CHAPTER 3

The Metaphysical Implications of Quantum Mechanics

SOMEWHERE BETWEEN SAM'S OFFICE and Dewhurst, William's musings are crowded out by thoughts of Dostoevsky and the new book. It will be a lot of work, a lot of research, but that's okay with William, because as far as he is concerned, work is not only one of life's first principles, it is also the chief good. William likes to work. He likes to teach, and he likes to write about people he finds interesting. Unfortunately, the people whom William finds interesting are often of little interest to others, so his books aren't exactly blockbusters.

When Kate was little, she asked, "Daddy, why don't you write a book about somebody famous like Marky Mark or the Spice Girls? Then everybody would buy it and we'd be rich!" William tried to explain that it didn't work that way, but the more he thought about it, the more he realized that was precisely how it worked. But he's doing all right, he thinks. He's written well-received monographs on Kurt Vonnegut, Gary Snyder, J. D. Salinger and Ken Kesey. His most profitable work, however, is an appreciation of Richard Brautigan called *Zen and the Art of Trout Fishing*, which became the basis for a docudrama that had been quite popular in Japan, where Brautigan had lived for a time. William knows it isn't a world-beater résumé, but it's not bad for a professor in a small private college.

When William gets back to Dewhurst, he enters through the front door, climbs a different flight of stairs and finds himself a few paces behind Janice Grant, the manager of Lothrup's campus bookstore. When she reaches Charles Lindbergh and the *Spirit of Saint Louis*, he calls out to her. "Hey, stranger, are you by any chance coming to see me?" There aren't many other places Janice can be going at that point, so William feels safe in asking.

Janice wheels around, surprised and smiling. "I most certainly am. My goodness, William, it's been forever since I saw you last." Janice is a lovely lady who, as far as William knows, has never spoken a cross word to anyone. They talk about the weather for a minute; then Janice clears her throat politely. "I didn't want to call or email you about this, but we haven't received a book order from you this spring." William tries to say something, but she puts up her hand. "No need to explain—I know your situation. I just wanted to tell you that you can call the bookstore any time over the summer, and we'll do whatever it takes to get your students' books here for fall semester. If, you know … you need any."

William is moved by her kindness and tries to thank her, but she won't let him. "It's nothing, really." Janice gazes at the Lindbergh mural. "I don't get over here much. It's very nice, but I'll bet you miss *Old* Dewhurst sometimes." Ninety-three years old at the time of the shooting, "Old" Dewhurst might have been on its last legs, but it was nothing if not charming, with its pressed tin ceilings, marble floors and foot-wide mahogany bannisters.

"I do miss it," William says. "But what I miss the most are the blackboards—they were real slate. Now I have a white board and a bunch of crappy markers that dry up the minute I take the cap off."

"It's the price of progress, William. It's what you pay to be hypoallergenic. Newhurst doesn't have a lecture hall, does it?"

"No," William says. "That's another thing I miss. Every time I walked into the lecture hall at Dewhurst, I half expected to see Professor Kingsfield at the podium, explaining contract law to his first-year students."

"I know what you mean," Janice says. "It had that look."

They do a walk-and-talk the rest of the way to his office, and because he knows that Janice would never spy for anyone, William asks if she would like to come in.

"Sure," Janice says. "I'd love to."

William unlocks the door and opens it for her. "Mi casa es tu casa."

"Wow, nice digs!" Janice says, looking around. "This is a lot nicer than your old office."

"About a million times," William says, "but my old office felt like home."

"This one will too—give it time."

They sit down, and although William is a little out of practice, he does his best to be congenial. "Tell me about your garden, Janice. I'll bet the early spring has you champing at the bit." William knows Janice and her husband are avid gardeners, and he's sure they have hundreds of little seedlings growing under fluorescent lights, probably in the garage, where they await the momentous occasion of their planting.

"You're right, William—I feel like I should already have the garden in—at least the potatoes, beets and carrots. If it weren't for the *Farmers' Almanac*, I probably would."

He enjoys talking to Janice, mostly because it's low-impact—she does all the work, and he doesn't have to say much, other than an occasional *Really?* or *Is that right?* After Janice talks about tomato blight and powdery mildew—topics that truly animate her—she mentions that she and her husband had talked about starting the seedlings in their safe room this year but decided against it.

"It's unused space," Janice says. "But the whole point of having a safe room is so it will be there when you need it. If it's filled up with plants, what good is it?"

William isn't sure he understands. "Is a safe room where you go if …"

"Yes. Exactly," Janice says. "It was terribly expensive—the security door alone cost a fortune—but we don't feel as safe as we used to."

"Who does?" William says. "A safe room is an excellent idea. In fact, I wish I could live in one. I'd wrap it around me like a blanket and never come out."

Janice's eyes fill up, and she tries hard not to cry. "I will never forget that poor little girl, William, not as long as I live. She was dressed in green for Saint Patrick's Day, and when I close my eyes, I can still see the little shamrocks on her scarf." Janice is referring to Amanda Norris, the second-to-last shooting victim. Amanda was from Bismarck, North Dakota. She was nineteen years old, and she had died in Janice's arms in front of the bookstore. No one really expected trouble on the south side of the campus, where the bookstore is, but the shooters had been on motorcycles, and SWAT had trouble containing them.

"It's okay, Janice. I understand."

Janice nods. "I know you do, William. You understand because what you went through that day is a hundred times worse than anything that happened to me, which makes me feel terribly guilty right now."

"There's no reason to feel guilty—absolutely none."

Janice struggles to regain her composure. She lowers her head for a moment and then looks up and changes the subject. "May I ask what you've been doing? You know—when you aren't here."

"Well, I'm thinking about another book," William says, "and I'm a closet carpenter."

Janice gets a funny look on her face. "Oh, you … build closets?"

"No, no. I meant that I have a sort of secret life as a carpenter—it's more of a hobby, actually."

"I see … So what are you building now?"

William tries to boil it down. "Well … about the time Jon started high school, we bought the lot next door to our place. There was an old carriage house on the property, and we began to remodel it with the idea of turning it into an apartment." Already, William wishes he'd gone down a different road, but it's too late. "Then … after Jon was killed, I didn't work on the place for a long time. I just wasn't in the mood. But a few months ago, I decided it was time to finish the job—I'm not sure why—so that's probably what I'm doing when I'm not here."

Janice is cautious and sifts William's remarks for the safest thing to respond to. "A carriage house—my word, how patrician."

William laughs. "Maybe a hundred and fifty years ago. To us it was just an old building that needed a second chance. When I get it finished, I'll rent it out—I'm told it will be a good write-off."

William doesn't mention the fact that he may never be done with the carriage house because every time he finishes something, he rips something else out—architectural deconstructionism, he calls it. In the last week, he's put in a skylight but taken down a bunch of vertical cedar paneling because he thought the wall would be more impressive as a starburst. He also removed twenty-two feet of rabbeted wainscoting and replaced it with tongue and groove because ... well, because he felt like it. Yes, the carriage house is the very definition of a self-licking ice cream cone, but William doesn't care.

"It must be very satisfying to build something like that," Janice says. "I'm sure it will rent the day it appears in the paper. What's your next book about?"

"Dostoevsky—if I actually write it."

"I've read *Crime and Punishment*." Janice makes a face. "I'm afraid that's the only one."

"That's the one that counts."

She looks at her watch again. "You know, speaking of books, I need to get back and check on the availability of a book for the Philosophy Department. It has a very pretentious title—something about quantum physics—but it's written by two men named Smith and Jones." Janice laughs. "I remember the names didn't really go with the title."

William knows the book. In fact, it's currently one of his favorites. "You're talking about *The Metaphysical Implications of Quantum Mechanics* by Phillip Smith and Bradley Jones. You won't have any trouble with availability—that book is a hot property right now. Smith and Jones were even on *The Daily Show* a while back."

"Is it a book I'd understand?"

"Of course," William says. "It's written for laymen like us. Smith and Jones believe that it's time to rethink the tidy Newtonian universe that we inherited from Einstein. They argue that our universe is neither orderly nor predictable because the atoms and subatomic particles that comprise it are not orderly or predictable. So quantum mechanics, not classical physics, is the way to unlock its secrets."

"What does that have to do with philosophy?"

William makes a sweeping gesture with one arm. "Everything! If the universe is unpredictable, the same must be true of human beings because we're made of the same unstable material. That means a lot of what happens in the world, and more importantly in our lives, has nothing to do with Providence or cosmic order—it's just random and chaotic. We need to come to grips with that philosophically—or so say the illustrious Smith and Jones."

"Hey, I'll go along with the chaos part, William—we had eighteen people for Thanksgiving—but I believe things happen for a reason."

William would like to know if this assumption extends to campus shootings, but he's too fond of Janice to ask. "You're in good company, my friend—so did Einstein. He never really bought into quantum mechanics. In fact, that's what he was talking about when he said, 'God does not play dice with the universe.'" William chuckles. "Of course ... Einstein was wrong. He approached the problem in terms of macrophysics, and that proved to be a mistake."

"Yeah," Janice deadpans. "Even I could see that. *Jeez, Albert—what were you thinking?*" She laughs and touches William's arm. "I'd better be going. It was good to see you, William. Remember what I said about your books."

"I will, Janice. Thanks. And thanks for stopping by."

Janice leaves and closes the door softly behind her. William hears her turn left and head for the open pit iron mine.

William looks around. *Now what?* Office hours without a teaching assignment is cruel and unusual punishment. But he knows this is part of Gardner's plan, to make him sit idly in his office with nothing to do but contemplate his sins. But at the moment, it isn't his sins that William contemplates—it's quantum mechanics and his conversation with Janice Grant.

"There's no doubt about it," William says out loud. "Quantum mechanics is the ultimate mindfuck. What is it they say? *If you think you understand quantum mechanics, then you don't understand quantum mechanics.*"

Unlike Janice, William has never believed that everything happens for a reason, and nowadays, he's even lost faith in cause and effect. And predictability. And order. Werner Heisenberg was right—there's just too much uncertainty out there. In fact, when Heisenberg was laying the groundwork for quantum mechanics, he went so far as to say it was impossible to know an object's location and velocity at the same time. This was the earthshaking assertion that came to be known as the Heisenberg Uncertainty Principle, and William found out how true it was shortly before noon on March 17, 2010. He was at Dewhurst, waiting for Jon to pick him up for lunch, when he got the notification on his cell phone—*Active shooters ... north side of campus ... take shelter in a locked room.* All he wanted at that moment was a little hard data, an infinitesimal speck of certainty. But there were only questions, the majority of which had to do with location and velocity: Where was Jon? Where were the shooters? Which way were they headed? And then, there was the Mother of All Uncertainties: given the conundrum of location and velocity, what were the odds that the shooters' vector would intersect with his or Jon's? Unless he was running late, Jon was almost certainly on the north side of campus because that's where Dewhurst is.

Yes, William thinks, uncertainty will nail you every time, and not only that—it also makes the past a wholly unreliable predictor of the future. You *think* an event will unfold in a certain way because it's happened that way a thousand times or because the odds favor it. And then *ka-pow*—it blows up in your face like a loaded cigarette. William continues to think about quantum mechanics, and before long, his thoughts become a letter.

19 April 2012

Dear Dr. Heisenberg:

This morning I was discussing quantum mechanics with a friend who said that she believes things happen for a reason. This was not offered as a theodicy or even as an article of faith. It was more of an observation on her part, but it struck me as one that quantum mechanics, with its emphasis on chance, would certainly repudiate.

Sometimes I wonder if extrapolation from quantum mechanics into the realm of philosophy is even valid, or are we talking about non-overlapping magisteria here? I mean, let's face it, quantum mechanics appears to explain a lot more than the movement of subatomic particles, and in my view, the random collision of these particles is no different than the random collision of people in a crowded subway or countries on the geopolitical stage. And if someone gets shot simply because he is in the wrong place at the wrong time, isn't this proof positive of a quantum universe? I would argue that it is, but I'd love to know what you think.

Sincerely,

William Kessler

PS: I'd also be interested in your opinion of *The Metaphysical Implications of Quantum Mechanics* by Smith and Jones—its premise is essentially what I'm talking about.

William reads the letter over and pronounces it finished. "Good enough, one eighty-eight." William does not regard the fact that Werner Heisenberg has been dead for thirty-six years as a problem. Truth to tell, William often writes to dead people, and because he never mails his letters, he is never disappointed when they don't write back. As he once explained to Dr. Spurling, "There are dead letters, and there are *really dead* letters. A lot of mine fall into the second category."

He files this letter with the others and wonders if perhaps, many years from now, someone will come across these electronic missives and think them worthy of publication, like Kerouac's letters or Plath's journal. But try as he might, he is unable to think of a single reason why this would happen.

William read recently that there's one chance in 182 trillion that a meteor will strike his house—an eventuality that, in his opinion, is far more likely than someone publishing his letters. The same article had said that a man has one chance in ten million of becoming president of the United States—roughly the same chance he has of being attacked by a shark. William had laughed out loud when he read that because he could only assume Mitt Romney knew the odds and liked them. Everything is about probability, William thinks, and the universe is just an enormous casino where the odds are stacked in favor of the house. For example, the odds of an American being killed in a terrorist attack are one in twenty million, about the same as becoming a saint. But in the final analysis, anything can happen because odds are just odds.

William closes his eyes, and suddenly it's two years ago. He's in Old Dewhurst, and he can hear the shooting and the screams, but Jon isn't there yet. After a moment or two Jon appears, out of breath, struggling to speak.

"This is bad. *Really* bad. We gotta—"

"Are you hit? Talk to me, Jon. There's blood all over your jacket."

"It's not mine ... I'm okay. We can't stay here."

"How many shooters? How many—"

There is a loud knock at the door, and William jumps a foot.

"Are you in there, Dr. Kessler?"

The question is followed by another knock that catapults William back to the present moment. "Yes, yes ... I'm here. Come in."

A young man enters and looks around. "Hello, Dr. Kessler. I thought I heard you talking to someone."

"There's no one here but us chickens," William says. "What can I do for you?" William points to a chair, and the young man sits down.

"Thanks. My name is Corey Knudsen. My sister graduated from Lothrup in 2008, and she said if I ever had the chance, I should take a class from you. She said you were the best professor she ever had."

William shudders, certain of what's coming.

"Her name is Gail. Do you remember her?"

Questions like this bite into William physically. "No, I'm terribly sorry. I have a little retrograde amnesia these days." He looks down at his desk, then at Corey. "But please thank your sister for the kind words." On a different day—or perhaps to a different person—William might have said, *I underwent electroconvulsive therapy in 2010, and there are still gaps in my memory you could drive a fucking bus through.* But he doesn't say anything.

And neither does Corey, at least not right away. Then he points out that although William's name appears in the registration guide for fall semester, there is no indication of what, if anything, he's teaching.

"So what's the story, Dr. Kessler?"

"The story? I don't know yet. I haven't been told if I'll be allowed to teach."

Corey shakes his head. "That doesn't make sense. You're a hero. You're the biggest—"

"I'm not a hero, Corey, and Lothrup has every right to determine who teaches in its classrooms. If they don't think—"

"Are they afraid because you were ... *institutionalized*?" Corey individuates all six syllables in a way that makes William laugh.

"Is *that* what happened to me? You know, when you put it like that, I wouldn't let me teach here either."

"I'm sorry, Dr. Kessler. I just wanted to take a class from you, but I can see—"

"I appreciate that, Corey. I really do. I'm confident the school will put something in the *Beacon* if they allow me to offer classes— they'll get the word out."

Corey looks unconvinced. "Yeah ... okay, Dr. Kessler. I hope everything works out."

"Me too. Thanks for stopping by."

No sooner does Corey leave than there is another knock at the door. This time, it's a young woman from Spooner, Wisconsin, named Tina Masek. Tina is an incoming freshman, and she wants to know what the best prelaw major is.

"I mean, I always assumed it would be criminal justice," she says. "That seemed like a no-brainer, and that's what I was going to major in. But then I read that criminal justice majors totally suck on the Law School Admission Test—that they barely score in, like, the top 50 percent. So ... what should my major be?"

"Something you truly enjoy," William tells her. And he explains that, statistically speaking, the five best majors in terms of LSAT scores are math, physics, philosophy, English and political science.

"But here's the thing, Tina—you have to pick something you love because GPA is almost as important as your LSAT score, so whatever you decide to major in, you have to excel at it."

Tina nods thoughtfully, but William has no idea what she's thinking. Then she exclaims, "Wow! I think you just changed my whole life!" And Tina Masek, who had walked into William's office uncomfortable at the thought of becoming a criminal justice major, walks out delighted at the prospect of becoming an English major.

And William is also pleased because he has long believed that a lawyer who has read Shakespeare is a better lawyer than one who has not. He applies that same thinking to plumbers, doctors, barbers—just about everybody.

CHAPTER 4

The Bahamian Jewel

AT ONE O'CLOCK, William drops all pretense, puts his feet up on the desk and thinks about the shooting. This happens at some point nearly every day, and he's learned not to fight it. It's impossible for him to get his head around what happened, but he never stops trying, and an important part of the exercise is remembering where people were killed. But the fact that the shooters had been on motorcycles makes this difficult because they covered so much ground.

Dewhurst was the only place where the two shooters had been together, so it had the highest body count—forty-one students, plus Professor Martin and Jon. But before Dewhurst, five students were killed in Hobart Hall, which is directly across the commons from Dewhurst, and four others were killed near the chapel, which is half a mile away. Two students—a young man and his fiancée—were gunned down on the steps of the library, and an unarmed security guard was killed in front of Watrous Auditorium. And then after Dewhurst, the young SWAT officer was killed at Wellstone Hall.

How many is that? William adds them up. *Four nonstudents and fifty-two students—I'm one short.* Then he remembers Amanda Norris, the girl who died in Janice Grant's arms. She had been killed by the second shooter after he left Dewhurst and headed for the other end of campus. As for the shooters themselves, William doesn't feel they should be counted, but one was killed in front of the administration building, and the other one, the one with dead eyes, William had killed in Dewhurst's lecture hall.

Besides Jon, William knew only two of the victims—a sophomore girl from Bigfork and the professor, Rupert Martin. The girl's name was Leah Nelson, and she had been a student in William's Victorian Novel class. Even with his fucked-up memory, William remembers three things about her with perfect clarity: she was one of the best students he had ever had; she had a captivating, crooked smile, sort of like Ellen Barkin's; and she loved *Wuthering Heights* more than any book she had ever read. Leah told William that she was a sucker for happy endings, and as far as she was concerned, *Wuthering Heights* had the happiest ending that could ever be. When she presented her paper to the class—*Wuthering Heights: A Model of Hegelian Dialectic*—she had worn a T-shirt that said *What Would Heathcliff Do?*

Leah was killed in Dewhurst's lecture hall. She had been shot in the chest and was almost certainly dead by the time William chased the first shooter back in there. But until the victims' names were released, William didn't know about Leah, and her death hit him hard. Leah was one of the four students whose families had brought the lawsuit against Lothrup.

The professor who had been killed was Rupert Martin. Martin was an odd duck, and a lot of people found him insufferable, including a good many of his students, who called him Dr. Martinet on account of his penchant for rules and classroom discipline. The nickname was well-earned—Martin had never met a rule he didn't like, and he was always coming up with new ones: rules about public displays of affection, rules about mobile devices, rules about everything. At faculty meetings he would prattle on and on about the need for more rules and increased discipline until someone would invariably tell him to blow it out his ass, at which point he would sulk or leave the room in a huff.

Despite all that, William liked Rupert and found his acerbic sense of humor refreshing. It's not that they were buddies or anything like that, but William and Rupert had done a little fishing together and had taken their wives to an MLA conference in San

Francisco. So there was a little history there, if not a close friendship. It was two weeks after the shooting—ten days after Jon's funeral—that Sam called to ask if it would be okay if the campus police dropped off Martin's briefcase and laptop.

"What the hell for?" William asked.

Sam was uncomfortable. "I need a favor, William—*Lothrup* needs a favor. I know the timing is awful, and I'm sorry I have to ask, but we need grades for Martin's students. Since he was a member of the English Department and a friend of yours, we were hoping …" Sam had waited for William to finish the sentence.

"You were hoping I'd do it?"

"Yes, we were. Martin's wife—what's her name?"

"Joyce."

"Right. I spoke to Joyce on the phone yesterday. Did you know she has cancer?"

"Yes, Marcia told me. I was very sorry to hear it."

"Yeah. Anyway … I explained to her that we needed Rupert's laptop and briefcase so we can get his grades on the server. I asked if I could send the campus police to pick them up, and she said that was fine, as long as they didn't bring them back. She said she can't bear to look at anything that was with Rupert when he was killed. So whaddya say, William? Can you help us out? Everything you need will be on his computer or in that briefcase."

"How many classes are we talking about?"

"Three."

"Do you want the grades based on current scores?"

"Yes—whatever the students had on March 17."

"Can I establish my own weights and parameters?"

"Yes, goddammit. Anything else?"

"Yeah—is anyone going to give me shit if every student receives a higher grade than the math supports? I mean, when you take a class that gets you shot at or killed, you should receive at least a B. In fact, we should put something in the school handbook that stipulates—"

"Look! Nobody gives a rat's ass what grades you give."

"You say that *now.*"

Sam started to bluster. "It's pretty freaking simple—we need to get the job done. Will you do it or not?"

"Yes," William said. "I'll be glad to."

Sam exhaled loudly. "Spoken like the hero that you are, William. Thank you."

So when two young men from the campus police had arrived, Marcia let them in, and William accepted the laptop, along with the briefcase, and thanked them for delivering the items to his home. The men, one of whom knew Jon from high school, offered their condolences and left.

When William realized a few minutes later that the briefcase had rotary locks for which he hadn't been given the combination, he called Sam, who couldn't really talk because he was already late to a meeting with Gardner.

"Punctuality is a very big deal with him, William."

"I don't care. This is important, Sam. There could be ungraded student work in that briefcase."

"It's possible," Sam said, "but what do you want *me* to do about it?"

"Is there any chance that Joyce would know the combination?"

Sam laughed. "Does Marcia know the combination to *your* briefcase?"

"No, I don't think so, but—"

"Look, William, we're not going to bother Joyce with this bull-shit. I gotta go. Try a BFH."

"Hang on—what's a BFH?"

"A big fucking hammer. Good luck."

"Yeah ... thanks for your help."

In the end, William didn't need a big fucking hammer to open the briefcase. He simply left it locked, and because he wasn't sure how much ungraded work might be in there, he simplified things by giving every one of Rupert's students an A or B, no matter what the laptop said. It felt good, and William had no trouble convincing himself that these were extraordinary times calling for extraordinary measures.

A week later, Sam called again. William, who was well into his hero period by then, took the call in the green room at ABC, where he was waiting to go on *Good Morning, America*. He tried to explain to Sam that he couldn't really talk, but Sam wouldn't be put off and asked if William had ever succeeded in opening Rupert's briefcase. William assumed his sky-high grades were being challenged, so he lied, telling Sam that he had indeed opened the briefcase and graded all the student work it contained prior to crunching the numbers.

"I did exactly what Rupert would have done," William said.

"Tell me about the briefcase," Sam said. "What else was in there?"

"Other than Marsellus Wallace's soul?"

"Look, William, this isn't funny. I need to know if—"

"There was nothing else, Sam—Scout's honor."

"Good … good. We'll talk later. Break a leg."

No one cared about the grades. They were never questioned, and William soon forgot about his moment of academic rebellion. Rupert's laptop and briefcase remained in a corner of his office for several weeks, and when he grew tired of looking at them, he carried them downstairs and put them in a little storeroom filled with other things he had grown tired of looking at.

William thinks about these events of two years ago until he gets the feeling that he's supposed to be doing something or, even worse, that he's forgotten to do something really important. Then he remembers the email from Marv Kreitzer—*please call me.* How could he forget the last friend he'd made in life, perhaps the last one he'd ever make? He and Marv had done time together—not jail time but definitely hard time. They had met two years ago at the Mason Crosswell Psychiatric Hospital in Glenfield, Minnesota. Or as he and Marv called it, the Hammond County Home for the Totally Fucked. That was unfair, though. Crosswell was a classy operation—nice rooms, great staff, beautiful grounds. It was situated in a lovely, verdant valley in west-central Minnesota, and, according to William's wife and daughter, movie stars went there all the time. It was like the Betty Ford Clinic of the upper Midwest, they said, adding that he was "sooo lucky" to get in there. But William didn't feel lucky. And he never saw any movie stars either.

Marv was at Crosswell because he suffered from clinical depression and kept trying to kill himself. William was at Crosswell because he got tired of everyone thinking he was a hero when he wasn't. Eventually, William got so tired of it that he tried to jump off a cruise ship somewhere between Montserrat and San Lucia. Yes, he'd done a few other things too, but attempting a header off the fourth deck of the *Bahamian Jewel* was definitely the kicker, the grand finale that greased the skids all the way to Crosswell.

Still, what everyone had said wasn't true—suicide never crossed William's mind. He just wanted off the ship so badly that he was willing to do anything, including jumping overboard, to make it happen. He and Marcia had no business on a cruise—it was too soon for anything like that. But they couldn't have known, and everything in their lives had sort of converged: they received a lot of money from Jon's Servicemembers Life Insurance; they were incapable of crying anymore; and everyone they knew was urging expensive, long-distance cures for their sorrow. So without really thinking about it, William and Marcia had booked a cruise.

William knew, almost as soon as the ship left Miami, what a bad idea it was—it demonstrated a complete failure of imagination, if nothing else. And it gave him too much time to think—to remember what had happened that day at Dewhurst and to hate the lie he was living. By the third day, William felt like a castaway, a solitary soul in the middle of the ocean. By the fourth day, he felt like an inmate, and the *Bahamian Jewel* had become his prison.

So on the afternoon of day four, William did the only thing he could think of—he made "a precipitous attempt to disembark." That's what he told the ship's doctor. He couldn't remember a lot of what happened, but Marcia told him that he had taken a decorative sword from the wall of the ship's casino and waved it around, yelling that he would take hostages if the ship didn't put into port immediately. Then he had threatened those who were trying to restrain him on the jogging track, where he had attempted to climb over the railing and jump. William doesn't remember this part at all, but he has no reason to doubt it.

The doctor kept him heavily sedated and strapped to a bed in the ship's infirmary until the *Jewel*'s captain could make arrangements for the Coast Guard to fly him and Marcia by helicopter to Barbados, where there was a real hospital. William doesn't remember how long he and Marcia were there—two days, maybe. Then from Barbados they flew back to Miami and on to Minneapolis.

After a week-long stay at the University of Minnesota Medical Center, William wound up at Crosswell. By that time, his pain had turned to numbness, and his life had become a sort of waking nightmare that didn't have much to do with him anymore. But the dark cloud definitely had a silver lining—his hero days were over.

William turns his phone on, finds *Marv Kreitzer* among his contacts and presses CALL.

Marv answers instantly. "Hey, my brother, where the hell are you?"

"In my office. I have hours Monday, Wednesday and Thursday."

"What about Friday?"

"I'm off."

"That's great because I have a follow-up at Cross next Friday, and I thought I'd come see you when I get through. Is that all right?"

"Hell yes!" William says. "You wanna go fishing?"

"I'd love to. Have you been yet?"

"No, but it's time to get the boat out of mothballs and try the crappies."

"God*damn*, it's good to hear your voice. How does the fishing opener look? Any problems?"

"None," William says. "We're gonna make it this year. I promise." William and Marv had planned to fish the opener last year too, but William, who was in the middle of his divorce that spring, wasn't really in the mood for fishing. Later that summer, they tried to make up for it by fishing half a dozen times in July and August.

"I'm gonna hold you to it," Marv says. "I've never fished the walleye opener, and I'm really psyched. Hey, are those effete little shits gonna let you teach in the fall?"

"I don't know. They're still chewing on it."

"Tell 'em to chew on my schlong."

"Good idea, Marv—that'll bring 'em around."

"Goddammit, you should come work with me—we'd be like Lennon and McCartney."

William laughs. "You're a jingle writer, Marv. I don't even play an instrument."

"You're forgetting the skin flute, my brother. I'll bet you can play that like nobody's business."

"Marv, you remind me of a Judd Apatow character—eternally adolescent."

Marv roars. "That's the *least* of it, William. Tell you what, though—I'll share your observation with Dr. Hanselman when I see him. I should get to your place around four. You haven't moved, have you?"

"Nope, same house."

"How the hell did you pull that off? I've been divorced three times, and I've never come close to getting the house."

"I gave Marcia all the insurance money that we got, minus the cruise. That really impressed the judge."

"That was a nice gesture, my brother. Look, please write a reminder to yourself that I'm coming to see you. I don't want to show up and find that you've forgotten all about it. I've never had electroshock therapy, thank God, but I know what it ... Is your memory improving?"

"It's called electro*convulsive* therapy these days, Marv—it sounds less barbaric—and, yes, my memory is getting better. I probably wouldn't forget that you were coming. It's more likely that, once you got here, I'd stare at you and wonder who the hell you were. It's called *jamais vu*—sort of the opposite of *déjà vu*—but it doesn't happen much anymore."

"Glad to hear it, Lenny. Maybe since it's your birthday, you can tend the rabbits."

William laughs. "How did you—"

"What the hell is going on up there? Lothrup is on the front page of the *Star Trib* every day. Are you guys gonna win?"

"The lawsuit?" William asks.

"Of course the lawsuit."

"First, the Minnesota Supreme Court has to agree to hear the case."

"What happens if they don't?"

"I don't know ... I suppose we try to borrow twelve million dollars, and if we can't, Lothrup College will give new meaning to the word *austerity*."

"That blows."

"Tell me about it. Hey ..."

"Hey what?"

"It's good to hear your voice too."

"I know, William. I gotta run."

"Okay, I'll see you on—" But Marv is already gone, vanished into the ether.

Marv's voice is like a tonic, an elixir that never fails to lift William's spirits. Marv is a brash, vulgar, philandering genius—a one-time Juilliard piano prodigy who was on a fast track to becoming the next Van Cliburn when he burned out in his early twenties. He disappeared for several years, played keyboards for some alternative West Coast rock bands and then reinvented himself as a jingle writer. By the mid-nineties, he was one of the best in the country. Marv's business has fallen off some since Crosswell, but William still hears his stuff on TV occasionally and on the radio all the time—Famous Dave's, Best Buy, Target. William loves the Target jingle—if you hear it once, you can't stop humming it: *Target, so much more than just a store / Lower prices, sales galore ...*

The first time William saw Marv, he was wearing a navy watch cap, shuffling down the main hallway at Crosswell in a burlesque of R. P. McMurphy in *One Flew over the Cuckoo's Nest*. William was on his way to the dining room, and as Marv passed by, he looked at William and winked, as if to say, *Hey, buddy, I'm trying to lighten the mood in this godforsaken place, and I can tell, just by looking at you, that you understand.* Marv was right. William did understand, and that's all it took for a tiny, precious spark to arc between them. Little things like that were second-order miracles at Crosswell because the patients were so damaged or so druggy that normal connections failed. It was as though all the wires were down, and no matter how hard you tried, you just couldn't get through.

Crosswell is one of those experiences that William tries to forget, a sort of hazy interlude between the cruise and everything that followed. But it is also a defining moment in his personal arc, so as memories go, it's hard to suppress. Crosswell was pure, unadulterated pain, and nothing about it was good, except for Marv, and he was released two months before William, which turned William's remaining months into what seemed like years.

Even William's release from Crosswell, major milestone that it was, didn't guarantee anything, and on the bad days—days when the shooting plays like a tape loop in his head, and the guilt is more than he can bear—William is sure he'll end up back there. That's mostly because when William was at Crosswell, his mind curled up in the psychological equivalent of fetal position, and he became as determined as Hamlet that no one was going to pluck out the heart of his mystery. After all, if he couldn't bring himself to tell Marcia what had happened at Dewhurst, he sure as hell wasn't going to tell anyone else. So he said almost nothing to his frustrated doctors—not in group therapy, not during one-on-ones, not even in casual conversation.

William's clinical diagnosis was a triumvirate of disorders: post-traumatic stress disorder, recurrent dissociative disorder and persistent depressive disorder. But a couple of his doctors were convinced that something else was going on too, something deeper and more sinister. But when they couldn't nail it down, they gave up on talk therapy and went the pharmacological route, trying dozens of different drugs and combinations of drugs on William in an attempt to "disrupt his negative ideation."

It was when the drugs didn't work that they resorted to electroconvulsive therapy, which didn't accomplish much either—except to turn William's memory into a sieve. But after four months, William began to show improvement. This may have had as much to do with the passage of time as it did with his treatment, but whatever the explanation, Crosswell cut him loose right before Thanksgiving of 2010, and things had been touch and go for William ever since.

Unlike Marv, William doesn't have follow-ups at Crosswell. In fact, he hasn't set foot in the place since he was discharged. William is terrified of Crosswell, and two days after he got out, he chose a local doctor from the Yellow Pages and had Crosswell send his medical records to the Chambliss Clinic. Marcia had been furious. So were the hotshots at Crosswell, but since they had certified that William wasn't crazy anymore, there wasn't a damn thing they could do about it.

William's last student visitor for the day is a young woman with a clipboard from Lothrup's Campus Empowerment Alliance. She introduces herself as Olivia Schmidt and explains that she has stopped by to see if William would be willing to sign a petition for their *Light It Up* campaign.

"It's really important that we get the signatures of as many faculty members as we can," she says.

William has no idea what she's talking about. "I'm sorry, Ms. Schmidt ... I'm not familiar with your cause."

"You're kidding, right?" Olivia points to her T-shirt, which bears the emblem of a stylized yellow light bulb, below which are the words *Light It Up*. William has seen the light bulb image around campus a lot this spring—in fact, it's been nearly ubiquitous—but he still doesn't know what it means.

He shrugs, and Olivia laughs. "You must have just returned from a sabbatical on the moon, Dr. Kessler. Most of the campus lighting is older than I am, and there isn't enough of it. The parking lots and the commons are barely illuminated at night, and some of our pathways aren't lighted at all. Lothrup's campus simply isn't safe, Dr. Kessler, especially for women. That's why the Campus Empowerment Alliance is advocating for new and improved lighting."

"And how is that going?"

Olivia sighs. "Not very well. Chancellor Gardner won't even hear us out. He just keeps saying that what we're proposing would cost too much money." She offers William the clipboard. "But you can still help."

William shakes his head. "I'm sorry. I don't sign petitions."

"Why not? Are you afraid?"

"Afraid? No, not really. It's just that petitions have always struck me as the death rattle of doomed causes—if you're circulating a petition, you've already lost."

"Ouch!" Olivia says. "That's terribly cynical, Dr. Kessler. I hope you're wrong, and I hope we can change your mind. It's very important that we improve the lighting on our campus."

"I wish you the best of luck," William says.

With that, Olivia Schmidt takes her leave, and William returns to doing nothing.

There are no more knocks on the door, so when it's finally time to go home, William tidies up the office and leaves.

It takes him twenty minutes to drive the twelve miles to his house. William used to think twelve miles was perfect—close enough that he could get to school quickly in the morning and far enough away that he could forget all about it on the way home. Now, none of that really matters. But William still misses the old days, when Jon would be waiting for him, football in hand, as he pulled in the driveway. Jon loved football, and many times he'd have William running a route before he'd even changed clothes— *Head for the mailbox and cut left.* Or *Let's try a button hook, Dad*—and William would do his best to become a wide receiver, that is, until his middle-aged body would bring him to his senses.

While Jon and William threw the football around, Kate would help Marcia in the kitchen and beg all the while for the car keys, so she could attend some event at her high school—or so she said. Kate was a live wire, a member of everything from Drama Club to the girls' softball team. She was happy, bubbly, always laughing. William enjoys thinking about those halcyon days with his family, but he knows that time is as dead as Camelot. And as he walks into his house, it seems even deader.

And it isn't just because of Jon. A lot of it has to do with Marcia and the fact that William misses her so much he can hardly stand it. They were married for twenty-eight years, and William enjoyed every one of them. He wishes he didn't still love her—life would be a lot easier—but his feelings aren't something he can turn off like a faucet, and he imagines there will be a jagged Marcia-shaped hole in his heart for the rest of his life. And he has only himself to blame. When he couldn't talk to Marcia about what happened at Dewhurst, she didn't understand and withdrew in self-defense. Soon, the two of them became so emotionally siloed that it was like they were living in different countries. And then it happened—*William, I just can't do this anymore. I'm sorry. I didn't plan it. I needed you, and you weren't there. Then Walter came along and …*

"I'm home," William hollers. He knows no one's there. He just gets a masochistic kick out of hearing the hard, bright sound of his voice bump up against all that emptiness. His home is largely devoid of furniture. Marcia had seen to that. At the outset, she had insisted that they were going to have an *amicable* divorce, and she used that word a lot. But after she'd met with her attorney a couple of times, *amicable* went right out the fucking window, and as a result, William has very little furniture. Marcia had even taken his bookcases, so after William tripped half a dozen times over stacks of books that were piled here and there, he made fifty feet of replacement bookshelves out of cinder blocks and two-by-eights. Just the bare essentials, he tells himself. *Simplify, simplify, simplify! Keep your accounts on your thumbnail. Let your affairs be as two or three.* Good old Thoreau, William thinks. What a bullshit artist.

William goes into the bedroom, pulls off his shoes and lies down on the bed. There is a picture of Jon on the nightstand, but unlike the photograph in his office, in this one Jon is wearing his dress blues and looks very serious. How Jon came to be in the Marines is a strange story and one William wishes he could forget. He had been at home, grading papers, when Jon called. Jon, who was a second-semester freshman at the University of Iowa, made a few minutes' worth of chaffy small talk, which was not like him, and this made William uneasy. He was about to ask Jon, point-blank, why he'd called, when his kid brought one off the hip.

"Dad, I'm not ready for college right now. I've decided to enlist in the Marines."

My God, no! William thought. You didn't say that—it's not even possible. That single sentence knocked the wind out of William. He remembers a strange pressure behind his eyes and a sort of underwater squeeze in his ears. He couldn't breathe, couldn't see, and in the darkness he fought to summon his unflappable professor persona—the calm, measured mien that just might save him.

"I'm a little taken aback," William finally said, finding the groove he was looking for. "It doesn't appear that you've given the matter much thought, Jon. I would have preferred that you subject such an important decision to a more thoroughgoing analysis."

"It's not a decision I made lightly," Jon said. "I'm sorry, Dad. My mind's made up."

Bullshit! William thought. Three years ago you wanted to be a football player. Two years ago, an archeologist. Last year, you enrolled at the University of Iowa to get a communications degree. And eighteen years before that you were a single goddamn cell. So don't tell me your mind's made up. But William knew he couldn't afford to lose his temper. If he did, Jon would shut down, and it would be game over.

"Look, Jon, I hope this decision isn't etched in stone, but even if it is, we're going to talk about it. You owe your mother and me that much. I should be there by dinnertime."

William hung up and explained to Marcia what had just happened, and she started to cry, saying, *Go, go, please hurry*, as though the sooner William got to Iowa City, the sooner this lunacy would end. Her sense of urgency rubbed off on William, who grabbed his coat and keys, a change of clothes, and was out the door in fifteen minutes. *I'll call you tonight, Marcia. It may be late.*

William drove like a madman, making it from Chambliss to Iowa City in seven hours. He picked Jon up at his dorm, and they went from there to the Red Lobster in Coralville. William was primed and ready. There had been plenty of time on the road for him to plan his moves, to formulate impeccably reasoned arguments that would leave Jon with nothing to say except, "I hate to admit it, Dad, but when you put it *that* way ..."

But after two and a half hours of butting heads—after dinner, dessert, coffee and more coffee—William was on the ropes, and he knew it. Jon wasn't kidding about his mind being made up—that was putting it mildly—and in the end, the episode turned out to be one of quantum mechanics' exploding cigarettes: William struck out, and Jon would join the Marines. When William had called Marcia that evening to tell her what happened, he felt like a complete failure, both as a father and a husband, and he drove home to Chambliss the next morning wondering what he could possibly say to Marcia that would comfort her. And all the way, images of Fallujah swirled before his eyes.

William regards Jon's story as the zenith of situational irony: he survives seven months in Helmand Province only to be killed twenty minutes from home by a self-radicalized shithead with a chip on his shoulder. But it's more than just irony. Jon's death was improbable to the point of being absurd. In fact, it's the quintessence of quantum mechanics, and it's easy for William to imagine all those subatomic particles whirling out of control, zigging when they should have zagged, causing an earthquake here, a miscarriage there, a tornado, an aneurism, a campus shooting.

William thinks if he could rewind the tape and play that awful day back ten times in a row, there would be ten quantum versions of it, each of them different. He believes this because the infinitude of tiny particles that comprise March 17 are endlessly arranging and rearranging themselves in different patterns. It's the antithesis of *Groundhog Day*, he thinks, so there might be versions of March 17 where Jon escaped injury altogether, versions where he was only wounded, versions where he was killed but in some other way, like an automobile accident or a convenience store robbery. Maybe there would even be a Hallmark version of March 17, one in which Jon saved several students' lives by getting them to safety. But while the day might have unfolded in any number of ways, there are two constants amid the sea of variables: everything is a function of chance, and chance is a function of the odds.

William knows it is the outsized role played by chance that prevents Jon's death from being a proper tragedy—chance and the fact that his death lacks anything resembling moral elevation. William also knows if there's a tragic figure, it's him, not Jon. But he tries not to think about it because it would mean thinking about what happened that day at Dewhurst, and he'd prefer not to do that.

William tries to stay calm, struggling to defeat the old feelings. He turns his phone on—no calls or messages—and because he has a little time before he leaves for Kate's, he goes out to the mailbox and retrieves the mail, along with the paper. The news is predictably awful: the North Koreans have launched another missile; Anders Breivik testified that he intended to kill *all* the children on the island of Utøya, not just seventy-seven of them; and the only thing weaker than the U.S. job market—with the possible exception of the U.S. dollar—is the U.S. housing market. *Is there anything that isn't fucked up?*

His phone rings—it's Kate. "Where are you?" she asks.

"I just got home. You said six o'clock."

"Yes, but if you're home, you might as well come over now."

"Yeah, okay. I'm practically on my way."

"Good. Hurry up. Bye."

Kate is up to something. William knows the signs. He tries to make a mental list of all the things it might be but soon realizes he's just guessing. Maybe she and Todd are going to offer him a drink when he gets there. Now *that* would qualify as a *big surprise*. Of course, it will never happen because Kate and Todd don't drink. Not a drop. Not ever. Todd had been one of Kate's counselors at LiveRight when she was drinking. Or rather, when she *quit* drinking. That is, if she ever *was* drinking. When she was twenty-one, Kate had become convinced she was an alcoholic, even though as far as William, Marcia and Kate's friends knew, all she ever drank was a beer once in a while or a glass of wine. William knew better than to play psychiatrist, but he couldn't help wondering if maybe Kate wanted to be an alcoholic so that someone—her parents, God, a strong-yet-vulnerable stranger with kind eyes and a twelve-step program—could charge over the hill like the cavalry and save her.

When William had called Kate's affliction "Munchausen syndrome, dry with a twist," Marcia had scolded him for not taking their daughter's difficulties more seriously. But there was one part of the problem they both agreed on—neither of them was willing to tell Kate she wasn't an alcoholic when she was thoroughly convinced she was. So they got her some help, Todd Benedict charged over the hill, and William would get a drink there when hell froze over.

But that's all right. He couldn't ask for a better daughter than Kate, and he loves her dearly. Kate had been religious before Jon was killed, but afterward, she took it to a whole new level, finding in God the answer to all of life's mysteries, especially the painful ones. As a lifelong rationalist, this sort of thing doesn't work for William, but he is happy that Kate has found a comparatively harmless antidote to despair. Perhaps someday he will find one, a metaphoric safe room with iron-clad walls and a door that opens only from the inside. But until that happens, or until quantum mechanics can help him make sense of things, the only way William can really understand his life is to pretend it's a five-act play. His marriage, career and the birth of his children are the essence of a rising action. The shooting is the dramatic climax, and all the events after that—the cruise, Crosswell, his divorce, his suspension—are elements of a falling action that will eventually lead to a pathetic denouement that savors of bathos and regret. It isn't a pretty picture, but it seems as plausible as anything else.

William, as he often does at home, begins to pace. He starts by pacing through the house from the front door to the kitchen and eventually finds himself standing in the doorway of the guest bedroom. This is where he and Marcia were together for the last time. Their marriage was over, Marcia was about to leave for Phoenix, and she had called to ask if the two of them could go through some boxes in the closet of the guest bedroom. William said yes, and for over an hour, things had gone pretty well.

"Are you still writing letters?" Marcia asked.

"I am, but not as many as before."

"Does it still help?"

"I guess so. It calms me down. If it keeps me out of Crosswell, I'll write letters till Christ comes again."

Not ten minutes later, Marcia opened an unmarked shoebox that was full of Jon's old report cards. She picked one up and looked at it, then another. William could see her shoulders begin to shake, and then, very quietly, she started to cry. Without looking at him, Marcia extended her hand, and he went to her, gathered her in his arms and held her, drinking in the fragrance of her Infusion d'Iris for what he knew might be the last time.

"You don't have to go."

"Don't start, William."

"We could work this out. I know we could. I love you and—"

"You promised me you weren't going to do this anymore."

"I know, but what's more important than our marriage? Isn't it worth fighting for?"

"It's too late, William. I don't have any fight left in me. It disappeared after all those months that you wouldn't speak to me, when all you did was stare into space. You should have let me in, William, but you refused to talk about Jon, the shooting or even what happened to you that day—you blocked out everything, including me."

"I was sick."

"And I was lonely. I'd lost a son, and then I lost you." Marcia pulled a tissue from her pocket and dabbed at her eyes. "I'm glad you're better, William, but it's over now. Walter and I are going to make a new life together. He makes me happy. He makes me laugh. Do you have any idea what that means? You have to let me go." A week after that conversation, Marcia moved to Phoenix with Dr. Burke, and William was on his own, going to his office and rattling around his empty house like a pea in a drum.

William's phone vibrates—a text from Kate: "If u havnt left yet plz get a mve on."

Yeah, this is bad, William thinks, but he's uncertain how nervous he should be. What is he about to walk into? His best guess: a female mystery guest has been invited to dinner tonight for his doubtful benefit. This sort of thing has happened before, and despite his protestations, it could easily happen again.

Dear God, William thinks. Anything but that.

CHAPTER 5

Baron Hürtgenvoss vom Hohenstadt

WILLIAM LIVES IN THE older part of Chambliss on the Agate River. Kate and Todd live in the newer part of town by Lake Ellen. But new and old, for the most part, are distinctions without a difference in Chambliss because very little is actually new— unless you're north of Dahlberg Road. Dahlberg, by a million different names, is that four-lane highway on the outskirts of all over-ripe Midwestern towns. It's where you find the big-box retailers, the fast-food joints and all the businesses that abandoned Main Street in search of better locations, only to discover that nothing, not even a shopping mall, could inoculate them against the ravages of e-commerce.

It's a little over six miles from William's house to Kate and Todd's, and he takes his time getting there. When he can see their house from the corner, he stops to check it out. It's a nice place—a four-bedroom Cape Cod on a half-acre lot—but it's the driveway that interests him because he's on the lookout for any car that shouldn't be there, any car that might belong to one of Kate's coworkers with no husband and a great personality. But there are no cars. So whatever the *big surprise* is, William is reasonably confident it won't be another woman that Kate wants him to meet.

William pulls in the driveway, and his two little grandsons,

Matthew and Jacob, are on him before he can get out of the car.

"GrampaGrampaGrampa." Matthew is six, Jacob five.

William hugs them both. "What's the word, men?"

Jake is jumping up and down. "We have a big surprise!"

"Yes, let's talk about that," William says.

Matt grabs his little brother's arm. "You're gonna get in trouble."

Jake looks at William and pretends to zip his mouth shut.

Kate comes out of the house and gives William a kiss. "Happy birthday, Daddy. I was beginning to wonder what happened to you."

"It's ten to six, honey. I'm early."

Kate takes his arm. "Let's go inside. Todd's in back, firing up the grill."

William follows Kate to the kitchen, where she opens the refrigerator and hands him an O'Doul's, which he looks at with disdain.

"Daddy, you shouldn't even have *that*. You're on Paxil."

"Not anymore," William says. "Effexor and Ativan, just like everybody else."

But Kate has moved on. "It's so nice today, I thought we'd have a summer meal and eat outside, even though it isn't really summer. The corn looked terrific, so we're having—"

"Kate—excuse me—where did the boys go?" William looks around. "They were right behind me, and they just ... disappeared."

Kate laughs. "I think they went downstairs, but they could be anywhere."

William puts his arm around her. "You look terrific, Kate. I swear you get a year younger every time I have a birthday."

"Thanks, Daddy. It isn't true, but it's nice of you to—"

"Hey, did you happen to tell anyone that it's my birthday today?"

Kate becomes girlish. "Maybe."

"Hey, birthday boy, is that you?" Todd is just out of sight on the patio, his voice coming from somewhere beyond the sliding screen door. "You guys should come out and join me—all the snacks are out here."

"We're on our way," Kate says. "Daddy, can you believe we're using the patio? This spring is almost spooky. This time last year there was a foot of snow out there."

"So far, this is the warmest spring since they started keeping track," William says. "I heard that on the radio."

Kate points to something in the yard. "I believe it—my azaleas are about to bloom."

It's a nice patio—more of a summer kitchen, really—with a wood-burning range, a monstrous gas grill and a covered dining area. Kate makes a lot of money, and the summer kitchen is her doing. She's an executive with a pension management firm called Merrimac Partners International, aka MPI, where she's quickly climbing the corporate ladder. Todd doesn't earn much as a counselor, but that's one of the things William likes about him—he isn't the kind of guy who gets upset because his wife makes more money than he does. William can appreciate that because Marcia was the CFO of Womack Paper, and five years after she took the job, her paycheck was bigger than his. In some ways, William thinks he has more in common with his son-in-law than he does with his own daughter.

Todd is holding a screwdriver in one hand and a can of WD-40 in the other.

"Anything serious?" William asks.

"Nope—routine maintenance. I had to replace the battery in the igniter, and a couple of the knobs were sticking. This is the first time I've used it this season." Todd presses the button, and the big grill comes to life with a reassuring *whoosh*. "Yeah—*that's* what I'm talkin' about."

"Try the dip," Kate says. "It's got some heat to it but—"

"And those little bacon things." Todd points to the table. "They're terrific."

From out of nowhere, Matt and Jake appear and sweep across the patio like a whirlwind, a blur of balls-to-the-walls kinetic energy that sets every atom within twenty yards thrumming. The table takes a hit, and everyone reaches for their drinks before they end up on the floor.

"Whoa!" Kate and Todd say together. "Slow down, guys."

"What are these? How old is Grampa? Can I have one? Matt hit me. You started it. Let's go." And then, as suddenly as they had appeared, they're gone. It is an instantaneous rate of change, and in the sudden quiet, William feels as though they have entered the eye of a hurricane. Kate and Todd set their drinks down and look at each other.

"It must be spring fever," Kate says.

But William suspects there's more to it than that. What he's witnessing has the freak-out feel of a manic episode or a monstrous glucose high—what he might expect if his grandsons had downed a pound of Skittles and chased it with Mountain Dew. Short of something like that, William can't imagine what could turn normal little boys into motile bundles of raw energy. It's quantum mechanics made flesh, he thinks—centillions of atoms moving this way and that in random, unpredictable patterns. But in this instance, he's sure the *big surprise* has something to do with it.

Kate goes inside to work in the kitchen while Todd and William talk. After they've covered the Twins and the unseasonable weather, Todd asks what William has heard about the fall term.

William frowns. "Nothing definite. But I'm reliably informed that if I teach in Oslo for a year, it could really help my cause."

"Hey, if that's what it takes to return to the halls of academe, you should give it some thought."

William doesn't say anything.

"Okay, bad idea ... how's the carriage house coming?"

"Good," William says. "I've decided I want to move a wall to make room for a bigger shower."

Todd laughs. "If you don't stop redoing everything and changing it around, you'll never get that place finished."

"That's true," William says, happy in the knowledge that Todd is almost certainly right.

Kate comes out with a big platter of hamburgers and brats, which she hands to Todd. "You're on."

"Okay," he says, and with long-handled tongs, he carefully covers the grill with the contents of the platter.

Kate stands there for a moment, making sure all is as it should be. "I've got to check on the beans and boil the corn. I'll be right back."

"How come you aren't using the wood stove?" William asks.

"I need more practice," she says over her shoulder. "I burn everything on it."

William turns to Todd. "What's with the boys? One minute they're flying around here like protons in a super collider; the next minute they're gone."

"Yeah, they're definitely amped up today."

Kate returns with a bowl of potato salad and sets it on the table.

"That really looks good," William says. "Have you seen the Visigoths?"

She looks around. "Not in the last five minutes." But at that moment Matt and Jake explode onto the scene, moving quickly from left to right. "Go wash your hands and get ready for dinner." As Kate speaks, she follows the boys with her upper body, like a trap shooter leading a clay pigeon.

William grabs Jake as he runs past. He holds him by the shoulders and stares into his eyes. "Are you in there, Jacob? You can tell me—have the pod people taken over your body?"

Jake screeches with delight. "Grampa, you're silly." And off he goes.

William looks at Kate. "I don't think we have any choice—after dinner we'll have to drive north and release them into the wild."

"No kidding," she says.

Dinner is soon ready, and Kate gets everyone, including the two boys, seated at the table with a plate of food in front of them. Kate and Todd have the boys under control, but it's like holding a wolf by the ears.

"Time for grace," Kate says. "Sing pretty."

William was hoping they might dispense with grace altogether, but Kate is going for the full Monty—a musical grace complete with hand holding. After a surprisingly snappy "Be Present at Our Table, Lord," dinner is served, and Kate has made one of William's favorite dishes: baked beans à la Marcia.

"These beans are incredible," William tells her between mouthfuls. "I know there's a secret ingredient in here, but I can't remember what it is."

"Unsweetened applesauce," Kate says. "It makes all the difference—at least, according to Mom."

Suddenly, the boys are yelling at each other. "It's Pelé, moron."

"*You're* a moron—it's Leo Messi."

"Pelé."

"Messi."

"Pelé."

"*Hey!*" Todd says in his knock-it-off voice. The boys look at him and, for the moment, fall silent.

The dinner conversation is fast and unpredictable, like a ricocheting pinball that bounces off one subject, caroms into another, then rattles around a bit before it drains. Only the shooting is off limits.

During a lull in the action, Kate sits up straight and sort of rearranges herself on her chair. "Daddy, I've been meaning to tell you about a friend of mine from MPI. Her name is Shelley, and she just transferred here from Madison. I think you'd like her. She's very—"

"Silence, demon!" William makes a cross of his index fingers and holds it in front of her face, as though he's warding off a vampire. "Stop playing Miss Matchmaker, Kate. What would your mother say?"

"I don't care," she says. "Mom has Walter Burke, but you don't have anyone. I want *both* of you to be happy." She looks at William, and for a moment, he thinks she might cry. "I refuse to believe that God's plan is for you to be lonely."

William never knows how to respond to Kate when she says things like that. She's so adorable and, at the same time, so full of crap.

Todd comes to his rescue. "Hon, let's leave God's plan to God for now. I'm sure your dad knows how to ask a lady out if he wants to."

"I do," William says. "I definitely do. I love you for worrying about me, Kate, but—"

"For your information, I'd quit playing Miss Matchmaker if you'd start dating on your own."

"I will. I promise. But until that happens, I want the dating thing to be my idea. We've talked about this."

Kate shakes her head. "I know, Daddy. I just don't understand. Women *love* you—you've got a great sense of humor, you look like you work out even though you don't, and—"

"And he can still bring the heat on his tennis serve," Todd says. "I know that for a fact. But this is something we should probably—"

"May we be excused?" The boys are nearing their breaking point. They're already half out of their chairs, trembling at the thought of escape.

"I want you back here in two shakes," Kate says. "We're about to have cake and ice cream."

The boys race into the house, and William can hear them thundering down the basement stairs. *What's the big attraction down there?*

William, Kate and Todd finish eating, and when they have discussed everything that needs discussing—Michele Bachmann's future, Adrian Peterson's knee, Garrison Keillor's semi-retirement—Kate asks Todd if he would please retrieve the kids.

He groans. "Okay. It was nice while it lasted."

William compliments Kate on a wonderful meal; she insists it was nothing, and soon Todd returns with Matt and Jake.

"It's time for dessert," Kate says. "Everyone please sit—I'll get it."

"I'll help," Todd says, following her into the kitchen.

William can hear them rattling around in there for a few moments. Then Kate comes through the door with a beautiful layer cake that has five candles on one side and two on the other.

"Fifty-two," she says, setting the cake in front of him. "Get it?"

"I get it," William says. "It's a gorgeous cake. Move over, Martha Stewart."

Kate points to the candles.

"Right, right." William turns to his grandsons. "Give me a hand, men."

Matt and Jake blow out the candles, and William removes them from the cake.

"Here, Daddy." Kate hands him a knife. "This is a White Russian cake. It's supposed to have vodka and Kahlúa in it, but I substituted white grape juice and chocolate extract."

"Of course you did," William says.

Todd looks at Matt and Jake, who are squirming in their chairs. "Maybe just this once, a shot of booze—"

"I hardly think so," Kate says. "The cake is in honor of your new book, Daddy—the Dostoevsky book. Did I say it right?"

"You nailed it. When did I tell you about that?"

"When we had lunch last month, remember? I had just talked to Mom … She and I had kind of a fight because I said her move to Phoenix was hard on … *certain people.*" Moving only her eyes, Kate indicates the boys.

"Oh, yeah. I remember." William cuts a piece of the cake and sets it on a dessert plate, which he passes to Todd, who adds the ice cream. "It's almost a shame to eat such a beautiful cake. Does it have a secret ingredient?"

"No," she says. "Secret ingredients are Mom's thing, but I think that's because she could actually taste them."

"That's a fact," William says. "Marcia Kessler—supertaster nonpareil."

When everyone has finished, Kate explains to William that this year is a little different, that they got him one big present instead of a bunch of little ones.

"I don't need *any* presents," William says.

Kate, who is practically glowing, stands up. "Oh, yes, you do." She looks meaningfully at Todd, then at the boys. William wonders if she's about to recite a Bible passage, but all she says is, "I'll be right back." She disappears into the house, and before William has time to be afraid, she returns leading a half-grown German shepherd on a leather leash. "He's yours, Daddy! Isn't he beautiful?"

William is horrified and certain that he's having a heart attack. "Yes, he's … beautiful … sweetheart. He's …"

The dog, unfazed by all the commotion, looks at William with calm brown eyes that aren't exactly trusting but which have no fear in them.

William tries to recover enough to feign excitement. "Wow … How old—"

"Seven months," Kate says, nearly beside herself. "He's completely housebroken, and he already knows how to sit and come when he's called. He'll be a lot easier than a puppy."

"Ye-es. Where did you—?"

"In Saint Cloud. There's a really good German shepherd breeder there—Hohenstadt Kennel. I called them about getting a puppy, but when they told me about Baron, I just couldn't resist."

"Baron? That's his name?"

"Yes, it's Baron something-or-other, but I can never remember the rest of it. Todd, would you please get his papers. They're in the manila envelope on the—"

"Table in the hall. Yep, be right back." Todd disappears, and Kate and the boys continue fussing over Baron, who has just discovered William's shoes.

"Anyway," Kate says, "Baron's story is really sad. The owner of the kennel said they had sold him as a puppy to one of the big shots at Electrolux, but the guy had a cerebral hemorrhage or something and dropped dead at work." Kate pauses, perhaps out of respect for the dead executive. "But the man's wife didn't really want a dog, so she asked the kennel if they would take him back, and … here he is!"

"Yes," William says. "Here he is."

Todd returns with the envelope and hands it to Kate, who removes Baron's AKC registration form and looks at it. "His name is Baron Hürtgenvoss vom Hohenstadt. Quite a handle, huh?" Kate replaces the registration form and hands the envelope to William. "Watch this, Daddy." Kate gives the leash a little tug. "Sit, Baron." The dog immediately sits down in front of William, who extends his hand so Baron can smell it. But Baron, misreading the gesture, raises his paw to shake hands.

"All right," William says. "I guess we can do that." William takes Baron's paw and gives it a little shake.

"See how smart he is, Daddy? His owner must have taught him that before he …" Kate supplies the fatal verb with a wave of her hand.

William looks down at Baron. "Is Kate right about you, Häagen-Dazs? Are you a smart dog?"

"*Hürtgenvoss*," Kate says. "It even sounds like the name of a baron."

William forces a smile. "Or a Nazi war criminal. Has he been downstairs the whole time?"

"Yes, in the laundry room. He was crying earlier, and we were afraid you'd hear him—that's one of the reasons we ate out here.

The boys have been going downstairs every few minutes to keep him company. Can I see that envelope a sec?"

William hands the envelope back to her, and Kate removes another document. "We don't want to forget this. It's a copy of Baron's health records and his vaccination history. The people at the kennel told me he doesn't need any more vaccinations until he's a year old, but they also said he should be started on heart-worm preventative no later than May first."

William nods. "May first—got it."

Todd hands Kate a second, much smaller envelope.

"Oh, thanks," she says. "I guess there are actually two presents." Kate hands the envelope to William.

William removes a single sheet of paper from the envelope and reads aloud: "Greetings from the Chambliss Kennel Club. This is to acknowledge that you and your dog/puppy are enrolled in our AKC obedience classes beginning Wednesday, April 25, 2012, in the Chambliss Armory from 7:00 to 8:00 p.m. All classes run for six weeks, by the end of which time ..." Someone had handwritten "Beginners Class" on the bottom of the page and circled it. William looks at Kate and Todd. "The twenty-fifth is next week. You already signed us up?"

"Yes," Kate says. "We wanted to make this easy for you." She looks at William and reads his mind, which, under the circumstances, isn't that difficult. "I know what you're thinking, Daddy, but having a dog won't be as hard as you think. You love dogs, you have a fenced-in backyard, and by the time Baron finishes obedience class—"

"He'll be reading Proust in French?"

Kate laughs. "It's more like he'll know the basic commands. Turn the page over."

William looks at the back of the page and groans. "Twenty-two questions? You'd think I was applying for a loan."

"They just want to know some things about your situation—Is this your first dog? Do you live in a house or an apartment? Stuff like that." Kate leans over and kisses her father on the cheek. "I think obedience class will really help forge your new relationship with Baron."

"I have no doubt," William says dryly. "You two thought of everything."

"We tried," Todd says. "The best thing is that German shepherds are really smart, so this will be easy-peasy."

William looks at Todd to see if he's actually serious, which he is. "Yes … a piece of cake." Baron, bored with William's shoelaces, is now trying to remove the napkin from his lap. *A walk in the fucking park.*

It isn't long before it's time to go. William helps with the cleanup, thanks everyone repeatedly and prepares to leave. The boys, who have finally begun to run down, have school in the morning, and William has had enough birthday party.

Kate hands him a five-pound bag of dog food. "Compliments of Hohenstadt Kennel."

"Oh, thanks," William says, heading out the door with Baron.

It's a classic Minnesota goodbye, executed in the driveway, with William behind the wheel of his car and Kate, Todd and the boys in a semicircle next to the driver-side window.

"I don't know how it happened," Kate says, "but we forgot to sing 'Happy Birthday.'"

"That's okay," William tells her. "You don't need—"

"Of course we do. All together, everybody."

So the four of them sing, and when they get to the part where they're supposed to fill in the blank with a name, it's a scumble of *Dad*, *William* and *Grampa*, which causes William a moment of existential angst as he's confronted by these overlapping identities. When it's over, William thanks his family one last time, looks over at Baron, and heads for home, driving slowly and defensively, as though he has a bowl of goldfish on the seat.

"Are you comfortable, Miss Daisy?" William asks. "Look, it's nothing personal. I just don't want a dog."

But Baron can hardly keep his eyes open and doesn't pay much attention. To William's surprise, his cell phone rings before he's gone a mile.

"Goddammit, I thought that thing was off." He looks at the display—Ruth Berman. "Hi, Ruth. It's so nice to hear from you."

"*Oy vey!* Already, he lies."

"No, I mean it. I was just saying to myself—"

"William, please tell me you're half done with the first draft of the Dostoevsky book."

William clears his throat. "I haven't actually started it yet, Ruth. I'm still doing the research and sort of a meta-analysis of what's out there. If I had an assistant, I could—"

"In your dreams, Velvel. Norton needs a finished manuscript from us by the end of August."

"I'm afraid that's impossible. How can I—"

"Find a way, William. I'm just telling you what the nice people at Norton told me. Happy birthday, by the way."

"Oh, thanks, Ruth. That's very—"

"We'll talk later, William. Write the fucking book. Buh-bye."

Baron, whose attention was riveted on William the entire time he was on the phone, continues to stare.

William looks at him and shrugs. "What can I say? It's complicated."

When they get home, William lets Baron out of the car and takes him into the backyard, where he sniffs around for a few seconds before peeing in the long rectangle of light cast by the kitchen window.

"Good boy," William says. "Aren't you supposed to lift your leg?"

Baron cocks his head and looks at him.

"You're right—that was out of line. Let's go to bed."

William places a folded-up blanket next to his bed for Baron to sleep on, but Baron puts his front feet on the bed and makes it clear that he would prefer to sleep up there with William.

"I don't think so," William tells him. "This bed is *way* too high. What if you fell off? You could really get hurt."

So Baron gives up, circles twice and plops down on the blanket. In less than a minute, he's sound asleep. William would like to fall asleep too, but he can't, and he soon finds himself thinking about Marcia and all the birthdays they spent together—quiet birthdays at home, birthdays at seaside resorts, even three or four birthdays in other countries, mostly for the sake of the kids. All those memories that used to give him pleasure now bring him nothing but pain because he no longer has Marcia to share them with.

Lying there in bed, he remembers the little things about her, like the way her eyes crinkled at the corners when she laughed and how she could always tell what food was seasoned with. *Can you taste the lemongrass?* she would ask. Or the saffron or juniper or whatever it was that would have eluded William altogether, had it not been for his wife's inerrant palate.

More than anything, he wishes he were still married, but after the shooting, his marriage didn't stand a chance. He should have seen it coming; every light was blinking red. But in his magnificent self-absorption, William had kept going, heedless and unaware, until the machine broke down. And when that inevitably happened, William wonders why he couldn't have been nuts for just a couple of months. Why did he have to leave such a big hole for Walter Burke to run through? It's as though the cosmos itself had it in for him—first his kid, then his wife. William thinks it's a good thing he didn't have servants or livestock—he probably would have lost them too, right before he broke out in Old Testament boils.

Yet man is born to trouble, William thinks, as the sparks fly upward.

CHAPTER 6

The Lothrup Writers Guild

WHEN WILLIAM WAKES UP, Baron is staring at him, his front feet up on the bed. It takes William a couple of blurry seconds to process the data, but once he does, he whisks Baron into the backyard without even putting on his robe. "I know you're supposedly housebroken and everything, but why tempt fate?" After making sure no one can see him, William walks to the edge of the yard and pees under the big Norway pine by the fence. Baron follows suit, looking up at him as though he's about to ask a question.

"It's called male bonding," William says. "Someday, you'll look back on this moment as a transformative experience."

A little later, after Baron has checked out everything in the backyard—and after the two of them have breakfast—William turns on the TV.

"Let's see what's in the news this morning, Baron." He knows it will be mostly campaign coverage, which it is, but there's also a story about the police digging up a SoHo basement—their latest attempt to find Etan Patz, a little boy who has been missing since 1979. And that story is followed by a piece about the Occupy movement that shows half a dozen young men in Zuccotti Park drumming on five-gallon buckets. William points to the TV. "Baron, if beating on a plastic bucket with a stick is the answer, wouldn't you love to know the question?" William shakes his head. "I don't think I'll ever understand the Occupy movement."

William checks his hands for tremors. They aren't bad, but they aren't rock steady either.

"Baron, I need to write a letter. Just so you know, when I need to write one and I don't do it, it sort of clogs the pipes, and all my other thoughts back up in my head until ... well, let's just say it isn't pretty." William and Baron walk down the hall to his office, formerly Jon's bedroom, and when they get there, William takes off one of his socks, balls it up and gives it to Baron. "Could you please play with this for a few minutes?" William sits down at his computer and turns it on. "Okay, who do you think—David Graeber or Judith Butler?"

Baron, who can somehow identify the lilt of a question, stops playing with the sock and looks at William.

"Yeah, you're right," William says. "We'll go with Graeber, anarchist that he is. Butler would want to grind some off-topic feminist ax."

A few minutes later, William reads the finished letter to Baron.

20 April 2012

Dear Professor Graeber:

I realize that the Occupy movement has neither leader nor spokesman—indeed, it appears to lack organization of any kind. But I've seen several of your interviews on TV, and you seem to understand this phenomenon as well as anyone. For that reason, I was hoping you might clear up a couple of things for me.

First, who are these people? Initially, I thought they might represent the Great Awakening of Marx's *lumpenproletariat*. But that may be simplistic. While it's true that the Occupy movement contains its share of delinquents and free-range troublemakers, it has also attracted graduate students, writers and more than a few professors. So again, who are these people, and what ideological glue could possibly hold such a diverse group together?

And more important, what do they want? The majority of Occupy—the self-proclaimed 99 percent—appear to be protesting the social and economic inequity engendered by corporate capitalism and rapacious banking practices. But most of these people don't appear to have jobs, so their grievances feel more personal than ideological. What's the story here?

Sincerely,

William Kessler

"So what do you think, Baron?"

William knows there's much more to Occupy than banks, capitalism and jobs, but he isn't kidding when he says he doesn't understand it. What's worse, he finds the Occupy movement deeply disturbing, especially the young people. William thinks it's their faces, the way they look as though they've realized, for the first time, that America doesn't need them. Not so long ago, these people would have poured through the Cumberland Gap in search of new lives in Kentucky or Tennessee or perhaps followed the Oregon Trail to the west. But now they sit huddled beneath blue tarps, tapping out some kind of encrypted message on five-gallon buckets—a message William isn't equipped to decode. It makes him feel out of touch and powerless, the way he felt when Hurricane Katrina flushed America's poor into the streets, pulling the curtain back on a stratum of society to which he had never given much thought.

And then, when the TV networks grew weary of Katrina, all of those people had disappeared, just as the Occupy people would soon do. But what bothers William is the knowledge that no matter what happens, both groups will still be out there, legion, angry, dispossessed. He wonders how many unhappy people America can assimilate before it bursts at the seams.

William looks at Baron. "If my Occupy letter meets with your approval, then it's time to give my sock back."

But Baron is having way too much fun to let go. And when William reaches for the sock, Baron plants his big feet and hangs on to it, growling and snorting.

William laughs. "Yes, I'm scared to death, Cujo. Don't be a jerk—give it back." Finally, William pries Baron's jaws off the sock and takes it from him. There are three holes in it, one of them quite large. "I can see we need to buy you some toys today." He holds up the sock and looks at it. "Something made of Kevlar, perhaps." He takes off his other sock and tosses both of them in the wastebasket. "C'mon, we'd better make a run to Field & Farm."

Ten minutes later, they're headed for Dahlberg Road. William needs a number of things for Baron—a safe crate for the car, a few toys, some bowls, a nice collar—and he knows Field & Farm won't let him down. William loves Field & Farm, even the smell of it, and he could spend hours there, checking out the hardware, the tools, the hunting and fishing gear. *Man stuff*, Marcia used to say, with a roll of her eyes. William wonders when he'll be able to think of something that doesn't lead to thoughts of Marcia. He also wonders, as he often does, which of the five stages of grief he's currently in and decides it's depression. Denial and anger didn't last long, and bargaining had ended in the guest bedroom. The final stage of the process is acceptance, of course, but William doubts he'll ever get there or if he even wants to.

Marv, who got to know Marcia at Crosswell, thought William should have fought harder to keep her. *Are you just gonna let that douchebag dentist run off with your wife?* But William didn't want to confront Marcia, even at her most brazen, even when she acquired, to his complete dismay, a host of sick friends in need of her constant ministration and a slew of professional responsibilities that kept her at work half the night. This was in addition to the fictitious meetings—book club, garden club, bridge club—that were consuming an evening per week by themselves. It was obvious that Marcia wanted to get caught, to have her affair with Walter Burke thrust into the open, but when William wouldn't accommodate her, she finally just told him. That was in January 2011, when William had begun teaching again after a four-month hiatus. A week later, Marcia moved out.

For months, William's reaction to his wife's infidelity was a rather typical combination of knee-jerk outrage and self-righteous indignation. But eventually, he was able to see that he had been so inaccessible, so emotionally carapaced that something had to give. William had actually considered the possibility that Marcia might leave him, but it had never occurred to him that she might leave him for another man. That came out of left field. Still, if he had been able to keep his head screwed on straight, it never would have happened. But back then, he was no match for the quantum chaos wrought by all those intractable atoms. Until Jon was killed, that degree of helter-skelter lethality was incomprehensible to him. Today, he can handle it. Today, he's like a Shaolin monk in kung fu training, always ready for his master—or even his dentist—to leap out of the shadows and try to land a crippling blow.

William pulls into Field & Farm's enormous lot and parks the car, making sure to crack the windows for Baron. "I'll be right back," he tells him. "Please don't destroy anything."

William moves through his favorite store at warp speed and heads back to the car, a plastic bag full of purchases in each hand. William is practically running, hoping against hope that Baron hasn't chewed a hole in the upholstery, shit all over the place or devoured every knob on the dashboard.

When Baron sees him coming, he goes nuts, beating his paws against the window as though he intends to tunnel through the Plexiglas. He even barks—something William hasn't heard him do before.

William drops the plastic bags and opens the door. "It's okay, Baron. Everything's okay—I'm back." But Baron is a wreck, trembling and crying as he tries to climb into William's arms. "Baron, what is it? You're shaking all over." Then William remembers how Baron's previous owner had gone off to work one day and never returned. He puts his arm around Baron and whispers in his ear. "I want to promise you something—I'll always come back."

After he gets Baron calmed down, William surveys the Jeep's interior for damage and finds none. "You're such a good dog! Look what I got you." He reaches into one of the bags and hands Baron a little ball made out of rope and rubber. "This is called a chewball. It's much better than a sock. I also bought you a nice crate so you'll be safe in the car, but it was too big to carry, so we have to pick it up at loading dock ..." William looks at the receipt. "Loading dock 17.

Let's go get it."

William drives around the corner of the building and stops at the security kiosk, where they look at his receipt and tell him what he already knows. At dock 17, a young man puts the crate in the back of the Wagoneer, and William heads for home. He's on Dahlberg Road when Kate calls to see how his first night with Baron went.

"It went fine," William tells her. "No problems."

"He was good?"

"Good as gold."

"Did he sleep straight through?"

"Yes. I couldn't believe it."

"I'm so glad this is working out. I think God brought you two together."

"You found Baron on Christian Mingle?"

Kate laughs. "You know what I mean."

William has no idea what she means, but they talk for a few minutes, and when they're done, William looks over at Baron. "Hey, I know what you need, Hürtgenvoss. How about a trip to the dog park? I've never been there, but I hear it's very nice."

Once again, Baron recognizes that he's being asked a question, and his interest piques immediately.

"I think it's over on Hjorth Avenue, just before it becomes Revere Road. Let's check it out."

It's a lovely spring morning, perfect for the dog park, and Baron has a wonderful time cavorting with the other dogs, especially a white mixed breed named Lenny and a yellow Lab named Hazel, whose owners, William learns, come to the park three or four times a week. William is surprised by how strangely satisfying it is to watch Baron romp and play, but after the three dogs have chased each other around for almost an hour, Baron is clearly tired, so William takes him home.

"Don't worry, Hürtgenvoss. We'll come back soon—I promise."

It's while they're having lunch that William looks at his watch and realizes that although Baron has been in his life for only seventeen hours, they are as comfortable together as a couple of Norwegian bachelor farmers. And William is feeling so well that he's actually surprised when he has a flashback that evening. Nothing explains it. There is no memory that triggers the event, no sound or smell that brings it on. William is watching TV, not paying much attention, when he feels sweat trickling down his sides. The next thing he knows, he's at Dewhurst, waiting for Jon to pick him up, and he's just received the active shooter alert on his cell phone. Then he hears shots, a lot of them, coming from Dewhurst's first floor.

"This is not real," William tells himself. "This is not fucking real."

But the shots continue, and when William opens his office door a crack, he sees Jon running flat-out down the hallway toward him. William grabs him and pulls him into the office.

"This is bad," Jon says, out of breath. "*Really* bad."

"Are you hit? Talk to me." William turns him by the elbow. "There's blood all over your jacket."

Jon pushes the door closed and locks it. "It's not mine ... I'm okay."

There is a fusillade of shots from the first floor.

"How many shooters are there?" William asks, his voice trembling.

Jon goes to the window. "Shit! Too far to jump. Why aren't there any police cars out there?"

"How many shooters—"

"Two—I saw two. Are we alone up here?"

"No. Unless they left, there are a couple classes at the far end of the hall, and I think Kaplan has office hours now. What the hell happened?"

Jon, who is still looking out the window, turns around. "I walked in with three or four people, and two guys on motorcycles drove up behind us and parked on the sidewalk. They were dressed in black and carrying knockoff M4s. One of them had a pistol—a nine, I think ... There wasn't much we could do. They came through the door yelling 'Allahu Akbar' and shot at everything that moved. I'm pretty sure the people I walked in with are dead. The girl on my right was hit in the head—that's her blood on my jacket. I was lucky. I made it up the stairs to the landing and got around the corner." Jon's face is the image of disbelief. "I expect this shit in Helmand, not in Chambliss, Minnesota."

They can hear screaming and the steady pop-pop-pop of gun-fire from the first floor.

"I don't think they're in the lecture hall yet," William says. "It sounds like they're shooting up the classrooms."

"Sure as hell, they're gonna come up here."

"We should barricade the door."

Jon looks around. "With what? We need to get out of here. Where are the cops?"

"Maybe they're waiting for SWAT. I can hear sirens."

And William knows he may *always* hear sirens. It was the sounds that day that had proven so difficult to forget. Most of the time, these sounds sleep quietly in the temporal lobe of William's brain, but it doesn't take much to wake them up, and when that happens, there's hell to pay. A couple of months after the shooting, William walked out of Orchestra Hall in Minneapolis when the undulant violins of Vivaldi's *The Four Seasons* had begun to sound like police sirens. By the time he got to his car, he was soaked in icy sweat. Fourth of July fireworks are also a problem. William doesn't attend fireworks displays anymore, but he can hear the Chambliss fireworks from his home, and the thunderous fina-les are always unnerving—the punishing explosions that come so close together it's hard to tell where one stops and another begins.

William waits for the episode to release him, which it does after a few more minutes, and he can't help thinking that his instruc-tions for dealing with these episodes are basically the same pro-tocol you'd follow if you were attacked by a grizzly bear—hit the deck and play dead. In both instances the premise was that, after a while, both a grizzly bear and a PTSD flashback would get tired of mauling you and move on. The trick, of course, was to be alive when that moment finally came.

Baron is staring up at him anxiously, and William reaches down to give him a pat. "It's over. I'm ... okay." William looks at his watch. "Are you ready for dinner?" Baron recognizes the word and leaps to his feet.

On weekends, Tuesdays and Fridays—days when he doesn't have office hours—William likes to work at the carriage house.

There are so many jobs to do. And undo. And redo. Also, William feels closer to Jon at the carriage house than he does anywhere else, and sometimes it's as though Jon is actually there, taping sheetrock around the corner or hanging a door in another room.

William is a far cry from a master carpenter, but he enjoyed teaching Jon what little he knew. It made him feel like a good father. And Jon—he was such a quick study! In no time he was framing up walls, building headers, trimming doors and windows with perfectly mitered joints. *He could do anything, that kid.* Since Jon was killed, work at the carriage house has become a lot more complicated. First, there's the list of things William wants to do: build a breakfast bar; hang the interior doors; finish the trim work; make a railing to the loft; put up faux beams in the bedroom. Then, there's the list of things he wants to *un*do: move the wall in the bathroom; replace the sheetrock in the bedroom with six-inch cedar; replace the sliding door in the kitchen with French doors; put different flooring in the kitchen. It's one step forward and two steps back at the carriage house—just the way he likes it.

On Saturday morning William takes Baron to the carriage house for the first time, and it goes very well. William brings Lamb Chop with them—one of Baron's favorite toys—but Baron has more fun playing with little pieces of scrap and running around with empty tubes of caulk in his mouth. Nothing seems to scare him, except for the table saw, and when William turns it on, Baron puts his ears back and leaves the room.

After working on the breakfast bar for an hour or so, William decides he can no longer put off hanging the bifold doors to the pantry. "It's time to face the music, Baron." William considers bifold doors a royal pain in the ass because they're almost always out of adjustment and rarely close properly. He realizes that they have their place, but bifolds are like certain people William knows: he appreciates their virtues; he just doesn't like them.

After William gets the bifolds installed, he fiddlefucks with the door panels for an hour, until both sides open and close more or less as the manufacturer intended. Then he trims the doorway, which takes him only half an hour, and after that, he tears the shelving out of the bedroom closet because he's thought of a better way to do it.

But the bifolds have left him jittery and nervous, and he can't seem to get past it. William knows from experience not to push his luck at such times, so he picks up the scrap and puts his tools away.

"I don't know about you, Baron, but I'm ready to do something else for a while. Should we try a little gardening? The place is getting overgrown."

Baron is up for anything, so the two of them go back home, and William begins uncovering Marcia's flower beds. What he really needs to do is mow the lawn, but his riding lawn mower is in the shop for repairs, and William doesn't remember which one. That's because it was something Marcia did when he was in Crosswell, and she had hired a lawn service after that. So wherever the lawn mower is, it's been there quite a while. William works diligently on the flower beds, which had seemed like a good idea until he realizes how much he's thinking of Marcia while he does it—especially after he finds little identification stakes with Marcia's handwriting on them beside some of the still-dormant perennials—*astilbe, coral bells, sedum.* For some reason, perhaps because he isn't expecting it, the handwriting really hurts, and William gives up on gardening after an hour or so.

That evening, while William is reading Dostoevsky and Baron is taking a nap, Kate calls again.

"Just checking in. Any problems?"

"Not a one," William says. "Everything is fine."

"Why are you whispering?"

"Because Baron's asleep. He had a hard day today."

Kate laughs. "Well, it's good to know who's running the show over there."

"Yes, it's a classic case of the tail wagging the dog, but he needs his rest." There is a lengthy pause, it's Saturday night, and William has a pretty good idea what's coming.

"Todd and the boys were wondering if you'd like to go to church with us tomorrow."

William is impressed. Using Todd and the boys in this way is a new gambit. Nevertheless, he knows the only person doing any wondering is Kate. "I'm gonna pass, honey, but thanks anyway." What William would like to say is that he doesn't believe in God, the probability of God or even in Baruch Spinoza's God. But his daughter already knows this, so all he says is, "Please convey my regrets to Todd and the boys."

Kate doesn't say anything.

"Are you still there?"

"Yes," she says, obviously miffed.

"I want to thank you again for Baron. What a wonderful birthday present!"

"You're not just saying that?"

"Hell no—I'd swear it on a stack of Bibles."

Kate laughs. "Daddy, you're so awful."

"I love you too, sweetheart. Have fun at church."

"Hang on a sec. Would it be all right if I stopped by around six, after the boys' soccer game on Tuesday?"

"Sure, I'll be here all day."

"Good. The boys want to see you, and they miss BearBear."

"Who?"

"BearBear—that's what they call Baron."

"Oh, okay. See you Tuesday."

Because obedience class is right around the corner, William and Baron spend at least thirty minutes, morning and evening, working on the basic commands. Baron likes his training sessions and loves learning things, but there's nothing he enjoys as much as going to Dewhurst with William. The first time William had taken him, Baron walked up all the stairs, somewhat tentatively, and then raced to the far end of the hall, past the *Edmund Fitzgerald*, past Judy Garland, all the way to where Bob Dylan was revisiting Highway 61.

"Too far!" William hollered. "*Come.*"

And like the good dog that he was, Baron wheeled around and scampered back to William, who opened his office door and let him in.

William's time at Dewhurst has taken on new significance because he's decided to use his office hours to work on the Dostoevsky book. He feels a little guilty about writing a book on Lothrup's dime, but he doesn't have anything else to do in his office, and his guilt lessens considerably if he thinks of his abridged position as a fellowship and his salary as a de facto grant from the Lothrup Writers Guild. Of course, no such group exists, but William is confident it would have awarded him a grant if it did. The only problem with the new arrangement is that in order to work both at home and at the office, William has to lug a suitcase full of books back and forth. But as the recipient of such a generous grant, he doesn't mind. And Dostoevsky's guilt-ridden characters are just as fascinating in one place as the other.

It was after another phone call from Ruth—*Get the lead out, Velvel*—that William actually went to work. He resisted the urge to hopscotch around and began at the beginning, writing a preface and introduction that explained how the primacy of guilt in Dostoevsky's work would be his book's intellectual center of gravity. William is happy to be writing again, and it will make it much easier to handle Ruth. *Yes, I'm well into the manuscript. Yes, I think you'll be pleased.*

William frequently discusses Dostoevsky with Baron, who now sleeps in bed with him. Because William had initially been concerned about the height of the bed, he dismantled the frame, carried the pieces to the garage and put the box spring and mattress directly on the floor. Together, they are no more than twenty inches high, a height that poses no threat to Baron. William's only objection to his newly chopped bed is that it's hard to get in and out of—he has to do it on his hands and knees—but it's worth it, and William enjoys having Baron right there to talk to. At first, William was uncomfortable with the idea of talking to a dog, and he wondered if he was guilty of the pathetic fallacy or some kind of mawkish anthropomorphism. But that feeling didn't last long, and because talking to Baron was so easy, so painless and uncomplicated, William soon found it addictive.

"You know, Baron, in *The Brothers Karamazov,* Dostoevsky uses original sin as a force for good. It's paradoxical in a way, but look at Father Zosima. His metaphysics are based entirely on the relationship between guilt and *philia,* a Greek word that translates loosely as *brotherly love.*"

Baron gives no indication that he cares, but William has spent too many years in the classroom to let that stop him.

"I think the key might be that original sin—at least as far as Dostoevsky is concerned—is *shared* guilt. And it's because we're all guilty that we must treat each other with humility and respect. And we need to remember that everyone we meet is engaged in a desperate struggle, just as we are." William yawns. "We'll have to continue this discussion tomorrow. Good night, Hürtgenvoss."

When Kate brings Matt and Jake by on Tuesday, they ring the doorbell, and Baron, who has never heard the doorbell before, cocks his head and looks in the direction of the sound.

"It's just Kate and the boys," William says. "They want to see you."

William lets them in, and suddenly the front hallway is filled with laughing, barking and salutations—*Hi, Grampa! Hi, BearBear! Hi, Daddy!* William's grandsons are dressed in their soccer uniforms. He gives them each a hug.

"How were the games?" he asks, giving Kate a kiss on the cheek.

"They're called *matches*, Daddy. They were fun."

William turns to the boys. "Well, men, did you win, lose or draw?"

Matt beams. "We won, 4 to 2."

"We got our asses kicked," his brother says, with no less enthusiasm.

"Jacob!" Kate says. "You know better than to talk like that."

Jake shrugs. "That's what coach said."

Matt is on the floor with Baron. "Look how much bigger BearBear is."

"He's gonna be a big boy," Kate says. "Why don't you two take him into the backyard and play?" So the boys and Baron head for the backyard, and Kate follows William through the house toward the kitchen, the usual venue for her visits. "You should have come to church with us on Sunday. The sermon was inspiring—it was about helping the spiritually challenged."

"So you're here to cut the grass? What a splendid gesture!"

Kate smiles. "No, I just stopped by to tell you how happy I am that things are working out with BearBear." She goes to the kitchen sink and looks out the window. "What is it about kids and dogs?"

"I don't know. You want something to drink? I've got Diet Coke, Sprite, Diet—"

"No, no thanks. Since your birthday, the boys have decided they want a dog. It's all they talk about. I guess they're old enough, but ..."

"You should get them a German shepherd, just like Baron."

"That's what *they* say." Kate pauses, then nods toward the back-yard. "The boys are having a ball out there, but before Todd and I take the puppy plunge, I'd like to see them assume responsibility for some of the not-so-fun aspects of dog ownership, like walks, exercise and feeding." She turns to William. "So please feel free to use us as dog-sitters. You'll be doing us a favor."

"Thank you," William says. "That's a generous offer. And since you mention it, how about the weekend of May 12? Marv Kreitzer and I have plans to fish the opener."

"You're giving it another try?"

"We are. We're gonna make it this year."

Like Marcia, Kate got to know Marv at Crosswell, and she doesn't like him much. In fact, the word she had used back then to describe him was *lusty*. "That's fine, Daddy. Just remind me a cou-ple days before." Kate turns away from the window and sits down at the table across from William. "Soccer was exciting today."

"Really?" William says. "They played without goalies?"

Kate smiles indulgently. "No, Daddy."

"They were allowed to use their hands?"

"Of course not."

"Then it wasn't exciting."

"It most certainly was. It's exciting to watch the children work together, to play as a team. It's a wonderful thing to see."

"Uh-huh."

Kate picks up the salt shaker, studies it for a moment, and then sets it back down. "I was thinking we should get together at Rafferty's or the Pasta House and have pizza. Would tomorrow work?"

William laughs. "Tomorrow is a school night—Baron and I have our first obedience class."

Kate touches her forehead with the heel of her hand. "Duh! How could I forget? Another time then—but *soon*."

"We'll work something out," William says.

After twenty minutes or so, Kate rounds up the boys and leaves. William returns to his office, and Baron, who is worn out from playing with the boys, falls asleep at his feet. But as William sits there, staring at the computer screen, he isn't thinking about Dostoevsky. Or Kate. Or even the shooting. He's thinking about Baron's upcoming obedience class, surprised by how nervous the thought of it makes him.

CHAPTER 7

The Hochstetler Method

WEDNESDAY, THE DAY OF RECKONING. William and Baron have office hours, but William is too apprehensive about class that evening to get anything done on the book. Even when he tries to read, his mind wanders, but he can't figure out what he's worried about. *It's dog school, for crying out loud.* He knows Baron is smart—he already obeys the basic commands, although *down* and *stay* need work. But even though William is confident that Baron will give a good account of himself, nothing is ever certain—Baron is so young and the world so unpredictable.

William can't remember what time the class starts, so when he gets home from school, the first thing he does is search through the pile on his desk to find the envelope with the Chambliss Kennel Club information in it. He finally locates it and sits down to read over the material. *Class starts at 7:00. Please bring your completed registration form, your dog's vaccination history, a leash and flat collar, and a few small treats for your dog.* He checks the items off in his head: *yep, will do, I'm all over it, no problem.* Then he answers the questions on the back of the registration form and tells himself over and over—until he almost believes it—that he and Baron are ready to kick ass and take names.

The classes are in the Chambliss Armory, and William allows plenty of time to get there. The armory is a beautiful old building,

Gothic revival, with Byzantine windows and crenelated parapets that make it look like a fortress. When he pulls into the parking lot, he sees two groups of owners walking their dogs on the grass at the far end. William notices that in the group closer to him, all the dogs are wearing gold bandannas.

"Should we have gotten you a gold bandanna, Baron? There's nothing in the kennel club stuff about it."

William gathers up the forms he's supposed to have; then he lets Baron out of his crate and puts a leash on him. When they get to the grass, they pass a woman who is tying a bandanna around the neck of her standard poodle.

"Excuse me," William says. "I was just wondering … what's with the gold bandannas?"

The woman smiles. "A gold bandanna means your dog has passed the intermediate class. It took Bonaparte here two tries, but he finally made it. When he passes the advanced class, he'll get a purple one." She finishes with the bandanna and looks at Baron. "Is he in the beginners class?"

"Yes," William says.

"When he graduates, he'll get a green bandanna."

"Green—good color symbolism," William says. "Thank you for clearing that up."

William joins the group of owners whose dogs do not have bandannas. He then crosses his fingers and walks Baron back and forth in the grass. Everyone there, including William, is praying his dog will do its business now, as opposed to later, in the middle of class. But all the dogs are too interested in each other to think about lower-world concerns. So the owners exchange pleasantries for a few minutes, compliment each other's dogs, and then head for the front door of the armory. William is eager to see what it looks like inside. He's driven past the armory a thousand times, but until now he's never had occasion to go in.

It's dark in the foyer, and it has the aura of an old high school. Even the smells are old—old, fusty and vaguely urinous. On one side of the main hallway is a long trophy case filled with photographs, flags and other memorabilia from the National Guard troops who have met and trained there over the years. On the other side is a bronze plaque commemorating soldiers from Chambliss who had been killed in action, two of them recently. William looks at the plaque for a minute; then he and Baron get in line behind a lady with a dachshund, and immediately, a man with a Newfoundland gets behind them. Baron is excited by all the other dogs, but he gives no indication of being overwhelmed or intimidated. He's just happy to be there. The line of dogs and owners leads to a check-in area in the hallway beyond the foyer, where two ladies seated behind a folding table are examining everyone's registration forms and vaccination records. The woman who checks William in is very friendly.

"A GSD," she says approvingly. "How nice."

The initials mean nothing to William. "What's a GSD?"

"A *German shepherd dog*—that's what they're called, you know. I've always loved them." She looks at Baron's paperwork, turns the registration form around so William can see it and taps on an empty box with her finger. "This is required information— we need your email address, please."

"Sorry." William takes her pen, thinks for a second or two, then writes his email address in the box.

"Almost done," the woman says. "Just one more thing." She hands William an adhesive-backed name tag and a Sharpie. "Please write your name on the name tag, and then you can take your dog into the gym." She points behind her. "Go right through those doors, hon."

"Thanks." William scribbles his name on the name tag, and he and Baron head for the gym. When they enter, William is momentarily blinded by the bright lights, but after his eyes adjust, he sees Marlene from Admissions across the room with a boxer. He feels as though he should say something to her, but he doesn't, just in case she's still angry about *amongst the lakes and pines.*

"Sir, may I help you? Which class are you here for?"

William turns to see a young woman with a clipboard standing beside him. "We're in the beginners class." He points at Baron. "No bandanna."

"Not yet, anyway," she says, smiling. "Beginners are at the far end of the gym, sir. This end is for the advanced class."

"Oh, okay."

"You two have a nice night." She reaches down to pet Baron. "Oh, and sir—please put your name tag on."

"Right."

William makes his way to the other end of the gym, where he peels the backing off his name tag and slaps it above his left pocket. Baron is pulling hard on his leash, wanting to meet a young black Lab who is no more than a few steps away. William recognizes its owner as Evan Ball, owner of Chambliss Marine, where William bought his boat a few years back. He walks over to him, and the two dogs greet each other excitedly.

"Haven't seen you in a while, Evan." William says. "Nice Lab."

"Thanks. Nice shepherd." Evan winks and gives William a smile. "Hey, isn't it about time for you to buy a new boat?"

Almost always, when William runs into acquaintances like this—people who know he went crazy—he feels as though they're checking him out for residual craziness. But Evan doesn't give that impression, and William is grateful.

"Not for a while yet," William says. "I need to replace one of my pedestal seats, though. I'll have to stop in and talk to you about that."

"Any time," Evan says. "I can give you a good price on Lund stuff—cost plus ten."

Already, there are a dozen owners and their dogs gathered at their end of the gym. "Do you know how many dogs are in this class?" William asks.

"Fifteen," Evan says. "And there's a long waiting list."

William is impressed. "I guess we've got the hottest ticket in town."

Evan nods. "The advanced class is maxed too. It's on account of the instructor—some hotshot trainer from Germany."

They talk for a few minutes. Then, an attractive woman, microphone in hand, walks to the middle of the gym. She waves to a couple of people, smiles and addresses the group.

"Good evening, everyone. Could I have your attention, please? Your attention, everyone … thank you. I'm Cheryl Torgerson, president of the Chambliss Kennel Club, and I want to welcome all of you to our AKC obedience classes." She really punches the last three words, and there is loud applause. "As most of you know, we are very honored to have Birgit Hochstetler, a renowned dog trainer from Germany, teaching this cycle of classes." Even louder applause. "Frau Hochstetler is in the U.S. for several months to assist our police in the training of their K-9 partners, and her résumé is ... well, just listen to this." At once, the intonation of Ms. Torgerson's voice changes, and she assumes the cadence of a motivational speaker, leaving certain words and phrases ringing in the air: *world famous ... Hochstetler method ... American military ... David Letterman.* After another minute or two, she brings it home. "So I am thrilled and honored to present Frau Birgit Hochstetler, dog trainer extraordinaire! Let's give her a great big Chambliss welcome!" Really, *really* loud applause.

When Frau Hochstetler walks over and takes the microphone, it's clear to everyone that she means business. She is a tall, unsmiling woman, her hair pulled back in a bun, wearing a belted beige suit with epaulets and pleated pockets that make it look like a uniform of some sort.

"Tank you and goot evening. I am Birgit Hochstetler. My English ist nicht so goot, but dogs, dey not care, ja."

This is supposed to be funny, and Frau Hochstetler waits until the remark compels a thin ripple of nervous laughter.

"Vee are going to verk hart, and you and dog vill go home ..." She searches everywhere for the word. "*Tired.* You vill go home *tired*, ja. No time talk. No time fun and game. Vee get started."

William and Evan exchange glances.

"Hermann Göring in drag," Evan says under his breath. "Whatever you do, don't piss her off."

"Not a chance," William says.

Frau Hochstetler gives the mic back to Ms. Torgerson and heads for the advanced class waiting at the far end of the gym. This causes William's group to breathe a sigh of relief. Their instructor is the young woman with the clipboard whom William had encountered earlier.

"Hi, everybody," she says. "I'm Jackie Carroll. I'm a certified AKC instructor, and we're going to begin by getting these rascals settled down. I'd like you to form a circle and walk briskly around this end of the gym, counter-clockwise, with your dog on your left side. Make him keep up with you. Let's go. And remember—this is *fun*."

Jackie seems very nice, and everyone likes her instinctively. The class begins to circle their end of the gym, and it goes well, except for two young dogs that seem determined to screw up the program. One is a little shih tzu who refuses to walk, forcing its unhappy owner to drag it across the floor like a lifeless clump of hair. The other is a brown-and-white Akita, who has grabbed hold of its leash and is growling and pulling on it, hoping for a game of tug-of-war. The dog's embarrassed owner has no idea what to do, and everything she tries only makes the dog more determined to be a world-class knothead.

Jackie reacts immediately. "Ladies, please bring me the shih tzu and the Akita. I'd like the rest of you to do another lap; then introduce your dog to the person in front of you. Please have them pet your dog while you pet theirs."

So William pets and Baron gets petted, but William is more interested in watching the two troublemakers at center stage. While the instructor works with the shih tzu, the Akita continues to yank on his leash, treating it like a tug toy. William is so focused on the Akita that he hardly notices its owner. But as she switches the leash from one tired hand to the other, William's eyes involuntarily follow the leash upward, like a leading line in a painting, and when he gets to the woman's face, his breath catches in his chest. She's pretty, but it's much more than that. It's the *way* she's pretty—the way her strawberry-blonde hair is such a perfect match for her complexion; the way her eyes, now staring daggers at her dog, are so wonderfully suited to her cheekbones.

"Yoshi," she hisses between her teeth, "if you ever want to see the park again ..." Then she forces a smile and looks around, as though she's waiting for Yoshi's real owner to show up and take the little bastard off her hands.

Jackie, having convinced the shih tzu that walking is better than the alternative, comes over to Yoshi, kneels down and blows gently into his ear. He drops the leash immediately, and his owner looks like someone who has been struggling with her computer for an hour, only to have her seven-year-old solve the problem with a single keystroke.

Jackie praises Yoshi and looks at his owner's name tag. "Amy, another thing you can do when your dog won't let go of something is place your hand across the top of his muzzle and press lightly against his gums, like this." She demonstrates on Yoshi, who is hardly appreciative.

Amy ... William thinks her name completes her perfectly. He supposes she's in her late thirties or early forties, but he's terrible at guessing ages. She isn't wearing a wedding ring, but he knows that doesn't mean anything, not anymore.

Class resumes, and Jackie has them form a line. "Okay, everybody—I want the first person in line to walk his dog past all of you and take a place at the end of the line. Then I want the next person to do the same thing, and so on. You want your dog to ignore distractions, so make him focus on you. Use a treat if you have to. Let's begin."

After the first five minutes of class, Baron calms down to the point where he doesn't pay much attention to the other dogs. Just like at home, he is concerned only with William and what William expects of him at any given moment. Baron trots down the line of dogs and owners like they aren't even there, turning his head only once—and with unaffected scorn—when a Pomeranian breaks ranks and jumps out at him.

After the "distraction" exercise, Jackie teaches the class what she calls *sit-down-stand* handling, which is all about where you put your hands when you have to make your dog sit down, lie down and subsequently stand up again. They practice this for a few minutes, but all that handling makes the dogs squirrelly, so Jackie has the class do a lap around their end of the gym to take the edge off.

But things don't go as planned. They *would* have, had it not been for a large, fuzzy caterpillar that is in the process of crossing the floor at that precise moment. Amy's Akita sees it first and throws an eight-cylinder conniption fit, barking as though he's just spotted a bear, three mailmen and a census taker. One by one, the other dogs see the caterpillar too—or pretend they do. They drop down on their elbows, stick their butts in the air, and join the glorious orgy of brainless barking. There are a few outliers, like Baron, who fight the urge initially, but soon they too get caught up in the moment, and in fifteen seconds, the class has degenerated into complete bedlam. But the thing is ... it's funny, and the owners are soon laughing in the same infectious way that their dogs had begun barking. Jackie has gone to get something to scoop the caterpillar up with when Frau Hochstetler appears out of nowhere. She looks at the group, then walks over to the caterpillar and squashes it beneath her shoe. The barking and the laughter die out instantly.

"No time for diss," she says angrily. She turns to Jackie, who has returned with a broom and dustpan. "I take over now. Better you go clean sumpting."

At that moment, the class hates her, and it doesn't matter how many dogs she's trained or how many awards she's won.

And she hates them right back, glowering at them as though, in the privacy of their homes, they dress their dogs up in little outfits and talk baby-talk to them.

"Dog training ist serious bisniss. Vee not stop for bugs, ja." She takes a deep breath. "Form circle. Dog on left side. I vant you take fife steps und stop. Dog must stop also. Vee go diss vay." She makes a counter-clockwise motion with her hand. "Let's begin—vun, two, tree—c'mon, efreebody. *I mean now!* Vun, two, tree, four, fife, stop. Goot. *Again.* Vun, two, tree, four, fife, stop. Goot. *Again.*"

The class does this perhaps a dozen times, and Baron blows the doors off the exercise because it's almost exactly like the one he and William do in the driveway every evening. Baron even sits when William stops walking, just as he's been taught to do. No other dog in the class does this, and Frau Hochstetler is clearly impressed.

She gestures to William. "I vant to see your *Schäfer.*"

Evan Ball, who is standing behind William, leans close. "I hope that means your dog, bro."

William laughs, but he isn't sure *what* it means. His ancient German is like a car trying to turn over at twenty below. Fortunately, a couple of cylinders fire, and he remembers that *Schäfer* means *shepherd.* He smiles and walks Baron over to her.

"Danke," she says. "Let me haff look." She runs her hands down

Baron's legs, examines his bite, checks his balls. "Goot, very goot." Then she addresses the group. "Vatch diss little *Schäferhund*. He knows vhat he's doing, ja." She instructs William to take Baron to the front of the line and points to a man with a Rottweiler. "Let me please to see Rottweiler."

After that, it gets embarrassing, and it's as though Baron and the Rottweiler are the only dogs in class. Frau Hochstetler singles them out for praise, uses them for demonstration and dotes on them at every opportunity. William knows what's going on. German shepherds and Rottweilers are Frau Hochstetler's stock in trade. These are the dogs she loves, the ones she trains on a daily basis. If there had been a Doberman or a Malinois in the class, William supposes it would have been singled out too.

If Baron and the Rottweiler are the stars, then Amy's Akita is the dunce. In fact, Yoshi doesn't do one damned thing the way he's supposed to. He grabs the hem of Amy's jeans and won't let go. Then, when Amy tries the muzzle squeeze that Jackie taught her, Yoshi breaks her hold on him and bites her hand. And when the class is doing a figure-eight drill, he pounces on a schnauzer in front of him, pinning the smaller dog to the floor. Yoshi is just roughhousing, but it's disruptive, and the owner of the schnauzer is not amused. And neither is Frau Hochstetler, though she says nothing.

Also having a bad night—although for different reasons—is a shy little borzoi who is very nervous around the other dogs and has a difficult time concentrating. At one point, Frau Hochstetler grabs her by the collar and says, "Vake up, Miss Muppet. Diss ist not beauty *con*test." This scares the dog half to death, and it promptly shits on the floor—not once, but several times in rapid succession. The rest of the class look, then look away, knowing that their secret fear is playing out before their eyes. The owner, an older lady who is clearly mortified, cleans up the mess, takes her dog outside and does not return.

A few minutes later, the group is working on an on-leash *stay* exercise when Frau Hochstetler walks over to Evan Ball, whose Lab, until now, has had a pretty good night. She looks at his name tag. "Your dog must obey all commands *first* time, Herr Ball."

Half the group bursts into laughter, and Frau Hochstetler doesn't get it. She looks at the class, confused and embarrassed, certain she's the butt of some joke that her limited English won't allow her to understand.

"Hairball," someone says to her. "Herr *Ball*. Don't you see? It's funny."

But Frau Hochstetler doesn't see, and her initial confusion quickly turns to anger. "*Was ist los?* You make fun at me?"

William summons his rusty German and tries to explain that they are not laughing at her. "*Sie lachen nicht über Sie, Frau Hochstetler.*" And then he tries to explain that *Herr Ball* is funny in English, but he can't think of the German word for *hairball*. He toggles between two possibilities for a hot second, then goes with "*Haarknäuel.*" He's sure the word has something to do with hair, but it could mean "wig" for all he knows.

"*Auf Englisch, Herr Ball ist Haarknäuel,*" he says, crossing his fingers. Then he waits, wondering if he's gotten through, wondering if his German is adequate to the task, wondering if he's just told the redoubtable Birgit Hochstetler that her hair looks like shit.

After what seems like an eternity, the corners of Frau Hochstetler's mouth turn up, ever so slightly, and she begins to smile. "Ah, yes. I understand. So … ist very funny, ja?" She gives William a little nod. "Danke. Vee get back to verk now—train dogs."

William had only wanted to clear up a misunderstanding, but the class despises Frau Hochstetler, and his gesture is costly. He was the teacher's pet before the hairball business. Now, he's an out-and-out traitor. The class would have been happy if Frau Hochstetler had been left to twist in the wind, wondering for the rest of her days what was so funny about Evan Ball's name. But it was the terrified look in her eyes, her inability to understand that struck a chord with William. He had seen that look a thousand times—at Crosswell.

The class, which had been tense before, is even more unpleasant now. Everyone wants it to be over. But there are ten minutes left, and Frau Hochstetler is making good on her promise to send everyone home tired. She asks that the dogs remain in place while she examines each one the way a judge would at an obedience trial or a dog show. Everything goes well enough until she gets to Yoshi, who bolts at her approach and slips his collar. He's at the far end of the gym before Amy can even react.

Frau Hochstetler looks at her in the same way she had looked at the caterpillar. "Get dog and get out."

"I'm so sorry," Amy says. "He's just having a bad night. He isn't really—"

"You und *Dummkopf* go have bad night someplace else, ja."

Amy is shocked. "Excuse me? What did you—"

"I vant you und your dog out uff here. He ist not ready. Needer are you."

Amy doesn't know what to say. She looks like a boxer who's been hit with a haymaker and no longer knows where he is. Amy nods and says she's sorry. Then she walks to the other end of the gym, trailing Yoshi's leash behind her.

"Well, I've had about as much fun as I can stand," someone says. "I'm outta here."

"Me too," says another. "This is like boot camp."

In all, four people leave early. Frau Hochstetler, who couldn't care less, finishes the exercise she had begun shortly before. When it's over, she dismisses the class. William kneels down and pets Baron, telling him what a good little *Schäferhund* he is. Then he heads for the door, wondering why every encounter he has with people leaves him more determined than ever to avoid the next one. Tonight, he'd seen—albeit briefly—a woman he would have enjoyed meeting. Now, he'll probably never see her again. When Birgit Hochstetler kicked Amy out of class, she destroyed an entire probability curve for William, a quantum universe where all things were possible. Now that was over, and *nothing* was possible, at least where Amy was concerned.

When William steps outside, the cool spring air washes over him, and he can't get enough of it. He inhales deeply, then exhales. He does this several times, as though he's purging his lungs of noxious vapor. William looks to the west. The sun is still up but just barely.

William is tired from all the interaction with people. Even the muscles in his face are weary from the workout imposed on them by the smiles, the talking, the array of facial expressions that must be conjured, modulated and then replaced with still more expressions in the endless continuum of social intercourse. It's hard to do that if you're out of the habit, William thinks. It's *very* hard.

He isn't far from his car when he notices a woman sitting beneath the open hatchback of a red SUV. She's leaning forward, head down, shoulders hunched. When he gets a little closer, he realizes it's Amy. This is an opportunity he never expected to have, so he puts Baron in the Jeep and walks over to her, trying to think of something to say. But all he can come up with is, "Tough night."

She looks up without interest. "*Ya think?*" Then she recognizes him. "Hey, if it isn't the brown-noser."

The remark is so childishly unaffected that William can't help laughing. "I haven't heard that expression in a while."

"Oh, really? I would've thought you heard it all the time."

William ignores the jibe. "I'm William Kessler." He extends his hand.

She hesitates but takes it. "I'm Amy Mattson."

"It could be worse, Amy. You could be the owner of that little bok choy with the spastic colon."

"It was a *borzoi*."

"The point is, I'd take Yoshi over him any day." William looks at Yoshi, who is in a crate behind her. He's lying down, being very good. "You know, he'll do better next week. Every dog has his day."

Amy's face is a mixture of anger and bewilderment. "There won't be a *next week*. Maybe you didn't notice, but your BFF Brunhilde kicked me out of class."

"She shouldn't have done that."

Amy looks at him, her face now contorted in disbelief. "And you helped her. How *could* you? She's so … *awful*."

William shrugs. "I don't know. Maybe I shouldn't have." He squints into the sunset. "It doesn't really matter—Frau Hochstetler won't be back."

"Oh, did she confide that to you?"

William shakes his head. "She didn't have to. How many calls do you think the Chambliss Kennel Club is going to get tomorrow? They might be impressed with her credentials, but they'll never defend her—there's no upside."

Amy is almost studying him now. "And you're an expert in these matters?"

"Sort of. But the thing is … Frau Hochstetler isn't really a dog trainer. That's why—"

"Not a dog trainer? What are you saying?"

William looks around and lowers his voice. "Frau Hochstetler's real name is Ludmilla Krieger. She was the East German phenom who took gold in the 100 and 400-meter hurdles in LA at the '84 Olympics. After she won her second medal, she defected, and then, a month later, it turned out she was actually a man." William shakes his head in sad remembrance. "It was an international scandal. I'm surprised you don't—"

"You're making this up, right?"

"Every word. You wanna get something to eat?"

"With you?"

William laughs. "Yes. No one in class ever has to know."

Amy's face reddens with embarrassment. "I'm sorry. I'm just … Where do you want to go?"

"Well, how about Ki's? It's close, and it'll be quiet there."

"Onion soup," Amy says. "They have the best onion soup in the world. I'll follow you."

CHAPTER 8

The Best Onion Soup in the World

WILLIAM FEELS AS THOUGH he's just won the lottery, and he drives the dozen blocks to Ki's with his eyes glued to the rearview mirror, afraid that if he looks away, Amy will disappear from his life forever. He'd been okay talking to her at the armory, but now that he's alone, his heart is going like a speed bag, and his palms are beginning to sweat. *Get a grip. Don't you dare screw this up.* When they arrive at Ki's, he's much better, and when Amy steps out of her car and comes toward him, he's as good as he's ever been.

She smiles, and it's like the sun coming up. "Imagine meeting you here."

"Yes, imagine," William says, certain that he has never seen anything so beautiful.

Amy points to the Wagoneer. "Cool car. It reminds me of a woody wagon."

William nods. "It's old. They haven't made 'em for years."

"Do you think we should put our windows down a little?"

"Yeah, probably." So even though it's cool, they lower the windows a couple of inches for the dogs before walking over to the restaurant's entrance.

Halfway there, Amy takes William's arm and turns him toward her. "I'm sorry, but I need to know right now if you're married, engaged, gay, in a relationship, on the rebound or … what's the other one? Oh yeah—trying to get back with your wife."

William's eyes open wide. "Wow … let's see … I'm recently divorced, but my wife and I were separated for quite a while before that. I'm lonely, and I miss my wife, but I don't think I'm on the rebound. If I were, I'd probably date more, and I hardly ever—"

"My God, an honest man," Amy says, letting go of his arm. "I shouldn't ask stuff like that. I've obviously spent too much time listening to my single girlfriends."

"No, you're right to do it," William says, thinking that if he were truly honest, he'd tell her he was still in love with Marcia. But instead he says, "I think you can rest easy when it comes to me. What about you?"

"Divorced—three years."

"Yes, I noticed in class that you weren't wearing a ring."

"You were checking me out?"

"I absolutely was." William holds the door for her, and they go inside. They're practically the only ones there, so the hostess seats them by a window. It looks out on a lighted pond full of ducks and geese, but most of them are asleep, their heads tucked neatly beneath their wings.

"So …" William says, in a way that means nothing in particular.

"So …" Amy replies, "I'm going to guess what you do for a living."

"Good luck. It won't—"

"You're a college professor at …" She presses her finger to her temple and furrows her brow. "*Lothrup.*"

William sits back in his chair. "I'm impressed! How on earth did you—"

"You have a faculty parking sticker in the rear window of your Jeep. It's expired, though—I noticed that at the last stoplight. What do you teach? German?"

"Actually, I teach—"

"How many other languages do you speak?"

"Three, if you count football, but I don't really—"

"How did you come to teach German? Let me guess—your grandparents came here from Germany."

William laughs. "My grandparents came here from Ohio." Amy starts to say something but William holds up his hand. "I know you've got your heart set on German, but what I teach, in various shapes and forms, is American literature. Oh yeah—the Victorian novel once in a while. And literary criticism."

"Theoretical or applied?"

The question surprises him. "Theoretical—Aristotle to Northrop Frye. Obviously, you've taken a few English classes."

"English has always been my favorite subject. Okay, your turn. What do *I* do for a living?"

William shakes his head. "I'm terrible at this. You are ... a personal trainer finishing a doctoral dissertation on Pre-Raphaelite poetry."

"Now *I'm* impressed. In a single sentence you complimented me physically and intellectually. But I'm afraid you're not even close. I'm the assistant principal at Hawthorne Elementary School."

"That was my second guess," William says. "Good old Hawthorne! Both my kids went there."

The waitress comes and takes their orders—a beer and a club sandwich for William, a bowl of onion soup and a glass of wine for Amy. The waitress experiments with a bit of small talk but leaves when she realizes she's dealing with two people whose focus at the moment is each other.

"How old are your kids?" Amy asks.

"Kate's twenty-nine, and Jon would've been twenty-four in July." He looks at Amy's stricken face. "Yeah, I've got a real knack for buzzkill."

Amy reaches across the table and touches his hand. "I'm so sorry. How did it happen?"

William looks out the window. "He was killed in the campus shooting. Jon was a Marine, and after serving in Afghanistan, he was shot by a wannabe jihadist right here in white-bread Middle America. I can hardly—"

"Oh, my God, William. That's so—"

"I know. Even now, even after two years, I can hardly believe it."

Amy's eyes are full. "William, I don't know what to say. I have a daughter named Lauren. She goes to school at Macalester, and if anything ever happened to her ..." Amy's expression changes, and she stares at William, transfixed. "You're *him*, aren't you? You're the Saint Patrick's Day hero!"

"I've never cared for that moniker."

"But it's true. This is amazing—I'm dining with a celebrity!"

William groans. "Let's just say that I've had my fifteen unfortunate minutes."

"I've actually read a lot about you," Amy says.

"Paul Bouchard's series, no doubt."

"Yes, I read that, but there's a lot of stuff out there. After saving all those people, didn't you sort of ... lose your way for a while?"

"My *mind*," William says. "I lost my mind for a while. I was in Mason Crosswell for four months. Just so you know, Amy, I don't usually get into this stuff until the second date."

"I'm sorry. I don't mean to be nosey. I just ..." Amy looks away, but William can tell she wants to ask him something.

"Go ahead," he says. "You'll never find out if you don't ask."

Amy looks relieved. "All right. I'm trying to remember what you did after the shooting that caused all the commotion."

"Well, there were several things, but my magnum opus was an attempted leap off a cruise ship north of San Lucia. That was right after I had failed to commandeer the ship with a sword."

Amy nods slowly. "Yeah ... I remember now. So ... what's the rest of the story?"

"I honestly don't know—the story doesn't have an ending yet. I was better by last spring—well enough that I was scheduled to teach the fall term—but then my wife left me, and I sort of relapsed. I made it through the rest of the year somehow, but everything fell apart after that. I never showed up for class last September, never contacted the college, and Lothrup was forced to put me on suspension. Now I'm hoping they'll let me teach *this* fall." William rubs his temples. "But there's this Norway thing in the mix, and if I don't teach for a year at our sister campus in Oslo, they may fire me."

"Can they do that?"

"Probably."

"No matter—I'd take the Oslo deal in a heartbeat."

"I'm not interested," William says.

"But why not? Oslo sounds like fun. After a year you could come back to Lothrup and ... begin anew."

"I don't want to begin anew."

"I don't believe you. Everyone likes to start over, to reinvent themselves, to ..." Amy thinks of something. "Hey, haven't you written some books?"

"A few," William says. "Nothing serious."

"Are you working on anything now?"

"Yes, a book about Dostoevsky."

Amy smiles. "Who has the film rights?" William starts to say something, but Amy gets there first. "I'm kidding, William. I'm sure it will be fascinating."

The waitress brings their food and asks if they would like anything else. When they say no, she nods and disappears into the kitchen.

Using a spoon, Amy cuts through the broiled cheese on her soup and tastes it. Her expression is pure bliss. "Oh, my God! This is unbelievable. Do you remember the Soup Nazi episode when Elaine says the lobster bisque makes her weak in the knees? That's *exactly* what this onion soup does to me. You've gotta taste this." She pushes the bowl across the table. "Go ahead—use my spoon."

"Are you a compulsive sharer?"

"I am. Try some."

"Am I tasting for anything special—fennel pollen, turmeric, wasabi root?"

Amy gives him a funny look. "You're tasting because it's good."

"Oh ... okay." William tastes the soup and agrees that it's delicious. "I think there's a little molasses in there—that must be the secret ingredient."

"Molasses? Really?"

"I think that's what gives it so much depth. It's terrific, Amy, but I prefer soup with a little meat in it." He pushes the bowl back across the table.

"Now we're getting someplace, William. These are the things people need to know about each other." Amy closes her eyes, takes another spoonful and then dabs the corner of her mouth with a napkin. "How's the club?"

William has to swallow before he can answer. "Excellent." He points to his plate. "Can you help me out?"

Amy laughs. "Since you're obviously new to this, let me give you a little tip. Sharing is always done for the other person's benefit, never your own. But thank you just the same." Amy accepts a quarter of the sandwich and places it beside her soup bowl. "All right, William, break time is over. Before our food came, I was about to ask if you're okay now."

William is slow to answer. "Yeah, pretty much. My memory is full of holes from shock therapy, but it's getting better." William has never called it shock therapy before, and he wonders why he just did. "The worst thing, though, is living with the fear that I'll end up back at Cross. Over half the people there—close to 60 percent—had been there before, so the odds are three-to-two against me." William pauses and looks out the window. "Every morning when I wake up, I wonder, just for a second, if this will be the day I lose my mind again."

Amy shakes her head. "Stop doing that. If you keep thinking you'll end up there, you probably will. William, look at me."

William stops staring out the window and looks into her eyes.

"You're not going back to Crosswell."

"I'm not?"

"No. But you need to think forward, not backward. I realize that I don't know you well enough to be dispensing advice, but there it is." Amy divides the toast on her soup in half, then in half again. "They make their own baguettes here."

William is uncomfortable. He hadn't wanted to talk about his past, but it was impossible to avoid. What if he clammed up and said nothing, only to have Amy realize, after the fact, that he was the crazy bastard in the *Saint Paul Herald*? That would be bad. That would look as though he were trying to hide something. William nervously rearranges the napkin in his lap. Then he picks up his fork and begins tapping it lightly against the edge of his plate.

"What are you doing?"

William freezes. "Uh … I don't know. Sorry." He sets his fork down. "Actually, I was just wishing you had a skeleton in your closet like I do. I'd even settle for a few disinterred bones. You have me at a terrible disadvantage."

Amy takes a bite of William's sandwich. "You're right—this is good. What kind of skeleton would you prefer?"

"Oh, I'm not fussy. Anything that makes you competitive—a misdemeanor conviction or maybe an outstanding warrant. Even an old drug bust would help level the field. I don't often get embarrassed about what happened to me, but ..."

"But what?"

"But I want you to like me, and if you think I'm nuts, I'm guessing the odds of that go way down." William looks out at the pond again. "Oops. I didn't mean to just ... blurt that out. Now, I've embarrassed you."

"It'll take more than that, William." Amy sets the sandwich down. "We can talk about my skeletons in a minute. Right now, I'm wondering if there's anything else I should know about you."

William rubs his chin. "No, that's about it—I don't really have a job, and my future is a big question mark."

Amy laughs. "You're every girl's dream, Professor."

"I know, but I look at it this way. If I get fired, and if the state supreme court refuses to hear our appeal, then Lothrup will have to cut so many professors that I'll just be another face in the crowd."

"How likely is it that the supreme court will hear the case?"

"It's hard to say. I'm told they accept only 10 percent of the cases referred to them, so ..."

"That doesn't sound very promising."

William shrugs. "It's better odds than the casino."

"That's a pretty low bar, my friend. It's four families, right?"

"Four families, three million each."

"And they say Lothrup didn't warn their kids about the shooters?"

William shakes his head. "Not exactly. Their position in both district and appellate court was that the school didn't warn their kids *in time*. The four kids whose families sued the school were among a couple of hundred students in Dewhurst who received the active shooter alert 182 seconds later than everyone else—after the shooting had already started. Those kids told police that they received the first alert as they were calling 911. But by that time, it was too late."

"Did you get the alert?" Amy asks.

"Yes, I was in my office at Dewhurst. I never had much trouble with my phone there, but for most people, reception was a problem. Nobody really knows why."

"I read it was because of the metal roof."

William nods. "A lot of people say that, but the metal roof was put on in 1997, and it was never an issue. Of course, it might have been the metal roof in conjunction with the pressed tin ceilings. But again—it was never a problem until 2009, when cell phone reception went to hell."

Amy gestures with her spoon. "Maybe it was fog. I also read that fog can affect your cell phone signal."

"I suppose it could, but whatever the problem was, it didn't seem to be related to weather or atmospheric conditions."

"Okay, what about electromagnetic interference? We had a lot of trouble at school when a ham radio operator over on Fairview replaced his antenna with one the size of the Eiffel Tower." Amy holds up her hand, her thumb and forefinger almost touching. "We came *this close* to going to court over it."

"I guess it could be something like that," William says, removing the frilly toothpick from the last quarter of his sandwich. "But nothing changed around campus that I'm aware of, and our signal strength had been iffy for months." William thinks of something and smiles. "Of all the theories, my personal favorite is the English ivy theory."

Amy laughs. "That sounds like something out of an Agatha Christie novel."

"It does, but there are experts who say the ivy on Dewhurst's walls was thick enough to scatter the RF signals, which is why some people got the alert immediately and others didn't. I like that theory, but it's got just as many problems as the rest of them."

"I like it too," Amy says. "But we'll never know, will we?"

William shakes his head. "Probably not. They tore Dewhurst down before any of the theories could really be examined, and there are no issues with cell phone reception in the new building."

Amy swallows her last bite of the gifted sandwich. "But do the theories and reasons really matter? I mean, wasn't Lothrup remiss when it failed to warn its students—some of them, anyway—of imminent danger?"

"Yes," William says, "according to the Ninth District Court and the court of appeals. But the controlling legal issue may turn out to be something else entirely. We're hoping the lynchpin of this case becomes the extent to which a college is required to be the guarantor of its students' safety. That's arguable, and if the Minnesota Supreme Court hears the case, I'm told that notion may become central to our appeal."

"It's a good thing for Lothrup that *in loco parentis* went the way of the dodo."

William looks surprised. "I almost forgot—you're a public school principal."

"*Assistant* principal."

"Assistant or not, you're right about *in loco parentis*. The Ninth District Court and the court of appeals both acknowledged that while today's schools no longer have the responsibilities of a parent, a reasonable person would still expect them to do everything in their power to protect the lives of their students."

"Who would dispute that?" Amy says.

William frowns. "The team of attorneys representing Lothrup College." He puts both hands flat on the table. "Enough of this—I want to hear about you. Tell me something about yourself."

"Like what?"

"Like ... why do you have an Akita?"

"That's easy," Amy says. "I did my junior year of college in Japan, and my host family had two Akitas. I just ... fell in love with them." Amy's voice goes up a couple of notes. "I suppose it's some kind of post-divorce thing, but I started feeling as though my life had become a routine—go to work, come home, go to bed, go to work. It was *way* too simple, so I got a dog. There was never any question about the breed."

William can relate, although in his view, simple is usually good. "Your instincts were spot-on, Amy. If you want to complicate your life, a dog is an excellent way to do it. Say something in Japanese."

Amy makes a face. "Why do people always ask me to do that? *Koko ni eigo o hanaseru hito wa imasu ka?*"

"Very impressive. What does it mean?"

"Does anybody here speak English?"

William laughs. "I imagine that line came in handy. How did you come to be divorced?" The absence of transition makes the question especially awkward, and William hastens to add a footnote. "In my case, my wife divorced *me*."

Amy pretends to wipe her brow. "Whew, that's a relief. I'd hate to think you're the type of person who goes around just … divorcing people."

"Absolutely not. I'm almost always the victim—the male Desdemona."

"I doubt that," Amy says, her smile fading quickly. "Did you know that only 12 percent of married men leave their wives for their girlfriends or mistresses or whatever they are?"

"I had no idea."

"Well, it's true. Unfortunately, I was married to one of the twelve-percenters, and he left me for another woman."

William smothers a laugh.

"You find that funny?"

"I do—but only because the idea of a man leaving you makes jumping off a cruise ship look like a rational act."

Amy's expression softens. "Thank you. That was very kind. You felt sorry for her, didn't you?"

"Who?"

"Birgit Hochstetler. You weren't trying to suck up or show off. You wanted to help her."

William nods. "It was the look on her face … the fear."

"So you're also a nice guy. Next, I'll see a unicorn. Hey, let's share a piece of cheesecake."

"Why would you say that?"

"Because I can't eat a whole piece myself."

"I meant about the unicorn."

Amy smiles. "I said it because nice guys are really, really rare. But unicorns are a bad example. Nice guys are more like … undecided voters. I mean, I hear about them all the time, but I've never actually met one. What about the cheesecake?"

"Another specialty of the house?"

"It is, but I'm mostly looking for a way to keep us here."

"Then I'm all for it." Immediately, William adds *candor* and *openness* to the growing list of things he likes about Amy. He raises his glass. "To dogs and chance encounters."

"I'll drink to chance encounters," Amy says as they touch glasses, "but I'll pass on the dog part, if you don't mind—mine got me kicked out of class tonight." Amy takes a sip of her wine and smiles. "Plenty of people get kicked out of bars and off airplanes—I even know a girl who got kicked out of Bed, Bath and Beyond. But how many people do you know who have been kicked out of obedience class?"

"Just one."

"And that's quite a coincidence because I only know one person who ever tried to jump off a cruise ship. I'd say that makes us even."

"I could challenge your notion of parity, but I appreciate the thought."

Amy brightens. "Oh—I thought of a skeleton. One time in seventh grade, I pulled the fire alarm."

William looks at her.

"There wasn't a fire. I just … pulled it. You don't seem to—"

"Yes, I get it—a gratuitous alarm-pulling. Is that really the best you've got?"

Amy looks disappointed. "It was a *very* big deal. We had an assembly about it."

"An assembly? Oh, my apologies—you are indeed a woman with a past." William pours the remaining beer into his glass. "Just for the record, why did you do it?"

Amy laughs. "I'm not sure. I was sort of a Goody Two-Shoes at the time, and I think I just wanted to see how the other half lived. Haven't you ever done something like that?"

"No."

"Well, you should try it. It's very liberating."

They stay until they're the only ones in the restaurant; then they stay a little longer. Soon, their little section is the only one still lighted, and at eleven o'clock, their waitress tells them what they already know—that the restaurant is closing.

On the way to their cars, William asks, "Would it be okay if I called you?"

"I'd be disappointed if you didn't," Amy says.

"I'll need your number."

"Let me see your phone. I'll take care of it for you."

"Thanks. I hate stuff like that." William fishes it out of his jacket pocket and hands it to her.

"It's off," she says. "Are you one of *those* people?"

"I'm not sure. Who are *those* people?"

She turns his phone on. "Technically, they fall into two groups. One group leaves their phones off because they want to call *you*, but they don't want you to call them. I call that group the artful dodgers."

"And the other group?"

Amy opens his contact list. "The other group is people like my ex-husband who keep their phones turned off because they're having affairs."

"What do you call them?"

"Two-timing rat bastards."

"I see," William says, laughing. "I think I'm probably in the first group."

"Not anymore, Professor. Join the human race—keep your phone on." Amy taps on the keypad for a few moments and hands the phone back to him. "Okay, you're all set. It says *Amy M.* I put in my cell phone number, plus my landline, which I've used, like, twice since the Bush administration—I'm not implying any connection. And I'll capture your number if you call me."

"You mean *when* I call you."

When they get to their cars, they stop and listen, but there is no sound from the dogs. "I think they're asleep," Amy says. "Hey ... I had a really nice time tonight—I mean, *after* class."

"Me too, Amy M. Good night."

They drive away from the restaurant, and as William heads for home, he's sure Chambliss has never looked so lovely. In fact, everything he sees is practically humming with beauty—the silent, stately houses; the purling river; the dark city breathing softly all around him. This is new, different and entirely unforeseen.

When he gets home, William goes straight to his computer. He's meant to write Walter Burke for quite a while now, and tonight seems like the perfect time.

25 April 2012

Dear Walter:

I'm not yet ready to forgive you for the role you played in ending my marriage (that may take a while). But I recognize that for too long, I was not there for Marcia, and you were—a fact for which I am honestly grateful.

I hope you and Marcia are enjoying Phoenix and that your new dental practice is flourishing. I go to Dr. Nordmeyer now, but if there is someone you recommend, I would certainly consider changing.

Best wishes,

William Kessler

It feels good to write the letter, and William believes it's more or less honest, except for the part about enjoying Phoenix, which he suspects is manifestly impossible. William is aware that a million and a half people live in Phoenix, but what he can't understand is why. When Marcia told him that she and Walter would be moving there, William had performed due diligence and done a little reading. Among other things, he learned that Phoenix has an average of 110 days a year when the temperature exceeds one hundred degrees—about the same number as Riyadh, Saudi Arabia. And if that isn't bad enough, Phoenix also has the highest skin cancer rate in the country and only eight inches of annual rainfall. But even that isn't the worst: Phoenix also happens to be smack-dab in the middle of Maricopa County, which is home to five species of venomous scorpions, nineteen species of venomous snakes, and a frightful array of venomous spiders—plus, Joe Arpaio. Talk about a fucked-up place.

William goes into the living room where Baron is stretched out full length on his side. "I can't believe how big you're getting."

Baron opens one eye and looks at him.

"C'mon, let's go out. Then we can hit the sack."

Baron gets to his feet and follows William sleepily through the kitchen and into the backyard.

"Frau Hochstetler wore you out tonight, didn't she?"

The night sky is beautiful and shimmers with stars. Without even looking hard, William finds both dippers, Cassiopeia and Orion, off to the southwest.

"Baron, if you follow the line of Orion's belt toward the horizon, it leads directly to Sirius, the Dog Star, which is part of the constellation Canis Major. He's the Great Dog that follows Orion across the sky. Did you know there were dog constellations?"

But Baron isn't interested. He's nearly too tired to stand. Even so, William has one more thing to tell him. "You know the lady who was with Yoshi? I want to see her again. I just thought you should know."

Again, William looks up at the sky. "Dostoevsky was right, Baron. 'The darker the night, the brighter the stars.'"

They go back inside, and Baron has a drink before heading for William's downsized bed, which he steps onto and lies down hard. William joins him a few minutes later, and Baron is already asleep, snoring softly like he does.

As he lies there, William tries to remember the last time he fell asleep thinking about a woman.

CHAPTER 9

A Black Bra and Panties

WHEN WILLIAM AWAKENS the next morning, his entire process of reconnecting with the world is different. Usually when he wakes up—even before he opens his eyes—William can feel the pain, and he knows that something is dreadfully wrong, even though it may take three or four seconds before he remembers about Jon and Marcia. But Thursday morning isn't like that, and in those intervening moments between sleep and wakefulness, William is reasonably sure he's happy, although he can't figure out why. Then he remembers about last night and Amy, and his unfamiliar feelings start to make sense. He would like to ask Amy out on a date—a *real* date—but he doesn't know what to propose until he and Baron pick up his mail in Dewhurst Hall later that morning, and there is a big poster by the mailboxes advertising Lothrup's spring play.

William reaches down and pats Baron on the shoulder. "That's perfect, Hürtgenvoss. What was it Blanche DuBois said? *'Sometimes there is God so quickly.'"* William realizes the unexpected solution to his date quandary has more to do with serendipity than with God, but either way, the play is a good idea, and he's happy with it.

Baron knows which door to run to now, and as soon as William lets him in, he checks the office out thoroughly, making sure everything is precisely as he left it. He has a few select toys there—a plush turtle, a set of Nylabone keys, a little pig that oinks—but tennis balls are his favorite because he can bat them around the office, and unlike at home, they never get lost under anything.

William decides to call Amy at noon, when he can catch her at lunch, so he takes his time going through the mail, which includes this week's copy of the *Beacon*.

"Shall we see what's in the local rag, Baron?"

The *Beacon*'s lead story is about Lothrup's intention to raise tuition, and the article is heavily interlarded with quotes from Chancellor Gardner explaining how a tuition hike is necessary because of the generous amount of student aid that Lothrup provides to its students. William goes from there to the *Beacon*'s editorial, which disputes the need for a tuition hike, arguing that if the amount of student aid is creating a financial burden on the college, then perhaps it should be reduced. William thinks this makes more sense than raising tuition, but the college will do whatever the hell it wants—he knows that for a fact.

William's favorite section of the paper is Letters to the Editor, but this week there is only one—a plea from *Light It Up* urging the college to install LED lighting in the commons, along the walking paths, and in the parking lots. It makes the same argument that Olivia Schmidt had made in his office when she asked him to sign the petition, but it concludes with a quote from Chancellor Gardner: "It is cost-prohibitive for Lothrup to transition from halide lights to LED lights at this time. We currently have nothing budgeted for a capital outlay of this sort, and none of our affiliated foundations is likely to underwrite an elective infrastructure project. So if you feel the campus is too dark, I suggest you buy a flashlight."

William smiles. "You were doing okay until you tacked on that bit about the flashlight. Way to stick the landing, Chancellor."

William saves the rest of the paper for later and works on the Dostoevsky book until it's time to call Amy.

But then the unexpected happens. When noon arrives, William finds that he's too nervous to make the call. By ten after twelve, he's in the throes of a panic attack, complete with cold sweats and a strange taste in his mouth. William knows what's wrong—he has no business calling Amy. In fact, the smart thing would be for him to forget about her, given the way he feels about Marcia. William doesn't understand how he can still be in love with Marcia and be half in love with Amy at the same time. Or maybe it's closer to three-fourths.

Whatever it is, until last night, William would not have thought such a thing possible. Now, he isn't so sure. Loving two women would be like living in two different universes, but this is only possible in a quantum multiverse, where everything imaginable is happening, not on a single linear timeline but on a vast web of timelines that overlap like Venn diagrams. In one of those quantum worlds, it is perfectly normal to be in love with two women at once. In fact, in one of those worlds, William has *always* been in love with two women at once. But it sure as hell isn't the world he's living in.

Suddenly, in the middle of all this cerebration, William has an idea. Maybe things aren't as complicated as they seem. Maybe he should forget about quantum mechanics for a moment and seek a more conventional answer to his problem. He types furiously.

26 April 2012

Dear Abby:

I am fifty-two, and even though my wife has recently divorced me, I'm still in love with her. This fact is problematic in itself, but now I find that I'm attracted to a woman I met recently quite by chance. Today, I'm on the brink of calling her and asking her out, but this is one of those impulses that feels ill-advised, like buying a lottery ticket or drawing to an inside straight. And yet I want to do it anyway. Considering my feelings for my ex, is this a good idea? —Manic in Minnesota

William looks at Baron. "Abby would probably say, 'Hell no, you idiot. It's a terrible idea. By the way, aren't you the guy who went bonkers on the cruise ship?'" He takes a deep breath and lets it out slowly, not at all surprised to find that the anxiety and the metallic taste in his mouth are gone. It never fails, he thinks—*write a letter, feel better.* That's what Dr. Spurling used to say, and for some weird reason, it worked. "To hell with it, Baron. I'm calling her." William turns on his phone, finds *Amy M* in the directory and presses CALL.

Amy answers right away, and when William hears her voice, he experiences a strange frisson of excitement. "Hello, Amy. This is William Kessler … from obedience class."

"Oh, hi," Amy says. "I'm so happy you called."

"I've been thinking about you all morning. Where are you? Can you talk?"

"Sure. I'm in my office having lunch."

"What are you wearing?"

Amy laughs. "Just a black bra and panties—I can't eat a baloney sandwich any other way. What about you?"

"Beige chinos and a short-sleeve shirt."

"I meant where are you?"

"Oh—at school. I have office hours today. Would you like to see a play with me on Tuesday night?"

"I'd love to. Which one?"

"Lothrup is doing *Buried Child.* It's student-directed, but—"

"Whose play is it?"

"Sam Shepard's."

"The *actor*?"

"Well, he's *also* an actor. A lot of people would say Sam Shepard is America's greatest living playwright. The curtain is at eight. Can I pick you up at seven?"

"Sounds great," Amy says. "I'm already looking forward to it."

"Me too." William is about to say goodbye when he realizes something. "I don't know where you live."

"We'd better fix that." Amy gives him directions, and after they talk for a minute or two more, she gets another call and has to go.

William rocks back in his chair, feeling as though he's in high school again. *A black bra and panties.* He closes his eyes and tries to imagine it. Then he *really* feels like he's back in high school.

Half an hour later, William is rereading parts of Dostoevsky's

The Idiot, wondering why, throughout the middle section of the novel, so many of the characters are readily—perhaps even *brainlessly*—forgiven by Prince Myshkin.

"Baron, I don't see how there can be forgiveness without atonement," William says. "That seems all wrong, like climbing a mountain without the pain." William closes the book but keeps his thumb in it. "Maybe that's Dostoevsky's point. Maybe Myshkin is *too* forgiving. All the people around Myshkin are guilty of something, but he abrogates their guilt without even acknowledging it. That can't be right."

William puts in a good day on the book—there are no knocks on the door—but just as he is about to go home, he receives two emails from *The Office of the Chancellor* that have been blind copied to every member of *The Lothrup Community*. His first thought is that one of the emails is an announcement about whether or not the Minnesota Supreme Court has agreed to hear Lothrup's appeal, but neither has anything to do with that. The subject of the first email is "Lower Parking Fees Approved," and it makes William smile. In January, not long after he was placed on probation, Lothrup was rocked by an unprecedented seismic event when Moody's downgraded the college's credit rating from Aa3 to A1.

The reasons for this, according to Moody's, were "questionable liquidity and enrollment stagnation," but everybody knew it was because Lothrup was potentially on the hook for a fuck-ton of money. Nevertheless, the *why* didn't really matter. What mattered—at least as far as Lothrup's administrators, regents and fatcat alumni were concerned—was the *how*, as in *how do we restore our credit rating even though we might have to cough up twelve million dollars to settle a wrongful death suit?*

Chancellor Gardner, eager to seize the bull by the horns, immediately fired the director of Financial Affairs and two other bean counters who had the misfortune of working in offices across the hall from his. But Gardner knew it wasn't enough just to fire people. He had to look like a problem-solver, so to that end he established a dozen committees, blue-ribbon panels and investigatory commissions charged with figuring out how to get Lothrup's credit rating back up to snuff.

Because William wasn't teaching, he assumed he wouldn't be tapped for a committee assignment, but Gardner surprised him by putting him on a committee called Student/Faculty Relations. William had been holed up in his office for a couple of weeks at that point, and he supposed this was Gardner's way of forcing him into the open, where people could get a look at him and decide for themselves how crazy he was.

After three meetings in which William never said a word, it was the committee's considered opinion that student/faculty relations were indeed important, and to prove it, they recommended a sizable reduction in student parking fees—a perennial gripe among Lothrup's upperclassmen. William couldn't see what parking fees had to do with student/faculty relations, let alone with Lothrup's credit rating, but it was pandering at its finest, and he wasn't about to get in the way of it. And now, according to Gardner's email, the reduced parking fees had been approved. This is inspired, William thinks. There's nothing like lower parking fees to show a credit rating agency that you really mean business.

Gardner's other email is an announcement that Clifford Wicks has accepted Lothrup's invitation to be its commencement speaker. Originally, the commencement address was to be delivered by conservative luminary Richard Weber, who had written several best-selling books and was a sometimes pundit on Fox News. Weber was a good public speaker with a national reputation, and Lothrup had booked him months in advance. Then somebody read his book, *Race, Ethnography and IQ,* and things began to unravel. Several hundred students protested on the commons, insisting that Weber should be prohibited from addressing the student body on account of his racist views. The area newspapers picked up the story, and in no time the Twin Cities papers had it on the front page. The whole thing was about to go national when Gardner reconstituted the Commencement Committee and instructed them to cancel Weber forthwith and find someone else—*pronto.*

The Commencement Committee turned the country upside down, but by then everyone they wanted was already spoken for. Finally, they settled on a long-retired Minneapolis news anchor named Clifford Wicks—*The News at Six with Clifford Wicks*—who

THE SAINT PATRICK'S DAY HERO

had won both an Emmy and a Peabody back in the day and who, by most accounts, still had all his marbles. But Wicks, knowing that he had Lothrup over a barrel, played hard to get and tried to negotiate his fee, which was a fraction of what Richard Weber would have earned, had he not insisted that people from Africa have lower IQs than people from other places. Finally, the Commencement Committee made Wicks an offer he apparently couldn't refuse, which meant the committee could once again be disbanded. That pleased William enormously because, for some reason, Gardner had put him on that committee too.

The next morning William wakes up happy again, and one of the reasons is that he has to get his boat ready so he and Marv can go fishing that evening. This is a delightful task, one of life's unrivalled pleasures, and as soon as he and Baron finish breakfast, William pulls his boat out of the garage and parks it in the driveway. It's a nice rig—a twenty-foot Lund with lots of bells and whistles. It's six years old, but as far as William is concerned, it's barely broken in.

First, William connects the hose, finds a bucket and sponge and washes the boat from bow to stern. This takes longer than usual because it turns out that Baron loves water, especially the kind that shoots out of a hose. He likes sponges too, but eventually Baron wears down, which means William can move on and check the trailer lights, charge all three batteries, change the lower unit lube, vacuum the floor and hook up the electronics. After that, William puts his fishing rod and tackle box in the boat and runs through a mental checklist of everything else: minnow bucket, landing net, hook disgorgers, running-light masts, flashlight, anchor, boat registration card, proof of insurance, drain plug, spare drain plug. Other than gas, that ought to do it, he thinks.

Getting the boat ready for the season is fun, but it also hurts because until Jon enlisted, it was a job they always did together, a spring rite filled with playfulness—*Oh, did I get you wet?*— and lots of good-natured ribbing about who caught more fish and who let the big one get away. And because Jon was a techie, this was when he would always make the case for another sonar, a

109

better GPS or some kind of whiz-bang technology that promised to put more fish in the livewell. That's how the boat came to be so tricked out. William doesn't know what half the stuff does. He just enjoyed watching Jon play around with it.

When William finishes with the boat, he and Baron go over to the carriage house, where William looks for a job he can do in a couple of hours. He considers putting the sink in the bathroom vanity, but because that would be a step forward, he removes about a third of the sheetrock in the bedroom instead. After he takes it off the wall, he breaks it into pieces and hauls it outside.

"I'm gonna need a roll-off on this job," he mutters.

On his return, William decides it's time to install the missing trim piece over the bedroom door, so he cuts a board, grabs the air nailer and quickly nails it in place—whap-whap-whap. The sound of the air nailer often conjures images of the shooting, but because it's a noise he's used to, William can usually suppress these memories intellectually. But not today. He sets the nail gun down and staggers blindly to the window, repeating his mantra—*This is not real. This is not fucking real.* But it's too late—the flashback has him in its grasp, and it is nothing like a bear. This one is a giant squid that wraps its tentacles around him and squeezes until William can hardly breathe. The shooting and the screams grow louder, and the terrible noise, which had been rolling up from the east stairwell, is now coming from the west one too. Jon is pacing like a caged animal.

"We have to go," Jon says. "We can't just wait for them to come up here and kill us."

"But the police will be here any—"

"We don't know that." Jon goes to the window again. "Look, I don't care where we go, but we can't stay here."

William stares at him. "It's not like we can go *down*."

"Is there any place we can hide?"

"No. There are only classrooms and offices up here. There's the janitors' closet, but ..."

Then, as he has done so many times before, William sees the dying student, his throat blown apart, turn toward him and collapse. The shooter at the end of the hall, backlit by the stairwell windows, doesn't look human. The refraction of warm rising air has turned him into a phantasm, a willowy black Slenderman with absurdly long arms and legs.

You have to run, Dad. He's reloading. Come to me, goddammit!

For ten full minutes, the flashback holds William in its grip; then the sound of shooting fades, and one tentacle at a time, the flashback lets him go. The episode is a bad one, and it has left William exhausted, worn out in the way he used to be after electroconvulsive therapy.

William sits on the stairs and tries to collect his thoughts until the air compressor kicks in, causing him another moment of unabated terror. He turns it off angrily, bleeds the tank, and then he and Baron go home, where he waits on the front porch for Marv and tries to recover.

CHAPTER 10

An Unimpeded Flow of Chi

WHEN MARV ARRIVES forty-five minutes later, the first thing he sees when he gets out of the car is Baron, lying at William's feet. "Duz yer dewg byet?" he says, doing a near-perfect Clouseau imitation.

William smiles. "No, he's a real sweetheart. Come say hello. His name's Baron."

So Marv steps up on the porch and kneels to pet Baron, whose initial caution quickly gives way to delight, once Marv proves he knows all the places that dogs like to be petted, scratched and tickled.

"He's a nice boy, William." Marv gives Baron a pat on the shoulder and stands up. "Did he follow you home from school?"

"No, he's a—"

"Goddamn! It's good to see you."

"Right back at you, Marv. It's been way too long."

William and Marv don't shake hands anymore. They used to, but somewhere along the line, they stopped. It wasn't as though one of them said, *Hey, this handshaking business is an empty gesture that doesn't have fuck all to do with our friendship.* But they both must have felt that way, or they'd still be doing it.

"I almost forgot," Marv says. "I brought dinner. Be right back." He goes to his car and comes back with a pizza box in one hand and a six-pack of Heineken in the other. He hands William the

THE SAINT PATRICK'S DAY HERO

pizza. "The house special from Allegretti's—no anchovies, just the way you like it. Tell me about Baron. Where did you get him?"

So William recaps the story about Kate and the birthday party, while Marv pets Baron and laughs.

"So how *is* Kate?" Marv asks.

"She's fine but about the same—very religious."

"I thought that might be a phase."

"Me too but not anymore." William shakes his head. "Kate really puts the *leap* in Kierkegaard's *leap of faith*. The way she sees it, when God isn't busy hurling gas balls around the firmament, he's tracking every atom in the universe and listening to the individual prayers of two billion people just like her, who think God is micromanaging every aspect of their lives."

Marv nods. "You know, the problem with people who think God is responsible for everything is that they think ... God is responsible for everything."

William smiles. "Splendid tautology. Another nugget from the Department of Redundancy Department."

But Marv isn't listening. He's staring at William's lawn. "Are you sure that au naturel is the look you're after here?"

"My rider is in the shop, so I'm cutting a section at a time with my old push mower." William holds up the pizza box. "Marv, the knowledge that there's an Allegretti's pizza in here is killing me. Not only that, we're in serious need of a bottle opener. Let's go inside."

As they walk into the house, Marv waves his hand at all the emptiness. "Are you ever going to buy any furniture?"

"I can see you know nothing about feng shui," William says. "If you did, you'd realize that my goal is to have an unimpeded flow of chi from one end of the house to the other."

"No shit?"

"Marcia took the furniture."

Marv laughs. "That's the usual way of it."

After they've had a beer apiece and a slice of pizza, William points to the clock on the kitchen wall. "We need to hit the road—they're getting away out there."

"I'm ready," Marv says. "We'll bring the beer and pizza with us. But there's one more thing." Marv pulls his jacket off the chair back, reaches into the pocket and removes a package wrapped in tissue paper that he hands to William. "Happy birthday, my brother. You're gonna love this."

William unwraps his gift and finds himself holding a round piece of heavy yellow plastic about the size of a small dinner plate. The "plate" folds neatly in the middle, and across the back is an inch-wide elastic band. William holds it up. "Marv, I have no idea what this is."

"But you will. Put it on your hand—your hand goes underneath the elastic."

William puts the piece of plastic on his right hand. "Like this?"

Marv nods. "Now move your hand."

William opens and closes the yellow object several times. "A Pac-Man puppet?" Suddenly, his face lights up. "I know what this is—it's for removing fish from the livewell."

"Winner, winner, chicken dinner!" Marv says, clapping him on the back. "Now you won't get finned anymore. Isn't it ingenious?"

William nods. "It sure is. And simple too, like most good ideas. Thank you very much."

"Aw, shucks, partner. 'Tweren't nothin'. I gotta put my stuff in the boat."

So while Marv does that, William takes Baron out before leaving him alone for what will be the first time. When they come back in, William has a little talk with him in the living room.

"Baron, I'm sorry about leaving you like this, but I made these plans before I even knew you existed." He tickles Baron behind both ears. "Here's Lamb Chop, and you've already got Mr. Monk and your chewball. Are you gonna be okay?"

"Don't worry about me, Mom. I'll be fine."

William turns around to find Marv standing behind him, laughing. "Where's your little blue cooler? It's not in the garage."

"I think it's downstairs. I'll get it."

On the way out of town, William and Marv stop at a Holiday station to gas up the boat and buy minnows. When they leave, William heads east, which causes Marv to sit up and take notice.

"Where are we going?" he asks.

"Lloyd Lake."

"I would've bet you'd want to go up north someplace."

"I thought about it, but it's really early, and we need the warmest water we can find. Lloyd has a lot of shallow, mud-bottomed bays that will heat up faster than anywhere else."

"Like I always say, you should have been a guide."

"Too much pressure."

Marv laughs and slides his seat back. "*There*—that's better. Take me to the big ones, William."

Marv isn't a very good fisherman. He's way too excitable and tends to set the hook too early, too late or not at all. And when he has a fish on, Marv pumps the rod without reeling, which creates so much slack line that a lot of Marv's fish get away without half trying. But what Marv lacks in ability, he more than makes up for in enthusiasm, and William would rather fish with Marv than with anyone else in the world. There's just no one who enjoys fishing more than Marv. And there's no one who enjoys Marv more than William.

When they get to the landing, they put the plug in the boat, disconnect the trailer lights, and William backs the rig down the ramp into the water. Even though the boat has been on the trailer all winter, it rolls off easily, and when William turns the key, the engine roars to life, purging its fogging oil in a few seconds of white smoke. Marv drives the Jeep and trailer to the parking area, and when he returns, he gets into the boat and takes his seat next to William. As they motor away from the landing, William trims the motor down and slowly increases the speed until the engine is running at three-quarter throttle.

"She sounds good," Marv shouts.

William nods.

They go all the way to the south end of the lake, where William pulls into a little bay half the size of a football field. He glances at the sonar and turns off the motor. "This bay and the one next to it have been in the sun all day today. Let's start here."

"Are we gonna troll?" Marv asks.

William looks at the water. "For a while … We'll see how it goes with jigs and minnows or maybe a Mister Twister."

William moves to the bow of the boat and uses the electric motor to work the weedline and the edge of the lily pads, which are visible but still several inches below the surface. He knows the crappies won't be very aggressive, so he moves as slowly as possible. For several minutes nothing happens.

Then Marv sets the hook, and William can feel it all the way in the front of the boat. "What have you got there, Mr. Linder? Do we need to strap you in?"

Marv is hunched over, laughing and reeling furiously. "It's not a crappie, that's for sure. He's big, my brother. He's got shoulders."

William looks at the line angle. "It's a northern."

"How can you—"

"Because he's making his fight out there, away from the boat. He's probably about to run. Just let him do what he wants."

The fish takes off and Marv's reel screams.

"What's wrong with your drag?"

Marv is still reeling, but he's not taking up any line. "It's Toulouse, Lautrec."

William laughs. "Then tighten it up. Just turn it." The fish peels off another ten yards of line. "The other way, Marv."

The northern puts up a good fight, but somehow Marv gets the fish close enough to the boat for William to net it. Marv is worn out but happy. "What a fish! Isn't he a beauty?"

"He sure is—eight pounds, easy. But not in season yet." William holds the fish with both hands and prepares to return it to the water.

"Let me." Marv takes the fish from him and releases it gently over the side. It vanishes with a swish of its tail. "Thank you, fish."

"Okay, back to work," William says. He catches a bass a few minutes later, but after an hour, they still haven't caught a crappie.

"Too early in the year?" Marv asks.

"Maybe just too early in the evening." William looks over his shoulder to the west. "If anything is going to happen, it will be when the sun touches the trees." He turns the boat toward deeper water. "How was your appointment?"

"Same old, same old," Marv says. "Hanselman tweaked my meds and took a thousand pages of notes. He said he bought a cabin on some lake over by Alexandria. You know his nurse? The one who looks like Jennifer Lawrence? She's engaged to a radiologist at North Memorial. Or maybe it was Park Nicollet. Oh yeah—

Dr. Spurling sends his love. So does Dr. Niles. Remember him, the Dr. Phil wannabe?"

"Of course. That guy was a walking catalog of off-the-wall bromides. A couple days before I was released, Niles came up to me and said, 'Remember, William, no dog ever peed on a moving car.' I *still* don't know what that means." William lets out another six feet of line. "What do they have you on?"

"Well, I was on Xanax and Zoloft, but Zoloft tended to … soften my resolve."

"Really? Zoloft is just sertraline. It's not exactly Viagra, but it shouldn't—"

"Well, it did," Marv says. "I told Hanselman, and he switched me to something that starts with a W. It's purple … The name is on every pill."

"Wellbutrin?"

"Yeah," Marv says. "That's it."

"I don't know what Wellbutrin will do for your head, but it shouldn't have any adverse effects on your sex life."

"Were you ever on it?"

"I've been on everything. Here's a bonus—Wellbutrin won't make you gain weight. It's not a serotonin inhibitor like Zoloft. What it does is regulate dopamine."

"Whatever *that* is," Marv says, laughing. "I've heard of a jailhouse lawyer before, but until I met you, I'd never heard of a nuthouse druggist."

"It was a hobby born of necessity. I decided if somebody was going to make me take a drug, then I should know something about it."

"Well, I'd put you up against any pharmacist I know. What are you on now?"

"Effexor and Ativan." William turns all the way around so Marv can see his face. "Pretty cool, huh?"

Marv raises his eyebrows. "*Very* cool. You're off Paxil—congratulations! I hear Paxil is as hard to quit as lithium."

"I don't know, but it was rough sledding there for a while." William steers the boat toward some lily root, which is sticking half out of the water. "Aren't psychotropic drugs amazing? We pop a few pills, and all of our problems go away. The entire world—all objective reality—restructures itself for our benefit."

"Or so it seems," Marv says.

William removes his sunglasses and rubs his eyes. "Has it ever occurred to you that if Hamlet had been put on Prozac, the most extraordinary conflict in world literature would've been reduced to dry mouth and drowsiness?"

Marv checks his minnow. "I never thought of it that way, but I suppose you're right. Prozac would have cost us 'The Raven' too."

"And *The Bell Jar*," William says.

"And whatever else David Foster Wallace would have written if he hadn't … you know."

William swivels his seat around. "Plus everything Baudelaire wrote and half of what Faulkner wrote."

"Not to mention the early work of Noah Kertzman," Marv says.

"Who's Noah Kertzman?"

Marv throws up his hands. "My fucking attorney. This game isn't fair—you're an English professor. I'll tell you what, though—I don't want my entertainment coming at the expense of *anyone's* suffering, not even a character's. I'd put 'em *all* on Prozac or whatever it took to stop the pain."

William thinks for a moment. "But maybe there's an upside to suffering. Aeschylus wrote that wisdom comes through suffering—it's a very Greek idea."

Marv shakes his head. "It's a very fucked-up idea, William. Suffering comes through suffering—that's about it. Where are the crappies?"

"Let's try the next bay over. Reel in." William raises the trolling motor, and they go around the point into a bay that, in most ways, resembles the one they just left. Both men switch to bobbers, and William anchors close enough to a small reed bed that they can cast to it.

"Can you believe what rotten luck that was?" Marv says.

"Could you be a little more specific?"

Marv leans back and puts his feet up on the gunnel. "I'm talking about Paul Bouchard from the *Herald*—the supercalifragilistic prick who just happened to be on your cruise ship when you freaked out."

"Yeah, that was kind of a bad deal."

"Bad deal? He made you look like the Son of Sam. What the hell was the name of that series he wrote?"

William switches off the sonar. "It was called *When Men Lose It*, and you're right—it caused me a lot of problems, professionally speaking."

"The little bastard had you in some good company, though—Mel Gibson, Charlie Sheen, Alec Baldwin."

William laughs. "You're forgetting Pee-wee Herman. You know, the chancellor actually quoted from that series when they suspended me."

"You're kidding. How's that going, by the way?"

William casts a little closer to the reeds. "Not very well. I mean, what can I say? I used up all my sick leave at Crosswell, and when I went back to work last year, Marcia left, and I barely made it through spring semester. Then, last fall, I didn't show up for my classes, I didn't contact the college, and I didn't take their calls. I just … disappeared. That's when they suspended me." William gives his bobber a twitch. "The latest development is that if I teach in Oslo for a year, Lothrup will forgive all my sins—or so I'm led to believe."

"That doesn't sound so bad—a year in the land of fjords, trolls and curvaceous blonde women."

William shakes his head. "Actually, most of the Norwegian women I met looked like Tilda Swinton. But it's nice of the college to give me a way out—especially since they think I was sticking my finger in their eye. The thing is, I wasn't exactly the poster child for rational behavior back then. If I had been, Marcia wouldn't have fallen in love with our dentist—what a bizarre coda."

"Yeah, that sucked." Marv reels in, shallows up his bobber and casts toward the reeds again. "I wish my third wife had left me for a dentist. That's kinda classy—I could live with that. But of course she ran off with a piano tuner. The little shit came to the house once a month to tune the Fazioli … but that wasn't all he was tuning."

William nods in the direction of Marv's bobber. "You've got a fish on. It's a crappie."

"How do you know?"

"By the way he dragged your bobber two feet before he pulled it under. Are you gonna set the hook?"

Marv rears back as though he's setting the hook in a marlin and starts to reel. By some miracle, the fish stays on, and Marv is nearly beside himself with excitement. "I think you're right—feels like a crappie. Keep comin', big boy. There he is—he's a nice one. Jesus, he's barely hooked. Get the net. Careful, careful—don't knock him off."

William nets the fish and lays it at Marv's feet. "That's a dandy—every bit of ten inches."

Marv winks. "Fo shizzle, my nizzle—that's what *she* said." He puts the fish in the livewell and watches it for a moment. Then he turns to William and sniffs the air theatrically. "It smells a little skunky in your end of the boat, my brother. Somebody needs to catch a fish."

William laughs. "I'm working on it."

"Look." Marv points across the lake. "The sun is on the trees."

In less than an hour, Marv has five crappies and William has six. The action is fast, and then it stops, as if someone had thrown a switch. It is very quiet as the sun sets, not a puff of wind, and William is thinking about Amy.

"Earth to William—I said I can't see my bobber anymore." Marv is on his feet, stretching.

William takes a breath, and he's back. "Yeah, it's getting pretty dark. But we did okay—eleven nice fish. I … met someone."

Marv turns and looks at William closely. "Aha! The old throw-away-line trick. Tell me more."

"There's not much to tell. I was at obedience class with Baron, and she was there. Her name is Amy. We went to a restaurant afterward."

"Attractive?"

"Very."

"What does she look like?"

"Strawberry blonde, a sort of peaches-and-cream complexion with—"

"You're describing a smoothie."

William laughs. "Let's just say she's pretty."

"Well, let's hear it! Did you bump uglies?"

William makes a face. "No, Lothario. I told you—I just met her."

"And at dog school, of all places. You know, I'm definitely getting a dog. Maybe I can rent one. Ordinarily, I like wine tastings and recitals for picking up women, but dog school could really broaden my horizons."

"It's called *canine obedience class*, and I thought you liked to meet women at the gym."

Marv nods. "That showed real promise for a while, but there are too many hats and headphones at the gym."

"I get the headphones," William says. "It's like reading a book on an airplane—a polite way of discouraging conversation. But what does a hat mean?"

"It means *consider yourself warned*," Marv says. "And when you see a woman with a hat *and* headphones, it's like she's got a sign around her neck that says, 'Look, I'm not wearing any makeup, my hair is a mess and I'm really trying to focus. So *fuck off!*'"

"I knew there was a reason I didn't go to the gym—it's *way* too complicated."

"True dat, my brother, but it doesn't matter. You're a dog school man now—stick with what you know. And best of luck with Amy. Keep me posted."

William shakes his head. "I'm not ready to start seeing anyone. Hell, most of the time I still feel married. In fact, my first impulse when I got home that night was to call Marcia and tell her all about it. How fucked up is *that*?" William turns on the running lights. "I don't know why I even mentioned it."

"Well, I'm glad you did," Marv says, "but you won't really know anything until you've—how shall I say it?—consummated the relationship."

"I'll keep that in mind, Captain Horndog. It's time to go."

Marv pulls the anchor, and they head back to the landing. It's a beautiful ride, and because the cabin owners haven't begun coming north yet, there are no lights on shore, which makes the lake seem less developed than it actually is. To the west, William can see flocks of ducks silhouetted against the red sky, all headed for the rice beds to the north.

After William and Marv get the boat trailered and leave the landing, William asks how Marv's son is doing. It's not a topic Marv enjoys discussing, but William wants to know, and he has a best friend's right to ask.

"Danny's doing great," Marv says. "He loves Boston, and he's still at Roth and Edelman. He'd like to do more trial law, but he's happy." Marv interlocks his fingers behind his head. "And of course he wants nothing to do with me."

William doesn't say anything. He figures Marv will go on, and after a few moments, he does.

"You know, Danny took the divorce hard, William. He was only sixteen. But it was my first suicide attempt that ended our relationship."

"When he was at Georgetown?"

"Yep, his second year." Marv takes a deep breath and lets it out slowly. "I'll tell you something, William—you probably know it already. When you try to kill yourself, everybody thinks it's about them, like it's their fault, or it's some kind of affront to them personally. That's sort of where Daniel is, and he won't allow himself to get close to me because it's safer that way—you know, in case I get it right next time."

"There better not be a next time."

"I sure as hell hope there isn't. Three times is enough. And the worst thing about it isn't the act itself—it's the prelude. It's like …"

"Like what?"

Marv stares into the darkness and doesn't answer right away. "After Juilliard, I played keyboards for a group called Dime Bag. I've told you about them."

"Yes, you said they were heroin addicts."

"You're thinking of False Arrest. I played with them for a while too. But this was Dime Bag, and we were in LA recording a demo. We had a little downtime, and I went to Santa Monica Beach so I could tell everyone back home that I went swimming there. But being a dipshit kid from Minnesota, I got caught in a riptide. It was such a helpless, powerless feeling. I swam for shore as hard as I could, but it was like running on a treadmill, and nothing I did to save myself made any difference. Finally, a lifeguard came out in a dinghy and rescued me. That's what suicide is like—getting caught in a riptide. It just grabs you and it won't let go." Marv looks over at William. "Danny doesn't understand that part. I wish to hell he did."

William nods. "You should try explaining it to him. I can see where he's coming from, though—you're a risky proposition. You'll just have to take the long view and convince him that becoming emotionally vested in you is a safe decision. It will take some time to do that, but what other options do you have?"

"Not too fucking many. There's a deer up ahead on the right."

"I see him."

Marv takes off his cap and rubs his head with both hands. "Terminal case of cap hair." He looks over at William. "You said on the phone that your memory was coming back from the electroshock therapy. Is that true or were you just bullshitting me?"

"Electro*convulsive*, and yes—it's getting better."

"No matter what you call it," Marv says, "I'm surprised Crosswell used it on you. Shock therapy is so … yesterday."

"It is, except in cases where the patient fails to respond to conventional treatment or exhibits violent tendencies—that was me on both counts."

"Violent? You?"

"The cruise ship."

"Oh, okay … I guess if you count that. Anyway, I'm glad your memory is getting better."

"Me too," William says. "But a lot of things are still scrambled. For instance, I have all these dates in my head, but I can't remember what they are. It's weird—for most of last year, I thought my birthday was October 11, but that's Marcia's birthday."

Marv reaches over and pats William on the leg. "I'm gonna let you in on something, just in case this thing with Amy gets serious. If it's *your* birthday, you get a blowjob. If it's *her* birthday, you take her to Kincaid's for dinner. It's hard to get the two confused."

William laughs. "I'll try to remember that. It isn't just dates, though. Movies are a problem too. I mean, there are a lot of them that I know I've seen, but I can't remember half the stuff that happens. I watched *Casablanca* last week, and it was like seeing it for the first time."

"That's not all bad, my brother. I assume you were shocked, *shocked* to learn that gambling goes on in Rick's Café."

William signals and turns into his driveway. "I was shocked, all right—six times. That's the root cause of my problems." He pulls up in front of the house, turns off the ignition and gestures. "I've gotta—"

"Yeah, I know. Go ahead. I'll take care of things out here."

William runs up the walk and bolts through the front door, convinced that something nonspecific yet horrifying awaits him within. But everything is fine. Baron is blinking as though he's been asleep, and there is no sign of any accidents. William takes him outside, and he does his business right away. "I can't believe what a good boy you are." But Baron, now wide awake, doesn't want to go back in the house, so William has to chase him down and practically drag him inside. "I may have to revisit the *good boy* remark," he tells him.

William makes Baron wait at the top of the stairs while he and Marv clean fish in the basement. William has a specially crafted board that fits over the laundry tubs, and he fillets the fish; then Marv washes the filets, inspects them for bones, and puts them into two Ziploc bags. Baron, who doesn't like being excluded, whines at first but soon gives up and stares indignantly down the stairs.

"He doesn't like being separated from you, does he?" Marv says.

"No, he's a little clingy, but that's okay—he has his reasons."

Marv seals the first Ziploc. "You know, I've been thinking … When we fish the opener next month, why don't we fish Monday too? Can we do that?"

William reaches for another crappie. "I don't see why not—that's a good idea. I'll have to talk to Kate and Todd, though—they're going to have Baron that weekend. I also have office hours on Mondays, but I can take the day off. That shouldn't be a problem."

"Good. I don't want to give those bastards an excuse to fire you, but it sure would be nice to fish an extra day." Marv is quiet for a moment; then he asks, "Are you doing okay, my brother? You seem good."

William answers slowly. "Yeah, I'm okay—at least, most of the time. I had a pretty bad flashback over at the carriage house this afternoon, but when that happens, I try not to blow it out of proportion. I just keep telling myself that what's happening isn't real, that flashbacks are a very common symptom of PTSD."

"I'm sorry that's still happening to you. When did you start working on the carriage house again?"

"A few months ago. I have the entire place sided. If it wasn't dark, I'd take you over there." William hands Marv the last two filets. "Okay, that does it."

Marv counts, then counts again. "Uh-oh."

William sighs. "Let me guess—we're short."

"Yep. One filet."

"Okay, I guess we know what to do."

So while Marv recounts the filets in each Ziploc, William checks the gut bucket. Half a minute later, he holds up a crappie with a perfectly intact side.

"Oops."

Marv laughs. "Usually it's on me. I like this better."

William finishes filleting the half-done fish, and then, to Baron's delight, he and Marv come back upstairs and have a beer. The two of them don't talk much when they fish, so this is a chance to catch up on things, to talk about baseball and make plans for the opener. After a while, William asks Marv to spend the night.

"I wish I could, my brother, but I've got a breakfast meeting with some suits from Nissen International. They're doing the new ad campaign for Radisson, and they want a jingle or at least some original production music."

"Well, they'll be talking to the right guy," William says. "Take the fish home with you."

Marv grins. "Thank you. I'd rather eat a crappie than any fish that swims."

Not long after that, Marv leaves, and William turns on the patio floodlights and takes Baron outside before they go to bed. But Baron is ready to play and soon finds an old gardening glove that he begs William to try to take from him. *C'mon, I dare you*, he seems to say.

"I'm gonna pay for that long nap you had, aren't I?"

Baron shakes the glove furiously, like a terrier shaking a rat.

"Yeah … that's what I thought. I'll get your tennis ball."

So William throws a tennis ball all over the backyard for Baron, and after half an hour, Baron begins to run out of gas. But by then, William is wide awake. "Hey, I've got an idea—I'm gonna make some popcorn. If you want, you can have a few bites."

They go inside, and William makes popcorn and takes it into the living room, which has an old TV and an even older sofa that he and a neighbor had brought over from the carriage house. He puts a few pieces of popcorn on the floor for Baron, turns on the TV and looks for a documentary—basically all he watches anymore. William loves documentaries. He loves them for their soothing, anodyne tone and the way they wash over him like the waters of oblivion, dulling his pain, erasing his past. The BBC's documentaries are the best, especially the ones narrated by David Attenborough. But in William's view, almost any documentary is better than anything else, provided the gazelle is allowed to escape the crocodile at the water hole once in a while.

CHAPTER 11

The Black Box

ON SATURDAY MORNING, Baron has an appointment to see the vet about heartworm prevention, but out of an abundance of caution, William thinks it best not to mention this to him. He simply puts Baron in the car, and off they go. William made the appointment at the same veterinary clinic he and Marcia used many years ago, when they had a little mutt named Snoofer that Kate brought home from somewhere. The place has changed a lot since then, and William doesn't recognize anyone, but they all seem nice, oohing and aahing over Baron, who enjoys the attention. William gives the receptionist Baron's health records and vaccination history, and she looks things over and makes some notes. Then she has William fill out a form, which she uses to enter Baron and William's data in the computer.

She types with blazing no-look speed, and when she's finished, she seems to see William for the first time. "Okay, Mr. Kessler, Baron is in our system now. He's already had his DA2PPC booster, in addition to his rabies, Lymevax and Bordetella vaccinations."

The only word William recognizes is *rabies*, so he feels like he should ask something. "What's that last one for?"

"Bordetella? It's an elective vaccine that will immunize Baron against kennel cough. We recommend it, and all good boarding kennels require it." She smiles and hands Baron's health records and vaccination history back to William. "So all Baron needs today is a checkup and some heartworm pills. Let me explain your options."

William and Baron listen attentively, and after they decide on chewable tablets, Baron gets weighed, has his checkup, and they leave.

When they get home, William gives Baron his breakfast and realizes that he's hungry too. But after rummaging through the cupboards, he discovers there's very little food in the house—a situation that has become the new normal. He has half a loaf of bread that hasn't molded but no jam or jelly. Then, behind a big jar of Ragu spaghetti sauce, he finds an old honey bear. There isn't much honey in it, and what there is has thoroughly crystalized, but William knows what to do. He puts it in the microwave—a little too long, as it turns out, because the honey bear has begun to melt by the time he removes it.

"Kinda looks like Jabba the Hutt, Baron. *Christ*, this thing is hot!" William digs around in the bottom of the melted bear with a spoon and comes up with a thimbleful of honey for his toast. "Baron, I think our difficulties this morning are a prophetic metaphor for the imminent global crisis." William is referring to the dramatic decline in the world's honeybee population, which has worried him, off and on, for a long time now. "The bees aren't just dying, you know. They're dying out—I've seen two documentaries about it, and the prognosis isn't good."

When William has finished his toast, he says, "Do you remember what I told you about writing letters? About how, when I feel the urge, I just have to do it, or bad things happen in my head? Well, buddy, this is one of those times, so follow me." William goes to his office and googles the Environmental Protection Agency and the Department of Agriculture.

"Lisa Jackson and Tom Vilsack—I *knew* that," William says, "and they're both guilty." Then he begins to type. He had intended to keep the letter short, but it gets away from him, and when he's done, it's seven paragraphs. William laughs. "*I would have written you a shorter letter, but I didn't have the time.* Who said that? Was it Pascal?" He edits the letter down to three paragraphs, and reads the abridged version to Baron.

28 April 2012

Dear Directors Jackson and Vilsack:

At this point, no one would deny the precipitous decline in the world's honeybee population that has been caused by colony collapse disorder, otherwise known as CCD. Although the cause of this epidemic was hotly debated a few years ago, most researchers now agree that CCD is the horrifying result of a new generation of insecticides called neonicotinoids, which are highly toxic to bees.

Yet somehow, both the Environmental Protection Agency and the Department of Agriculture remain implausibly unconvinced by the mountain of data pointing to neonicotinoids as the foundational cause of CCD. Even worse, the EPA has proffered a medley of explanations for CCD that includes everything *but* neonicotinoids.

The EPA and the USDA are regulatory agencies responsible for protecting the American people, and it's high time they stop obfuscating and start doing their jobs, which, regardless of what Monsanto and Cargill say, does not include shilling for Big Business. It's also time for you to acknowledge what scientists already know—that neonicotinoids are the new DDT. There is no time to waste: if we lose the honeybees, we lose one in every three mouthfuls of food we will eat today.

Sincerely,

William Kessler

William finishes reading, looks down at Baron and laughs. "Every word is true, but I sound like a whacked-out vegan in a tin foil hat. Oh well, could be worse, I guess." He saves the letter to his "Letter" file and stands up. "Shall we head over to the carriage house?"

The two of them work at the carriage house until late afternoon. William nails up most of the new wainscoting, tears out the rest of the sheetrock in the bedroom, and replaces some window trim. Then curiosity gets the better of him, and he decides to check out the five cardboard boxes that Marcia stashed there before she left for Phoenix. For weeks, ever since William had begun working on the carriage house again, he has moved the boxes from room to room, wherever they weren't in the way, but he never gave much thought to what was in them. Each box has SAVE written on it in black Magic Marker, but there is nothing on the boxes indicating what they contain. That strikes William as odd, considering how organized Marcia is. In fairness, though, she was in a hurry at the end. She had been putting things in Kate's basement, but then Kate—who had been biting her tongue—finally let fly, giving her mother a First Corinthians earful about marriage and divorce. After that, Marcia had decided to store the last five boxes elsewhere.

William and Baron look in each of the boxes, and mostly what's in them are kitchen items for the carriage house. There's an old microwave, some copper-clad Revere Ware, a hauntingly familiar set of dishes with red apples on them. *If you kids want dessert, you'd better polish those apples.* There are also several pairs of salt-and-pepper shakers and an assortment of funny coffee cups from Marcia and the kids: *Give Me Some Time to Overthink This*; *Don't Make Me Use My Lecture Voice*; *And IIIIIIII E IIIIIIII Will Always Love You.* It makes William sad to run into these relics from his former life, but in the last box is an old blender that's nothing short of a gut punch.

"Is that really *you*, Gerardo?" William removes the blender from the box and holds it up. "Jesus, amigo, I thought you were dead." He sets the blender on the kitchen counter and stares at it.

One summer, when William was completing his PhD at the University of Minnesota and teaching a grab-bag class called American Fiction, he and Marcia had bought the blender at a garage sale. The plan was to have a milkshake now and then, but before long, William was making so many frozen daiquiris in the blender that they gave it a name—Gerardo Esteban, on account of the large GE logo on the blender's face. It was hot that summer, hotter than anyone could remember, and as the steamy afternoons reddened into early evening, he and Marcia would start speaking in code, saying things like, "Gerardo probably wonders what happened to us," or "I told Gerardo we'd meet him at the *Nacional* in half an hour." Then William would make frozen daiquiris, throw something on the grill, and he and Marcia would sit on the back porch of their rented home and pretend they were in Havana *antes de la revolución*. Years later, they would joke about Kate being conceived one hot summer night on the beach at Santa María del Mar.

William puts the blender back in the box, but when he goes home that afternoon, he takes it with him and places it in the cupboard. He wonders why he keeps doing this to himself, falling into emotional quicksand everywhere he turns. He misses Marcia, but Marcia is no longer part of his life. William *knows* that, at least on an intellectual level, but he's like an amputee who continues to feel the pain of a missing limb, an aching reminder of his former completeness.

The next day, Sunday, begins unremarkably enough. As he so often does, William has a to-do list, but it isn't long—he wants to replace two rotten boards in the deck, take Baron to the dog park, and then mow a section of the lawn with the push mower. The mowing alone would earn him the right to work on the Dostoevsky book for the rest the day. But William never gets any further than the deck boards because when he looks in the basement storage room for the can of matching stain, he hears the insidious drip-drip-drip of water. It doesn't take him long to find the problem. Running diagonally overhead, suspended from the floor joists, is the intake line for the water heater, which is on the other side of the storage room wall. And right where the line angles hard to make the turn, there is a green, corroded copper elbow that, from the look of it, has been leaking for some time.

"Goddammit," William says. "I should stick my head in here once in a while." He moves things around to assess the damage and finds that for the most part, it isn't bad—a retired lampshade, an old dartboard, somebody's straw hat. But also among the casualties are Rupert Martin's laptop and briefcase. William is casually sorry about that, but in truth he hasn't given a thought to either item since he carried them to the basement two years ago.

William opens the computer, tips it to one side, and water pours from the keyboard. "Not a good sign," he says, almost laughing. "I hope all your little ones and zeros can tread water." He sets the computer down and reaches for the briefcase, but the handle comes off in his hand. "I believe I'm seeing a theme here." William picks the briefcase up with both hands and carries it into the laundry room, where he sets it on a small table. In its prime, it had been a nice leather-covered attaché case, but it's completely ruined now. The leather, which is white with mold, has split and is curling at the edges, and the Masonite infrastructure is swollen to the point where it has separated at every seam. The lock is still holding, but it hardly matters—William could poke his finger through the briefcase anywhere he really tried.

"I guess it's finally time to see what's in here," he mutters. "I hope it isn't student work I should have graded back in 2010."

William pulls the top panel off the briefcase, and at first he isn't sure what he's looking at—a black box, roughly the size of a pocket book novel, with four antennae on top. Then it hits him, and when it does, it takes his breath away. "Oh Christ! This can't be!" He picks the thing up and, just to be sure, reads what's on the back of it. Then he returns the box to the briefcase, raises his hands halfway and backs up slowly, as though he were retreating from a snarling animal. The black box is a cell phone signal jammer.

William goes upstairs and begins pacing, with Baron at his side. It's crazy, he thinks, but it also makes perfect sense. Poor Rupert, the man who had campaigned ceaselessly for more and more rules, was driven to distraction by cell phone use in his classroom. This was especially true in the lecture hall where, because of its size, students could text and monitor their Facebook pages with impunity. "I'm supposed to be teaching Intro to Lit," Rupert would say, "but it's more like Social Media in the College Classroom." Most of Lothrup's students would never risk the ire of their professors by using a cell phone in class. But "Dr.

Martinet" didn't command that type of respect, and a lot of his students walked all over him. So a jammer was Rupert's horrible solution to a problem he couldn't solve any other way.

As William paces, he remembers the phone call he got from Sam the day he had appeared on *Good Morning, America.* To William's relief, Sam wasn't interested in the inflated grades he had given Rupert's students. The only question Sam asked was about the briefcase—*What was in there?* Because William had been preoccupied at the time, he forgot all about it, and yet now, thanks to a leaking pipe, that question had been answered. But there are so many others: Did Sam *know* about the jammer? What made him suspect Rupert? And why, if Sam thought there was something important in Rupert's briefcase, did he send the brief-case to William? William knows he will be paying Sam a visit first thing in the morning.

He and Baron go outside, where William continues to pace while Baron watches from the patio. William thinks about Rupert and how horrified he would have been by the unintended conse-quences of his actions. Rupert wasn't a bad person, but he was definitely unlucky. Had he been anything else, he would've been caught using the jammer *before* the shooting took place. That way, Rupert would have been disciplined by the college and per-haps fined a few hundred dollars by a judge, like the restaurant and theater owners William had read about who pretended not to know that blocking authorized radio transmissions is a violation of federal law. But of course nothing like that had happened, and in his maniacal rage for order, Rupert got students killed when he blocked Lothrup's active shooter alert for three minutes. William stops pacing. *Why just three minutes?*

"Baron, where are you? Oh—okay. Listen, I need to take another look at that jammer. Was it *on* or *off*? That could be important."

William returns to the basement, retrieves the jammer, and car-ries it upstairs to his office, where he places it on the desk and sits down. Baron, who knows just what to do when William is at his desk, lies down on the little rug next to his chair, his head between his paws. William picks up the jammer and looks at it. "It's turned off. Who do you suppose did that? And *why?*"

William closes his eyes and pretends he's Rupert Martin at that moment when all hell broke loose. Witnesses said they didn't receive the first alert in the lecture hall until there was actually shooting in the hallway—in other words, when it was too late to matter. William thinks about this for a while, then opens his eyes and looks down at Baron.

"I think I know what happened, Hürtgenvoss. I think when Rupert was teaching, he turned the jammer on and kept it in his open briefcase, maybe under a sheet of paper or something. On the day of the shooting, as soon as he heard gunfire in the hallway, he probably turned it off so his students could call 911. Of course, when he did that, everyone in the lecture hall received the active shooter alert, but it would have been late—*three minutes late*." William raises his finger in a way that indicates he's still thinking. "And then … after Rupert turned the jammer off, he probably closed his briefcase, which explains why no one ever saw it—not his wife, not the police, not whoever gathered up the personal property of the victims." William puts his hand on Baron's head. "That was probably the last thing Rupert ever did, Hürtgenvoss— he was killed right there at the lectern."

Rupert Martin had done an astonishingly stupid thing, and William knows if it should become public knowledge, Lothrup would have to withdraw its appeal to the state supreme court before the justices had even determined if they were willing to hear the case. There might be additional lawsuits too. William doesn't know what kind of exposure Rupert's estate would've had, but Joyce had died seven months after the shooting, when William was in Crosswell, so both she and Rupert were beyond everyone's legal reach.

William puts the jammer into an empty toner cartridge box and takes it back to the storage room, where he sets it on a shelf. He puts the laptop next to it and slides the moldy briefcase into a plastic bag that, moments before, had been home to a Vikings foam finger, circa Daunte Culpepper. He places the briefcase beside the laptop and steps back. "You remind me of the three wise monkeys," he says, looking at the little tableau. "But just to be safe, let's not *do* any evil either."

His Sunday plan disrupted, William walks over to the carriage house with Baron to get his plumbing toolbox and a spare copper elbow. It doesn't take long to fix the leak in the storage room—William is a fair-to-middling plumber—but all the time he's working, he thinks about the jammer, how it could impact the future, and what Sam knows about it.

Monday morning dawns bright and clear, and at five minutes to eight, William is looking for a parking space behind the administration building. He eventually finds one, not far from where a construction crew is getting ready to start work. They're putting on green high-viz vests, and one of them is spray-painting lines on the curb and sidewalk that run along the west side of the parking lot. William assumes they're part of the wheelchair accessibility project that he read about in the *Beacon*. The article said that all the six-inch steps from street-level up to the sidewalks were going to be replaced with ramps in an effort to make Lothrup's campus more wheelchair friendly.

"This is good, Baron. While I'm gone, you can watch these guys work." William locks the doors and cracks the windows. "I won't be long. I have to do this."

When William gets to Sam's office, his secretary isn't at her desk, so he glances around the corner and sees Sam watering one of his plants with a little plastic watering can.

"Your philodendron has seen better days, Sam."

Sam turns around and smiles. "Hi, William. Yeah, I don't think it gets enough light in here." William braces for another hug, but Sam turns back toward his plant and gives it a final shot of water. Then he sets the watering can on a file cabinet and points to a chair. "C'mon in. Take a load off. To what do I owe this rare and unexpected pleasure?" Sam sits down at his desk.

William closes the door and takes the chair directly across from him.

"Uh-oh," Sam says, nodding toward the closed door. "Whenever someone does that, I know it's gonna be bad."

"That depends," William says. "Do you remember when you called me two years ago and asked what was in Rupert's briefcase?"

Sam chuckles. "William, I have long admired your talent for social chitchat. Yes, I remember. You were about to appear on *Today*, and you told me there was nothing in there but some student work."

"It was *Good Morning, America*," William says. "And I lied. I told you I had opened the briefcase and graded what was in it because I thought you were going to chew me out over the grades I gave Rupert's students. But the truth is that I never opened the briefcase until yesterday—and I think you know what I found."

Sam is impassive. "A cell phone signal jammer?"

"That's right," William says. "But how did you know?"

"A lot of things pointed to it … I'm talking about things two years ago."

"Like what?"

"Well, student complaints, for one thing. Before the shooting, we received a lot of complaints about Dewhurst's erratic signal strength, and some of them even speculated it was being caused by a jammer. Of course, most of those students thought *we* were behind it."

"Who's *we*?"

"*Us*—the college, the administration, the same fascists who make them study dead white poets and won't allow gender-neutral bathrooms. Anyway, we investigated." Sam remembers something and laughs. "We made IT the tip of the spear—what a goatfuck *that* was. The most those nerds were willing to say was that Dewhurst's fluctuating signal strength was—how did they put it?—*not inconsistent with the effects of a signal jammer*."

"Not inconsistent? How litotic of them."

"Yes, and how unhelpful," Sam says. "To their credit, though, they did tell us how jammers work, and they said a medium-sized jammer could theoretically block the phone signal in Dewhurst's lecture hall and probably in adjacent classrooms. They said that jammers don't typically penetrate roofs and ceilings, so I'm betting you didn't have much trouble with your phone on the second floor."

"I didn't. How were you able to identify Rupert as the culprit?"

Sam smiles. "I take full credit for that, and I'm rather proud of it. It was three weeks after the shooting, basically on a hunch, that I ran the class schedule of every student who had put his name on a complaint about the signal strength. Guess what I found?"

William shrugs. "Nobody takes Linguistics at eight in the morning?"

"I found that three-fourths of the names belonged to students who had Rupert Martin as an instructor."

"And *that* made him your prime suspect?"

"It wasn't *just* that. Let's face it—nobody had more problems with students using mobile devices in the classroom than your erstwhile buddy Rupert. And it made sense to me that if he was using a jammer, it was probably in his briefcase." Sam makes a face. "That's where I blew it, though. By the time I figured that out, I'd already had Rupert's briefcase delivered to your front door so you could put his grades on the server."

"And that's when you called to ask what was in it?"

"Yes. I didn't know what else to do. But you said there was nothing in there, so I sort of ... ran out of runway."

"And that was it? That was the end of your investigation?"

Sam nods. "Yeah, pretty much. But technically, the investigation ended when we got slapped with the lawsuit. Once that started, the last thing I wanted to do was prove that one of our profs had been using a cell phone signal jammer in Dewhurst. My God, that would have put the final nail in our coffin." Sam rocks back in his chair. "It's my turn to ask a question—how did you happen to look in the briefcase after all this time?"

William laughs. "I wish the explanation was more dramatic. I had some water damage in my basement, and the damn thing got soaked and fell apart. It was just ... one of those things."

"Where is it now?"

"The jammer? It's in a safe place."

Sam frowns. "You should get rid of it."

"I don't think so."

"Then give it to me, and *I'll* get rid of it."

"It's fine where it is."

Sam presses a button on his phone. "Nicole, could you please bring me another cup of coffee?" He turns to William. "Want anything?"

"No, thank you."

Sam takes his finger off the button and points it at William. "Here's the thing, buddy. I don't think you're seeing the whole field. Lothrup may be headed back to court—this time for all the marbles—and nothing has changed. If it should get out that one of our professors was illegally blocking cell phone signals in Old Dewhurst, it would be over for us—game, set and match. So ... I'm sure you understand that it's best if you don't mention the jammer to anyone."

William can hardly believe his ears. "Oh ... I see. Help me out here, Sam. Are you asking me to withhold evidence, or are you asking me to become an accessory after the fact? I get the two confused."

Sam scowls. "I'm asking you to be *smart*. Nobody's suggesting that you break the law. You're under no obligation to come forward. You're not a witness to anything. Hell, there isn't even a trial going on. I'm just saying it would be better for Lothrup if you kept the jammer to yourself. Jesus H. Christ! We're down twelve million dollars as it is. We don't need you trying to run the number up."

"I hear you," William says, "but I don't like it."

"You know, I wish I hadn't said anything. This entire discussion is academic, anyway. The jammer won't even matter unless the supreme court decides to hear our appeal, and like I told you, they only accept one case in ten. And they almost never take a case where the district court and the appellate court are in agreement. So you don't have much to worry about, William. Just don't get self-righteous—that's all I'm saying."

Sam's secretary comes in with a cup of coffee, which she sets in front of Sam. "Here you go, Sam."

"Thanks, Nicole."

"Can I bring you anything, Dr. Kessler?"

William shakes his head, and she leaves. He feels that his conversation with Sam has gone far enough, and he takes advantage of the interruption. "Did you happen to watch the Twins beat the Royals yesterday?"

Sam nods. "I caught some of it. Marquis really had his sinker working, didn't he?"

"Yeah, he looked good, but the Twins are still in last place. They're 6 and 15."

"Somebody told me that Blackburn is out of the pitching rotation. Is that true?"

"I'm afraid so," William says. "They think he has the yips."

"My God, what will it be next?"

William stands up. "I'd better get over to my office, Sam. It was nice talking to you."

"So that's it?" Sam says.

"You know how it is. I don't want Gardner to think I'm fudging on the terms and conditions of our agreement."

"Speaking of Gardner, we should talk about Norway."

"All right," William says. "Did you know that Norway gets 98 percent of its electricity from hydro?"

"No, nor do I give a shit."

"Then perhaps it would interest you to know that Norwegians invented both the aerosol can and the cheese slicer. So long—I really have to run."

"We'd better talk soon," Sam says. "You need to make some decisions."

"And I will." William doffs an imaginary cap and heads for the door.

"Hey."

William turns around. "What?"

"Do we need to worry about you?"

William gives him a tight-lipped smile. "Have a nice day, Sam."

As William heads back to the car, he can see Baron through the wire mesh of the crate, anxiously awaiting the moment when William will reenter his life. When William is a few feet away, Baron begins to whimper and tremble in apparent amazement, as though William's return is an act that has defied all odds and expectations.

"See, I told you I'd be back," William says as he opens the door. "You got all upset over nothing, didn't you?"

William gets in and fastens his seat belt, but he doesn't start the car. Instead, he thinks about what Sam had just asked him to do, and he can't quite believe it. William doesn't know if it was legally wrong, but there's no question that it was ethically wrong, and William doesn't need any more ethical dilemmas than he's already dealing with. Keeping quiet about the jammer, no matter how you sliced it, was a chickenshit thing to do. But if he had to, he could do it. After all, he'd done worse.

Suddenly, one of the men on the concrete crew attacks the curb with a jackhammer, and William's insides turn to ice. *This is not real. This is not fucking real.* But it happens so fast that William is unable to fight back or mount a defense. If he had *seen* the jackhammer before he heard it, it might have helped. But he didn't, and he's instantly in Old Dewhurst, listening to the screams and the gunfire. He's saying something to Jon, but Jon is shaking his head.

"Look, Dad, s*helter in place* might be okay for a tornado, but we need to get outta here. Tell me about the janitors' closet—does it have a steel door?"

"No, it's no better than here. And it's exactly the sort of place those bastards would check." Then William has an idea. "But if we can't go down, maybe we can go up."

"Up *where?*" Jon says. "We're on the top floor."

"The roof. There's a little stairway in the janitors' closet that leads to an observation deck. The janitors go up there and smoke. Not many people know it's there."

"I'm in," Jon says. "How do we get there?"

"It's down the hall on the other side."

"How far?"

"Twenty yards, maybe a little more."

"Jesus, twenty yards is a long way."

"It's our only option—unless you want to stay here."

"Not a chance," Jon says. "Let's do it."

And the shooting and the screams, which had begun as two distinct sounds, begin melding into one.

But there is another sound, a dull percussive sound that William doesn't recognize as part of his flashback. It stops and starts again, and through it all, William can hear a dog barking. By degrees, he becomes aware that someone is tapping on the car window, but he can't see them.

"Are you okay, buddy? Can you hear me? Do you need help?"

William fights his way out of the darkness. "No, I … Baron, knock it off!" He tries to focus his mind, then his eyes, and when William turns his head toward the voice, he sees a profusion of fluorescent green that slowly morphs into one of the workmen.

"Are you all right? Should I call 911?"

"No ... I'm okay," William says, lowering the window. "Everything's fine."

"Are you sure? We noticed that you were just sitting here, and it looked like ... like you were having a little trouble. That's why I walked over."

"I appreciate it—I really do."

The man points to Baron. "Your dog doesn't like me."

"He's just confused. Thanks for checking on me."

"Hey, no problem. Glad you're okay. Have a good one." The workman heads back to his crew, and when William has his wits about him again, he starts the car and heads for his office.

Because he's running late, William parks behind Dewhurst, which means he and Baron have to forgo their walk across the commons.

"Don't worry, Baron," William tells him. "We'll get back to our routine on Wednesday."

William is still a little shaky, but he's recovering quickly and feels okay on the stairs. As he unlocks his office door, he can hear the phone ringing, and he almost doesn't answer it, for fear it's Sam wanting to talk about Norway or Gardner wanting to fire him. But it's Kate, and she's not happy.

"Daddy, you turned off your cell phone again. Why can't you just leave it on like everyone else?"

"Because then people would call me."

"Isn't that the idea?"

"Not exactly."

"Why do you even *own* a phone?"

"In case I need to call someone."

"Oh, then you should get one of those new one-way phones."

William, suddenly interested. "They make a phone like that?"

Kate groans. "Do you have any idea how frustrating you can be?" But before William can answer, Kate follows that question with another. "I was wondering if you'd like to meet us at the Pasta House for pizza tomorrow night."

"I can't, honey. I have a date."

There's a pause, then a torrent of questions that Kate can't ask fast enough. *Do I know her? What's her name? Did you meet at the college? Where does she work?*

"Calm down, sweetheart—deep breaths. Her name is Amy, and she's the assistant principal at Hawthorne Elementary School. I met her last week at obedience class." William hears what sounds like a muffled gasp. "Kate ... are you all right?"

"Oh, my gosh! Did you say *obedience class*?"

"I did. Is that significant in some—"

"And you really like her?"

"Yes, I do."

"Daddy, do you realize that God's fingerprints are all over this?"

William braces himself. "He has fingerprints?"

"The idea to get you a dog was part of God's plan. Think about it. If I hadn't gotten Baron, you wouldn't have been in obedience class. And if you hadn't been in obedience class, you wouldn't have met ..."

"Amy."

"Right—a woman you say you like. How can you possibly argue that this isn't providential?"

William can't decide if Kate is channeling Jonathan Edwards or Joel Osteen, but either way, her cause and effect aren't within shouting distance of one another. "I'm not sure, honey, but I'd probably begin by drilling down on the part where God told you to get me a dog."

Kate laughs. "I don't see why. If God can tell Noah to build an ark, he can certainly tell me to get you a dog."

"I suppose you're right, Kate," William says, hoping to bring an end to the biblical comparisons. "As for pizza, how about Thursday?"

"Great!" Kate says. "We'll meet you there at six. Don't forget. Bye, Daddy."

"Wait, wait—don't hang up."

"What is it?"

"Are you still willing to babysit Baron on the weekend of the twelfth?"

"The fishing opener?"

"Yes."

"Of course. Why?"

"Well ... Marv and I would like to fish on Monday, so I was

wondering if you could take Baron to the kennel Sunday afternoon. I called the one nearest to your house—it's Priscilla's Pampered Pet Palace over on Hazlehurst—and they said they'll have plenty of room. I think they're a good outfit. I haven't been there, but when I spoke to them on the phone, I asked a few questions.

Kate laughs. "I'll bet you did. Daddy, I hate to put BearBear in a kennel. Don't you take him to work with you?"

"Yes, he's here right now. Did you want to talk to him?"

"I don't need to. My point is that if BearBear goes to work with you, then there's no reason he can't go to work with Todd. He'd be a big hit at the clinic."

"Well, you'd better talk to Todd about that," William says. "What I'm saying is that you shouldn't hesitate to put Baron in the kennel if Todd says no or if you get sick of having him around. The kennel will take him—he's had his portabella vaccine."

Kate laughs. "You had him vaccinated against mushrooms?"

"Hell, I can't remember the name of it. The point is that he's current on everything."

"That's fine, Daddy, but there's no need to take BearBear to the kennel. I'll tell Todd that you're going to pick him up at LiveRight Monday afternoon."

"Thanks, honey. I really appreciate it."

Now that he has a plan for Baron, all that remains is for William to inform Lothrup of his impending absence, and he does so in strict accordance with faculty policy because he's sure they're watching him for that sort of thing. First, he calls the automated phone number that faculty members are required to use when they're going to miss class or office hours. Then, he enters his four-digit PIN followed by O16, the code for personal leave. As soon as he enters the date of his absence, an email goes out to William's advisees, telling them that he won't be in his office on Monday. If he's lucky, someone will run over from the administration building and put a sign on his office door, but that's up to them. William has met his contractual obligation. Monday is his.

William settles in and begins to outline a chapter of the book that examines the relationship between dreams and guilt in Dostoevsky's work. It's a relationship that holds a morbid fascination for William, and he's been looking forward to exploring it. Raskolnikov and Stavrogin both commit heinous crimes—murder and rape—in the hope that these crimes will allow them to transcend their frail humanity and become something akin to Nietzsche's Übermensch. But both characters are haunted by dreams of their victims, undone by visions that, according to both Freud and Jung, are nothing more than repressed manifestations of their own guilt. But it was different with Ivan Karamazov. He didn't kill anyone. But he came to believe that he had, and in his dream, he encounters the devil incarnate, who, as it happens, turns out to be Ivan himself. But William wonders how it could be otherwise, since we are perforce every character in our dreams.

Even the characters we hate, William thinks. Even the ones we kill.

CHAPTER 12

A Glorious Romp through Symbol Land

THE NEXT DAY, if William isn't thinking about the jammer, then he's thinking about his date with Amy, and both things make him nervous. He tries writing, but that doesn't go very well, so he walks over to the carriage house, but none of the jobs awaiting him there seem especially interesting. Finally, he and Baron walk down to the river—this year little more than a stream—and find carp running in the shallows. Judging from Baron's reaction, this is what he has waited all his young life for, and he splashes after the fish with abandon, chasing one, then another, throwing cascades of water in all directions. William sits on a log, laughing and shouting encouragement, but after forty-five minutes, Baron, exhausted and half-drowned, gives up on the fish. He shakes a couple of times, climbs up the bank and lies down beside William.

"Not as easy as it looks, is it?"

Baron glowers at the water.

"Hey ... don't feel bad because you didn't catch one." William pats him on the shoulder. "They have a huge home-field advantage—ask anybody." William stands up and stretches. "C'mon, buddy—time to go."

When the two of them get back to the house, William checks his email, and there's one from Marv.

Hey William—

Thinking about the opener—totally stoked. Went to Cabela's yesterday and bought a ton of shit, including a fishing license.

Here's a little mood music: https://www.youtube.com/watch?v=0PPsIOfMTHU

Later. Marv

William clicks on the link, and it's Doc Watson and his son Merle playing "I'm Going Fishing." William listens to the song and then calls Marv, who explains that he's "going south on the Crosstown like a bat outta hell."

"Well, slow down," William says. "I want to ask you something."

"Ask away."

"Your email said you bought a fishing license. Don't you already have one from when we went crappie fishing?"

"Oh, shit," Marv says. "That's right. Well, now I've got two of 'em. Jesus, I never know what I'm doing anymore. I'm like a fucking tweaker—I can't sleep, and most nights I don't even go to bed."

"I don't like the sound of that."

"It's nothing. I go through stretches of it now and then. It never lasts long."

"You should tell Dr. Hanselman."

"Yeah, I will. How are things going with Amy?"

"Good—I've got a date with her tonight, so I'd better get cleaned up. I'll see you Friday."

"Hooah! Over and out."

William thinks about Marv for a few minutes; then he takes a shower, shaves and gets dressed. He dresses a little better than the play requires—J. Crew khakis (dark brown with pleats) and a linen-blend camel sport coat over a light-blue polo shirt. He wants to look good. It's been a long time since he cared about things like that, and the feeling pleases him. He and Amy actually live near each other, on opposite sides of Hawthorne School, so there's no need to hurry. He apologizes to Baron for deserting him for the evening and leaves his house shortly after six because he has an errand on the way. It's the first of May, and William thinks it would be fun to give Amy a May basket, so he stops at a florist shop and picks one up—lavender, yellow daisies and white lilac.

At two minutes to seven, he's pulling into Amy's driveway, and her house looks exactly the way he imagined it—a charming one-and-a-half-story Craftsman bungalow with a gabled dormer and a large front porch. There are lots of flower beds, and her tulips are up, but the only flowers in bloom are some daffodils. Or maybe they're jonquils. William can never remember the difference or even if there *is* a difference. He grabs the May basket, walks up the stairs to the porch, where Amy meets him and lets him in.

"Hello, Professor. You found the place, I see."

"Yes, I …" William can't help staring. There's something about the way Amy's olive-green blazer accentuates her hair, her eyes, her everything. "You look lovely."

"Why, thank you. You clean up pretty good yourself." Amy looks at the May basket that William has forgotten he's carrying. "Is that … for me?"

"Oh, yeah. Sorry." He hands her the basket, slightly embarrassed.

"It's beautiful. Thank you. No one has given me a May basket since I was a little girl." Amy smells the flowers and smiles. "C'mon, let me give you the cook's tour."

William doesn't know if it's fate, pheromones or some quantum alignment of subatomic particles that draws him to Amy. But whatever it is, he definitely feels something when he's with her, something significant. "Your daffodils are up."

Amy nods. "They're jonquils. Yes, they came up last week. Sheep manure, William—that's the secret to growing nice flowers. A lot of people use cow manure, but—"

"How can you tell the difference?"

Amy gives him a funny look. "The packaging—sheep manure has a sheep wrapped around it and cow manure—"

William laughs. "I meant the difference between daffodils and jonquils."

"Oh, that's easy. Daffodils are a deeper yellow and have only one flower per stalk. Jonquils are kind of cream-colored and have lots of flowers on a stalk." Amy waves her hand. "This is the living room, as you can see. Follow me."

"Where's Yoshi?"

"Safely sequestered for the evening. I took him to the park after school so he's really tired." Amy motions William into a small room off the living room. "This was a little bedroom, but I turned it into my office."

"I did something very similar."

Amy's house is neat but not too neat. It's orderly without being symmetrical, understated without being plain. William is not surprised that every room is like her in some way—the warm colors, soft edges and casual mash-up of accents.

"You have a beautiful home," he says.

"Thank you. My dream is to completely remodel the kitchen, but that isn't going to happen for a while." She puts her hand on his arm. "We should probably be going."

Amy says goodbye to Yoshi, who is consigned to the laundry room, and they leave. When they get to the Jeep, William opens the door for her, walks around to his side and gets in. "Well, are you ready for our big date?"

"I am, Professor—fired-up and ready to go!" Amy sniffs the air. "Your car smells very … masculine."

William puts the Jeep in reverse. "Now I'm worried—that sounds like code for something else."

"No, not really. You car smells like Field & Farm, which has a very distinctive guy aroma—a unique blend of tires and animal feed." She sniffs again. "I also smell … fish." She wrinkles her nose. "Rather *old* fish."

"You're two for two, Amy. There's a dog bed in the back from Field & Farm that I need to return because it's too small—Baron really likes to stretch out. And there's an empty minnow bucket that I think has a minnow or two stuck in the bottom of it. I keep meaning to—"

"I'm very happy that you called me, William."

"Did you think I wouldn't?"

"No, I'm just glad you did. Tell me about the play."

William signals and changes lanes. "*Buried Child*? Well, it won a Pulitzer in '79. It's vintage Shepard."

"How so?"

"Oh … you know. It's kind of an autopsy on the American dream, the nuclear family, the idealism of the Midwest. It's like a lot of his stuff—very mythoclastic."

Amy laughs. "Oh, no—not mythoclastic! *Anything* but mythoclastic." She makes a face. "That's a very campusy word, Professor."

"Sorry," William says. "It must be left over from a lecture."

"No harm, no foul."

William stops for a stop light and looks over at Amy. "Do you feel like you've known me a long time? I feel like I've known you forever."

"Yes, it's weird. It's like we have some kind of karmic connection from a past life."

"But is that a good thing or a bad thing?"

"We're about to find out, William."

A few minutes later, William and Amy are walking up the steps to Watrous Auditorium. Lothrup College has three auditoriums, but small productions and student-directed plays are almost always staged in Watrous, otherwise known as the Matchbox, due to the fact that it seats only two hundred people. In the pediment of the auditorium are the words *nam gravis populo ut perfrui*.

Amy looks up at the inscription. "Can you read that?"

"Yes. It says, 'Please turn off your cell phone.'"

"Seriously."

William has to think for a moment. "It all depends on how you translate *gravis*. Either it means 'for the enjoyment of *serious* people,' or it means 'for the enjoyment of *overweight* people.' There's a story that the Matchbox was a Jenny Craig endowment."

Amy laughs. "I guess if you were *seriously overweight*, either translation would be appropriate."

"I suppose so."

No one is being seated yet, and the lobby is quickly filling with people who are kibitzing in little groups. William and Amy stand beside one of the marble columns next to the balcony staircase, and

William explains that he has to pick up their tickets at will-call.

"Please wait here. I'll be right back."

William weaves his way through the lobby, and when he returns, Amy is leaning against the column, smiling at her cell phone. "I just sent my daughter a text about you, and she says, 'Don't let him get away. He sounds perfect!'"

William smiles. "Your daughter is a young woman of unimpeachable judgment." He looks over Amy's shoulder. "Ohhh, shit."

"What is it?"

"My boss and his wife are heading this way. He's seen us, and he wants to say something. *What the hell is her name?*"

"I'm sure he just wants to say hello."

"You don't know him—he's probably wondering if I'm packed for Norway." William closes his eyes. "It's either Kristen or Kirsten."

Chancellor Gardner and his wife—a dead ringer for Barbara Bush—make their way quickly across the lobby through a crowd that seems to part magically for them.

"Hello, Kessler," Gardner says. "I've been wanting to thank you for your work on the Commencement Committee. It couldn't have been easy coming up with another speaker on such short notice." Gardner is smiling, but it's a smile that never quite makes it to his eyes.

William nods politely. "Good evening, sir—and thank you. Yes, it was challenging, but I believe Clifford Wicks will do an excellent job for us. Permit me to introduce my friend Amy Mattson. Amy is the assistant principal at Hawthorne Elementary School." William puts his hand on Amy's elbow. "Amy, I'd like you to meet Chancellor Herbert Gardner and his wife, Kristen."

"*Kirsten*," his wife says coolly.

"Forgive me," William says, wishing desperately that he were in the quantum universe where her name was Kristen.

"I'm honored," Amy says, shaking Mrs. Gardner's hand, then her husband's.

Gardner beams and looks closely at Amy, clearly liking what he sees. "It's always gratifying to meet another overworked, underpaid educator."

Amy smiles. "Thank you, Chancellor, and congratulations. I

read recently that you were awarded a Mellon Foundation grant for your Town-and-Gown Initiatives program."

Gardner, both delighted and surprised, puffs up like a toad. "Well, yes, yes. That's true. The Mellon Foundation recognizes, as I do, that the, uh, primacy of campus/community relations cannot be overemphasized." He looks at Amy as though he's just knocked over all the milk bottles, and she's the prize.

William turns to Mrs. Gardner, avoiding her first name altogether. "Do you like Sam Shepard's work, Mrs. Gardner?"

"William, the only thing I know about Sam Shepard is that he was married to Jessica Lange. The Langes lived down the street from us in Cloquet."

"You don't say! Were you and Jessica—"

"No, we were never really friends, but—"

"I saw a couple of his plays when I was at New Haven," her husband says, not caring that he is interrupting his wife. "But I'm afraid Mr. Shepard is a tad macabre for my taste."

William is confused. "Then why—"

"Kessler, I haven't missed a play here in ten years, student-directed or not. I have no intention of missing this one."

William nods. "Yes, of course. I hope you enjoy it, Chancellor."

Mrs. Gardner looks over Amy's shoulder. "They've started seating people, Herb. We should go."

"Yes, let's see what Mr. Shepard has on his mind this evening." He turns to Amy. "It was a pleasure meeting you."

"It certainly was," his wife echoes.

"Thank you," Amy says. "It was nice to meet you too."

When the Gardners are out of earshot, William breathes a sigh of relief. "Why the hell couldn't I have gotten her name right? I had a fifty-fifty chance." He looks at Amy and smiles. "A Mellon Foundation grant? How would you know that? You had Gardner eating out of your hand."

"It was dumb luck. There was an article about it in the paper, but I only read it because the headline struck me funny—it said, 'Herb Gardner Gets Mellon Grant.'"

William laughs. "Well, you definitely made a conquest there. He'll probably divorce his wife, wait a decent interval, then propose."

Amy takes William's arm. "We should find our seats. There are quite a few people here."

"Yes, let's hear it for the Lothrup Drama Department."

William is pleased to see such a good turnout on a week night, especially in the spring, with finals week approaching and students focused on the end of the year. He and Amy find their seats and hardly have time to settle in before the house lights dim, come back up, then dim again. A few moments later, the theater goes black, and there is the sound of heavy rain. Slowly, the stage is illuminated, and the audience is looking at an old man, whiskey bottle in hand, seated in the living room of a dilapidated farmhouse. He is bathed in the flickering blue light of a silent television. One by one, his family is introduced, and the play lurches forward, driven by their awful secrets.

It isn't that the play pleases, exactly; it's more like each scene is an automobile accident from which the audience cannot bear to turn away, and for nearly two hours they are held spellbound as they watch the deconstruction of the heartland and its moldering values. They want the play to go on forever, and when it ends, they give the cast a standing ovation.

"My goodness!" Amy says, reaching for her purse. "That's the only play I've ever seen that actually becomes what it's about. The third act was ... anarchy."

William nods. "*Buried Child* packs a punch—it's Norman Rockwell meets Norman Bates."

"And what a glorious romp through symbol land," Amy says.

They file slowly toward the exit, with Amy in the lead. William leans forward. "Would you like to get some dinner?"

"Could we go to Seven Dwarfs?" Amy says. "I love that place— their sundaes are unbelievable."

William laughs. "Is there any restaurant you *don't* love?"

When they reach the car, Amy gets in and fastens her seat belt. "Longy's on Roosevelt Road."

William looks at her. "What about it?"

"You asked if there was a restaurant I didn't love, and there is—it's Longy's. I got food poisoning there once. Or maybe it was too much mezcal." Amy's expression is thoughtful. "Then again, it could have been the worm—you know, the worm in the bottle."

"You swallowed it?"

"There were unconfirmed reports."

"You're a party animal."

"It was right after my divorce," Amy says. "I went a little crazy for a while."

"An attempt to find yourself?"

Amy laughs. "William, if I'd wanted to find myself, I would've taken a ceramics class."

Seven Dwarfs is a family restaurant known for its burgers and its ice cream, and other than three or four couples rounding off their evenings, it's nearly empty by the time William and Amy get there. They are seated in a booth across from an enormous mural depicting Snow White and several of the dwarfs dancing in front of their cottage. One dwarf plays an accordion while a deer, a rabbit and several squirrels look on.

William and Amy order cheeseburger baskets and sundaes—butterscotch for William, chocolate fudge for Amy—and when the waitress leaves, Amy looks closely at the mural. "The dwarf without a beard is Dopey, and the one with the big nose over by the tree is Grumpy. The one laughing is Happy. But who is that playing the accordion?"

William glances up at the mural. "That's Weird Al Yankovic—the guy tours nonstop."

"Not current on your dwarfs?"

William shrugs. "It's not my area of expertise, but if it's something I knew before Crosswell put the zap on my brain, it may come to me—that's the way it works. How is it that you have such a command of the subject?"

"I'm an elementary school assistant principal, William. We have to know every character in every kid movie ever made—it's mandated by the state."

William points to the mural. "See the arch-top door on the dwarfs' cottage? I have one almost exactly like it on the carriage house, except mine has sidelights. And it's bigger, of course."

Amy tilts her head. "What carriage house?"

"I guess I haven't told you about that. I'm remodeling a carriage house next door to where I live, turning it into a little apartment. It's something I started with my son."

"So you're also a carpenter. You are truly a Renaissance man."

William laughs. "It takes talent to be a Renaissance man. I'm strictly a dilettante."

"Whatever you are, the carriage house sounds like a huge job. And carpentry takes such patience—all those boards and nails and—"

"I've always thought that patience is what it takes to teach little kids to read. I've often wondered how you people do it."

"It has more to do with love than patience," Amy says.

"Either way, I wouldn't stand a chance."

Amy breaks the paper band on the napkin that holds her silverware. "I know what you mean, Professor. I couldn't do what you do, either. I can't even imagine being a part of that publish-or-perish, smart-people world you live in. Speaking of which, how's the book coming?"

Just then, the waitress arrives with their burgers and says, "I'll bring your sundaes when you're done. Enjoy your meal."

William, happy to have dodged the Dostoevsky bullet, thanks her and she leaves. "These look really good." William removes the pickles from his cheeseburger, squirts a little ketchup on it and raises it to his mouth. Then he makes a face and lowers it.

"What's wrong?" Amy asks.

"I was just wondering … if we're eating the same thing, do we still have to offer each other a bite?"

"May I?" Amy takes William's discarded pickles and puts them in her basket. "Here's the deal, my friend. *Sharing for Beginners* clearly states that unless identical food items have been prepared differently, they need not be shared."

"Whew, that's a relief! For a second there, I thought I'd screwed up."

"Nope. You're okay."

As they eat, they talk with the easy grace of a married couple, and William, who can't take his eyes off Amy, wonders how he can possibly feel the way he does about her. *I mean … I hardly know her. This is our second date.*

When they're almost finished, Amy says, "I can't eat all these fries. You want some?"

"Sure."

Amy hands her basket across the table, and William helps himself. "Thank you."

Amy nods, and her expression becomes serious. "I thought I'd wait until we were done eating to mention this—you know, in case I start crying or something—but I was told this afternoon that I won't have a job next year."

William had been smiling, but his expression changes instantly. "Oh, no. I'm so sorry."

"Me too," Amy says. "The district is looking at a two-million-dollar shortfall next year, and my position is one of the recommended cuts."

William shakes his head. "That's awful, Amy. Have you been notified in writing?"

"My principal gave me the letter today. She had to—it's May first. But I saw this coming two months ago. People with *assistant* in their title always get the ax when money gets tight."

William doesn't know what to say. "Don't worry. You'll find another job."

Amy nods. "Yes, I suppose so. But it probably won't pay what I'm making now, and that's going to impact Lauren. She loves Macalester—*loves* it—and I have to tell her that she'll be going somewhere else in the fall." Amy lowers her head.

"Hey, I'm nobody's idea of an optimist, Amy, but I believe in you, and I know everything will be okay."

"I appreciate the vote of confidence, and I ... I sure hope you're right." Amy clears her throat and glances to her left. "Don't look now, but have you noticed that couple seated across the room?"

"Yes. The guy keeps looking over here."

"They *both* keep looking over here. What's their problem?"

"It's nothing. They'll come over to our table in a few minutes."

"Whatever for?"

"You'll see."

"Okay, if you say so ..." Amy thinks of something and smiles. "Hey, I figured out why signal strength was so bad at Dewhurst, and it had nothing to do with the ivy or anything like that."

"Did this come to you in a vision?"

"Kind of."

"Lay it on me."

"Sunspots."

William smiles.

"I'm serious. I read online that sunspots can cause all kinds of—"

"It wasn't sunspots."

"It wasn't?"

"No."

"But how can you be so sure?"

"I just am." In that instant, William wants to spill his guts, to tell Amy about the jammer, about the bind he's in, about how he could drop a dime on Lothrup and cost them a fortune. But he doesn't say anything. Amy has her own problems, and she sure as hell doesn't need any of his.

"A penny for your thoughts, Professor."

William smiles. "I was just wishing we could turn the clock back a few minutes to where we were talking about the Seven Dwarfs, and I was imagining the two of us in bed."

Amy laughs. "How cheeky of you! Were we having fun?"

"I don't think a one-syllable word could possibly describe it."

Amy takes his hand and pretends to read his palm. "Hmm … it could definitely happen for you, William. I see it right here in your heart line."

"Any idea when?"

She looks again. "Oh, that's very hard to say."

"Why?"

Amy squeezes his hand and releases it. "Because I don't know the first thing about reading palms."

When they get their sundaes, Amy dips her spoon in hers and tastes it. "Mmmm … you've gotta try this." She pushes the tulip-shaped glass to where he can reach it.

William tastes the sundae and nods. "It's excellent. There's something special about the ice cream here." He slides it back across the table. "Look at all the little pieces of vanilla bean. And that golden color … I'm guessing it's some kind of French vanilla."

"It's bad luck to overthink ice cream, William." Amy takes another spoonful. "I can't believe how good this is." She sets her spoon down. "You're sort of analytical about food, aren't you? When we were at Ki's, you were wondering if molasses was the secret ingredient in their onion soup."

"I get that from my wife," William says. "She's a supertaster. Do you know what that is?"

"More or less."

"Well, my wife can taste one part per million of *anything*—the kids used to say she could taste color and sound." William laughs. "This is a true story. One time we were in New Mexico for a wedding, and we stopped at a little café for a bowl of chili. I kept saying how great it was, and Marcia—that's my wife's name—Marcia said it was because of the cocoa powder. I said, 'Hey, you're good, lady, but nobody puts cocoa in chili.' So we bet ten dollars, and I lost—Marcia asked the cook. It was actually kind of funny. He didn't speak English very well, and at first he thought she was asking if he put cocaine in his chili."

"You refer to Marcia as your *wife*."

William doesn't understand. "Yeah …"

"She's your *ex*-wife."

"Oh, sure. But … you know what I meant."

"William, my overall sense is that you like me, but …"

"I *do* like you. Calling Marcia my wife, that was just—"

Amy laughs. "I'm not talking about that. You haven't asked me to taste your sundae."

William scrambles, nearly pushing his sundae into Amy's lap. "Sorry. Here you go. I forgot they aren't the same."

Amy tries it and thanks him. "It's wonderful … and I'm usually not big on butterscotch. This has been a lovely first date, William."

"Yes, it's been fun, but … isn't it a *second* date?"

Amy shakes her head. "The first one was more of an impromptu hang-out date, so even though it was fun, it shouldn't really count."

"Oh, okay. Then, yes—this has been a lovely first date. I'm hoping I can see you tomorrow."

"You will, William—we have obedience class."

"It's Doc, by the way."

Amy is confused. "You have a nickname?"

"I'm talking about the dwarf playing the accordion—it's *Doc*. He's the only dwarf who wears glasses."

Amy laughs. "I can't tell you how relieved I am to know that."

The couple on the other side of the room get up to leave, but instead of heading for the door, they walk directly toward William and Amy.

"How did you *know*?" Amy whispers.

"Experience."

When they reach the table, the man speaks first. "We're sorry to interrupt, but aren't you ... the Saint Patrick's Day hero?" He looks at William hopefully.

"You look just like him," the woman adds.

William nods, and the couple are relieved. "I told you!" the man says. "I'm Blake—Blake Kirby. This is my wife Debbie." He extends his hand, and William shakes it. "Now I've shaken hands with two heroes—John McCain and ... I'm sorry—I can't remember your name."

"William Kessler, and I'm no hero—not by a long shot."

"Oh, but you are," Mrs. Kirby says, reaching for William's hand. "You saved all those lives. God bless you for what you did."

"Yes, that was really something," her husband says. He looks down at the table. "We know you had some trouble after that, and we're very sorry—hope things are better now." He says this quickly and looks up again. "We'll let you get back to your meal."

"It was an honor to meet you," his wife says, turning to leave. "You were very brave."

William gives her a wan smile and says nothing.

When they're gone, Amy tries to speak to William, but at first he doesn't respond. She moves her hand up and down in front of his face. "Why the thousand-yard stare, William? Are you okay?"

William turns slowly toward her. "Yes ... it just does something to me when people who have no idea what happened at Dewhurst call me a hero."

"I could see how uncomfortable you were," Amy says. "But when you do something heroic, people are bound to call you a hero. That's just the way—"

"But there's a lot more to this than people realize."

"More than killing a terrorist and saving lives?"

William nods.

"Okay ... do you want to talk about it? I'm a very good listener."

"Thanks but ... no thanks."

"Fair enough, but I hope someday you'll tell me."

"Why?"

"Because then I'll know you trust me, and I want that for both of us."

"I do trust you. It's just that—"

Amy holds up her hand. "It's okay—really. By the way, William, when you were imagining the two of us in bed, where were we? I need to know."

William makes a little sound of uncertainty. "I can't say for sure, but it kinda felt like my house. Why?"

"I just want to be ready ... you know, in case it actually happens."

"Yeah ... I'm 95 percent certain it was my place."

"Good. On the strength of that, I won't run out and buy new sheets and pillow cases."

William is still thinking. "I guess we could have been at a motel."

"We weren't."

"How do you know? It's my fantasy."

"Of course, but it's not like I wasn't there."

After William takes Amy home—and gets a long good-night kiss—he races home to let Baron out. Baron, who is excited and wants to play, chases imaginary rabbits around the yard while William listens to the night sounds and marvels at the newly risen moon. It's full and refulgent, bright enough to read by, and it makes everything in the backyard appear luminous and other-worldly. After a couple of minutes, Baron shows up with a large stick that he wants William to throw for him.

"First things first, my friend." William points to the sky. "Did you know that May's full moon is called the Milk Moon? I think that's because May is when there's enough new growth to put the cows out to pasture, which dramatically improves the quality of their milk. But it could be some Native American thing, so don't quote me on it."

Baron, who has no plans to quote William on anything, has dropped his stick and is now digging a hole at the base of the fence.

"Knock it off, Hürtgenvoss. I can see you."

William looks up at the moon again and thinks about the way his life is struggling to improve, to disentangle itself from a grievous past. This is not something that he willed or even imagined. It's simply the quantum wheel beginning to turn, and as far as he's concerned, it's about time. He thinks of Amy, how her green eyes have so many different depths, how her laughter reminds him of music. And then there's Baron, who has quit digging and is now dragging a shovel around by its handle. The night is pulsating with the sound of spring peepers, crickets and the calls of whip-poor-wills. Down by the river, a heron croaks, its raucous voice scraping against the moonlight.

William smiles. *What is all this juice and all this joy?*

CHAPTER 13

I Know Nothing. Noth-ing!

THE NEXT MORNING after breakfast, William, as he does every Monday, Wednesday and Thursday, puts Baron in the backyard while he gets ready to go to the office. When it's time to leave, he joins Baron to see how many holes he's dug—a new habit that William is trying to discourage. But Baron is sitting quietly beside the bird feeder, watching a squirrel make its way along the top of the fence.

"Slow day at Hürtgenvoss Excavation?"

Baron glances at him, then refocuses on the squirrel.

"Look, if you want to come with me, let's boogie."

The instant Baron hears that, he races to the back door and waits—his nose to the crack—for William to open it. *Let's boogie* is the phrase William uses whenever he takes Baron with him in the car, so it's become one of Baron's favorites, second only to *Hey, it's chow time.*

They leave the house but make it no farther than the end of the driveway, where William stops, puts the Jeep in park and reaches for his phone. All week he's been meaning to call the vet to ask which tick collar they recommend, but he can never remember to do it. So he turns his phone on to make the call but is immediately sidetracked by a text from Marv: "am @ whisky junction. gr8 band. b4 that i was @ cabooze. band so-so. im drumk. mk."

William turns to Baron. "It seems that mk was on the West Bank last night. He says he got drumk." He looks at the time stamp on the message—1:46 a.m. "I guess Marv's not kidding when he says he can't sleep." William knows that if he doesn't answer Marv's text immediately, he never will. He hates texting, mostly because he's lousy at it, and he's thoroughly convinced of two things: one, that thumbs are meant for grasping, not for pressing buttons; two, that texting represents the devolutionary nadir of written expression. But slowly, painstakingly, William's thumbs lunge and jab at the keyboard until he has a short reply: "Marv, for a hangover try coconut milk if you can get it. Gatorade if you can't. Center yourself, Gautama—Mille Lacs in 10 days."

William looks the message over, not at all pleased. He hates the way his texts always read like little letters, the way they exhibit none of the cool *CUL8R* insouciance so fashionable in texting. But there isn't a damn thing he can do about it—he just isn't comfortable using the language that way. "And it doesn't stop with cyberslang, Hürtgenvoss. I feel the same way about emojis—the lingua franca of our brave new world that finds the concept of actual words too challenging."

When they get to Dewhurst, Baron runs full tilt down the hall to William's office door, where he sits and waits for William to catch up. Once inside, Baron makes sure no one has played with his toys, and William opens one of his many casebooks on Dostoevsky and begins to read. Forty-five minutes later, Sam walks through the door.

"As I live and breathe!" William says. "If it isn't Sam Richter!"

"Hello, William. Who do we have here?" Sam reaches down to pet Baron, who has come over to say hello.

"Why, that's visiting professor Ernst Edelweiss from the University of Hamburg. He's here on the Sister Campus Exchange."

"Is that a fact?" Sam kneels in front of Baron and pets him with both hands. "I've said for a long time that we need to police that program better."

"Actually, his name is Baron. Kate gave him to me."

Sam nods. "Nice dog. I guess it's okay if you bring him to work in the summer, but I'm not sure how that will play once school starts."

"If you and Gardner have your way, I'll be in Norway by then.

Hey, is that what you're here to talk about?" William chuckles. "I'll bet you had to ask someone where my office is."

"Don't be silly," Sam says, sitting down. "I looked it up in the campus directory. And Norway is just one of the reasons I'm here. I told you on Monday that we'd talk soon."

William takes the chair next to Sam, turning it in order to see him better. "So ... are we going to talk about Rupert's jammer?"

Sam sits up straight, his feet flat on the floor. "William, before we even get started, I want to make something clear. The only thing I know about a jammer is that you say there was one in Rupert's briefcase. I don't know if that's true, and I don't want to know. So let's get on the same page here—I'm not advocating anything, and I'm sure as hell not telling you what to do. In fact, it would be better for me if this conversation never took place, so—"

"I get it—plausible deniability."

Sam furrows his brow. "What?"

"You want plausible deniability. If you're sufficiently insulated from this mess, you can pretend you're Sergeant Schultz—*I know nothing. Noth-ing!*"

"Listen, William. I don't—"

"You've changed your tune a bit from Monday, Sam, so I assume you've spoken to Gardner."

Sam smiles. "Did you and I talk on Monday? I don't recall."

"No, of course you don't," William says. "For what it's worth, the line you'll want to use is, 'At this moment in time, and to the best of my recollection, I do not remember.'"

"Yeah ... I like that."

"It's very popular in courtrooms," William says. "Okay, bring it! Tell me something that you aren't really telling me."

"All right," Sam says. "You can be a real pain in the ass. How's that?"

"Direct and probably true," William says, "but I meant about Rupert's jammer."

Sam leans back in his chair. "I'm just spitballing here, sort of thinking out loud, but has it occurred to you that whoever has the jammer can write his own ticket? Hell, they're sitting in the catbird seat."

William looks at Sam askance. "Is that mixed metaphor your way of saying if someone gave you a *quo*, you might respond with a *quid*? I was right—you *have* talked to Gardner."

"Who's Gardner?"

William laughs. "Gardner is the hubristic SOB who wants to send me to Norway for my sins."

"Not so much anymore."

"I'm not following you. Are you saying that I *don't* have to go to Norway?"

Sam smiles. "I'm saying it depends on you."

"And all this talk about firing me if I don't go … that was bullshit?"

"Oh, no—you could still get fired. That also depends on you—on the choices you make."

William can feel the noose tightening. "What choices?"

"Well, if you choose to live in the real world and be a team player, that's a good choice. If you choose to go rogue and continue living in your own private Idaho, that's a bad choice. Like it or not, William, you're a member of our Lothrup family, and we have to look out for each other."

"I haven't felt the love lately, Sam."

"Maybe that's about to change. Like I said, everything is up to you." Sam studies William's face. "Do we understand each other?"

"You should avoid asking direct questions like that, Sam. If I were to answer—" William blows across his open palm—"that could be the end of your plausible deniability."

Sam looks at his watch. "No matter. I have to go. I have a meeting in a few minutes."

"Would that meeting have anything to do with this meeting?"

Sam stands up. "I know nothing. *Noth*-ing! Hey, good talk—see you later."

After Sam leaves, William thinks about their conversation. Two days ago, Sam had asked him not to say anything about the jammer. Today, that request had turned into a bribe. Their exchange had been almost cryptic at times, but for all its three-cushion phrasing, the bottom line was clear: if William kept his mouth shut, he would be rewarded. If he spilled the beans, he would be punished. William appreciates the opportunity to keep his job, just as he appreciates not having to teach in Norway. Naturally, the idea of succumbing to bribery makes him uncomfortable, but his misgivings aside, William has no desire to rock the boat or antagonize his employer. And this is because William knows what everybody knows: if you don't have a job, America will chew you up and spit you out. That's one of those nasty little truths that really helps focus the mind.

And it doesn't hurt that the math is on his side. What Sam had said on Monday was true—the supreme court was unlikely to hear the case. The fact that they reviewed only 10 percent of the cases referred to them meant there was a 90 percent probability that if William didn't say anything about the jammer, it wouldn't matter anyway. In a quantum universe, it was foolish to ignore odds that ran nine to one in your favor—that sort of thing didn't happen very often.

William's phone rings, and it's Ruth. "Hello," he says. "I was just going to call you."

"*Schmegegge*, William. Tell me about the book."

"I've been fine, thanks. So nice of you to ask. And you?"

"Can we dispense with the pleasantries, Velvel? I need to know if you're making progress."

"I'm about a quarter done," William says.

"I want that you should send me a hundred pages. Is that a problem?"

"I'll send you seventy-five pages—for your eyes only. How's that?"

"You're making me nervous, William. Yalla, yalla—let's pick up the pace. I want you to finish this project so we can do something that will make some money."

"Like what?"

"Like a book about the shooting."

"Not a chance," William says.

"Why not? Who's got better bona fides than you?"

"I don't care. I couldn't do it."

"I don't believe that, William. When I think about the book you could write ... holy shamoka!"

"I've gotta go, Ruth. I'll get the pages to you."

"Do that, William. Shalom."

William knows he can't meet an August deadline, but he doesn't really care. Publishers like August deadlines because it puts their books in the stores by Christmas, but academic books don't appear on retail bookshelves anyway, so William isn't worried. Just the same, he isn't looking for trouble, so before he forgets, William emails Ruth seventy-five pages.

William is hard at work when Baron goes to the door and barks, his way of saying that he needs to go out.

William gets up and clips a leash to his collar. "Lead on, Macduff."

After Baron pees and sniffs around behind Dewhurst, William takes him for a short walk. They are almost to the science building when a young woman passes them from the opposite direction and hands William a flyer. "*Light It Up*, sir. Have a nice day."

"Yeah … thanks." William glances at the flyer, folds it twice and stuffs it into his pocket. It's ten minutes later, when William and Baron stop at a bench on the commons promenade, that he actually reads it, mumbling the key words so fast that it sounds like chanting. When William is done, he looks at Baron, who is staring up at him.

"Okay, partner, here's the gist of it. The first paragraph is *Light It Up*'s usual boilerplate about Lothrup having one of the darkest campuses in Minnesota—we have an *inexcusable lumen deficit,* they say. And the remedy for this deficit is LED lights— lots of 'em. But in addition to talking about security and safety, the flyer makes an environmental argument." William smiles. "That's smart, Hürtgenvoss—you gotta do that these days. So it says that if Lothrup were to do everything *Light It Up* is urging, not only would we all be safer, but we would also reduce energy consumption on campus by …" William checks the page. "3,446,162 kilowatt hours per year, which means a consequent reduction in carbon dioxide emissions of 1,388 metric tons. Hang on … there's something I want to read you."

William searches the page, scanning the print with his finger. "Yeah, here it is. 'The reduction in carbon dioxide emissions is the equivalent of taking 318 cars off the road or planting 39,216 trees.'" William laughs. "Those little data points are specifically addressed to Gardner, which tells me that *Light It Up* doesn't get it. Gardner doesn't give a damn about trees, cars or carbon dioxide. If they want Gardner onboard, they'll have to talk to him about money or explain how he can get his picture on the cover of *Minnesota Monthly*. Reducing pollution and hugging trees isn't Gardner's thing—you feel me, dawg?"

Baron is stretched out with his chin on William's shoe, but he looks up with one eye because William has asked him something.

"You know, as long as we have a few minutes, we should probably talk about tonight's class. You were brilliant last week, but we could do better on the *down* and *stay* exercises. Whaddya say we do a little work on them before we go back?" So William and Baron practice those two commands until Baron does each one three times in a row without making any mistakes.

Like before, the thought of obedience class makes William nervous, but this time the nervousness is suffused with excitement because he will get to see Amy again. William had to work hard to convince her to give the class another try, and he succeeded only after he sent her links to several articles that explained how obedience classes were indispensable to the socialization of young dogs.

"These articles don't mince words," William told her. "If you don't take Yoshi to obedience class, he could become alienated to the point where his sense of self desiccates. In time, he could even start drinking out of the toilet. And you know what? For the rest of your life, you'll wonder if it was your fault."

"All right already," Amy said at last. "I'll go. But if Frau Hochschnitzel is there, I'm leaving."

"*Hochstetler*—and she won't be there. I'll meet you on the beginners' side of the parking lot."

When they get home that afternoon, William and Baron try to take it easy. It's hot and humid, and William is a little frazzled by his efforts to eat, shower and leave for the armory in time for class.

"It's not as hot as last week," he tells Baron, "but it's sure as hell hot."

He meets Amy in the parking lot, and when he sees her, he can hardly believe how lovely she looks, how crisp and cool. He wants to take her in his arms, to kiss her and hold her close, but he knows the relationship isn't there yet, so he gives her a hug instead. "Why does the sight of you always take my breath away?"

"I'm not sure," Amy says, turning the hug into a kiss. "But it's probably the same reason that when we do this, I feel dizzy."

"Hey, maybe we should skip class tonight and go back to my place and talk about it. We could open a bottle of wine, slip into some comfortable—"

"Not a chance, Professor. Yoshi and I have been working all week on the long stay, and he's about to make me proud."

William laughs. "Well ... I took a shot."

"Yes, you did. We have to see if the Frau is here."

"She isn't."

"I need proof."

They take the dogs into the armory and look around. There is no sign of Birgit Hochstetler, and William wishes they had bet something. "Toldja," he says.

"Yeah ... maybe." But Amy isn't convinced. "I'm going to ask one of the kennel club people. The Frau could be hiding in an office someplace, plotting a comeback."

But the person Amy asks plays it very cool. He shrugs his shoulders and pretends to know nothing about Frau Hochstetler. It isn't until Amy talks to some of the people in the class that she begins to relax. They're gathered in small groups, leaning toward each other meaningfully and speaking in coded phrases. *Did you hear? Eva Braun has left the building. Yes, the Reich has fallen.* In their excitement, everyone seems to forgive William his trespasses of the week before, and now they include him in their conversations, even soliciting his opinion about who will teach the class now that Frau Hochstetler is gone. This is a big question, and the group is delighted when Jackie Carroll, the girl everyone liked from last time, walks down to their end of the gym and announces that she will be their "facilitator" for the rest of the course.

"I have to admit it," Amy says. "You were right about the Frau. How did you know?"

William smiles. "It's no mystery. I just happen to know a thing or two when it comes to personae non gratae."

Baron and Yoshi both have good nights, but William's head really isn't in the game. He spends most of the time watching

Amy—her facial expressions, her body, the way she moves around the ring—and it nearly kills him to be so close to her and yet be unable to reach out and touch her. He can hardly believe that a week ago, he didn't know who she was.

In the middle of class, a storm rolls in, accompanied by explosive claps of thunder that frighten the dogs, especially some of the older dogs in the advanced class. Their fears are heightened by the fact that they aren't at home, which means they can't hide under the beds or in the shower stalls that have protected them so well over the years. After the storm passes, it takes a few minutes to reassure the dogs and get them calmed down to the point where class can resume. William is glad that Baron doesn't care about loud noises or thunder. In fact, if Baron has any quirks at all, like an aversion to hats, beards, strange noises or microwave ovens, William hasn't discovered them.

When William and Amy walk out of the armory, it's much cooler, and the humidity has dropped considerably. There are large puddles in the parking lot, and happy robins are singing and scoring worms on the sidewalk and the edges of the asphalt. When they get to their cars, William and Amy crate the dogs, and William drops the endgate of the Jeep so they can sit down.

"Don't you just love the way it smells after a thunder shower?" Amy says.

William inhales deeply. "Yes, it's nice—there's even a name for it. It's called petrichor."

Amy shakes her head. "It scares me that you know that. Name your three favorite smells—no fair thinking about it."

"Okay ... canvas tents, burning leaves and old books." He thought of the way Marcia smelled after a shower but kept that one to himself. "Your turn."

"Baking bread, new shoes and my grandmother's attic. She dried herbs up there—lavender, sage and basil. I'll never forget that smell. It was so earthy and complex."

"It smells good just to hear you describe it." William would like to do something, to go back to his place or maybe get a cup of coffee, but before he can suggest it, Amy leans close and puts her arm around him.

"I'd better be going. I have a seven o'clock meeting tomorrow morning."

"Bummer. What about?"

"Well … we're meeting about a fifth grader who is either EBD or PDD—we're not sure which—and we need to change his IEP so that his MCA doesn't impact our AYP. We don't want the state stepping in, because if they do—"

"You'll be SOL?"

"You got it. I have to go."

They hop off the endgate and kiss, but Amy soon pulls away.

"Like I was saying, Professor. I'd better be going." She kisses him one more time and gets into her car.

William reaches in the window and touches her face, tracing the line of her jaw with his finger. "I'll be thinking about you—*a lot*."

Amy smiles. "Good. I'll be thinking about you too."

"I've got a family thing tomorrow night. Can we do something Friday?"

"Of course," Amy says. "Give me a call."

"I will, but in the meantime how am I going to make it forty-eight hours without seeing you?"

"Well, you can do what I'm going to do."

"And what's that?"

"I'm going to enjoy missing you. I'm going to enjoy every minute of it because I know I'll see you soon. Good night, William."

William watches Amy's car pull away, thinking what good advice she just gave him. Having someone in your life to miss—someone you'll actually see again—is about as good as it gets.

CHAPTER 14

The Seventh Applicant

THE NEXT DAY, May third, is a scorcher. It's hot even at nine o'clock in the morning, and as William and Baron head to campus, it even *looks* hot—the haze, the breathless trees, the wavy lines on the pavement. William can feel the back of his shirt sticking to the car seat, and if he didn't know better, he'd swear that Chambliss had been picked up in the middle of the night and dropped into southern Alabama.

He and Baron spend most of the day at the office, but William knew, even before he left the house, that he wasn't likely to get much done. And it isn't because of the heat. It's because May third is his and Marcia's anniversary. The concept of anniversaries is confusing to William, and he wonders if he even has one anymore, since he's no longer married. But either way, he can remember his wedding as though it were yesterday. William's bride—the lovely Marcia Ellen Hastings—was from Brainerd, Minnesota, and on May third, twenty-nine years ago, the two of them were married north of town at a fancy resort on Gull Lake.

Mrs. Hastings had died when Marcia was in high school, so Marcia assumed almost all of the responsibility for planning the wedding, and it was the first time William had seen her in action. He knew she was organized, but as he watched her orchestrate the details of the ceremony and reception, he couldn't help being impressed by how executive she was. She worked out budgets for everything (including postage), negotiated with the vendors, and could tell you which guests were vegetarians, who was allergic to shellfish and how much a videographer should be tipped. William had been very proud of her. And of course, thanks to Marcia, their wedding came off without a hitch.

Their honeymoon had come almost entirely out of their own pockets, which made it doubly hard for them to choose a destination. May was too early for Banff and too late for Mexico. Hawaii was four thousand miles away, and Caribbean beach resorts were prohibitively expensive. So after a great deal of discussion and research, they finally settled on Key West, which seemed perfect—it was the off season, accommodations were cheap, and there were no crowds.

William tries to remember the name of the little boutique hotel where they stayed, but he's unable to come up with it. Whatever it was called, they loved it there, and he and Marcia found the Keys delightful. They rented paddleboats, bicycles and kayaks. They hiked, snorkeled and saw the sights—Hemingway's house, Tennessee Williams' cottage, Sloppy Joe's Bar. They even went deep-sea fishing, and he caught a little sailfish that they released, and Marcia caught a mahi-mahi that the kitchen staff prepared for their dinner that evening. It was a magical time, and William cannot imagine how anyone could have had a better honeymoon.

But now he hates May third. And when he thinks about his life with Marcia, it makes him uncomfortable, as though he's being unfaithful. But he can't decide what he's being unfaithful to—the memory of Marcia or the reality of Amy.

William writes a quick note to Marcia that he wouldn't mail in a hundred lifetimes, and when he's done with it, he can't tell if he feels better or worse.

3 May 2012

Hi Marcia—

I'm wondering if you remember the name of the place where we stayed in Key West on our honeymoon. So many times questions like this come up, and you're the only person in the world who knows the answer. I wish our relationship was such that I could occasionally ask you things, like which repair shop has our lawn mower, but I know better than to do that.

I've been working at the carriage house when I can, and it's coming along nicely. I found Gerardo in one of the boxes you left there, and it was quite a shock—I felt like that guy in Saint Paul who was raking leaves and uncovered a severed hand.

Anyway ... it's our anniversary today, and I was thinking about you. I do that more than I should, I suppose, but it's not something I can control.

Love,

William

PS: Kate gave me a dog for my birthday. His name is Baron. I wish you could meet him.

William would like to tell Marcia about Amy, but what would he say? That he met a woman he really likes, but nothing will ever come of it because he can't get past the twenty-eight years he was married? Twenty-eight years is a long time. It took only twenty-three years to build the pyramid at Giza; twenty to build the Taj Mahal; ten to dig the Panama Canal and eight to put a man on the moon. A lot of things happen to a couple in twenty-eight years, things that are impossible to forget. William thinks that if his mind were a computer, he'd find someone to erase the hard drive. That was the answer—to become a *tabula rasa*. Then again, he'd lost enough of his memory already.

At eleven o'clock William is thinking about the shooting like he does, calling the roll of the dead, when that old trapdoor opens in his mind, and he falls through it.

Jon is staring at him. "This observation platform ... can we secure it?"

This isn't real. This isn't fucking real.

"I said, can we secure it?"

William looks at him. "I don't … I don't know."

"We have to be able to keep the shooters from getting up there. Is there one stairway, one door?"

"Yes. I called it a stairway, but it's more like a library ladder."

"It doesn't matter," Jon says. "C'mon, we gotta go. It may already be too late."

William always hopes to skate across his recollections of the shooting, like a waterbug darting across the surface of a pond. But it doesn't always work that way, and now William is in too deep—deep enough to hear the shots, the screams and the sirens. Eventually, he hears a burst of gunfire and sees the student with his throat blown away, trying to hang onto the drinking fountain. This is right after he sees the first shooter, an underexposed image, black and anamorphic, standing in front of the windows at the top of the stairs.

"Run, Dad! He's reloading. Come to me, goddammit!"

Most of the time, when he hears Jon telling him to run, it's a good thing because it usually happens near the end of the flashbacks, when William can sometimes force himself back to reality as though he were willing himself to awaken from a bad dream. That's how it is this time, and by one o'clock, William is okay again. He takes Baron for a short walk, but the heat, which was bad four hours ago, has become unbearable. It's humid, oppressive, and even though it's early May, William can hear the unmodulated whine of cicadas that normally wouldn't be around for another month or more.

William wipes his brow. "It feels positively tropical out here, Baron. And what's weird is how everything seems so confused by the heat. Yesterday, I saw black-eyed Susans in bloom, and I think they're supposed to bloom in July." William points to the ground. "And have you noticed this fuzzy stuff? It's poplar fluff, and you don't usually see it until mid-June. Like I said, everything is confused, including me." But William is talking about more than the weather. He's talking about the jammer, hoping he's doing the right thing or at least the more intelligent thing.

It isn't long before the heat drives the two of them back to William's office, where they try to revive themselves in the air conditioning. William gets Baron a fresh bowl of water from the drinking fountain and then begins to pace. "It's a good goddamn thing we're not experiencing climate change, Baron. Can you imagine how hot *that* would be?"

Baron looks up at the question, but William's sarcasm is lost on him.

"You know, these climate-change deniers amaze me. How can they keep saying that the scientists are wrong and that human beings have nothing to do with the planet heating up? Hell, some of them—one of them in particular—won't even acknowledge that climate change is happening."

William is referring to Oklahoma's senior senator, James Inhofe, whose book, *The Greatest Hoax*, had come out in February. Someone put a copy in his mailbox at school, and William had actually read it, even though he felt it was unmitigated hooey from first page to last. Even worse, William thought the book was dangerous, given the current milieu, and that it had the potential to do for ignorance in America what the Catholic Church's ban on condoms had done for AIDS in sub-Saharan Africa.

William looks at his hands, and there is a slight tremor in the fingers. "I think it's time to write Senator Inhofe, Baron. I should have done it a long time ago."

The reason Senator Inhofe had thus far been given a pass was simple: William liked him. He had seen Inhofe on TV a number of times, and he always came across as a gentleman, even when he was being slapped around in combative interviews. But gentleman or not, Inhofe had it all wrong when it came to climate change, and that was a problem because the nation's anti-science devotees—a new and disquieting voice in America—were in complete agreement with him.

"Baron, how do I tell a basically nice person that he's full of shit without sounding snarky?"

William reads online for fifteen minutes and then types his letter.

3 May 2012

Dear Senator Inhofe:

I recently finished *The Greatest Hoax*, and I take respectful issue with a number of your assertions, especially those regarding science and scientists, 97 percent of whom believe three things that your book flatly denies: one, that climate change is a real and serious problem; two, that human activity is largely responsible for it; and three, that the 38 billion tons of carbon dioxide we pump into the atmosphere every year is causing our planet to become warmer. I would add that you do not buttress your arguments very convincingly by quoting Genesis, Rush Limbaugh and your friends at the Cato Institute.

You state repeatedly in *The Greatest Hoax* that climate change is nothing more than a big-government conspiracy designed to steal our freedom, raise our taxes and create an insidious world order. What's more, you claim that global warming is a left-wing ploy to increase regulation, which you believe will supersize the budget and inflate the cost of living. And yet nowhere in your book do you offer a scintilla of proof for these notions.

Senator Inhofe, America is a country where you can deny climate change with impunity and shout your denial from the rooftops. Likewise, you are free to reject science, scientists and any scientific theory that offends your sensibilities. But I would ask that you remember something when you're cashing all those checks from the Koch brothers and the fossil fuel industry: denying the truth never changes the facts.

Sincerely,

William Kessler

William reads the letter over three times.

"Well, Baron, it's snarky but hopefully not *too* snarky." He saves the letter to his letter file and swivels his chair around. "It doesn't matter anyway because Thomas Swift was right—you can't reason a man out of an idea he wasn't reasoned into. I would add that it's also impossible to get a man to understand something when his income depends upon his *not* understanding it. But goddammit, I tried." William feels better, and there are no longer any tremors in his fingers, so at least therapeutically, the letter was a success.

Because it's Thursday, the end of the week for William, he schleps his suitcase full of books home, and that evening he meets his family for dinner at the Pasta House, a little Italian restaurant downtown. Kate arranges something like this a couple of times a month, and in the past, William has always been happy to go. But now that he has Baron, he hates to leave him alone unless he has to.

I'm sure BearBear can survive without you for an hour or so.

Yes, it's just that—

Daddy—you're going.

So William goes. They order an extra-large pizza with nothing but cheese on one side (Kate and the boys) and everything but anchovies on the other (William and Todd). The boys are well behaved in restaurants—Kate and Todd have worked hard on that—and it's a pleasant-enough outing. William talks about soccer and *The Lorax* with Matt and Jacob, and he talks about work with Todd. Kate wants to know about Amy, and William does his best to answer all the questions that, in her excitement, she forgot to ask when they spoke on the phone—*yes, very pretty; divorced; a daughter in college.* But the most interesting part of the evening, at least to William, is when Kate discloses that she talked to Marcia for an hour the day before.

"So ... what's new?" William asks, trying to sound casual.

"Oh, I don't know," Kate says. "I thought Mom sounded a little down, but she's having fun remodeling the house she and Walter bought. It's a little Spanish colonial with a tile roof. She said she hired a contractor to knock down a wall and add a—"

"Is she working?" William asks.

"She hasn't found a job yet. I think that's part of the problem."

"Jobs are hard to come by right now," Todd says, reaching for another slice of pizza. He turns to William. "I've been meaning to ask—did you ever find your riding lawn mower?"

"Not yet," William says. "It's in a repair shop someplace, but Marcia never told me which one. Or if she did, I forgot."

"Why don't you just call her and ask?" Kate says. "Wouldn't that be the sensible thing to do?"

"Oh, I don't know. I just don't know …"

"Don't be a baby. Call her."

William shakes his head.

"It'll turn up," Todd says. "What about Norway? You gonna go?"

William puts a loose mushroom in his mouth. "Tell you what—I'd rather wear a tin beak and pick shit with the chickens."

"Daddy!" Kate is horrified and points to the boys, who are giggling at the s-word.

"My bad," William says, not especially sorry.

Todd is struggling to keep a straight face. "Is that a line from Chaucer? Or Burns, perhaps?"

"No … it's something my father used to say. It just popped into my head."

"Well, pop it out again," Kate says angrily. "Good heavens!"

Order is soon restored, the conversation moves on, and the boys want to know about Baron.

"He's growing almost as fast as you guys," William tells them. "I took him to the vet on Saturday, and he weighed fifty-eight pounds."

"The vet?" Matt says, his face clouding over. "Is he sick?"

"No, he's fine," William says. "He just needed a checkup."

"We're getting a puppy," Matt says. "Mom said we could." He turns to Jake for confirmation, and his brother nods excitedly.

"A German one, just like BearBear."

"Whoa! Not so fast, guys," Kate says. "I said *maybe*. Your father and I haven't made that decision yet."

The boys slump in their chairs.

"Buck up, men," William tells them. "I think you have the puppy thing in the bag. Once you get to *maybe*, the rest is all downhill."

Kate, wide-eyed, looks at her father. "Thanks, Daddy. That was very helpful. Whose side are you on?"

"I'm on the side of oppressed people everywhere, sweetheart. Wherever there's a fight so hungry people can eat, I'll be there. Wherever there's a mom who won't let her kids have a puppy, I'll be—"

"The puppy issue is complicated," Kate says. She turns to Todd. "You're not exactly helping me out here."

"Sorry," Todd says. "You know, I had a dog when I was a kid. His name was Rusty, and he could catch a Frisbee no matter how—"

"You're worse than *he* is." Kate puts her hands to her head. "I don't want to talk about this anymore. What about the opener, Daddy? Is Marv Kreitzer still coming up?"

"Yes. Are you guys still willing to babysit Baron?"

"We'll be glad to," Kate says. "Marv Kreitzer ... I'll never understand what you see in that man."

"No, probably not."

Todd cuts a piece of pizza in half for the boys and sets his knife down. "I understand it perfectly. You and Marv are like war buddies."

"We *are* war buddies," William says. "Are you going to take Baron to the clinic with you on Monday? I told Kate it's okay to board him if you'd rather not—"

"No, he's coming with me. It'll be fun. The patients will love it."

"Thanks for taking care of him."

The rest of pizza night unfolds without incident, and when William gets home, it's less than a minute until his landline rings. He grabs the phone and accompanies Baron into the backyard.

"Hi, William. It's me."

"Amy! I'm so glad you—"

"Your cell phone isn't on. I thought we talked about that. I had to look up your home phone in an old phone book."

"I'm sorry. I turned it off because I was in a restaurant with my daughter and her—"

"I had a very important phone call this afternoon. Guess who?"

"I don't know ... your ex-husband?"

Amy laughs. "Why would you guess *that*? Are you projecting?"

"No, I just thought—"

"Chancellor Gardner. He called me at work just as I was getting ready to leave. Did you know that Rita Abernathy took a job at Tulane?"

"No. Who is Rita Abernathy?"

"You really don't know? She was the director of Lothrup's lab school. You're not exactly dialed in to the news at school, are you?"

"No, I guess not. What does Rita Abernathy have to do with your call from Gardner?"

"Everything—he wants me to apply for her old position. They're interviewing candidates this month."

"Wow! And to think you met him only two days ago—no flies on Gardner. I knew he was smitten, but—"

"Wait, there's more. Lothrup has already done two rounds of interviews and reduced the field of applicants from twelve to six. But Gardner said not to worry about that. He told me it didn't matter. He said he wanted me in the hunt—those were the words he used—and he said I could be the seventh applicant."

"You realize that you're going to be offered the position, right?"

"Oh, my God, William—I hope so, but don't jinx me. That job would be a huge step up for me. And the *money* ... Lauren could stay at Macalester, like, *forever.*"

"Amy, I know how Gardner operates. He's an autocrat, and if he wants you to be the director of the lab school—and he clearly does—then it's a done deal. Look, he's already rejiggered the interview process for you."

"I know, but ..."

"But nothing. Congratulations!"

"Stop it."

William believes everything he's said about Amy being a shoe-in, but he also knows her prospects for becoming director of the lab school are inexorably linked to him. If he keeps quiet about the jammer, there won't be a problem. But if he says anything, Amy can kiss the directorship goodbye. That possibility, much more than the prospect of his own dismissal, makes William nervous.

Amy sighs. "So you're happy for me, right? You seem sort of ... distant."

"Of course I'm happy. It's wonderful news. I guess I'm wishing that Lothrup was a better employer, but I know this is no time to get fussy."

"You're right—it isn't, not with an opportunity like this on the line. From what I hear, the lab school is well run and has an excellent board of directors."

"It probably does, but how come my boss is the one who called you?"

"Herb is an—"

"Oh, it's *Herb* now?"

Amy groans. "All right—*Chancellor Gardner*. Maybe you don't know this, but the lab school board is six regents plus the college Chancellor, who is an ex officio board member. There was nothing unusual about him making the call." Amy pauses for a moment. "You're so suspicious sometimes, so ... *cynical*."

"I get that a lot—it probably comes from hanging around with Ivan Karamazov. But remember something, Amy. I have a lot of experience when it comes to Gardner and Lothrup, and it isn't all good."

"Point taken, Professor. Let's move on. I missed you tonight."

"I missed you too. What would you like to do tomorrow night?"

"Umm ... how about dinner and a movie?"

"Could I make dinner here?"

"Of course—what a great idea! That way I can see where you live. I need directions, though."

"Well, wear something sexy—I like buttons. I also like lacy underwear. It doesn't have to be black but—"

"Directions to your house, William."

"My house ... right. Let's start from Hawthorne School. Once you're there, go five blocks east on Beechwood Lane, turn left on Newton and go three-quarters of a mile to River Road. Turn right on River Road—I'm the fourth driveway on the left. Got it?"

"Yes. River Road. Fourth driveway. I can be there at six-thirty. Is that okay?"

"It's perfect," William says.

"Oh, and please keep dinner light."

"Ten-four. No roast goose with dumplings or—"

"William, are we a *thang*? My daughter asked me that on the phone, and I wasn't really sure."

William laughs. "We are most definitely a *thang*. Tell Lauren I'm your *bae-thang*—she'll understand."

"*Bae*?"

"Before anyone else."

"It's true," Amy says. "You are."

CHAPTER 15

A Latter-day Sisyphus

WILLIAM DOESN'T SLEEP MUCH that night. Part of the reason is the heat, and part of it is the way Dostoevsky's conscience-stricken characters chase each other through his thoughts, their patronymics tangled in a thicket of Russian diminutives and nicknames. But mostly what keeps William awake is the jammer and the possibility, however slight, that the supreme court will defy the odds and decide to hear Lothrup's appeal. William doesn't *think* they will, but in a quantum universe, it doesn't matter what you think or even what the odds are. One chance in a billion is still a chance.

It isn't that William regrets his decision to keep quiet about the jammer or that he's second-guessing himself. He knows staying mum is the smart thing to do, and it's good not only for his future but also for Amy's. And then there is Lothrup itself to consider. It wouldn't be easy for the college to come up with twelve million dollars, and even if it did, there would still be deep cuts that would impact Lothrup's students for several years—class size would increase, programs would be eliminated, financial aid would be reduced. Looked at in that way, the moral calculus of his predicament isn't so confounding, and there is no shortage of reasons why it's best if William keeps the jammer to himself. The problem is, despite William's rationalization, it doesn't always feel like the right thing to do. In fact, there are times when it feels like a mistake, but not like fat-fingering a phone number or wearing stripes and plaids. It's more on the scale of invading Russia in winter. But William is sure of one thing—he made the best decision he could, given the circumstances and the ethical clutter.

When William lets Baron out, they walk from the front yard to the back, and William scowls at the lawn. It doesn't look bad in the few places where he has mowed recently, but everywhere else it's overgrown and going to seed.

"Baron, how the hell am I supposed to keep up with this job without the riding lawn mower? It's impossible!" William jabs at the air with his finger. "I'm a latter-day Sisyphus, condemned to push a twenty-one-inch rotary mower around my yard for all eternity."

But Baron isn't listening. He has other things on his mind, which include a little painted turtle that has found its way under the fence. Baron would like to check it out, to give it the *Schäferhund* sniff test, but he's afraid to get close enough.

"C'mon, Hürtgenvoss. Leave him alone. Let's go in."

Baron gives up on the turtle, and they go inside for breakfast. But William, cranky from too little sleep, is still fuming over the lawn mowers—the one he has and the one he can't find. Eventually, he subdues his choler, and things are better until he goes out to cut a piece of the lawn, and the lawn mower won't start.

"Goddammit, that's the last straw! If I have to call Marcia to find the riding lawn mower, then so be it." Filled with purpose—and more than a little pique—William stomps into the house and grabs his phone. He hasn't spoken to Marcia since she and Walter moved to Phoenix, but he would never remove her from his contact list. So before he gets cold feet—before he can even think about it—he finds her name and presses CALL. When she answers, William is surprised, although he couldn't have said why.

"Uhh ... hi, Marcia. I ..."

"William? Is that really *you*? When I saw your name in the display, I just ... I couldn't believe it. How have you been?"

The sound of Marcia's voice is beautiful and beguiling, like an old love song, and William is not prepared for it.

"William … are you there?"

"Yes, yes," he stammers. "I'm here. Can we talk, or is this a bad time? If it is—"

"No, it's fine. I'm just sitting here at the kitchen table, having coffee and watching the peccary eat my quail food. They come right into the yard in the mornings and—"

"There's something I need to tell you, Marcia."

"You're scaring me, William. Are Kate and the boys all right? Is Todd—"

"Yes—everybody's fine. It's nothing like that. I'm calling to tell you that I never picked up the riding lawn mower from wherever you took it to be repaired. Could you please tell me where that was?"

Marcia laughs. "Is that really why you called?"

"Yes. The lawn is out of control. If I can't locate the rider—"

"It's at Holmgren's—at least it was."

"The place by Five Corners?"

"That's right. It wouldn't start, remember?"

"Sort of. Thanks. I'm sorry to bother you."

When Marcia speaks again, her voice is different—still beautiful, but even softer and warmer. "You're not bothering me at all. You sound good, William. I've missed you this spring."

William doesn't know what to say. "You have?"

"Yes. Does that surprise you?"

"A little, yeah."

"Well, it shouldn't. Yesterday was our anniversary, and I thought about you a lot. If you say you didn't think about me, I simply won't believe you."

There was a time when William might have lied, but he doesn't bother now. "I did think about you … I thought about the two of us in Key West."

"We had fun there, didn't we?"

William's palms are beginning to sweat. "Yes, we did. How's Walter?"

Marcia laughs. "You're changing the subject, William. Walter is fine. He's very busy getting his new practice on its feet."

"Are you getting much rain there?"

"Rain? It doesn't really rain here, William."

"No … I guess I knew that. Look, I'd better be going. It was nice to talk to you."

"I enjoyed it very much, William. Thank you for calling."

William presses END CALL and shudders. "Not my proudest moment, Hürtgenvoss. Don't say a word."

He replays the conversation in his head, and his end of it is even worse than he thought. *Are you getting much rain there?* What an idiotic thing to say—a Minnesota non sequitur right up there with *Cold enough for you?* Marcia was doing her best to be open and friendly, and he'd acted like an addled schoolboy. One thing's for sure: he still has feelings for her—just the sound of her voice reduced him to jelly. And what about Marcia? Maybe she has some leftover feelings too. It certainly seemed that way—*I've missed you this spring.* To William, that's a simple declarative sentence not amenable to interpretation. But even so, he knows he's being foolish because when Marcia had told him that, she was sitting at another man's kitchen table in the city they moved to after she had fallen out of love with him—her husband of twenty-eight years—and filed for divorce. Those were the facts. Everything else was airy-fairy bullshit. But still …

As soon as William recovers, he calls Holmgren's about the lawn mower and, not surprisingly, Marcia is right. Holmgren's, who had lost the ticket on it months ago, apologizes profusely and is so happy at the prospect of getting the lawn mower out of their shop that they offer to deliver it for free. William is pleased to be getting his lawn mower back, to chalk up even a tiny victory, but he has moved on to the next item on his list, which is dinner with Amy—*something light.*

William looks over Marcia's recipes, surreptitiously acquired through Kate, and then he and Baron make a quick run to the grocery store. When they get home, William sets about making "Thirty-Minute Tomato Soup," which he's positive that no one, not even Marcia, has ever made in less than forty-five minutes. Moving quickly, he places all the ingredients in a soup kettle: vegetable broth, olive oil, heavy cream, garlic, flour, a chopped onion, basil, thyme, two big cans of peeled tomatoes, unsalted butter, salt and pepper. Then he stirs everything with a big wooden spoon.

"'Double, double toil and trouble / Fire burn, and caldron bubble.'" William stares into the kettle. "Turn into soup, goddammit. I'm going for the record."

Next, he reads over Marcia's recipe for "Grown-up Grilled Cheese Sandwiches" and laughs. "Ah, yes, the secret ingredient."

He cubes the cheese, gives three pieces to Baron, and puts the rest in a blender—along with the secret ingredient, of course. After twenty seconds on BLEND, the cheese has become a thick paste, which he places in the refrigerator. With dinner now on autopilot, he is free to spend the rest of the afternoon on Dostoevsky. But at two o'clock, Holmgren's drops the lawn mower off, and the man who delivers it insists that William try it out, which he does. The lawn mower starts easily and runs fine, so William smiles and gives the man a big thumbs-up. Holmgren's is the only interruption that afternoon, and once the delivery man leaves, William returns to Dostoevsky and his favorite theme.

William is beginning to understand that guilt in Dostoevsky's work is not an end in itself but rather a means to an end. Guilt causes pain, which, if it is ameliorated by love, leads to forgiveness and redemption. This thematic progression is central to Dostoevsky's thought, and William has no trouble seeing it in his novels. In *Crime and Punishment*, Raskolnikov, an amoral precursor to Nietzsche's superman, murders two people, only to discover he is not "extraordinary" at all. Raskolnikov is consumed with guilt and is miserable for years, until his love for Sonya leads to his eventual redemption. In *The Brothers Karamazov*, the same basic mechanism leads to the redemption of Dmitri. In *Notes from Underground*, the young prostitute Liza offers the promise of redemption to the novel's anonymous narrator, but he foolishly rejects it. William frequently feels like one of Dostoevsky's characters, especially when he thinks about Jon, and although he hopes redemption might someday be a possibility for him, he knows he's undeserving.

Right in the middle of all this, Ruth calls.

"I loved the seventy-five pages, William," she says. "You can make *anything* interesting, like when you compare Dostoevsky to Saint Peter—I laughed out loud."

"Thank you. I—"

"And I love how you describe Prince Myshkin—a real mensch, but smart he isn't."

"I'm glad you—"

"It's time to start thinking about a title."

"Okay, but I don't want anything flashy ... How about *Guilt and Redemption in the Novels of Fyodor Dostoevsky*?"

"Too dry, Velvel—it sounds like a dissertation."

"You're right," William says. "Or a subtitle."

"You know, a subtitle might be the answer, but we need to lead with something lyrical ... What about *Regaining the Garden: Guilt and Redemption in the Novels of Fyodor Dostoevsky*?"

"Works for me," William says.

"Good. Of course, the nice people at Norton get a vote, but let's use it for the time being. I gotta go, William. Send more pages. Shalom."

Amy arrives right on time. William and Baron both hear her pull in the driveway and go outside to greet her. The instant she sees William, her face lights up, and they kiss as soon as she gets out of the car.

"Just so you know, Professor, I've waited all day to do that." Amy nods at the house. "'Is this absolutely where you live, my dearest one?' What famous character said that?" Amy reaches down to pet Baron. "Sorry—Yoshi couldn't make it. I'll bring him next time."

William pretends to think. "It was ... Daisy Buchanan. She says that to Nick Carraway when she comes to his home for tea—and to reunite with Gatsby."

"Boy, you're no fun. I'll have to pick something harder next time." She takes his hand as they walk to the door. "Do I look tired? Be honest. I didn't sleep a wink last night."

"You look ravishing. Are you worried about the lab school job?"

"Of course I'm worried. Anything could happen. What if—"

"It's in the bag, Amy—relax." William opens the front door, and they step inside.

"Oh, my God! What is that wonderful smell?"

"C'mon. I'll show you."

As they walk through the house to the kitchen, Amy looks around, fascinated.

William points to the soup kettle, now on the stove's simmer burner. "It's tomato soup."

"Wow!" Amy says. "A forty-eight-inch Wolf stove. You must be one serious cook."

"My wife, not me."

Amy lets it go. "My dream is to have a stove like this someday." Amy points to the covered kettle. "May I look?"

"Of course. It's hot, though. Use the mitt."

Amy slips on the oven mitt, removes the kettle's lid and looks inside. "It's beautiful! And I can't believe how good it smells."

"Thank you. It's one of those super-fast soup recipes, but it's not bad. It's a lot better with fresh tomatoes—you know, *garden* tomatoes."

"The entire *world* is better with garden tomatoes," Amy says, her voice full of longing. "By the way, I like your house."

William is surprised. "Really?"

"Yes. It has an interesting aura, but … it's a little spare, don't you think?"

"I do," William says. "I call it Bleak House."

Amy nods. "Yes, I suppose the House of Usher would be over the top. But your furnishing is nice in its own way—postgraduate minimalism with a touch of divorce."

William points to his bookcases. "But nicely leavened by Home Depot."

"That's true," Amy says. "A whole new riff on shabby chic."

"Someday, I'll buy more furniture and restore this place to its former glory, but right now it's a fitting analogue to my soul—or what's left of it." He puts his arms around Amy and kisses her. "Are you hungry?"

"Starved," she says. "What are we going to do about your soul?"

"Not to worry. 'All sorrows are less with bread.' What famous author wrote that?"

"I don't know … Julia Child?"

"Cervantes. Let's get this show on the road."

They have a glass of wine, and after he feeds Baron, William begins making the sandwiches. Amy watches closely as he microwaves the cheese for fifteen seconds and then spreads it onto buttered slices of sourdough bread, which he slathers with still more butter before placing the sandwiches in a skillet.

"You put the cheese in a blender first," Amy says. "I've never done that."

"These sandwiches are made with Brie, cheddar and Gruyère, and each cheese melts at a different temperature. When you blend them together, they behave like one cheese."

When the sandwiches have browned evenly, William puts one on Amy's plate and the other on his own. Then he gets them each a bowl of soup. "We're eating the same thing, so no sharing, right?"

"Right—sharing is mostly a restaurant thing." Amy cuts her sandwich in half, takes a bite and closes her eyes. "Absolutely, positively, out of this world!"

"Can you taste the secret ingredient?"

Amy takes another bite. "I'm not sure. I taste *something*, but with Gruyère in there—"

"It's vermouth. I put a slug of vermouth in the blender, along with the cheese. That's why my wife calls these 'Grown-up Grilled Cheese Sandwiches.'"

"Your *ex*-wife. That's the second time you've said that since I got here."

"I'm sorry, Amy. It's a hard habit to break."

Amy nods. "You know, I'm not really sure what vermouth tastes like, but I've never had a better grilled cheese sandwich." She lifts a spoonful of soup to her lips. "And the tomato soup is delicious too—every bit as good as it smells."

William takes a bite of his sandwich and then stares at it. "I *think* I taste the vermouth, but … maybe it's just because I want to."

Amy sets her spoon down. "William, are you really supposed to *taste* a secret ingredient? I mean, it wouldn't be much of a secret if you knew what it was. Isn't the important thing that it adds something special to whatever you're eating?" Amy picks up her spoon again. "You shouldn't be so scientific about food. It's like life—the object is to enjoy it, right?"

"Yeah ... I guess." William shifts uneasily. "I called Marcia today to ask her where the lawn mower was."

"You misplaced your lawn mower?"

"Not exactly. It was in the repair shop, but I didn't know which one."

"I see. How did it go?"

"Great!" William says. "I found it, and it runs like a top."

"I meant how did your phone call with Marcia go?"

"Oh ... not very well. I was ridiculously nervous."

"Why?"

"I'm not sure. When I heard her voice, I just ... got flustered."

"You're still in love with her," Amy says matter-of-factly.

William sits up straight in his chair, his expression one of guilt commingled with surprise.

Amy laughs. "Hey, relax—it's okay. If you want to pine after a woman who doesn't love you, that's your business." Amy picks up her sandwich. "But you should remember something—Marcia divorced you and ran off with another man."

"Actually, she ran off with another man and *then* divorced me, but ... yeah."

"She should lose points for that, William, don't you think?"

"Yes. Absolutely."

"I mean, it was a shitty thing to do."

William nods. "The shittiest."

"But you don't care?"

William puts his hands in the air. "Of course I care. But we were married a long time, Amy. I put a lot of my life into that marriage. It's hard to just set it aside and say, 'Well, that took a bad bounce.'"

"Marcia managed to do it."

"That's true," William says. But he wonders if it really is. He doesn't tell Amy that Marcia had said she missed him, mostly because he doesn't know what to make of the remark. It may have been an empty pleasantry. Then again, it may have been something else. Either way, he'll never know. And when he's with Amy, he doesn't care. He looks at her, and she holds his gaze.

"What?" she asks.

"Amy, I honestly don't know how I feel about Marcia anymore, but I know how I feel about you, and … I think I'm falling in love with you."

Amy smiles. "I know, William. I can tell by the way you look at me sometimes … like right now, for instance."

"It's that obvious?"

"Yes—but that's a good thing because I feel the same way about you. I have for a while now." Amy tilts her soup bowl to capture the last spoonful. "You're an excellent cook. I had no idea you—"

"Whoa! Wait a minute," William says. "Can we rewind the tape? I think we just glossed over a climactic interpersonal moment."

"I'd say it was more cathartic than climactic," Amy says, finishing her soup. "We said we were falling in love with each other. But I think we both knew that anyway."

"I didn't," William says. "I had no idea how you felt."

"Oh, no," Amy coos. "That's simply unforgivable." She gets up and puts her arms around him. She kisses his face, his neck and finally his lips. "I haven't done a very good job of conveying my feelings."

"Actually, you're doing much better now," William says, trying to pull her into his lap. "But convey them some more."

"I would," Amy says, "but we're going to a movie."

"This is more fun," William says.

"C'mon, let's figure out which one we want to see."

They move to the patio, and Amy scrolls through the movie options on her phone while Baron, who hasn't figured out that he'll soon be left behind, patrols the backyard for squirrels.

"*The Three Stooges*," Amy says without enthusiasm.

William shakes his head. "Nyuk, nyuk, nyuk—no thanks."

"Okay … *Hunger Games* is at the Glen, but … that's more violent than I had in mind." She continues to look. "*Windfall*—that sounds pretty good. It's won a lot of awards."

"It's good if you're in the mood for a documentary about wind energy."

"Hmmm … I guess I'll pass. Hey, here we go—*Salmon Fishing in the Yemen*. I liked the novel, but I can't remember who wrote it. He's British."

"Paul Torday," William says. "I think Lasse Hallström directed the movie. He's one of my favorites."

"What else has he directed?"

"Lots of stuff—*The Cider House Rules, The Shipping News, What's Eating Gilbert Grape* ..."

Amy continues to look at her phone. "It doesn't say anything about the director."

"No matter. It's about fishing, so it gets my vote."

"Mine too. It's settled—*Salmon Fishing in the Yemen*. It's at the Cineplex, and it starts in an hour and a half, which means there's time to show me that carriage house you told me about at Seven Dwarfs."

"Yeah, we can do that," William says. "C'mon, Baron. Let's show off our work."

The three of them walk over to the carriage house and when they get there, Amy looks up at the cupola. "I love that, especially the weathervane. And I see what you meant about how it has a door like the Seven Dwarfs' cottage." Amy nods toward a pile of broken sheetrock. "What's this?"

"The old ceiling."

"It doesn't look that old."

"It isn't," William says, looking a little sheepish. "I used more sheetrock than I probably should have in there, so I took some of it out."

Amy points to a loose stack of three-foot boards. "And this?"

"That's the old wainscoting. It's rabbeted, and I decided to go with tongue and groove instead."

"You're going to have a fortune into this place, William."

"I already do, but I don't care—I've gotten pretty fussy, especially when it comes to things Jon wanted that I vetoed, like copper gutters or a French door instead of a slider. When I run into things like that, I take my stuff out and replace it with whatever he wanted."

Amy nods. "And by doing that, you get to see the place *he* imagined."

"I do," William says. "And in a way, it makes me feel as though Jon and I are still working together."

"And if you keep redoing everything, the job will never end, right?"

William is embarrassed by the way Amy sees right through

him. "I don't know … I guess I'd like to see it finished someday, just not right now."

Amy touches his arm. "Hey, it's okay. Build the carriage house forever if you want to."

William nods. "Let's go inside." He opens the front door and the three of them enter. Amy walks to the middle of the living room and turns around slowly, taking everything in.

"This is beautiful," she says. "I love how it still looks like a carriage house—you used a lot of the original wood, didn't you?" She looks around. "Where's Baron?"

William laughs. "He's probably looking for a piece of round scrap. A piece of two-by-two will work in a pinch, but he prefers closet dowel—something about mouthfeel, I guess." William takes her arm. "I have to show you the kitchen."

William takes her into the kitchen and then upstairs to see the bedroom, bath and walk-in closet. Amy is very impressed.

"I had no idea you were so talented. This place sure doesn't look like an English professor built it."

"I accept the half of that observation that's a compliment," William says.

At that moment Baron comes upstairs, carrying a tube of construction adhesive. "I'll take that, Baron, if you don't mind. No more closet rod around?" William removes the tube from his mouth.

Amy gestures to the bedroom floor, most of which has been ripped up and stacked at the top of the stairs.

William shrugs. "It's laminate. I decided to go with real hardwood."

"I see. Thank you for showing me this place. I love it." She takes William's hand. "We've got a movie to see."

When they get back to the house, William has to deal with Baron. "I'm sorry, partner. Can you make it on your own for a while? Amy and I are going to see a movie." Baron, realizing that he is about to get left behind, lays his ears back, flattening them against his head like an angry horse.

"Don't be that way, Hürtgenvoss. We won't be gone long."

Ordinarily, William wouldn't go to a movie on a Friday night because he'd assume the theater would be too crowded, the audience too young, and the untutored laughter too annoying for the experience to be enjoyable. But *Salmon Fishing in the Yemen* isn't exactly packing the house—there's no line to get in and no crowd at the concession counter, where he and Amy buy big boxes of popcorn.

"I hope the size of the audience isn't a reflection on the movie," William says, looking at the handful of people in the theater. "I wonder if we should go around the room and introduce ourselves."

Amy smiles. "The movie has probably been here a while. Maybe everyone has seen it by now."

He and Amy enjoy *Salmon Fishing in the Yemen*. It's a good date movie—light on its feet, clever, and exactly what they were looking for. Afterward, on the way to the car, William says, "I'm not sure that in real life people would give up on each other so easily."

"What do you mean?"

"Well, do you think Ewan McGregor's wife would really let him go without a fight? And what about Emily Blunt's boyfriend? He doesn't even try to win her back."

"That's because he knows it's over, William. They both do."

"It just seems strange to me."

Amy takes his arm. "The book was a lot edgier and much less of a romance, but I liked the movie too. I was surprised by how British it was."

"I assume you're referring to the political satire and the dry, self-deprecating wit."

"Yes," Amy says, "and all those buttoned-down English characters."

William nods. "Shot through with eccentricity yet plucky to the end—even the salmon."

"I believe the salmon were Scottish."

"Ah, but the Scots are Brits; they just aren't English. So it's still a British comedy."

"Yes, and you know what they say about British humor."

William opens the car door for her. "I don't, actually. What do they say?"

Amy laughs. "I have no idea, but I'm sure they say something. I think we should go back to your place and look it up online—right after we make love."

William shakes his head as if he's trying to clear it. "I'm sorry—I'm not sure I heard you correctly. Did you say—"

"I most certainly did."

"What about Yoshi?"

"My neighbor owed me a favor." Amy looks straight ahead and tries not to smile.

"You planned this, didn't you?"

"Don't ask so many questions. You gonna talk or drive?"

"I'm gonna drive." William walks quickly to the driver's side and gets in. "We're outta here." But before he can back the Jeep out of its parking space, he and Amy are kissing—deeply kissing, seriously kissing. Neither of them really initiates it. It just happens, like the sudden onset of a summer storm.

"William, this is crazy."

He pulls her closer. "I've been crazy—this is *way* better."

"But we're in a mall parking lot ..." After a few more moments, Amy ends the interlude. "Let's go, William. As much fun as this is, we are *not* going to have sex in front of the Cineplex."

"Party pooper," William says. He re-positions himself behind the wheel and points to the Jeep's console. "Don't you hate these things? They just get in the way. I liked it better when—"

"Start the car, William."

When they get to William's house, he hustles Baron into the backyard, and he and Amy start kissing again, removing each other's clothes as they clutch and fumble through the darkened house toward the bedroom. William is entirely consumed by the moment, yet he is also aware, in some strange, out-of-body way, that his first sexual encounter in almost two years is unfolding perfectly, like a scene from a romance novel. That pleases him, and everything is fine until Amy unbuttons his shirt and pushes it back over his shoulders without undoing his cuff buttons, an oversight that turns his shirt into a straitjacket. At that point, the romance novel, for a moment or two, degenerates into good old mimetic realism.

"Hold it, Amy. Wait. I can't—"

"Oh, God. I'm sorry. Turn around so I can ... Yes, that's better." Amy struggles to find the cuff buttons and bursts out laughing. "I don't think this is what Erica Jong had in mind."

"You mean a sexual encounter where clothes fall away like rose petals?"

"Yes … Okay, this sleeve is done. Let me see the other one. Good. Hold still … *Got it!* My turn." Amy raises her arms, and William pulls her top over her head, her vest having been removed two rooms earlier.

At the bedroom door they kiss, and William is unfastening Amy's bra when he suddenly thinks of something.

"My bed is on the floor."

"And God is in his heaven, William. Make love to me."

"But you don't understand." He reaches inside the door and turns on the light.

Amy stares. "I'll be damned."

"Yeah, I thought you should know before we … I was worried that Baron might fall off, so I—"

"I appreciate the heads-up, William—tell me later."

Amy turns off the light, and they fall onto the bed and finish undressing each other. As William's hands move on her, Amy arches her back, pressing herself against him, and he can feel the passion raging in his veins, tugging at his body like current. They make love urgently at first, then tenderly, and William is outside of time, tumbling into a world he isn't sure he remembers. But it's thrilling, and he and Amy are good together, and it pleases them to please each other—giving, taking, and finally coming together explosively. As he lies beside her afterward, listening to her breathe, William doesn't know where he stops and Amy begins. It all feels like the same thing. They make love again just before sunrise, and a short time later, Amy puts on William's shirt and reaches for her phone.

William rubs his eyes. "Who are you calling at this hour?" He looks at Amy's face, illuminated by the soft light of her phone, and suddenly he understands what Aquinas meant when he wrote that true beauty will always exhibit *claritas,* a Latin word that has puzzled William until this moment.

"I'm not calling anyone. I'm just checking my messages."

"Come back to bed."

Amy pulls the duvet back and snuggles up beside him. "I want you to know that was wonderful."

"*Better* than wonderful … a little rocky at the outset, but our recovery was the stuff of legend."

"You know something? I'm happier with you than I've been in a long, long time. And I feel so … safe."

"Safe from what?"

"I don't know … from everything. It's like being on the buddy system at camp, only better. I know that nothing will happen to me because you won't let it. It's a wonderful feeling." Amy rolls over on her side and faces him. "That's how you make *me* feel. How do I make *you* feel?"

"Good. Great."

Amy wrinkles her nose. "You can do better than *that*."

William thinks about it for a moment. "Okay … I feel the same way about you that Richard Brautigan feels about his girlfriend in the poem 'Rural Electrification Project.'"

"Wow! Great tease! Go on."

"Well, when Brautigan looks at his girlfriend, all he can think of is electricity coming to rural America in the 1930s. He says it was like a young Greek god who came to the farmer and took away the darkness of his life forever. Suddenly, there was light everywhere, even on the coldest, blackest mornings. After the Rural Electrification Project, Brautigan says he wanted electricity to go all over the world and light everyone's darkness. He says he gets the same feeling every time he sees his girlfriend's face."

Amy kisses him. "And that's really how you feel about me?"

"Pretty much. The electricity trope is a little dated, though. I should probably say you're like 4G wireless internet access."

"I like electricity better," Amy says, stroking his chest. "You wrote a book on Richard Brautigan, didn't you? A book that was made into a movie?"

William turns to her. "How would you …" His eyes open wide. "You *googled* me. I'm sleeping with a woman who googled me."

"Haven't you googled me?"

"Absolutely not."

"Are you really angry?"

William kisses her. "Furious. But I'll get over it."

"I have an idea," Amy says. "Let's fall asleep, and when we

wake up, we can be happy all over again that we're together."

"Okay," William says. "But I'd better bring Baron in. He probably thinks I don't love him anymore."

Baron, who is sleeping by the back door, gives no indication that he has such thoughts, but he's glad to come inside, even though William won't allow him in the bedroom. "You'll understand when you're older," William tells him.

Amy has fallen asleep, so William climbs quietly into bed beside her. He doubts that sleep will come easily for him because every neuron in his brain seems to be firing at the same time. But he's happy, so it's okay. In fact, he's happier than he's been in two years, and when he looks over at Amy, he wonders if this is what redemption feels like. He tries to chase that thought, but the next thing he knows, the sun is slanting hard through the window, and Amy is shaking him by the shoulder. He squints at the clock in disbelief.

"I couldn't tell you the last time I slept this late, but I was probably eleven or twelve."

"I know," Amy says. "Same here. I've gotta run. I have to pick up Yoshi and get him to the groomer in forty-five minutes." Amy sits on the edge of the bed and puts on her top. "I had a good time, William."

"Me too."

"No, I mean … I had a *really* good time."

William tries to pull Amy back into bed, but she gets away from him. "I'm serious—Yoshi needs this appointment. What do you and Baron have planned for today?"

"I thought we'd work on the carriage house. Why don't you come by?"

"All right. I'll bring lunch. See you later." Amy kisses him on the cheek and leaves. And the instant she does, William feels as though he's in a bell jar with all the oxygen sucked out of it. Already, he misses her and needs desperately to be a part of her. As he watches Amy drive away, he wishes he could live deep inside her body, like the beautiful blood that pulses in her veins.

CHAPTER 16

The Sandra Bullock Self-Destruct Button

WILLIAM AND BARON have breakfast in front of the television, and they're about to head over to the carriage house when William gets an email from Marv.

Hello William,

Bad news, my brother. I lost my driver's license, and I won't be able to get up to Chambliss for the opener. I'm very sorry. I don't know what else to say.

Marv

William has him on the phone in less than ten seconds. "I just got your message. Where are you? I hear music."

"I'm sitting at the piano, playing dirges and short fugues in minor keys."

"How did you lose your license? Please tell me you didn't get a DWI."

"I didn't. I got pulled over for speeding, and it turned out I didn't have insurance—I could've sworn I did. Anyway, they fined me two hundred bucks and suspended my license for thirty days, so I don't have a way to get up there for the opener. I thought about taking the bus, but with fishing gear it would be damn near impossible and—"

"I'll come down and get you."

"It's too far. I would never ask you to do that."

"You aren't asking—I'm volunteering. It's no big deal."

"I appreciate the offer, but—"

"The talking's over, Marv. We've looked forward to fishing the opener for a long time, and I'm not going to let anything get in the way of it again—certainly not the fact that you don't have a driver's license." William really wants to drop it. "So how fast were you going, Mario?"

"Pretty fast, but it was the lack of insurance that … I feel funny about this."

"Don't worry about it—I'll pick you up. Nuff said."

There's a long pause. "All right, William. Thank you."

"Everything else okay?"

"Yeah, mostly."

"What does that mean?"

"Everything's fine."

"Glad to hear it." William tries an old line from Crosswell. "You wanna make talk, Kemosabe?"

"Not really."

"Okay, then. I'll see you Friday."

"Thanks again, my brother."

William hangs up the phone and turns to Baron. "Well, this may not be all bad, Hürtgenvoss. It'll be hard for Marv to raise hell in the Cities if he can't drive. I'd better call Kate."

Because it's Saturday, he's a little worried that he'll catch her at a bad time, but Kate is doing laundry and eager for a break.

"I can't believe the mountain of dirty clothes a family of four generates," she says. "What's up?"

"I've got a problem," William tells her. "Marv just lost his driver's license, which means—"

"DWI?"

"No, he was driving without insurance, so I'll have to go get him before the opener and take him home afterward. That means I won't be able to pick Baron up on Monday like we planned. I think you should put him in the kennel on Sunday, and I'll get him on Tuesday, when I get home from Marv's."

"I don't want to do that, Daddy, and Todd wouldn't like it either. Just plan on picking Baron up at LiveRight on Tuesday afternoon instead of Monday. It's not a problem."

"I can't tell you how much I appreciate this, Kate. But remember—if you need to put him in the kennel for a couple of nights, take him to Priscilla's Pampered Pet Palace."

"Okay, but that won't be necessary."

When William gets off the phone, Baron is staring at him.

"Please tell me you didn't understand what that call was all about." Baron wags his tail and comes over to get petted. "Listen, buddy, before we go over to the carriage house and make sawdust, we need to stop and see our friends at the lumberyard. We need finishing nails for the air nailer and an eighty-tooth blade for the miter saw. I'll be ready to leave in about fifteen minutes."

On the way to the lumberyard, William pulls over to check out a new home that's going up on a backlot about a mile from his place.

"They're flying on that job, Baron. It seems like only yesterday they were framing it up. Now, they're almost done with the siding." William looks at the gable end facing him, which is covered with cedar sidewall shingles. "I like that look, don't you? I wish I had put shakes on the gable ends of the carriage house—it would've enhanced the cottage feel of the place, but ... it's too late now."

After they pick up what they need at the lumberyard, the two of them have a pretty good morning at the carriage house. William works on a face frame for the breakfast bar and then knocks down a wall in the bathroom. At one o'clock, Amy shows up with lunch.

They kiss and William asks where Yoshi is.

"He's still at the groomer. I don't pick him up until later this afternoon—he's getting the works."

William points at Baron, who is standing behind Amy's car, waiting for her to let Yoshi out.

"I'm sorry, Baron," she says. "I know I keep saying this, but I'll bring him next time—I promise."

William looks at the plain brown bag in Amy's hand. "You went to Rocky's. What a great idea!"

"Yeah, I love that place. I got you an Italian beef, but the hot dogs looked so good I couldn't resist. Where are we eating?"

William gestures to the big oak in the side yard, beneath which is a round metal table and some old lawn chairs. "Baron and I take our breaks over there. How about lunch al fresco?"

They walk over to the tree and sit down, and Amy hands William his sandwich and a can of pop. Then she unwraps her hot dog and takes a bite. "Oh, you *gotta* try this." She hands it to William, who takes a bite and hands it back.

"That's really good," he says. "It beats the hot dogs at Target Field, and that's not easy to do." William unwraps his Italian beef part way and hands it to her. "Because I love you, you can have the first bite—and as good as that hotdog is, you're gonna wish you'd gotten one of these."

Amy tries it and smiles. "Mmm … this *is* good. You've come a long way, William. Sharing is almost second-nature with you now."

Amy becomes quiet, and William can see tension building in her features, especially around her mouth. "Anything wrong?"

"No, not really. I'm just worried about getting the lab school job. The application process is very intimidating."

William nods. "I'll bet it is. Tell me about it."

Amy takes a deep breath and lets it out. "Well … it's very corporate, and everything has a point value. First, there's an interview with the regents' committee—that's on Wednesday. Then on the fifteenth there's a breakfast meeting and a campus visit, followed by some one-on-ones. After that—I don't remember when—there's a dinner meeting with community leaders, where I'm supposed to deliver twelve to fifteen minutes' worth of 'remarks.' And the end of May, if I haven't washed out, there's a mock problem-solving exercise—a sort of Q-and-A—where the regents and a couple of attorneys present me with theoretical problems that I have to solve using 'means and methods consistent with state statutes and the school handbook.' I think that's how they put it."

"And then it's over?"

"Hardly. The last thing I have to do is teach a class for half a day with a bunch of people evaluating me—teachers, regents, Lothrup professors—everybody but the Salvation Army." Amy becomes pensive. "Actually, I believe there was talk about inviting them too."

William laughs. "That's a lot of hoops to jump through, but I know you're gonna knock 'em dead."

"I don't know about that, but I plan to give it everything I have. The first thing I need to do is get my résumé to the chancellor's office ... like *yesterday*."

William is quiet for a moment. "Would it be the end of the world if you didn't get the job?"

Amy nods slowly. "I don't have a plan B, so ... yeah, it would." She looks at William closely. "Do you know something I don't? Aren't you the guy who keeps saying I have this job sewn up?"

"You do. You definitely do. I don't know why I said that. I was just ... wondering."

"Enough with the negative vibes, Professor." Amy takes a bite of her hot dog. "Speaking of jobs, what do you hear about Norway? Is that still a condition of your employment?"

William is unprepared for the question. "Umm ... not so much. It seems ... I guess they found someone else who was—you know, willing to go."

Amy reaches for her Diet Coke. "That's good, then."

"Yes ... very good."

There is no more talk of jobs, and after lunch William shows Amy the breakfast bar he's been working on.

"It's lovely," Amy says. "I wish I had a breakfast bar ... maybe when I remodel the kitchen. What are we going to do?"

"Do?"

"Yes. I'm here to help. What job are we going to tackle?"

William looks at her, so excited, so eager to lend a hand. He isn't used to having help anymore, so at first he doesn't know how to answer.

"There must be *something*," she says.

"Yes, yes, there is. I made five decorative beams that are ready to put up in the bedroom." He points to the living room ceiling. "They're just like these, only shorter. Would you like to help with that?"

"I'd love to." Amy puts her hands on her hips. "Let's git 'er done."

Because William has the ceiling blocked and ready, he and Amy are able to install all five beams in under two hours. After they have the last one in place, they step down off their ladders and check out the ceiling from different vantage points around the room.

"The beams look terrific," Amy says. "And they match everything."

"That's because they're cedar," William says. "I used a lot of it in here."

"I'm going to be really angry with you if I'm here a week from now, and you've taken all our beams down and thrown them away."

"It'll never happen," William says. He takes off his tool belt and hangs it over the doorknob. "That's enough for one day." He turns to Amy. "Any chance we can do something tonight?"

Amy frowns. "I wish we could, William, but I have to attend a retirement dinner tonight for three of Hawthorne's finest." She brightens. "I know—you can come with me."

"Thanks for asking, but ..."

"You'd rather stick needles in your eyes?"

"I'm not a big fan of retirement dinners—or *any* dinners, for that matter."

"All right, William. I'll let you off the hook tonight. But next time, you won't be so lucky."

William always notices when Amy says things like "next time" that suggest a future in which the two of them are still together. But right now he's thinking short term. "What about tomorrow? Do you like to fish?"

"I love to fish," Amy says, "but my ex-husband didn't, so I never got to go. Are you inviting me to go fishing?"

"I am. Are you interested?"

"Yes! And thank you. What a wonderful idea!"

"You'll have to buy a license."

"I'll get one on the way home. What else do I need?"

"Sunglasses and a hat. I'll pick you up at ten."

"I can't wait! I'd better be going, William."

"Thanks for helping me. And thanks for lunch."

After Amy leaves, William returns to the bedroom of the carriage house with Baron and stares at the new beams. The bedroom is nearly finished, and in a way, it's frightening. This is how it will happen, he thinks—one room at a time. If he isn't careful, someday when he least expects it, he'll come over here intending to work and find the entire carriage house is finished.

"Baron, let's go outside. I want to check something."

The two of them step outside, and William walks to the nearest gable end and looks at it. "I don't see a problem, but I need to get up there."

William doesn't want to take the time to set up scaffolding, so he puts his longest extension ladder against the gable end, climbs up with a pry bar and tears off two pieces of siding up near the peak. One of the pieces breaks, but it isn't hard to remove them, even on a ladder.

"I'm gonna do it," he hollers down to Baron. "I'm putting shakes up here."

William doesn't anticipate any trouble replacing the lap siding with shingles, and he's pleased with his decision. He leaves the ladder up against the house, and he and Baron go home, where William calls the lumberyard and orders enough cedar shakes to cover the two gable ends.

When he gets off the phone, he updates Baron. "They're gonna be delivered on Tuesday. I didn't know this, Hürtgenvoss, but the shakes come in panels, kinda like plywood—how cool is that? Hey, where's that orange Chuckit ball you always want me to throw for you?" William and Baron play until they're both tired, and after dinner they fall asleep in front of a History Channel documentary on the Falklands War.

The next day, William and Amy fish Blackwell Lake just north of town, and it's almost magical. The weather is perfect, the action fast, and with the possible exception of Marv, William has never seen anyone who gets as excited about fishing as Amy. William's plan was to still-fish with minnows and focus on panfish. But northern pike and bass are also feeding in the shallows, so when their bobbers go down, there's no telling what kind of fish it is. Since neither William nor Amy wants to keep any fish, William flattens the barbs of their hooks with pliers, so the fish can be unhooked quickly and returned to the water.

Later that afternoon, as Amy is hoisting a big bluegill into the boat so William can grab it, she says, "I'll bet I've caught over a hundred fish today."

William pulls his sunglasses to the end of his nose and looks at her.

"Okay, maybe not a hundred, but I'll bet I've caught over fifty."

"I'll bet you have too. You're a very good fisherman." William releases the bluegill and rebaits her hook.

Amy brings her rod back to cast but stops in the middle of it. "You know, if anyone else told me that, I'd probably think they were just kissing up or trying to make me feel good. But you don't know how to lie, so it must be true."

"It is," William says. "You *are* a good fisherman. But ... I can lie with the best of 'em."

"Really? You don't even lie about Marcia, not even when it's in your interest. You say that you love me—and I totally believe you—but you've never once said that you don't love her. And it would be the easiest thing in the world to do, but you just hem and haw and eventually change the subject—you never lie."

William nudges the control with his foot, and the electric motor pushes the boat's bow back into the wind. "Not true—I lie as much as the next guy."

Amy laughs. "Only if the next guy is Abraham Lincoln. Look, I'll prove it to you. Let me give you a little test."

"Go for it."

"Hang on." Amy casts toward shore, reels up a little slack and turns toward William. "Okay, what's the biggest fish you ever caught?"

"A freshwater fish?"

"Yes."

"A twenty-four-pound northern."

"Do you believe in prenuptial agreements?"

"After Paul McCartney's divorce? *Hell* yes."

"Do you think Sandra Bullock is pretty?"

"I do."

"How old do you think I am?"

"I don't know ... forty?"

"Is that your final answer?"

"Yes."

"Then I rest my case. First of all, only someone who's pathologically honest would tell a woman he's sleeping with that he believes in prenups—there's no upside to that. As for Sandra Bullock being pretty, of course she's pretty. But honesty is the enemy in situations like this. What you want to do is scrunch up your face and say, 'Sandra Bullock? Pretty? I just don't see it.' And when you said—"

"Hold on a second. What's wrong with saying Sandra Bullock is pretty?"

Amy presses her finger to her chin. "Gee, let me think. Three days after a guy says that, imagine him having breakfast with his wife. Maybe because he's half asleep, he says something stupid, like he doesn't really care for turkey bacon or that he prefers jelly to jam. And what do you think *she* says?" Amy looks at him expectantly.

"I don't know," William says. "What?"

"She says, 'Maybe you should get Sandra Bullock to make your breakfast.'"

William nods thoughtfully. "Wow ... you're right. That poor bastard pressed the self-destruct button and never even knew it."

"Sad but true," Amy says. "He was a dead man walking." She furrows her brow. "Where were we? Oh yeah—and when you said I was forty, most men wouldn't have crossed that line. They would have said late thirties no matter what they thought. But not you— you're incapable of lying."

William laughs. "Don't be so sure. That twenty-four-pound northern I just told you about was actually closer to twenty-two pounds. But I weighed the metal stringer he was on, and even then I rounded up. What about that?"

"That was just a control question. It doesn't count."

"I see. So how old are you?"

"Forty-one. But what really matters is that I'm a very good fisherman—you said so yourself, so it must be true."

William points to her bobber. "A good fisherman would set the hook."

"But my bobber isn't down."

"No, but it's sort of tipped over—take him."

Amy sets the hook, and the fish makes a run, then leaps out of the water. Amy moves to the back of the boat and bends over the motor in an effort to keep the fish away from the prop.

"Nice bass," William says, laughing.

Amy turns around. "I beg your pardon?"

They fish for another hour or so, and then William takes her home. At Amy's house they kiss in the Jeep, and Amy smells wonderfully of Coppertone, sun and fresh air. It's an intoxicating combination, and William can't get enough of it. "Whenever I'm with you, I don't want it to end."

"Neither do I," Amy says. "I loved today. Thank you for taking me."

"I loved it too. And I especially enjoy kissing you in the daytime like this—we need to do it more often."

"Then you should take me fishing again."

"You can count on it. How about dinner tomorrow?"

"Sure. Where?"

"I don't know. We'll figure something out."

William walks her to the door. They kiss one more time, and then he heads home. On the way he calls Kate. It's not something he does often, but he wants her to know that he asked Marcia about the lawn mower, that he wasn't afraid to call her. When he gets Kate on the phone, they talk about the boys for a few minutes, and then William mentions, as nonchalantly as he can, that he called Marcia.

"Hey, good for you," Kate says. "I didn't think you had it in you."

"Yes, you made that clear, daughter. So now I have the lawn mower and—"

"How did she sound?"

William wonders if that's a trick question, but he answers honestly. "She sounded good. We didn't talk very long, but—"

"Where are you?"

"On the way home. I just dropped Amy off. We went fishing."

"*Fishing*. This is getting serious."

"Could be," William says.

THE SAINT PATRICK'S DAY HERO

Kate laughs. "You don't do coy worth beans, Daddy. By the way, I asked Todd about taking Baron to LiveRight on Tuesday too, and he said it wasn't a problem."

"That's very nice of him," William says. "Tell Todd I owe him one."

They're still talking when William pulls into his driveway, so he parks in front of the garage, and they talk a while longer. Kate keeps doubling back to his phone call with Marcia, and William keeps trying to steer the conversation in other directions because his disastrous Marcia call had lasted no more than three minutes and didn't exactly turn him into a font of information. *You know, Kate, we didn't really talk about that ...*

On Monday William and Baron go to the office, and he works on the Dostoevsky book for two hours without interruption. William's authorial MO has always been to read, take notes, and finally to write, with the interval between reading and writing often being as much as a week. But he's finding this approach doesn't work well with Dostoevsky because the intellectual terrain is so rugged that it's better if he writes a little bit every day—even if it's only a few hundred words.

For the last couple of days, William has been puzzling over the term *Russian soul*. All the Dostoevsky critics use it, but none of them explains what it means. From what William can infer, the *Russian soul* has something to do with anti-European nationalism and a belief that Russian peasantry is not only the true embodiment of Russian character, but also the best hope for the fulfillment of Russia's national destiny. But it's a vague term, to say the least, and William suspects there's a thick streak of Russian nihilism in it.

There is a knock on the door that causes Baron to bark, which yanks William out of tsarist Russia and drops him foursquare in the New World.

"It's okay, Baron," William says. ""'Tis some visitor, tapping at my office door—only this, and nothing more.'" He hollers for whoever it is to come in.

A young man enters, and Baron trots across the room to check him out. "I was right—I *did* hear a dog." He pats Baron on the shoulder. "What's his name?"

"It's Baron," William says. "We share the office. I'm Dr. Kessler."

"Hi, I'm Jared Harding. Nice to meet you." They shake hands, and Jared explains that he's a prelaw transfer student from Mankato State. "The thing is, I earned six credits at Mankato that Lothrup may not accept. So until they decide what they're going to do, I don't know which classes to sign up for next fall. Since you're my advisor, I thought maybe …"

"You've come to the right place," William says. "What we should do is work out two schedules—one that includes the credits and one that doesn't. Once we've done that, you and your major will be covered either way." It doesn't take them long to create the schedules, and in half an hour, Jared is a man with a plan.

"Thank you, Dr. Kessler. I really appreciate your help."

"Glad to do it, Jared. I'll talk to the Registrar's Office and find out what's going on with your Mankato credits."

"That would be great. Thanks again." Jared looks down at Baron. "My grandfather had a German shepherd. He was a really cool dog."

William nods. "Take care, Jared."

William returns to Dostoevsky but not for long, because twenty minutes after Jared leaves, another advisee knocks on the door. This time it's a farm boy from Cedar Rapids who has the worst case of junior blues that William has ever seen. His name is Brandon Metzger, and Brandon is burned out. He's sick of school and can't understand why he should subject himself to another minute of it when everything he wants is right there in Cedar Rapids, waiting for him—his girl, a job at the Deere plant, his friends from high school, his family.

"I even miss my dog," Brandon says, reaching down to pet Baron. "I just can't *do* this anymore."

As a faculty advisor, William is never *ever* supposed to recommend that an advisee drop out or transfer, but that's what he does, suggesting to Brandon that he might be happier in a school closer to home, maybe even one in Cedar Rapids, like Coe or Cornell College.

"They're smaller than we are," William tells him, "but they're excellent schools, solid in every way."

Brandon doesn't jump up and down and say yes, but William can tell he likes the idea. And when he shakes William's hand and thanks him, he's happy—at least happier than when he walked in.

After Brandon leaves, William takes Baron for a walk. They're almost to the science building when William says, "I'm wondering if you should become a therapy dog—students relate very well to you. You're like a little piece of home to them."

Baron, who is watching a flock of geese overhead, appears not to hear him.

"Hey, I don't need an answer right away. Just think about it. I'll have my people talk to your people."

On the way back, they walk past a beat-up Honda Civic with a bumper sticker that reads, *Honk If You've Felt the Recovery.* You got *that* right, William thinks, and it reminds him of something. Just before their second obedience class, he and Baron were out for a walk when he stopped to talk to a neighbor who was washing his car—the same neighbor who had helped him move the sofa from the carriage house. The man's name was Hank Ennis, and he told William that he'd been laid off. Hank said he was still in shock because he'd worked twenty-two years for the same company— an outfit that made electric motors for small appliances—and he thought he was high enough up the food chain that he would be able to keep his job. But thirty people were cut, and he was one of them. Hank said a security guard had escorted him from the building, and as he described walking out the door with a cardboard box full of his personal belongings, Hank's eyes filled with tears.

William felt terrible and didn't know what to say. Hank had sensed this and with forced bravado said, "Hey, don't worry about me. I'll find another job." But he was older than William, and they both knew what the odds of that were. William thinks about Hank as he makes his way across the commons, and when he gets to his office, he sits down at his desk, looks up a few things online and begins writing the letter that has been taking shape in his head for a long time.

7 May 2012

Dear Treasury Secretary Geithner:

Last month's jobs report was even more dismal than usual and showed the smallest employment increase in six months. And it gets worse: over 40 percent of the unemployed have been out of work for over half a year, and the portion of the working-age population participating in the job market is now at its lowest level since 1980. This so-called recovery—the weakest one since World War II—may have begun in July 2009, as you maintain, but America's middle class still isn't feeling it.

I appreciate that you did not cause the economic collapse, but you have missed several opportunities to lessen its severity. For instance, you went to considerable lengths to rebuild bank balance sheets, but you ignored households altogether. You have also done nothing to alleviate the housing crisis—a debacle that has already cost five million families their homes, and economists predict that number could easily double. And finally, you supported a series of budget cuts last summer that have all but strangled our incipient recovery—and this just to get a deal with Republicans on the debt ceiling.

I think you should be locked in a room with Bernie Sanders until you get your mind right.

Sincerely,

William Kessler

William, growing angrier by the minute, reads the letter over. No, Timothy Geithner didn't cause the collapse. The big bankers did that—men like Fuld, O'Neal and Blankfein. What William can't understand is why, four years after these Masters of the

Universe had destroyed thirty-five trillion dollars of global wealth, none of them is in jail. He thinks Timothy Geithner should be in jail too, although for different reasons.

Geithner forgot to pay his income tax for three years, but he apologized, and the Senate made him Secretary of the Treasury. Wesley Snipes also forgot to pay his income tax for three years, but when *he* apologized, he was sent to federal prison for income tax evasion. Maybe he didn't do it right, William thinks. Apologies can be so tricky. William tries to put the whole thing out of his head, afraid that if he doesn't, he'll end up writing a letter to Attorney General Holder, and he isn't in the mood to write another letter just now. In fact, since he met Amy, he hasn't felt the need to write many letters at all. His hands still shake once in a while, but not very often, and his life, which a month ago felt like an onerous chore, now has an almost embarrassing, Zip-a-Dee-Doo-Dah exuberance about it.

William files his letter and cleans off his desk. Then he remembers to call Sam Richter to see if Sam can pull a few strings and get Jared Harding's credits approved.

"I'm the academic dean," Sam says, "not the registrar."

"It's not like I'm asking you for a kidney," William tells him. "Just make a phone call. You're better connected than I am."

After a little back-and-forth, Sam finally gives in. "Look, I'll see what I can do. In the meantime, Gardner wanted me to ask if you have any interest in being English Department chair. Dr. Kaplan is retiring in 2014, and Gardner said he'd back your play if you wanted the job."

William laughs. "Why doesn't he just offer me a gym bag full of nonsequential hundred-dollar bills?"

"Don't look a gift horse in the mouth, my friend. It sounds like a good deal to me."

"Bleeping golden," William says. "Tell me something—how come Gardner never speaks to me directly? Why is it always through you?"

"I don't think Gardner feels it's in his interest to have any contact with you—it wouldn't be smart."

"What an asshole."

"My advice is to forget about him. You have to think of your future, William."

"Until you and your buddies found out that I had Rupert's jammer, I didn't *have* a future."

"At this point in time, and to the best of my recollection—"

"Yeah, yeah."

"Just don't be stupid." Sam says this with a ring of finality and changes the subject. "Have you done any fishing?"

"A little. How about you?"

Sam makes a loud exclamation of disgust. "I *would* have, but my genius kid borrowed the boat and tried to run E85 in it. Do you have any idea what that shit does to an outboard? Long story short, my motor's in the shop."

"Bad time of the year for that, Sam. I hope you get it back soon."

"You and me both."

They talk for a while about the strange weather, the jet stream, El Niño and how to fish a thermocline. Finally, Sam says, "I don't know how to say this without pissing you off, William, but the last couple of times we've talked, you've sounded good—*really* good."

"As in *normal*?"

Sam laughs. "I'm not sure *normal* is the word I'd use, but … something like that."

"Things have been going very well for me, Sam."

"Yeah, that's what I hear. Gardner tells me you have a knock-out girlfriend who has applied for lab school director—Amy something."

"Amy Mattson."

"Right. And she's the principal at Hawthorne Elementary?"

"Assistant principal. Please don't forget to get Jared Harding's credits approved."

"Anything else I can do for you, William? How about a private parking space with your name on it?"

"No thanks, but you can tell Gardner to kiss my ass."

"Oh, that's great, William—very mature."

"Bye, Sam."

William hangs up and is thinking about Gardner when Amy calls his cell phone, which, fortunately for him, happens to be on.

"What a wonderful surprise!" he says.

"Oh, William, it's so nice to hear your voice. I'm having an awful day."

"Did a mean little boy put gum in your hair?"

"It's worse than that. All day I've been dealing with crying teachers who are losing their jobs, and it's too depressing for words. When you get put on unrequested leave, you lose a lot more than your income. You lose your health insurance, your self-esteem, your credit rating ..." Amy pauses for a moment. "I'm sorry, William, but if we were going out tonight, I'm not really in the mood anymore."

"I understand. Why don't you come to my place and bring Yoshi? We'll order Chinese, drink wine and watch a movie."

"I can't tell you how wonderful that sounds. But I've got a lot to do before I can leave—I haven't gotten much done today."

"That's okay. Take your time and just get there when you can. I'll tell Baron he has a playdate."

"I've missed you so much."

"I've missed you more. See you tonight."

They hang up, and William returns to the *Russian soul*, which is just as vexing now as it had been earlier. After two hours of reading and note-taking, William leans back and rubs his eyes.

"Baron, one of the reasons the *Russian soul* is so damned confusing is that Gogol, Tolstoy and Dostoevsky all understood it differently. But Belinsky—he's the worst. I have no idea what he's talking about." William sighs. "Let's get out of here for a few minutes. I need to clear my head."

Baron jumps up and dances around while William attaches his leash.

"Remember—heel nice and no lunging at squirrels."

They walk behind Dewhurst, past the football stadium to the practice field, where they look through the chain-link fence at the thin, sere grass. No one is around, but the irrigation system is on— ten big sprinklers going *tisk, tisk, tisk, tisk* as they soak every inch of the field. Baron is transfixed, quivering with excitement at the sight of so much water moving in so many directions at once.

"I suppose you'd give anything to get in there," William says.

Baron whines, his head moving from one arcing jet of water to another.

"Tell you what—I'll set up a sprinkler for you at home, maybe a couple of them." William nods toward the field. "It won't be as exciting as *that*, but it'll be better than nothing." He looks down at Baron, who has jumped up against the fence and is peering through it like a kid at a construction site. "C'mon, Baron, we'd better get back."

At four o'clock William and Baron go home, and at five Amy calls to say she's about to leave school and should be there in an hour and a half. "I'll pick up some wine."

"Great," William says. "I can't wait to see you."

"Me too. But first I have to go home, feed Yoshi, take a shower, iron a blouse for tomorrow and—"

"Don't hurry. Whenever you get here is fine."

"Okay, it'll probably be between six thirty and seven. I'm so—" Amy breaks away, and he can hear her talking to someone—*What? You're kidding! Oh, my God!*—then she's back. "Sorry, William. Better make it seven thirty. It seems that a pipe burst in the cafeteria, and the kitchen is flooding. Gotta go."

CHAPTER 17

Never Judge a Book by Its Color

WILLIAM HAS A BEER and tries to straighten up the place. Then he remembers his promise to Baron and goes to the garage, where he finds two oscillating lawn sprinklers that he sets up next to each other in the backyard. Baron is thrilled and runs back and forth through the sprinklers the way a child might, except that he bites and barks a lot at the water.

"You're easily amused, Hürtgenvoss." William watches him for a while and eventually goes inside. At seven thirty, Amy and Yoshi arrive.

"I got the wine," Amy says, holding up a bottle in each hand. "Is Riesling okay?"

"It's perfect," William says. "Two bottles—you *did* have a bad day."

"Yes, but it's over now, and I'm so glad to see you." She hands him the wine and plants a lingering kiss on his lips. "Really, *really* glad."

"We're going to forget all about today," he says. "I promise."

"The sooner the better. Where's your roommate?"

"In the backyard, playing in his water park. C'mon, I'll show you." William looks at Yoshi. "He's so clean and fluffy—he looks like a different dog."

"He'd better, considering what his grooming set me back."

Amy and Yoshi follow William through the house to the kitchen, where he sets the wine on the counter and lets Yoshi out. After a brief search for the corkscrew, he says, "Ideally, we should put the Riesling in the refrigerator for a while before we open it."

Amy shakes her head. "Not today, Professor—let's suspend the rules."

So William opens one of the bottles, and they take it to the patio, where they watch Baron and Yoshi run through the sprinklers and chase each other around like long-lost litter mates.

"So much for Yoshi's bath," Amy says. "I'd ask you to turn the water off, but he's having way too much fun. Did you work on the book today?"

"I did. I'm attempting to come to grips with the *Russian soul*. It's a pivotal concept in the study of Russian literature, but it's tricky."

"Do we have one? I mean, is there an American soul?"

William reaches for her glass and refills it. "Yes, I think so. It's a little scuffed up since 9-11, but it's still there. It's that pioneer idealism you see every now and then glinting through the moral outrage and political tribalism." William points to Yoshi. "Your friend is having a fit."

Yoshi, who isn't used to having so much room to run, has begun racing madly from one end of the yard to the other. Baron watches for moment and then takes off after him.

"Yoshi has the zoomies," Amy says, laughing. "Look at his eyes."

Yoshi is running as though a mountain lion is hot on his heels, but he's overstriding so much he can barely keep his balance. He finally spins out on a turn, and when he gets up, the craziness is gone, and Yoshi is Yoshi again. A few moments later, he picks up one of Baron's toys and a minor scuffle breaks out.

"What are they fighting over?" Amy asks. "Is that a bone?"

"It's a deer antler. Baron found it down by the river." Baron wrests the antler away from Yoshi and parades around the yard with it. "I think they're both going to sleep tonight."

After another glass of wine, Amy begins to unwind, and William asks if they should go inside and order dinner.

"What about Baron and Yoshi? Will they be all right?"

"You're a helicopter parent, aren't you? We can keep an eye on them from the kitchen."

William turns the sprinklers off and they go in. Amy stands in front of the sink and looks out the window. "That's good—they're lying down."

"They'll be fine. Have a seat and let me do something about that empty glass." He fills both their glasses and opens the second bottle of wine, which he sets on the table between them. "I'm sure this is a stupid question, but do you have a favorite Chinese take-out place on this side of town?"

"Of course—Chin's. It's the best by far, and it has great Yelp reviews. It's also fairly authentic—no peas, carrots or broccoli."

"You're like having a food critic on speed-dial. So what's good at Chin's?"

"Anything Cantonese."

"Okay, let me find a pen."

The two of them put an order together, including chopsticks, and William calls it in. The call itself doesn't go very well—neither William nor the woman he's speaking with seem to understand each other—but eventually the order gets placed, and William gives his address, enunciating with jaw-breaking precision. *Forty-five minutes? Yes. Thank you.*

He taps END CALL and shakes his head.

Amy is trying hard not to laugh. "That went well."

"Nothing to it," William says, putting a finger in his shirt collar and pulling it away from his neck. "I was talking to an old woman who can hardly speak English. What's more, I got the distinct impression it was my fault."

Amy nods. "That was the grandmother—yeah, she's tough."

"I should have had you talk to her."

"I spent a year in Japan, not China. *Watashi no hobākurafuto wa unagi de ippai desu.*"

"Translation?"

Amy thinks for a moment. "My hovercraft is full of eels."

William laughs. "Don't you just hate when that happens?"

"This wine is excellent," Amy says, emptying her glass. "I don't remember much Japanese. You know, sometimes I wish I'd gone to France instead of Japan—the language is more fun. The Japanese language is so *big*." Amy holds her hands far apart, and William grabs the wine bottle, which narrowly escapes her gesture. "And so *nuanced.* The Japanese have, like, a hundred words just for *hello,* and each one is different—Hello, I really like you; Hello, I *think* I like you, but the jury is still out; Hello, I *used* to like you, but now I realize you're a total *manuke*—that means *loser.* Of course, if I *had* gone to France, I'd probably have a poodle or a French bull-dog instead of Yoshi—what an awful thought! I'm sure I would have learned how to make better hollandaise sauce, though—mine tends to separate." Amy wets her finger and runs it around the rim of her glass. "Wow! Hear that? It's crystal." She looks at William and giggles. "I think I'm getting drunk."

"I certainly hope so," William says. "If not, we'll have to get you checked out for hypomania."

"What's that?"

"It's when a person changes the subject every five—"

"Maybe I should have bought *one* bottle."

"Seconds. You just need some food, and it's on its way."

When dinner arrives, William is amazed that it's all there, including chopsticks, which Amy uses beautifully, even on the fried rice. "Your year in Japan is showing," he tells her.

"Thank you. *Hashi* were easy for me—that's *chopsticks* in Japanese." She shakes her head. "What a shame to eat just when I was getting a good buzz on."

When they finish dinner, William makes some coffee and pours them each a cup.

"Hey, we don't want to forget these." Amy hands William a for-tune cookie and breaks her own in half, withdrawing the strip of paper. She reads it and bursts out laughing. "This is perfect. *Never judge a book by its color.*"

"Its *color*? What inspired advice."

"What does yours say?"

William holds his fortune up to the light and squints at it. "*To him who is in fear, everything rustles.*" He hands it to Amy. "The attribution is Confucius, but I believe it's actually Sophocles."

"It doesn't matter, Professor. It's true either way." Amy crum-ples up the fortune and sets it by her plate. "Just so you know, things are rustling pretty loud for me today."

"Because you're afraid you won't get the lab school job?"

"Because I'm worried about my daughter. Macalester is very expensive, and the selection process for lab school director is a meat grinder—I have the interview with the regents day after tomorrow, and I haven't interviewed for a job in years."

"You're going to get the job, Amy. Gardner *wants* you for that job. It's going to work out fine. You'll see."

Amy looks at him. "Aren't you ever afraid of anything? Please say that you are."

"Of course I am. We've talked about it."

"Having another breakdown?"

"Yes." William leans forward, his elbows on the table. "I'm afraid that one day something will pull the rug out from under me, and I'll end up back at Cross. It's the most terrifying thought in the world— and the most depressing. And it has the strangest way of sneaking up on me. I mean, I can be making breakfast, backing out of a parking space, opening a window, and suddenly, there it is—my worst fear, staring me in the face."

Amy shakes her head. "But you're fine. It isn't like you're going to slip on a banana peel and land in a mental institution."

"That's what I keep telling myself," William says. "But going crazy is like having one of those diseases that goes into remission— it disappears for a while, but it can come roaring back at any time."

"I know I'm partial, William, but my money is on you. And for what it's worth, I think your odds of staying out of Crosswell are better than my odds of getting the lab school job."

William shrugs. "Maybe. But now were talking about two unrelated probability sets—in other words, statistical apples and oranges. And the thing is, nobody really knows what his electrons are going to do—or when."

Amy gives him a funny look. "I don't like this conversation, William. Let's not talk about it anymore."

"Good idea."

They put the leftovers away and bring the dogs in, and it isn't long before Yoshi and Baron have crashed on the living room floor.

"Hallelujah," Amy whispers. "The kids are asleep."

"I remember a time when those four words were the most

beautiful in our language."

They tiptoe back to the kitchen, and Amy sits down, but William stands with his back to the sink, staring at her.

"You look like you're about to give a speech or something," Amy says.

"Well ... there are some things that I need to tell you. One, I—"

"William, please don't number things when you talk to me. And unless you're about to say we won't be seeing each other again because you've met a twenty-five-year-old yoga instructor who's leading you to a spiritual awakening, lighten up a little. You're making me nervous."

"Lighten up—right. What I want to say is that this weekend is the fishing opener, and I'll be fishing Saturday, Sunday and Monday with Marvin Kreitzer, my crazy friend from Cross. Marv told me Saturday that he lost his driver's license, so I'll have to go down to the Cities to pick him up on Friday, and I'll have to take him home on Monday. Naturally, I'd rather be with you, but Marv and I made these plans before you and I—"

"Hey, don't worry. It's fine." Amy reaches out and touches his hand. "Fishing is good for the soul. So are crazy friends. And you don't need to feel guilty—Lauren is coming home this weekend, so I'll be busy anyway."

"Thank you for understanding. Marv and I had plans to fish the opener last year, but it didn't happen."

"You'll be home on Tuesday, right?"

"Yes. I'll spend Monday night at Marv's and come back Tuesday morning." William knows that Tuesday is important, but he can't remember why. "What's the significance of—"

"Tuesday is the fifteenth. It's the day I have the breakfast meeting followed by 'informal chats' with parents, faculty members and support staff."

"I'm sorry, Amy. I forgot about that. Maybe I shouldn't fish Monday. That way I could be here."

"William, don't be ridiculous. How would *that* help me?"

"I don't know. It just seems—"

"Look, call me when you can, and on Tuesday I'll tell you all about my day when I see you."

"Yeah ... okay." William goes silent.

"I can tell you're not finished," Amy says. "What else is on your mind?"

"I'm wondering if you could join Marv and me for dinner Friday night. It's important to me that you two meet."

"I'd love to, but it depends on whether Lauren is coming home Friday night or Saturday morning. I'll have to let you know. What else?"

"That's it, except …"

Amy makes a rolling motion with her finger.

"Except that I met this twenty-five-year-old yoga instructor who's got the nicest *asanas* I've ever—"

"Tell her to get a real job," Amy says, laughing. "And some real pants. Let's get back to us. What movie are we going to watch?"

"That's up to you," William says. "I'll show you the options." They go into his office, where he points to one of his homemade shelves. "Behold, my collection." The films, many of which are documentaries, take up about six feet of shelf space, and it pleases William to think that he never bought any of the DVDs himself. A few years ago, for reasons unbeknown to him, his family had tired of giving him neckties and switched to movies. They even enrolled him in a movie-of-the-month club. So it wasn't long before William had quite a few of them.

"Let's see what you've got here." Amy removes several films, commenting on each of them in turn. *Oh, I love this movie—I laughed till I cried. This one too—great soundtrack. Hey, here's a classic—can you believe this didn't get Best Picture?* Amy stops. She turns to William, puts her arms around him, and they kiss. "I like your movies, but … I'd rather see your etchings."

"And I'd love to show them to you," William says. They kiss again, hungrily, as though they've been separated by oceans and vast deserts. Then William guides Amy down a darkened hallway to the guest bedroom. At first she doesn't understand. Then she remembers about his bed.

"Right—your bed is on the floor. I don't mind though, really."

"I know," William says, "but it's hard to get in and out of. Let's be civilized tonight."

"All right," Amy says, whispering in his ear, "but not *too* civilized."

Their lovemaking is even better than the first time—something William would have thought impossible—and there is no nervousness or uncertainty. William is amazed at what he feels, and he and Amy make love as though they have discovered some part of themselves they hadn't known was missing.

Afterward, Amy catches her breath and snuggles against him. "My God, William …" She lowers her voice as if someone might overhear. "That was unbelievable."

William laughs. "Are you sure it was us?"

"Oh, yeah. It was us all right."

The next morning when William wakes up, Amy has already put the dogs in the backyard and is getting dressed. He looks at the clock on the nightstand. "It's six o'clock. Are you leaving?"

"I'm afraid so. I have to go home, feed Yoshi, get cleaned up and turn myself back into the assistant principal at Hawthorne Elementary." She sits down on the bed and kisses him. "I wish I could stay."

"Me too. Have a cup of coffee, at least." With that, William jumps out of bed, makes coffee and fills a Tupperware container with leftover Chinese food for Amy's lunch.

"Oh, William, this is wonderful. Thank you."

"You're welcome. Think of me at lunchtime."

"I will. But I'd do that with or without the Chinese food." She gives him a kiss. "I can't see you tonight—I have to prep for my interview tomorrow."

"It's in the morning, right?"

"Ten o'clock at Wellstone Hall."

"Do you know anything about the format?"

"There are six regents on the committee, and they each get one question and a follow-up. I get five minutes to respond."

"When they ask you what your weakness is—and they will—tell them it's kryptonite."

Amy smiles. "You got it. I'll call you the minute I walk out of there."

"Don't forget."

"Keep your phone on."

Amy and Yoshi leave, and William, who had planned to work

on the Dostoevsky book at home that morning, realizes he left his suitcase full of books at Dewhurst. But it's not a big deal. It just means a trip to his office, and William decides he might as well work there, since there will be no interruptions.

"Let's boogie," he says, and Baron, who is always up for a ride in the car, runs to the front door.

When they get to the office, Baron bats his tennis ball around, and William reads a little online news before tackling the *Russian soul* again. One of the articles he reads is about the current heat wave, which the author, a well-known meteorologist, describes as a hundred-year event. This kind of talk used to confuse William because so many of these "hundred-year events" were occurring only a few years apart, like Camille and Katrina. But now William realizes that the *hundred-year-event* descriptor is just quantum shorthand for something that has a 1 in 100 probability of occurring in any given year—in other words, a 1 percent chance. William understands this, but he wonders what the implications are. Does it mean that anything—bad weather, accidents, school shootings—can happen at any time? Sort of, he thinks, but it's more complicated than that. It means that at any given moment, an almost infinite number of possibilities exist, yet the one that actually occurs is a matter of chance—a function of the random, clattering machinery of the universe.

William thinks of Janice Grant and how she had said that things happen for a reason. And yet what happened that day at Dewhurst was nothing more than malignant chance. Ever since the shooting, quantum mechanics has never been far from William's thoughts, and this is because life, at least as the quantum theorists understand it, is driven by chance, dumb luck, blind fate—whatever one chooses to call that unpredictable element in the universe that creates chaos yet lacks assignable cause. William can relate to that—it's basically "shit happens" in a fancy suit. The difference is that in a quantum world, the shit isn't just happening now. It's happening in the future, the past and perhaps even in parallel universes. And the shit will *keep* happening because the laws of probability, in a voice like an off-stage whisper, say it will. Yes, the odds against a particular outcome may be long, but that doesn't mean it's impossible. Consider the man who was struck by lightning seven times. Or the family whose dog returned home after three years. Or the earthquake victim who was buried for twenty-seven days yet managed to survive. Anomalies aren't the exception, William thinks. They are the rule.

William has a pretty good day on the Dostoevsky book, and by the time he goes home, he's well into a chapter he's calling "The Beaten Horse," which deals with one of the most famous dreams in literature. In the dream, Raskolnikov sees an old horse beaten to death by a drunken peasant—something Dostoevsky had witnessed as a child—and the episode becomes an emblem for life in Mother Russia, an existence filled with cruelty, oppression, helplessness and, most of all, guilt. William has tears in his eyes when he rereads the dream, but he knows it's impossible to understand anything about Dostoevsky, let alone the *Russian soul*, until he comes to grips with the horror of that episode. The problem is that William's brain has quirky wiring. It's a place where sadness often begets more sadness until his thoughts breadcrumb back to the shooting. Once that happens, his mind is like a tire that catches a rut and can't climb out of it.

"Dad, did you hear me?" Jon asks.

"Yes. You asked about the janitors' closet."

"I asked if you could see it from here." Jon opens the door a crack. "Where is it?"

"It's the third door down on the far side of the hall. It's just past the drinking fountain."

Jon opens the door a little wider. "Yeah, I see it. Is it unlocked?"

"I don't know," William says. "You might have to break the glass, reach in and open it."

"Okay. I'm gonna go first. When I get there, I'll signal when it's safe for you to make a run for it."

"Understood," William says. "Be careful."

Jon nods and sprints out of the office. When he gets to the janitors' closet, the door is unlocked, so he opens it and backs into the doorway. Then, seeing no one at either end of the hall, he motions for William to join him. William is like a racehorse coming out of the gate, but he's wearing leather-soled shoes and struggles to gain traction on the marble floor. But he keeps his feet under him, and he's halfway to Jon when he sees a male student running toward him from the end of the hallway. Jon sees him too, and begins waving him in like a third-base coach. Then one of the shooters appears, shimmering in the thermal current at the top of the stairs, and when he opens fire, the student's throat explodes. There is a quantum moment before the boy actually falls, a moment in which William's past and present coalesce. And when it happens, the boy and the beaten horse become the same terrifying thing. As the dying boy struggles to stay on his feet, William wonders if this isn't exactly what Dostoevsky was trying to convey—the savage destruction of innocence, the inability to prevent it, the cavernous depths of human cruelty.

Don't stop, Dad. Please don't stop. Come to me, goddammit!

Late that afternoon, the lumberyard delivers the shingle panels, and William and Baron walk over to the carriage house to take a look. They're wrapped in white plastic, but William opens up a corner and sees a beautiful cedar shake shingle underneath. He bends close and inhales. "My God, Baron—does anything smell better than fresh-sawn cedar? This is gonna be a fun job, once we pull the lap siding off."

The next day, while Amy has her interview, William returns to the office and completes "The Beaten Horse." He also has a short session with Baron because that night is obedience class, and they haven't practiced as much as usual. In between the writing and the obedience work, William thinks about Amy and wonders what question she is answering at that exact moment: *Why are you the best candidate for the job? What sorts of things make you angry? Where do you see yourself in five years?*

At a quarter to twelve, Amy calls. "Hi, I just got out of there. I'm on my way to the car."

"How'd it go?" William asks.

"I thought it went well," Amy says. "I don't know how it could have gone much better."

"Did they like you?"

"I think so," Amy said. "But you never really know."

"What were the questions like?"

"They were good. They'd put some thought into them."

"Tell me one."

"Umm … *Are you the type of person who checks her work email on vacation?*"

William chuckles. "That's like asking, 'When did you stop beating your wife?' How did you answer?"

"It's a health and wellness question, William. They want to know if I'm going to overstress and burn out. I explained that I am perfectly willing to go above and beyond when it comes to fulfilling my responsibilities, but I also told them it's important that I take care of myself in order to ensure my long-term success."

"Wow! You crushed it!" William doesn't say anything for a moment. "Of course … you've got this job in the bag anyway."

"I've warned you about that, William." Amy yawns. "Are we meeting in the parking lot for obedience class tonight?"

"Absolutely. In the meantime, you should crawl under your desk like George Costanza and take a nap."

"I might give that a try. See you tonight."

When they meet that evening, they've been apart for only forty-eight hours, but for both of them, it feels like weeks.

Amy throws her arms around him. "When I'm away from you, I'm only half a person."

William kisses her. "I know what you mean. Could you feel me missing you?"

"I could—I really could."

He kisses her again and then nods toward the armory. "Shall we?"

The theme of tonight's class is distractions, and in some ways it's fun. Jackie Carroll had told everyone that it was important for them to find out what their dogs are afraid of before it's too late to do anything about it. So that evening, while the owners try to heel their dogs around the ring, Jackie calls out directions—*left turn, fast time, right about turn*—as members of the Chambliss Kennel Club ride around the gym on bicycles, hobble about on crutches and push each other in wheelchairs. They also dribble basketballs and drop objects on the floor, like clipboards and coffee cans.

"Keep your dogs focused," Jackie tells the group. "And make those rascals heel. Okay, fast time. Keep it smooth." Baron and Yoshi aren't bothered by any of the distractions, but some of the dogs cry, and a little Brittany spaniel piddles on the floor when a wheelchair gets too close.

That night, Amy insists that William and Baron stay at her house—venue nondiscrimination, she calls it. Their lovemaking is wonderful, but the next morning when William wakes up, he's alone and doesn't remember where he is. This causes him a few moments of low-grade panic because it's something that happened all the time at Crosswell. But then Baron, who senses William is awake, puts his front paws up on the bed to say hello, and right after that, Amy comes into the room with a cup of coffee and kisses him.

"If you take the dogs out," she says, "I'll make breakfast."

William props himself up on one elbow. "Breakfast? You've got a deal—I don't deserve you."

"Probably not, but get up anyway." She gives his foot a shake. "'It's daylight in the swamp, slugger.' That's what my father used to say."

"Really? Mine used to say, 'Get your ass out of bed.' I guess he wasn't into metaphor. Then again, that expression is an obvious synecdoche, so maybe—"

"C'mon, Professor. *Chop-chop.*"

William pulls on his clothes and takes Baron and Yoshi outside, where they chase each other around and double-check everything in the yard to make sure no stray dogs sneaked in there and peed under the cover of darkness. Finally, they do what they're supposed to, and William takes them back in the house.

"It's not quite ready," Amy says. She points to the breakfast nook. "Have a seat."

William sits down and thumbs through *Time* magazine's *100 Most Influential People* edition. In a very few minutes, Amy sets a plate of food in front of him.

"This is wonderful," William says. "Scrambled eggs, sausage, toast … Having breakfast together makes me feel like we're a couple."

"It takes breakfast to do that?" She kisses him on the cheek and sits down.

"It helps." William takes a couple bites and looks across the table at her. "I love being with you in the morning, even though it's never for longer than a few minutes."

Amy smiles. "I second that emotion, Professor."

"These eggs are terrific, by the way. What am I tasting? Tarragon?"

"No."

"Ricotta?"

"No."

William takes another bite. "I know—it's some kind of designer mustard."

Amy laughs. "You're tasting eggs. I'm sorry to disappoint you, but there's no secret ingredient. I used two extra yolks and a little milk—that's it."

"Hmmm ... it's hard to believe eggs could taste this good."

Amy looks at him as though she's about to say something. But she doesn't.

After breakfast Amy gets ready for school, and William leaves for home, where he gets cleaned up and feeds Baron before they go to the office. William isn't kidding himself—he knows he won't get any work done because he's too busy thinking about everything he has to do before he leaves tomorrow to pick up Marv. There's the boat, of course—he must remember to charge the batteries—but it's also important that he inventory his tackle. How many barrel swivels does he have? How many number 6 octopus hooks? There are so many delightful questions to be answered, so many splendid little tasks.

William struggles to read an essay on Dostoevsky by Milan Kundera, but he can't get into it. "I think Joseph Brodsky is right about this guy, Baron—too much obscurantist argle-bargle." William sighs and puts the book down. "Or maybe I'm just not in the mood."

William goes through his mail and picks up the *Beacon*, where he finds an open letter from Chancellor Gardner that appears to be a point-by-point refutation of the *Light It Up* flyer about kilowatts and carbon dioxide that William had been handed a week ago. William has no idea whose numbers are correct, but Gardner's letter, condescending and paternalistic, takes special delight in mansplaining the mysteries of data analysis to women who, in Gardner's view, need to be led back to the shady groves of reason. At one point he calls the *Light It Up* women "puerile and opinionated," and in the last paragraph, he writes, "I understand that many of you were offended by my suggestion to buy a flashlight, and for that I apologize. I should have told you to eat more carrots." Gardner is clearly angry and looking for a fight he can win. But William isn't sure he's found it.

"Easy does it, Chancellor," he says aloud. "You may be punching above your weight."

At one o'clock Ruth calls, wanting a progress report and additional pages, and William tells her that *Regaining the Garden* is proceeding apace. "It practically writes itself," he says, lying blackly. "I'll send you more pages next week."

By two o'clock, William can't take it any more, and the fishing opener is tugging at his sleeve like an importunate child. He looks down at Baron. "To hell with it," he says. "Let's go home."

CHAPTER 18

So Much for Isaac Fucking Newton

THAT AFTERNOON AND EVENING, William works hard to get everything ready. At seven he turns on the radio in the garage and listens to the Twins get shellacked by Toronto, and after the game, he keeps going until he's too tired to do any more.

William knows it's a mistake to go to bed with his brain in high gear, but he does it anyway, and it takes him a long time to fall asleep. First, he thinks about Amy—her gentle humor, her smile and how badly she wants the lab school job. Then he thinks about Marcia, about her concrete sequential thought processes, so different from his, and the way she could divide fractions and multiply large numbers in her head. He continues thinking about her until he realizes that she is probably lying beside Walter Burke at that very moment. It isn't until he begins to think about fishing that he falls asleep.

The next morning, William is hoping to give the newspaper a leisurely once-over before he has to leave to pick up Marv, but then he remembers he has to check the fluid level in the boat trailer brakes. One thing leads to another, and before long, it's time to go.

When William gets to I-94, it's as though he and Baron are the only ones traveling south. The rest of the world is heading up north to go fishing. Marv lives three-plus hours southeast of Chambliss in an affluent Minneapolis suburb. But three hours and change isn't bad, and William doesn't mind driving, especially if he has things to think about, which he almost always does. He decides to call Amy, but because he's trying to keep his eyes on the road, he touches the wrong number and gets her home phone answering machine: *Hi, this is Amy Mattson. Either I'm having an out-of-house experience, or I'm unable to answer the phone right now ...* William loves listening to her voice, but he hangs up before the beep because he doesn't really have a message. He tries again—more carefully this time—and Amy answers right away.

"Hi, William," she says. "I'm so glad you called. Where are you?"

"On my way to Marv's. How 'bout you?"

"I'm hiding in my office. I don't want to talk if you're anywhere near the Cities."

"It's okay—not much traffic yet. I yearn for you tragically."

Amy laughs. "Who said that?"

"Chaplain Tappman in *Catch-22*. But I'm serious—I feel like we've been apart for months. Can you meet Marv and me for dinner?"

"Yes, I talked to Lauren about an hour ago, and she said she's coming home tonight, but it'll be after nine, which probably means after ten. I was going to call you on my lunch break. Where should I meet you guys?"

"Meet us at the Yellow Horse Diner at ..." William looks at his watch. "Seven o'clock."

"I'll be there with bells on."

"You know, I've never understood that expression, but I love the image." A big semi blows past, and William can see another one in his rearview mirror. "Amy, the traffic is picking up. I'd better get back to business—unless I can interest you in phone sex."

"William, as hard as it is to say no, I'd rather you concentrate on your driving."

"Okay. See you at the Yellow Horse."

In addition to being one of Marv's favorite places to eat, the Yellow Horse Diner is an ancient Chambliss landmark that's listed in the National Register, although no one really knows why. The diner is actually a repurposed streetcar from the old Duluth Street

Railway, which went out of business during the Great Depression and sold its big yellow cars—horses, as they were called—to the highest bidders. Marv loves the diner's art deco design and its unpretentious food. William likes the Yellow Horse too, though not as much as Marv does. But then Marv wasn't around to see the place half underwater during the flood of 2008. In that part of Chambliss, the water didn't go down for almost two weeks, and William thought the diner, iconic though it was, occasionally smelled musty after that.

William pulls into Marv's driveway at two fifteen, and before he can even get out of the car, Marv is standing beside it.

"It's good to see you," he says. "What time did you leave Chambliss?"

"Around eleven."

"Then you made good time, my brother."

William gets out of the car and stretches. "It was easy—everyone in the state is going the other direction."

"That's true. You could probably steal Marshall Field's right now."

"Marshall Field's is gone, Marv."

"See what I mean? Hey, can I let Baron out?"

"Sure."

Marv walks to the rear of the Jeep, opens the tailgate and lets Baron out of his crate. Baron greets him happily and heads for Marv's backyard.

William looks around. "Your place looks great."

"I'd get kicked out of this subdivision if it didn't. C'mon in and have a beer."

"Don't mind if I do. Did you see which way Baron went?"

At that moment, Baron comes around the corner of Marv's house with the end of a garden hose in his mouth. He stands there, his tail wagging, and stares at the two men.

"What does he want?" Marv asks.

"He wants us to turn the water on, but we aren't going to—I don't need a wet dog." William convinces Baron to drop the hose, and the three of them go inside.

Marv's home is fancy—swimming pool, wine cellar, recording

studio—and Marv himself is a neat freak, so William is surprised by the uncharacteristic disorder he sees everywhere. The kitchen table is covered with pizza boxes, beer bottles and assorted fast-food containers. The countertops are piled high with mail, most of which appears to be unopened, and the kitchen garbage has over-whelmed its receptacle and is now piling up around it.

"Sorry about the mess," Marv says. "It's the maid's day off." He opens the refrigerator, takes out two beers and hands one to William. "Here you go."

"Thanks. Do you have something I can give Baron a drink in?"

"You bet." Marv fills a large mixing bowl with water and sets it on the floor. "Let's take a short break before we head out."

"I'm definitely down with that." William follows Marv into the living room, where they sink into Marv's big accent chairs. After his drink, Baron joins them, stretching out on the cool stones in front of the fireplace.

"He's gotten a lot bigger since we went crappie fishing," Marv says.

William nods. "He has, and the vet says he'll probably grow for a couple more years." He sets his beer on a coaster that looks like a big Alka-Seltzer tablet with *Plop Plop, Fizz Fizz* printed on it. "How's the jingle-writing business?"

"It's good. I'm working on the Radisson project. What do you hear about your future at Lothrup? Is it still Norway or the highway?"

William shakes his head. "No, they've cooled on that idea—at least for the time being."

"Lucky you! Hey, I know you don't want to go, but Norway seems so … idyllic and peaceful."

"Do you realize that you're four times more likely to be mugged in Oslo than in New York City?"

Marv rubs his chin. "What a strange thought … getting mugged by a Norwegian. I'll bet after they take your wallet, they offer you coffee and krumkake. *Here—still varm—I yoost take out of uffen.*"

William laughs. "I don't know—and I have no intention of find-ing out."

The two men talk for a while, and William knows that if he's ever going to tell Marv about the jammer or how Amy became unknowingly entangled in the cover-up, this is the time to do it. But so far, he hasn't told anyone, and William decides it's probably best to keep his own counsel. He looks at his watch. "We'd better hustle, or we're gonna get stuck in rush-hour traffic. Where's your gear?"

"In the garage." Marv gets up. "We'll go out that way."

On the garage floor, in addition to Marv's fishing tackle and duffel bag, are a cooler, two cardboard boxes and several brown paper bags full of groceries.

"Boat food?" William asks.

"Correctamundo, my brother—smoked salmon, Twizzlers, sunflower seeds, Double-Stuff Oreos, beef jerky, cold cuts for sandwiches, gingersnaps. I had to take the old people's bus to Byerly's ... It was like meeting the ghost of Christmas future."

"I hope you'll let me pay for half of this stuff," William says, looking at the bags and boxes.

"Not a chance. You got room for everything?"

"Room to spare." William puts Baron in his crate, and then he and Marv pack what they can around it, putting the rest in the back seat.

When they're finished, Marv says, "I'll be right back—gotta get something." He disappears for a minute, and returns wearing a beautiful honey-colored leather jacket.

"Very nice," William says. "Gucci?"

"Nope, Cucinelli." Marv takes a step back and does a full-pivot turn like a runway model. "It was a gift from an admirer."

"Pretty fancy jacket for fishing."

"My fishing clothes are in my duffel bag. Let's do this."

Almost as soon as they leave Marv's subdivision, they find themselves in an unbroken line of northbound cars and RVs that stretches out of sight. But fortunately, the traffic is moving pretty well in all lanes. As they approach downtown Minneapolis, William exits 35W, and when he does, they can see the old Metrodome on the left, its fabric roof very white against all the gray buildings.

"The house that Kirby built," Marv says, meaning Kirby Puckett, the Twins one-time star center fielder. "God, I miss baseball in the Dome."

"It was too noisy," William says. "I used to have a twenty-four-hour headache every time I went to a game there."

"I know, but ... all those memories." Marv ducks his head so he can see out William's window. "I was there with Danny when Dave Kingman hit the pop-up that never came down. Danny wasn't more than five or six. It was the funniest thing I ever saw."

"I remember reading about it."

"Yeah, the ball went up, all right—but it *stayed* up. So much for Isaac fucking Newton." Marv laughs and makes half an arc with his right hand, demonstrating how the wayward ball had vanished into thin air. "Frankie just kept looking up at the—"

"Viola?"

"Yeah. He was pitching, and he kept looking up at the ceiling. Kingman was standing over by first, wondering what the hell happened. Danny and I were laughing our asses off—everybody was. Even old Frankie started to laugh, and finally Hatcher got a ball—"

"Who?"

"Mickey Hatcher, the first baseman. He got a ball from the ump and dropped it on the ground. Then he sort of looks around like, 'Oh, *here* it is,' and he picks it up and tags Kingman out. The whole place was in hysterics—thousands and thousands of people—and my son and I ... we ..." Marv quits waving his hands around and looks at William. "We got to see it together. It never happened before, and ... we got to share it." Marv is suddenly quiet, and William, not sure how or even *if* he should respond, is afraid to look at Marv, for fear he might be crying.

"I don't mean to meddle, Marv, but ... are you taking your pills? They only work if you take 'em."

"So now you're gonna give me the pill lecture? Jesus Christ, William, it's not about pills. It's about memories—they *hurt*."

"I'm just worried about you, Marv."

"Well, you don't need to be. I'm fine."

"Okay ... sorry."

William doesn't say anything more. He knows about the pain, about the aching weight of memories. Hell, that's all he's got when it comes to Jon—a few recollections, random fragments that bleed in and out of each other like watercolors: Jon on a Shetland pony;

a little older in his Batman costume; then much older, hitting a three-pointer to beat Moorhead at the buzzer. Sometimes, William can see everything but Jon's face, which frustrates him and makes him feel guilty at the same time.

It's quiet in the car for a while; then William presses the Minnesota reset button. "How 'bout them Twins? Did you catch the game last night?"

"Yes," Marv says. "It was a blowout—the Twins made six errors."

"And basically handed the game to Toronto, which means the Twins are now 8 and 23—ten games out of first in the ALC."

Marv groans. "Can anything break your heart like the fucking Twins?"

"Yes," William says. "The fucking Vikings."

"Amen to that. When you get right down to it, why would anyone want to be a Vikings fan?"

"I don't know," William says. "It builds character, I guess."

Marv laughs. "To hell with the Vikings—they're a snakebit franchise. I want to hear about Amy. The last time I saw you, you'd just met her. You hadn't even done the deed."

"Everything is going great. I really like her, Marv."

"I'm happy for you," Marv says. "How is she … you know, *practically* speaking?"

"We're not having that conversation."

Marv searches William's face until he sees the tiniest suggestion of a smile. "I know that look, you stud. That's the look of a man who's getting his—"

"We're absolutely not going there."

"We'll see about that. When do I get to meet her?"

William looks at his watch. "In about two hours. I asked Amy to join us at the Yellow Horse."

"The Yellow Horse! That's terrific. I promise I won't steal her from you."

And two hours later—after dropping off Baron, his food and a box of toys with Kate and Todd—William and Marv are driving around the Yellow Horse Diner, looking for a place to park.

"We're a little late," William says. "I suppose Amy—hey, there she is! That's her standing by the door." William honks and waves, and Amy, all smiles, waves back.

"Wow, that's what I call hot!" Marv says. "Absolutely *en fuego.*"

"That's what I've been telling you."

"You weren't lying, my brother." They park the car and join Amy.

"I was beginning to wonder what happened to you two," she says. She kisses William, and he introduces her to Marv.

"It's so nice to meet you," Marv says.

"Thank you. It's nice to meet you too. I've been hoping we'd be able to get together. I know you and William share some serious history."

"That we do," Marv says, almost but not quite staring. Marv's expression reminds William of all the Renaissance art he has ever seen in which shepherds experience a visitation by angels. There is that same look of disbelief and wonder.

"Amy is an assistant principal here in town," William says.

"That's wonderful!" Marv says. "I have nothing but admiration for educators, but what an awful time to be one! Everyone in America seems determined to cut your pay, take your health insurance away or destroy your unions."

Amy nods. "You're right. It's a lot different than when I got into this game."

"Shall we?" Marv holds the door, and they go inside. Because of the fishing opener, the Yellow Horse is crowded, and the three of them have to wait briefly before being seated.

"I love this place," Marv says. "It's so ... *retro.* Look at the cherrywood paneling, the brass fixtures—we're revisiting America's Gilded Age."

William points to the menu board. "And it's serving biscuits and gravy twenty-four/seven. But I know what you're saying."

"My daughter and I used to come here a lot," Amy says. "But that was a while ago."

"Before the flood?" William asks.

"No, it was after that—sometime between the Tower of Babel and the Ten Commandments."

William and Marv laugh.

"I meant the *Chambliss* flood."

"I know, sweetheart," Amy says. "I'm just messin' wit' ya."

The Yellow Horse has a typical diner menu with eight to ten entrées, but for those in the know, the choice is simple—Yankee pot roast or the meatloaf platter.

All three of them order meatloaf, and after their waitress leaves, William turns to Amy. "Guess what Marv does for a living."

"Umm … are you a professor of something?" she asks.

Marv shakes his head. "Nothing so dignified, I'm afraid."

"I'll give you a hint," William says *sotto voce.* "In your entire life, you've never met anyone who does this."

"Oh, my God—you're a bullfighter! I've always wanted to meet one."

Marv laughs. "I'm a jingle writer. William finds that unusual."

"I'd have to agree," Amy says. "You're the first jingle writer *I've* ever met."

They talk about famous jingles until their food arrives. Amy is familiar with some that Marv has written, including an old Spam jingle.

"Yeah, that's always been one of my favorites," Marv says. "It might not be 'You Deserve a Break Today,' but those sixteen notes paid for my first house."

"The Spam jingle is a classic," Amy says, "but I like your Target jingle best—it's that reggae beat." Amy moves her upper body to the rhythm. "*Target, so much more than just a store … something, something sales galore.*"

"*Lower prices,*" Marv says. "Thank you. This discussion has been wonderful for my self-image."

"I'm glad I could help," Amy says, taking a bite of meatloaf. "This is really good!"

Marv and William nod in agreement.

"So where are you boys going to fish in the morning?" Amy asks.

"Mille Lacs," William says.

"Great. Maybe if you figure out where the walleyes are, you'll take me next week."

"Do you like to fish?" Marv asks.

"I *love* to fish," Amy says, and she and William give a rollicking account of their outing on Blackwell Lake.

"William, you should invite Amy to come with us tomorrow."

"I would but ..."

"My daughter's coming home for the weekend," Amy says.

"From college?"

"Yes. I haven't seen her since Easter."

A discussion of kids and colleges ensues, followed by a discussion of Minnesota politics that somehow turns into a discussion of Lake Waconia, where Governor Dayton plans to fish in the morning.

"You ever fish Waconia?" Marv asks William.

"A few times when I was at the U," William says. "I guarantee they'll have the governor fishing Pillsbury Reef tomorrow with a Lindy Rig and a leech."

After dessert and coffee, it's time to leave. Everyone has had a good time, and William is glad, not just because he engineered it, but because there's something inexplicably satisfying in the knowledge that the people you love enjoy each other's company.

The men walk Amy to her car, and when they get there, she and William kiss, and he promises to call. *Nice to meet you, Marv. Nice to meet you too, Amy.* Then she's gone, and William and Marv are standing in the parking lot, watching her turn left onto Crescent Boulevard.

Marv shakes his head. "She's seventeen on a scale of ten, my brother—totally fly. You're a lucky man." They walk across the lot in the direction of William's car.

"I think I love Amy," William says. "But it's like I told you—sometimes our relationship feels like an illicit affair."

"You really are cray-cray—you know that, right?"

William shrugs. "I can't help it. I still feel married sometimes."

"My problem was exactly the opposite—I *never* felt married, not even when I was." Marv laughs softly. "Be honest—do you ever fantasize about being in bed with both of them at the same time?"

William looks at him, open-mouthed. "I can barely manage to have both of them in my *thoughts* at the same time. You have a one-track mind."

"Hey, I was just curious. One time I met two sisters from Milwaukee at a Yuja Wang concert, and—"

"The two redheads—you told me about them. What I'm trying to say is that I love Amy, but if I had a chance to turn back the clock and stay married to Marcia, I'd probably do it. Marcia and I go back a long way." William laughs softly. "Ronald Reagan was president when I met Marcia, and it wasn't long after the Twins played their first game in the Metrodome that we rented *Tootsie* and watched it in my apartment in Dinkytown. Naturally, I don't remember much about the movie, other than the implausible premise, but there's one thing I'll never forget."

"What does any of this have to do with—"

"We watched it on Betamax, Marv—*Betamax*! Most people under thirty wouldn't know what that is."

Marv smiles. "Okay, I get it—you and Marcia were together a long time, maybe too long."

"Don't go all Joyce Brothers on me, Marv." They're standing on opposite sides of the Jeep. William unlocks the doors and they get in.

"You can rest easy," Marv says, fastening his seat belt. "I rarely give relationship advice—that would be like Woody Allen giving parenting tips—but you should realize that just because a couple has been together a long time doesn't mean they should be together forever." He settles back in the seat. "Besides, you're not running this show. Marcia is, and she's shtupping your dentist."

"Thank you for the delicate expression of that thought."

"Well, it's true, my brother. She left you for another man. But look on the bright side—he could've been a weasely little piano tuner."

When they get to the house, Marv points to the suitcase full of Dostoevsky books just inside the front door. "Going someplace?"

"No, those are books that I haul back and forth from the office."

"A new exercise regimen?"

William laughs. "I'm doing research for another book."

"Oh, that's terrific! What's it about?"

"Fyodor Dostoevsky. After you were discharged, I'd tongue my pills and stay up all night rereading his novels. It was amazing—they affected me in a way they never had before. I can't really explain—"

"William, I'd be suspicious of anything that happened at Crosswell."

"I am, but I have to write this book."

"Well, good luck. I probably won't understand it, but I'll sure as hell try. You know, we should unload the Jeep. That stuff in the cooler should go in your refrigerator. Plus, I've got something in one of the boxes that we really need."

What they *really need* turns out to be a bottle of Talisker, which Marv locates very quickly. "Seek and ye shall find," he says, holding it up.

"Let the games begin," William says.

The plan was to do some serious damage to the bottle of Scotch, but after two drinks, neither of them can keep his eyes open.

Marv yawns and looks at his watch. "Only ten thirty. Goddammit, William, it's official—we're pussies." He swallows the last of his drink and sets it down. "Am I sleeping in the guest room?"

"Yes, it's all ready for you."

"Thanks." Marv heads for the hallway. "Please tell me we aren't leaving for Mille Lacs at the crack of dawn."

"We aren't. There's no point doing that when we're gonna fish until late tomorrow night."

Marv laughs. "This is really happening, isn't it?"

"Yes, it is. Good night, John-Boy."

"Good night, Grandpa."

Although William is tired, he doesn't fall asleep right away, and at first he can't figure out why. Then he realizes that he misses Baron lying against his right leg. But William is also thinking a lot about tomorrow, wondering where the fish will be, feeling the live weight on the line when he sets the hook. He's been like this about the opener since he was a kid, and although the tingly, anticipatory feeling had disappeared for a couple of years, it's back now, and William is glad. During the long nights at Cross, when he grew tired of reading, he would lie there in the dark and refish every lake he knew. Sometimes he fished for lake trout, other times for walleye, but he was always fishing, moving slowly along the drop-offs and weedlines, presenting his bait with textbook precision. But then, when he got out of Crosswell, he didn't think much about fishing until he and Marv started doing it. William knows if it weren't for Marv, he probably would have quit fishing altogether. It was part of another life—until Marv blended his two lives together.

CHAPTER 19

The Break

BY EIGHT O'CLOCK the next morning, William is making breakfast, and Marv is making sandwiches. They move quickly, and by nine thirty he and Marv have bought bait and launched the boat at Pike Point landing on the north end of Mille Lacs Lake.

"I like this landing," William says, "but only when I know the wind isn't going to blow." He steers the boat between the channel buoys toward the big water.

Marv holds up his phone. "The Weather Channel says five to ten out of the southwest for Garrison, Wealthwood and Malmo."

"Yeah, it doesn't get much better than that. You know, as warm as it's been, we should probably start fishing out on the mud flats."

"The flats? Really? Well, you're the guide, my brother."

William pushes the throttle forward, and the boat leaps across the water. The mud flats—at least the two that interest William— are nine miles away, roughly in the middle of the 207-square-mile lake. Fifteen minutes later, when William's GPS tells him that he's reached the first flat, he stops, lowers the trolling motor, and they scope things out with the sonar.

"There are fish on-bottom here," William says, looking at the screen. "They're probably feeding. What do you think?"

A quarter mile away, three boats are bunched up on a piece of the same flat that William and Marv are on. And two hundred yards beyond the three boats is a commercial launch.

Marv points to it. "I like that there's a launch fishing out here. But it sure feels funny being on the mud flats this time of year. Maybe if it was July …"

William nods at the screen. "But the water temperature is seventy-two degrees. Those fish think it *is* July. Let's give it a try." So they bait up and troll very slowly in twenty-eight feet of water, staying on the edge of the flat as much as possible.

"I don't think I'll ever get used to fishing with leeches," Marv says. "They give new meaning to *gross*—especially putting them on the hook."

William laughs. "Remember when you used to make me do it for you?"

"I categorically deny that ever happened."

"I'm turning right—watch your line." William turns slowly, then proceeds straight again. "I'm still seeing a lot of fish, Marv. I don't know why we haven't—" William feels a sudden tap. "There's one." He turns off the trolling motor and gives the fish line for a full fifteen seconds.

Marv reels in and watches. "Are you going to set the hook eventually or just wait until he shits it?"

"I'm gonna set the hook," William says. "Riiiiight … *now!*" William snaps the rod back, and there's no give at all. "He's decent, Marv. We're gonna need the net."

William fights the fish for quite a while before Marv is able to net it safely and lift it into the boat.

"It's a nice one!" Marv says. "Skinny, though."

"A post-spawn female—she's probably just starting to feed again." William removes the hook and measures the fish before carefully releasing it. "So long, sweetheart."

"How big?"

"Twenty-four inches."

"Very nice. What's the slot again?"

William wipes his hands. "We're allowed to keep four walleye apiece under seventeen inches. But we may have trouble catching fish that small, especially out here."

William's suspicion turns out to be true. They fish mud flats, rock piles and reefs all over the north end of the lake, but most of the fish they catch are way too big to keep. By early evening they have only four fish in the livewell.

"It's frustrating," Marv says, "but it's still a nice problem to have. I've lost track of how many big fish I had to throw back today. How many fishermen get to say that?"

"Just the ones out here." William points to the cooler. "Would you please dig around in there and find me another sandwich?"

Marv opens the cooler. "Pastrami okay? There's one right on top."

"Yeah, that's fine—thanks. I think we should fish the break for a while, and then move in really close when it gets dark—I'm talking five or six feet of water."

"Sounds like a plan."

The "break" is an underwater escarpment 150 yards offshore, where the shallow water of the beach drops off sharply from eleven to twenty feet. A lot of walleyes congregate there, especially in the early evening, and William trolls back and forth across the drop-off, hoping they can pick up a couple of fish under seventeen inches. Almost immediately, Marv hooks another big one that William scoops up in the landing net and lays gently at his feet.

"*Booyah!*" Marv says. "That's the biggest one I've caught today."

"That's the biggest one either of us has caught."

Marv measures the fish and releases it. "That one was twenty-six and a half inches. What's the equation for converting inches to pounds?"

"The one I use is length cubed, divided by 2,700."

"Jesus, I'd need a calculator to figure that out."

William checks their depth and turns toward shore. "There's an easier way, but it only works on big fish—just subtract twenty from a walleye's length."

"Twenty *what*?"

"I don't know—just *twenty*. If your fish is twenty-six and a half inches long, and you subtract twenty, it leaves six and a half. Ergo, your fish weighs approximately six and a half pounds."

Marv shakes his head. "Sorry I asked. It's a sacrilege to contaminate fishing with mathematics." He wags a finger at William.

"And no more *ergos*, my brother."

"Sorry. I lost my head there for a moment."

As the sun sinks lower, William keeps moving into shallower and shallower water. They each catch another big walleye, but legal fish are just as elusive in close as they are everywhere else on the lake. At dusk, Marv sets the hook, and his rod bends in a deep, unrelenting arc that suggests he's snagged one of the lake's larger specimens of Precambrian granite. But even so, the optics are beautiful—the bending rod in relief against the pink sky; Marv, a darkened silhouette in the back of the boat, more totemic than human. Initially, when Marv set the hook, William thought he saw a tiny twitch at the rod tip—barely a quiver. But when several seconds pass and he sees no further movement, William doesn't know what to think. It was probably nothing, but ...

Marv, however, has no doubts. "Goddammit, every time we make that turn, I get rocked up." He stands and tries to reel.

William turns off the trolling motor and stares behind the boat. "Marv, hold on a minute. Let's play this one as a fish."

Marv looks at him and makes a face.

"Just humor me—keep enough tension on the line that it bends the rod a little. Let's watch it for a minute." So Marv pulls back against whatever he's hooked, and the two of them stare at his rod tip. After five or six seconds it moves, ever so slightly. "Did you feel that?"

Marv shakes his head. "No, but I sure as hell saw it."

"It's a fish." William says. "A big one."

The rod tip moves again, twice as much as before. "That time I felt it."

William points to Marv's reel. "What pound test do you have on there?"

"I don't know—nine, I guess. Is that bad?"

"Let's just say I wish it were twelve."

Marv stands up, careful to keep a bow in the rod. "He's back there about fifteen yards, William. I can't do a damn thing with him."

"That's all right. We can deal with that." William turns the trolling motor on. "If the mountain won't come to Muhammad, then Muhammad must go to the mountain."

"I thought it was the other way around—not that I give a shit." Marv starts to reel. "Look, Muhammad, all I ask is that you not back over my line."

William laughs. "Don't give him any slack." He backs the boat up, and the fish never moves. Marv reels the entire time, and when his line is running nearly straight down into the water, William turns off the trolling motor. "See if you can move him now."

Marv tries to hoist the fish up a little but to no avail. "I just can't *doo* it, Captain. I don't have the *poower.*"

William is nervous about the bend in Marv's rod, as well as the relatively light weight of his line. "Okay, enough of that—nine-pound test isn't exactly ski rope."

"I've been trying to remember who was president the last time I changed it."

"Don't tell me things like that," William says.

"How long can he just sit on the bottom?"

"I don't know, but eventually he'll get bored or remember that he has to be someplace, and he'll just swim off and break your line—unless we can get him to make a mistake."

"Like what?"

Before William can answer, Marv's rod bounces up and down half a dozen times very quickly. "Jesus! What's that all about?"

"It's okay," William says. "He's just shaking his head, trying to spit the hook."

"Well, I wish he'd quit doing it—holy shit! He's coming up." Marv begins reeling frantically. "I don't get it ... he's just coming up ... like a sack of potatoes."

The fish could easily have peeled all the line off Marv's reel, but he doesn't. There is no fight in him, no anger. He is just dead weight hauled ignominiously upward. When he reaches the surface, he rolls over on his side next to the boat, his gills opening and closing very slowly. William guesses that he's well over thirty inches. In his entire life, he's never seen a walleye that big—not on a wall, not in a photograph, not anywhere. He makes a move with the landing net.

Marv, who is closer to the fish, waves him off. "Please don't net him. We have to keep him in the water." Marv sets his fishing rod down, and turns to William, his face filled with sadness. "My God, William. He's sick. Look at him."

William leans over the boat. "He's old, Marv—really old."

"Why does this hurt so much? Look … look at his eyes."

Daylight is fading fast, but William can see that the fish, instead of being spectacular shades of green, black and gold, is mostly brown and mottled with fungus. His skin is scar upon scar—the newer ones from Indian nets and spears, the older ones from muskies and big northerns. His eyes, nearly the size of quarters, are cloudy with cataracts.

Marv takes a hook disgorger and removes the hook as the big fish lies quietly beside the boat, gulping and moving its gills. "He just gave up, William. He didn't want to fight anymore. He couldn't do it. He was so tired and sick that he just … gave up. I know what that's like. I know …"

The timbre of Marv's voice isn't right, and it makes William nervous. "Get him upright, Marv. Move him back and forth through the water so he can breathe. I'm going to start the trolling motor. Hang on to him." So Marv holds the fish while William moves the boat forward very slowly. After thirty seconds, William asks if the fish is able to remain upright on his own, but Marv doesn't answer.

"Marv, answer me. I can't see anything back there."

Marv never takes his eyes off the fish. "I think he's … doing better. Should I let go of him?"

"Yes. Let's see what happens."

Marv lets go, and the fish swims slowly down and away from the boat.

"Talk to me. What's going on?"

Marv turns to William, and there are tears running down his cheeks. "He swam away. I feel so bad. I … I hope I didn't hurt him, William. He's such a magnificent creature—so much better and braver than I could ever hope to be."

Marv is crying hard. William moves quickly to the back of the boat, and Marv collapses into his arms. "I'm sorry, William. It's just so sad, so awful. I can't explain it—"

"It's okay, Marv. You don't have to explain anything to me, not ever."

"I wish I hadn't caught him."

William is rocking Marv in his arms. "I know, I know. But it's all right. We didn't hurt him. He's okay." William is frightened, but nothing frightens him as much as the fact that he understands what Marv is feeling. "I want to tell you about something that happened to me. Are you listening?"

Marv is still crying. "Yes."

"Good, because this is important, and I never told you before. One morning last spring, I was sitting at the kitchen table, reading the sports section, and there was a sappy article about a hotshot women's lacrosse player who was about to play her last game for some East Coast college—I don't remember which one. And whoever wrote the article was lamenting the fact that this poor girl would never play lacrosse again after this game because professional women's lacrosse doesn't exist. Anyway, I'm sitting at the kitchen table, reading the article, and suddenly I'm crying—literally *sobbing*—over the story of this girl I'd never heard of, who played a sport I've never watched, for a university I can't even remember. It scared the shit out of me, Marv, because I thought I was well on the road to recovery by then. But that little episode forced me to accept that I was still fucked up—monumentally fucked up. You know why?"

Marv shakes his head.

"Because I hadn't been taking my meds. What about you? Are you taking *your* meds?"

"Some of the time. *Most* of the time." Marv is trying to compose himself. "It isn't about pills, William. When you're like us, everything hurts. We're like those poor bastards at the museum with all their skin peeled off and their insides on display for the whole world to see. My God, if I can get through the day without screaming, it's a major accomplishment."

William nods, his head moving against Marv's. "I know. And it isn't just because of the sad things that happen, like when a child goes missing or some guy beats up his wife. Sometimes, it's the other things that hurt the most. I've got scar tissue on my soul from beautiful things I've seen."

"Like what?"

"Oh … like the time I was hiking north of Ely, and a wolf stepped into the middle of the trail—I could feel his stare pass directly through my body. Or the time I picked Jon up after football practice, and I saw him break up a fight between two little kids and make them shake hands."

Marv nods. "These are the things you never forget, but you're right—they hurt too."

"But maybe a little bit less if you take your meds."

"Yeah, yeah." Marv has stopped crying. "Thank you, my brother." He glances around and tries to laugh. "I'm getting dizzy, William."

William looks up and realizes that when he scrambled to the back of the boat, he left the trolling motor running, and they've been going in tight little circles ever since. "We're quite a pair, aren't we, Marv? We're like Mutt and Jeff."

"Or Barnum and Bailey."

"Or Abercrombie and Fitch."

"Or Lerner and Loewe."

William laughs. "I think you might be pushing the envelope with that one." William goes to the front of the boat and turns off the trolling motor. "Hey, should we go over to the casino and lose a little money?"

"Might as well. Maybe we can beat the mayflies."

"Too late for that." William points toward Garrison, where clouds of mayflies swirl in the distant lights, making it look as though a May blizzard has roared out of the Dakotas and is sweeping across northern Minnesota. McDonald's arches are a golden blur, and on Highway 169, the traffic has slowed to a crawl.

"Mayflies only live a few hours," Marv says. "Every one of those little fuckers will be dead by morning."

"I didn't know that, Dr. Doom. It gives new meaning to carpe diem."

"Good," Marv says. "It could use some."

CHAPTER 20

The Easiest Piece

WILLIAM AND MARV FISH Sunday and do very well, but Monday is windy, and by noon everyone but the big launches has been blown off the lake. But William and Marv don't mind. They've had enough; plus, they've eaten a lot of walleye, and both of them have their legal limit, which was hard to do on Mille Lacs this weekend, at least according to the other fishermen they talked to. When they get back to William's house, they have lunch, and Marv asks about the carriage house.

"It's coming along really well," William says. "You want to see it? You haven't been over there in a long time."

"Yeah, I'd love to."

So the two of them walk over, and William begins the tour by showing him the outside of the building, which is more or less finished, except for the gable ends.

"There's nothing like cedar siding for warmth and rusticity," Marv says. "What happened up there?" He points to the peak, where William had ripped the two boards off.

"Woodpecker."

"Big sonofabitch," Marv says. "He even brought a ladder." He looks at William. "What's going on?"

"Nothing. I just decided to go with shakes up there. The exterior needed something—more texture, more charm ..."

"More cowbell?"

"Exactly."

Marv smiles. "Well, you're the boss."

Even though William has ripped out almost as much work as he's completed, Marv is surprised at the progress inside the carriage house and even more surprised by William's talent for carpentry. *Where did you learn to build cabinets? How did you get all those boards to meet in the center like that?* And William explains that when he runs into something he doesn't know how to do, he either asks at the lumberyard or watches YouTube tutorials until he can handle it.

"You're a good carpenter, my brother. You'll never starve."

William laughs. "But you don't know how slow I am."

They walk back to the house, and by two o'clock they're on the road to Marv's.

"It was a great opener," Marv says. "We caught a lot of nice walleyes."

"Yeah, but that slot is a killer. We'll have to try again next month. Can you believe this traffic? A lot of people must have fished today."

Marv looks at the crowded lanes of southbound vehicles, most of them with boats in tow. "Wait until tonight—I-94 will look like a parking lot." Marv takes off his jacket and tosses it in the back seat. "Christ, this spring has been hot."

"The hottest on record," William says. "Before long, we'll have palm trees growing along Nicollet Avenue."

"And alligators on the golf courses."

Four hours later, they still haven't made it to Marv's house, but neither of them cares. They're happy to have the time together. When they finally exit the interstate, they stop at an A&W and get burger baskets to go, which they eat on Marv's front porch.

"I don't think I've had a Papa Burger since I was in high school," William says, trying to take a bite of the impossibly large hamburger.

Marv nods. "There's nothing like A&W for keeping you in touch with your inner child."

"And your cardiologist," William says. "But it sure is good."

After they finish eating, they unload the Jeep, freeze Marv's walleye and sit by the pool.

"You wanna go for a swim?" Marv asks. "The water is eighty degrees—it's perfect."

"No thanks. You know what I'd *really* like?"

"You're fairly predictable, William. You'd like me to play the piano."

William smiles. "Any chance?"

"When have I ever refused you?" Marv gets up and heads for the studio with William right behind him. As they pass through what Marv calls the hearth room, William sees several pictures of Danny on a little Pembroke table by the fireplace.

"Hang on a sec." William stops and looks carefully at the photos. There are three graduation pictures—high school, college and law school—as well as a few candid shots. "I like this one." William points to a grainy picture of Danny and several other young people at a table in a bar or restaurant. They are all holding up glasses and beer bottles, laughing and smiling as though they've been there a while.

"That was taken on the day Danny was hired at Roth and Edelman. His mother sent it to me."

"He looks just like you, Marv."

Marv shakes his head. "He's a lot better-looking than I am. Smarter too. C'mon."

Marv's studio is completely soundproof, and when he opens the door, there is a little rush of air as the pressure equalizes. They enter through the control room that, in addition to a large audio console, has a playback system with woofers so powerful they can blow out a match—William has seen them do it. A second sound-proof door leads to the studio itself, and in the middle of the room is a grand piano, its lid open, as though it's about to say something but can't remember what. Marv walks over to it and sits down. William sits in one of the five theater seats right below the control room window.

"What would you like to hear?" Marv shakes his arms theatrically and cracks his knuckles like Ed Norton warming up on *The Honeymooners*.

"Anything," William says. "I'm not fussy."

"How about Tchaikovsky?" And with that, Marv's hands, like two animals released from a cage, begin to race each other up and down the keyboard. Marv is good—*really* good—and there's nothing William enjoys more than listening to him play, especially a piece like this, with such ringing highs and thunderous lows. To William's ear, it's like bells chiming one minute and waves crashing the next.

When Marv finishes the movement, William leaps to his feet and claps. "That was magnificent—too good for words!"

Marv smiles. "You're hardly impartial, but thank you. That was from Concerto no. 2. I love it on this piano."

"I've never heard a piano that sounds like that," William says. "I've never heard *anything* that sounds like that."

Marv touches the dark wood of its cabinet. "Yes ... kudos to Paolo Fazioli." He follows the Tchaikovsky with a Chopin etude, then the fast section of Liszt's Hungarian Rhapsody no. 2. It's punchy and loud, and Marv interprets it beautifully. Then he plays a piece that is unfamiliar to William.

"It's a Scarlatti sonata," Marv says. "You always seem to like the faster stuff."

"I like it all." William cups his hands around his mouth. "More, more."

"All right," Marv says. "But enough with the highbrow crap—here's 'Maple Leaf Rag.'" He plays it perfectly—not crazy-fast, the way people usually play it, but at an even march tempo. William keeps time, alternately tapping both feet. When Marv is finished, he doesn't move and appears to be staring at the keyboard.

"Bravo!" William says, applauding. "I'll bet they didn't teach you that at Juilliard ... What's wrong?"

Marv looks up. "Nothing. I was just thinking how much Danny loved the Joplin rags when he was little. He used to dance around the house whenever I played one."

William knows only too well what Marv is feeling. "I think every parent has memories like that—memories that make them happy and sad at the same time."

Marv nods. "Memories are tough, but it's the regrets that get me down." He sits up straight and stretches, raising his arms above his head. "Okay, William. One more … something soothing before bed—'Meditation' from *Thaïs*."

When Marv finishes, William gives him a standing ovation. "That was wonderful. I can't tell you how much I enjoyed it."

"But did you hear the *ma*, my brother?"

"The *what*?"

"The *ma*. I had an instructor at Juilliard, a little Japanese guy named Ishida, and he always used to say, 'You must hear the *ma*, Marvin-san. Music not only what you play. Music also what you *not* play.'"

William laughs. "I'm not very good with Zen paradox."

"Neither am I, and I left before I figured it out. But I think Ishida was saying that music is about negative space—the silence in a piece, as opposed to what we hear as music. The *ma* is the interval between the notes, a special kind of beauty that we hear only with our imagination."

"I'm sure he was right, Marvin-san, but I don't think I hear it. I'm just an untutored *gaijin* who loves it when you play. How about an encore?"

"All right. You'll know this one. Listen for the *ma*."

Marv plays a delicate, haunting piece in which the treble line sounds like a violin solo accompanied by a chorded piano. It is sad but lovely, and William is sure that if tears could be heard, they would sound just like this. The piece is short—no more than three minutes—and when Marv is finished, he turns to William.

"Well?"

"That was one of the most beautiful things I've ever heard," William says. "I think it was used in a movie soundtrack years ago, but I don't remember which one."

"It was the easiest piece in *Five Easy Pieces*," Marv says. "It's Chopin's Prelude in E Minor. Jack Nicholson's character plays it for his brother's fiancée, right before they decamp to the bedroom. Did you hear the *ma*?"

"I don't know. I was too busy being blown away."

"That's good too, I guess." Marv pushes the bench away from the piano. "Do you ever hear music in your head?"

"No," William says. "Just voices."

"Seriously. Does it ever happen that you're driving along, minding your own business, and suddenly you hear … Verdi's 'Va, pensiero?'"

William laughs. "Everybody hears music in their head. I probably wouldn't hear opera, though. I'd be more likely to hear Eric Clapton."

"That's even better … And when Clapton is pulling the blues notes out of a minor chord, like only he can do, you hear it perfectly because it's in your head, right? It isn't real."

"I suppose so. Music is like Plato's notion of form—its perfection exists only in our minds."

"Well, the *ma* is like that," Marv says. "I don't think you even need real music to hear it. Sometimes it's easier to hear with our imagination than with our ears." Marv stands up. "Ready to turn in?"

"Yes, it's time. Thank you for playing."

That night in Marv's guest bedroom, William lies in a big four-poster beneath a pair of Benson-Cobb prints and thinks about the *ma*—what Marv had described as the unfulfilled promise between musical notes. To someone in William's line of work, the *ma* was a close cousin to the caesura—the strategic pause that Mallarmé had used in his poetry, JFK in his speeches, Marlon Brando in his acting. The *ma* was a lot of things. It was even the comedic comma between a joke's setup and its punch line—a moment of nothingness that shapes the whole.

But William thinks the *ma* is more than a simple hiatus. He suspects it is the purest form of space itself, like the interval between our heartbeats or those sublime moments onstage when the dancer stops moving. In sculpture, the *ma* isn't mass; it's the all-important void. In a painting, it's the emptiness that generates form—the barren landscapes of Andrew Wyeth or the unoccupied triangle in *The Last Supper* that is created by Jesus leaning left and John right. You could see the *ma* easily enough. That wasn't a problem. But *hearing* it was altogether different, and William had never done it—not at a concert or in a recording or even in his head. But he hoped the *ma* was like redemption—something he might experience someday if he was lucky.

The next morning, Marv gets up early to make coffee and to see William off. He's wearing a red cashmere robe with little polo players on the pockets and matching red slippers with more polo players on the vamps.

"Hey, Hugh Hefner called," William says. "He wants his robe back."

"Eat your heart out, my brother. You're clearly jealous." Marv points to William's coffee cup. "Do you have a travel mug in the car? I'll fill it for you."

Twenty minutes later, William is on the road, and before he's even made it to Richfield, he calls Amy at home.

"I just wanted to wish you luck with today's campus visit and the one-on-ones."

"Thank you. I'm just getting ready to leave. Did you catch a lot of fish? It seems like you've been gone for a month. Did you miss me?"

"*Your absence has gone through me like thread through a needle. Everything I do is stitched with its color.*"

"Oh, I *love* that poem. It's W. S. Merwin, isn't it?"

"It is. And yes, we caught plenty of fish."

"Where are you?"

"Just north of Eagan. I'm on my way home, but I have to pick Baron up at LiveRight."

"What shall we do tonight?"

"Well, I have an excellent documentary on Madagascar that I'll bet you haven't seen."

Amy laughs. "I guess that was a stupid question."

"Why don't you come over?"

Amy doesn't say anything.

"I can hear you breathing," William says. "What are you doing?"

"Oh, I'm sorry. I'm standing in front of the mirror thinking about Coco Chanel. She said before a woman leaves the house, she should take one thing off."

William laughs. "She may not have realized it, but Mademoiselle Chanel was talking about the *ma*, about using negative space to advantage."

"I think I can get by without this pendant. I *like* it, but …"

"What about coming over?"

"Absolutely. I'll bring dinner. Lauren and I made lasagna, and there's a lot left over—lots of salad too."

"Great," William says. "Remember to bring Yoshi."

"Is that code for *I want you to spend the night*?"

"It is."

"How could I refuse such a smooth talker? What time?"

"Does six thirty work?"

"Yes. I'll be there with—"

"I know—with bells on."

William pushes the speed limit all the way home, arriving at LiveRight around eleven fifteen. The receptionist hardly looks up when she tells him that Todd is with a patient, but when William asks where Baron is, she gives him a big smile and points down the hall. "The last time I saw that precious thing, he was in Dr. Benedict's waiting room."

"Oh, okay. Thanks." William walks into Todd's waiting room, where Baron is being petted by a girl with tattoos all over her arms and neck and more hardware in her face than William would have thought possible—hoops, rings, studs, even bolts. When Baron sees him, he practically leaps into William's arms, whimpering, talking, making all kinds of happy little sounds.

William hugs him. "I missed you too, Hürtgenvoss. Calm down. Everything is okay."

"Cool dog," the girl says. "Is he yours?"

"Yes … we haven't seen each other for a while."

"What's his name?"

"It's Baron," William says, looking at her face. Over the years, William has trained himself never to look at girls' tattoos or try to read what's on their T-shirts, since it's impossible to do either one without being misunderstood. But he has no rule to follow when it comes to piercings, probably because he's never needed one before.

"You're staring," the girl says.

"I'm sorry. I was just wondering if they hurt."

"My piercings? Not at all. My nipples are pierced too. So is my—"

"Hey, that's terrific—really. I gotta go." William snaps a leash on Baron, and they're about to beat a hasty retreat when the door to Todd's office opens and a young man wearing a Punkadelic Forever T-shirt walks out with Todd not far behind.

"I'll see you next Tuesday," Todd says. "Try to get here on time."

The young man gives him the *rock on* sign over his right shoulder.

When Todd sees William, his face breaks into a surprised smile. "I see you found Baron. How was the fishing?"

"It was good. Thanks for taking care of my friend here."

"It was our pleasure, William. In fact, we really ..."

Another young woman, this one with a baby in her arms, walks into the waiting room and sits down.

"Hi, Yolanda," Todd says. He turns to William. "I wish we could talk but—"

"Hey, I know you have appointments. I'm not here to hang you up."

Todd looks relieved. "Okay, we'll talk later." He motions to the girl with all the piercings. "Please come in, Gloria—sorry I'm running late."

William leaves, and once he gets outside, he walks Baron around for a few minutes.

"Baron, you couldn't pay me enough to do Todd's job. I mean, what do you say to a girl who feels compelled to tell you that her nipples are pierced? I submit that when you're bringing *that* up in a conversation, there are some topics you've overlooked."

William puts Baron in the car, but before they leave LiveRight, he calls Kate, who actually picks up.

"Hello, this is Kate Benedict, Chief Accounting Officer. How may I help you?"

"I love the way you say that. Bad time?"

"Oh—hi, Daddy. No, it's a good time. I just got back from a meeting."

"I want to thank you for babysitting Baron. I just picked him up at LiveRight. Todd was really busy."

"Yeah, I guess this spring has been crazy. Did he give you the box with BearBear's toys and food in it?"

"No. Like I said, he was busy, but it's okay. I have another bag of—"

"Darn it," Kate says. "He promised he'd remember."

William can tell Kate is angry, and he can practically hear Todd getting his butt chewed.

"By the way," she says, "you have the boys to thank for taking care of BearBear. They were trying to prove to Todd and me that they're ready for a puppy of their own, and I think they proved it."

"Good for them. Listen, I won't keep you—I'm sure there's a spreadsheet or two that need tweaking."

"Try a hundred of them. Let's get together soon, Daddy."

"We will, Kate. Bye-bye."

When William and Baron get home, they play in the backyard for a long time—William even turns on the sprinklers—but eventually Baron gets tired, and they go inside. William sits down at the kitchen table with Baron at his feet.

"I've got to make a call," William says.

He takes out his phone and punches "Roth & Edelman" into a search field. Then, when he's on the firm's website, he taps on "Our People" and scrolls down until he finds "Daniel Kreitzer." There's a short bio and a thumbnail photo of Danny, and William is not at all surprised to learn that he's a partner. There is also a phone number, which takes William directly to "the voicemail of Daniel Kreitzer," who, he is told, will return his call as soon as possible.

William is prepared for this, so he takes a breath and does his best to lay down a coherent message: "Daniel, this is William Kessler. I'm a friend of your father's, and I've been a little worried about him lately. I don't think he's taking his medication regularly, and this weekend he seemed a bit unstable. I just thought you should know. And, uh ... it's okay to tell him I called you." William laughs. "He'll be angry, but he'll get over it. Thanks, Danny. Bye." William taps END CALL and cringes. Goddammit! He didn't mean to call Daniel *Danny*—it was out of his mouth before he knew it. But other than that, the message seemed okay, and William feels better for having left it.

Before he can turn his cell phone off, William hears the desk phone ringing in his office and runs down the hall to answer it. It's Sam, and he's calling to tell William that the Minnesota Supreme Court has agreed to hear Lothrup's appeal.

"I thought you'd want to know, buddy—we're gonna get one more bite at the apple. Is this good news or what?"

William doesn't say anything.

"Are you still there?" Sam asks.

"It wasn't … it wasn't supposed to happen. The odds were—"

"I know," Sam says, "but this is a good thing. Gardner is doing his happy dance, and everybody here at Wellstone is ecstatic."

"I'm sure they are, but—"

"Look, William, there's another reason why I called."

"I know."

"Now that we're headed back to court, it's imperative that there aren't any surprises. We can't afford to be blindsided by something unforeseen."

"Like Rupert's jammer?"

"I didn't say that."

"You didn't have to," William says.

Sam is annoyed. "Just don't do anything stupid. If something should happen in the middle of our case … if we get hit by some bolt from the blue, things would go pear-shaped in a hurry."

"*Bolt from the blue?* You can't even say it, can you? We're talking about a cell phone signal jammer."

It's several seconds before Sam responds. "Just remember which side your bread is buttered on, William."

It's clear to William that Sam doesn't understand his situation at all. "Look, I know why you called, Sam, but you have nothing to fear from me. Remember, even if I had the courage to do the right thing, my hands are tied because Amy is interviewing for the lab school job."

"The right thing?" Sam says. "That kind of talk makes me nervous, William. Have you considered the impact that a twelve-million-dollar settlement would have on our students? You should be thinking about the greatest good for the greatest number—*that's* the right thing."

William groans. "Spare me your utilitarian bullshit. Look, I gotta go, Sam. I can't talk about this right now." He can hear Sam saying something, but he hangs up anyway.

Numb with dread and practically shaking, William walks quickly to the bathroom and vomits into the toilet.

The odds that the supreme court would review the case might

have been nine to one, but as long as those odds were, they weren't long enough, and William's free ride is over. He had hoped to sit in the cheap seats and watch the supreme court do what they did 90 percent of the time, but they'd thrown a monkey wrench into everything, and suddenly, the jammer mattered. In fact, the only thing that mattered more than the jammer was what William was going to do about it. Keeping his mouth shut had been a reasonable option before, but it would be more difficult now. Now, his silence could have serious ramifications, perhaps even legal consequences.

He splashes some water on his face and rinses his mouth. "Fucking supreme court."

William still has a couple of hours to kill before Amy arrives, so he turns on the TV just in time to hear CNN's Soledad O'Brien tell the story of a twenty-eight-year-old Egyptian waiter named Hamdi al-Nubi who supposedly died of a heart attack, only to awaken at his funeral the next day. As one might imagine, the mourners were overcome with joy, and the funeral turned into a party. William enjoys the story, but he's a sucker for any story that's amenable to a quantum interpretation, and a man who exists in two opposing biological states at the same time is about as quantum as it gets. William understands this on a uniquely personal level, because before Amy came into his life, he too was simultaneously dead and alive—the human equivalent of Schrödinger's cat.

It isn't long before William gives up on TV and collapses on his bed. He awakens at six o'clock and lets Baron out. Then he takes a shower. At twenty to seven, Amy and Yoshi get there, and ten minutes after that, William and Amy are making love in the guest bedroom.

Afterward, as they lie in the gathering darkness, Amy exhales loudly. "Whew! If that's what happens after four days, can you imagine if we'd been apart for a week?"

"I don't even want to think about it." William sits up, folds the pillow in half and places it behind his head. "How did the Big Interview, Part Two go?"

"It went fine. I especially enjoyed the tour of the lab school. I attended a meeting there two years ago, but until today, I'd never really seen it. They didn't allow enough time for the one-on-ones, though—it was like speed dating. One of the people I sat down with had worked at Hawthorne from 2003 to 2007."

"Then that was a good thing," William says. "An added bonus."

Amy shakes her head. "Not exactly. She was always late to work, and after about a dozen warnings, I put a letter in her file. She was furious."

"She probably forgot all about it."

"Nobody forgets anything, William. You know that as well as I do."

Neither of them speaks again until Amy asks about the opener. When William doesn't respond, she tries again. "I said, tell me something about—"

"I'm sorry, Amy. I heard you. I was just thinking."

"About what?"

"A lot of things. I was thinking about the lab school job and how much you want it. I was also wondering if Lothrup will ever let me teach again. And I was thinking about how I walked into the Chambliss Armory as an emotional basket case and walked out with you in my life. I've waited so long for the wheel to turn that I'm terrified I'll jam the gears somehow."

"I don't think that's likely, but it's important to maintain your strength. Could we continue this conversation over lasagna?"

William laughs. "Of course. What goes better with neuroses than lasagna?"

The next morning, William puts Baron and Yoshi in the back-yard, and he and Amy have a quick cup of coffee.

"Don't forget obedience class tonight," Amy says. "Meet me in the parking lot."

"We'll be there. Have a nice day at school."

Not five minutes after Amy and Yoshi leave, William's phone vibrates, and he pulls it from his pocket. When William sees Marv's name in the display, he assumes Marv is about to read him the riot act for calling Danny yesterday, and he braces for it.

"Hi, Marv. Look, I hope you're not—"

"Good morning, my brother. I'm glad your phone is on."

"Yeah, I ..." William realizes he forgot to turn it off after leaving the voicemail for Danny.

"Hey, I was wondering if I left my jacket in the back seat of the Wagoneer. I'm pretty sure I did."

William breathes a sigh of relief. "I don't know, but it's parked right outside. I'll take a look." William heads for the door. "The Twins play Cleveland today. You gonna watch?"

"The game isn't televised, William."

"Goddammit, why do they do that?"

Marv laughs. "It would be easier to explain Schenkerian harmony, but basically, it's about money and network ratings."

"I really wanted to see that game—it's the Twins' chance to climb out of the cellar."

"Yeah, but that probably won't happen against Derek Lowe. He's 5 and 1."

"Okay, I'm at the car." When William opens the passenger-side back door, he sees Marv's jacket on the floor behind the seat. "Yeah, Marv, it's right here. What do you want me to do with it?"

"Wear it in good health, William. I'll get it eventually. I just wanted to make sure it was there." Marv pauses for a moment. "The opener was great. I'll never forget it."

"Neither will I, Marv. You take it easy."

"Ditto, my brother. Hasta la vista."

William turns off his phone and holds Marv's jacket up by the shoulders, impressed all over again by the flawless calfskin and exquisite stitching. "I'll bet this thing cost three or four grand," William says aloud. Then he goes back in the house, checks his Rolodex and copies down Marv's address. That done, he lets Baron into the kitchen.

"You up for a ride to the UPS Store, Hürtgenvoss?"

Baron, who enjoys both questions and rides, looks up and wags his tail.

"Good. I don't like having Marv's jacket here—I'm sure it cost a fortune, and I don't want to be responsible for it. Let's boogie."

William knows that UPS is the way to go—they'll even put the jacket in a box for him. But it's been several years since he was there, and he isn't sure where the store is. He *thinks* it's in a little strip mall south of Dahlberg Road, but this is the sort of situation where his mind sometimes play tricks on him. This time, however, he gets lucky, and the UPS Store is exactly where it's supposed to be. William walks in and hands the jacket across the counter to a young woman in a brown uniform and a matching cap with her ponytail pulled through it.

"Nice jacket," she says.

"Yes, it is. A friend left it in my car."

"Can you believe this weather? We've had the air conditioning on since April."

"Hottest spring on record," William says, trotting out the line that has become his default response to all weather-related small talk.

The girl wraps the jacket in tissue, puts it in a box and places the box on a scale. "So where would you like to send this?"

William gives her the address, says yes to additional insurance and hands over his credit card.

"The jacket will be delivered before five o'clock on Friday," she says, applying a label to the box.

And in no time, William is back in the car, wishing everything could be so efficient. Fifteen minutes after he leaves the UPS Store, he's trundling his suitcase full of books up the stairs to his office, and by one o'clock, he's written twelve hundred words about *The Brothers Karamazov*—specifically, how the ability to feel guilt or shame is a necessary prerequisite to feeling love for others. William isn't sure he believes it, but Dostoevsky does, and that's what counts.

Because he and Baron have class that evening, William takes Baron outside, and they go over a couple of things. First, when he heels on a leash, Baron's shoulder must remain perfectly even with William's knee; second, on the *long stay* command, Baron has to sit until William gives him the *okay*. "You can't just sit for a while," he explains, "and then decide to stand up or raise your butt off the ground—that's not cool."

When the two of them head for home that afternoon, William notices a couple of dozen *Light It Up* activists meeting in an outdoor classroom at the far end of the commons. They are at least a hundred yards away, but William knows who they are by the bright yellow light bulbs emblazoned on their T-shirts. How do they do it? he wonders. How can they believe in personal agency and their impossible goal with such surety and conviction?

Naïve though they are, William knows he's looking at the avatars of faith's perfection.

CHAPTER 21

Separation Anxiety

WHEN THEY GET HOME from school, William mows a section of the lawn, takes a quick shower and has dinner with Baron. Then it's time to leave for obedience class.

When they get to the armory, William drives to the beginners' end of the parking lot, but Amy isn't there yet, so he joins a few people who are walking their dogs back and forth along the edge of the weeds. After a few minutes, everyone but William is making their way to the armory, but Amy still hasn't shown up, and William is determined to wait for her. Just when he's beginning to worry, she pulls in and parks next to the Jeep.

"Sorry I'm late," she says, getting out of her car.

"We're okay. It's two minutes to seven."

"I got hung up at school."

"Anything serious?"

Amy takes a quick look in her compact mirror. "It could be. Just as I was about to leave, a mother walked into my office and told me that her son is being bullied. We take bullying very seriously at Hawthorne, and I spent over an hour explaining to her how we're going to handle it." Amy lets Yoshi out of the car and walks him around for a minute. "Okay, William, let's go. I wonder what Jackie has in store for us tonight."

Amy and William are late, but class hasn't started because there are two bats flying around the gym, swooping and diving in a way that frightens a lot of the women and more than a few of the dogs. Three National Guardsmen try to help by opening the doors at the south end of the gym—doors big enough to drive a tank through—but the bats won't fly out. In a few minutes, however, they disappear into the dark recesses of the ceiling and stay there, which is almost as good.

With the bat problem under control, at least for the moment, Jackie explains that tonight's class will focus on three things: first, practice drills for the final exam, which in two short weeks will test each dog on the Big Five—*sit, come, heel, down* and the dreaded *long stay*; second, the unsupervised separation, which is something new; and third, three "good manners" exercises that Jackie insists will make life easier for both dogs and owners.

"Okay," she says. "That's the plan. Let's start by doing a couple laps to remind these rascals who's in charge."

Baron and Yoshi both do well in the practice drills, with the exception of the *long stay*, a two-minute exercise that is a minute too long for every dog in the class. But where things really break down is on the unsupervised separation. In this exercise the owners, two at a time, tell their dogs to sit and stay. Then they hand their leashes to Jackie's helpers and leave the gym for what is supposed to be three minutes.

Jackie probably knew what would happen, but no one else did, and after a few moments—often before their owners were out of sight—the dogs began to whine, cry and bewail their abandonment so pitifully that it was painful to listen to. Yoshi held out for maybe half a minute before he raised his head like a wolf and started howling, his lips pursed in a little O. Baron was worse. The instant he could no longer see William, he started barking and dragged the poor girl who was holding him across the gym in the direction of the door that William had disappeared through—*forever*, in Baron's mind.

The unsupervised separations prove so loud and disruptive that the advanced class begin to stare, and at that point Jackie halts the exercise. "It seems we have some minor issues with separation anxiety," she says, laughing. "The good news is that it won't be on your final exam, but it's very important, so try to work on it at home."

Amy lines up behind William for the obligatory one-lap heeling exercise that Jackie uses when she wants to calm the dogs down. "I had no idea Yoshi would behave like that," Amy says. "Were you surprised by Baron?"

William shakes his head. "Not really. Baron's first owner died unexpectedly. I think that's why he gets so upset if I leave him."

Jackie raises her arm overhead and swings it in a circle. "All right, everybody, heel 'em around the ring—I want to see slack leashes."

After that, as advertised, Jackie shows the class how to teach their dogs some "good manners" skills that are basically behavioral habits that no dog would acquire on its own in a thousand years. The first one is *leave it*, and as Jackie explains, this is the command you want your dog to know when you drop your blood pressure pill on the floor. The second one is *me first*, and the dog that has been taught this behavior will sit six feet in front of every door before it's opened, so its owner can pass through the doorway first and see what's on the other side of it. The third skill is *settle*, a command accompanied by a short leash and lots of assurance that helps excited dogs get control of their emotions. By the time Jackie has taught the class how to begin teaching these commands to their dogs, it's almost eight thirty, but no one seems to care.

After Jackie dismisses the class, William and Amy are getting ready to leave when one of the kennel club ladies comes up to William and sticks out her hand. "Someone told me it was you, but I didn't believe them. You're Dr. Kessler, aren't you—the Saint Patrick's Day hero?"

"I'm Dr. Kessler," William says, shaking her hand. "But I don't lay claim to the hero part."

"Well, you should," the woman says. "I'm Muriel Skogsberg, and I've always wanted to thank you for what you did. My nephew was in Dewhurst that day. He says he's alive because of you." She looks at Amy. "You must be very proud of him, Mrs. Kessler."

"I couldn't be prouder," Amy says, not bothering to correct her.

Muriel smiles. "Some people say we don't have heroes anymore, but around here we know better."

William doesn't know what to say. "Thank you, Mrs. Skogsberg. Please ... please give my best to your nephew."

"I will, and thanks again." She leaves, and William and Amy head for the door.

Amy gives him a nudge. "She meant what she said—they all do."

"I know," William says. "I just hope that someday people will quit coming up to me like that. Maybe after five years they won't feel like they have to—"

"Are you ever going to tell me what happened?"

"At Dewhurst?"

"Yes."

"I don't know … I've never told anyone."

"Not Marcia?"

William shakes his head.

"Marv?"

"Nope."

Amy gets to her car and turns around. "You know, William. I don't mind that you won't tell me—I really don't—but I hope it isn't because you don't love me enough or trust me enough or value me enough to share it. I'm not sure I could handle that."

"It isn't any of those things, Amy. It's just …"

"Hey, it's okay." Amy looks at her watch. "Wow! We really ran over. Good class, though."

"Yes, it was—I think Baron is going to be sitting six feet in front of the door from now on."

After they put the dogs in their cars, William ventures a suggestion as though he just thought of it. "Hey, as long as you have Yoshi with you, you might as well follow me home and spend the night."

Amy laughs. "So you're saying we should sleep together because it's expedient?"

"Not at all," William says. "I'm saying we should sleep together because it's the only thing I cherish more than being with you, and sometimes I think if I can't touch you and hold you in my arms, I'll die of incompleteness, and it's like—"

"Whoa! Time out," Amy says, making a T with her hands. "Is *incompleteness* a word?"

William nods. "It's also a feeling. I know this because it's the feeling I get when I'm not with you."

"Then I suppose it doesn't matter if it's a word. By the way,

William, that was an excellent elevator pitch—very persuasive—but in fairness, I was already planning to spend the night." She kisses him on the cheek. "Let us away, my love. I'll be right behind you."

The drive to his house reminds William of the drive to Ki's on the night he and Amy met, with two exceptions. This time, William is reasonably sure that Amy won't disappear from his life if he takes his eyes off the rearview mirror. And tonight, William has feelings for Amy that he would not have thought possible three weeks ago.

At William's house, they let the dogs out and go inside, and when he turns on the lights, William is barely able to process the scene before him.

"Oh, my God!" Amy says. *"Oh, my God!"*

William's belongings, the few that he has, are strewn about the floor. Every drawer has been rifled, every closet tossed, every shelf emptied.

"Goddammit, I've been burglarized!" William takes Amy's arm. "Listen, there may still be someone in the house. I want you to get in your car and lock the doors until I come for you. I'm going to put the dogs in the backyard and take a look around."

Amy leaves without a word and William gets the dogs to the kitchen, where he shoos them out the door into the backyard. Then he begins a walk-through of his violated home. The place is a mess, but it doesn't appear to have been damaged or vandalized, and for a few minutes, William can't see that anything is even missing. Then he notices that the TV in the kitchen is gone. William checks the garage, then the basement, which received only cursory treatment from whoever had broken in. When he heads back upstairs to the kitchen, he sees Amy on the landing with a tire iron in her hand.

The intensity of her expression causes William to smile. "I thought you were supposed to—"

"Wait in the car—yeah, I know." Amy lowers her weapon. "I would have, but when you didn't come get me, I got worried."

"Where did you get the tire iron?"

"Oh ... *this*?" Amy looks at it sheepishly. "I keep it under the seat of my car."

"Good idea," William says. "You sure had your war face on. You looked like you were ready to brain somebody."

"I was, but I didn't know that was you coming up the stairs and—"

"Hey, it's okay. I'm just glad you're on my side. From what I can tell, whoever it was got in through the garage service door and gained access to the house from there."

"William, you have to call the police."

"I know, but it hardly seems worth it. The only thing missing is the television in the kitchen. Why would somebody steal a five-year-old TV? And why *that* TV? The one in the living room is bigger."

"I don't know. Please call."

So William calls the police, and they tell him that while he's waiting for a squad car to arrive, he should go through the house again and make a list of everything that was stolen. *And sir, please try not to touch anything.*

So William and Amy do another circuit of the house, and this time William notices that his toaster is gone.

"That's even weirder than the TV," he mutters.

It's only a matter of minutes before William starts to wonder if Lothrup is involved—an idea that does not require a huge intellectual leap. By all appearances, someone had ransacked the house looking for something—the signal jammer, perhaps—and when he couldn't find it, he took the TV just to make the break-in look more like a burglary. William thinks the "burglar" was probably heading for the door, the TV in his arms, when he decided it would be more believable if he took something else too, so he turned around and grabbed the first thing he saw, which was the toaster. It was like, *What the hell—this will do.* The way William sees it, the stolen TV and toaster were just props, yet they failed to convince, and the break-in resembled a no-holds-barred Easter egg hunt more than it did a robbery.

William wonders if perhaps he spooked Sam yesterday with his *do the right thing* remark. Maybe the higher-ups were afraid that Birnam Wood was getting a little too close to Dunsinane, and they decided to take the jammer before William had a spasm of rectitude that cost them their appeal. It was certainly possible, but at the same time, it was patently absurd—the idea that a bunch of fuddy-duddy college administrators were capable of behaving like managing partners in *The Firm*. They were right to worry, though. Everything was different now that the supreme court had agreed to hear Lothrup's case. Even William was different. If he had previously been a known commodity, non-threatening and predictable, he was now a loose cannon capable of blowing an enormous hole in Lothrup's future.

"I'll be right back, Amy," William says.

"Where are you going?"

"I want to check something in the basement."

"You were just down there."

"Yeah … but I forgot to look at something."

William returns to the basement and finds that the jammer is still in the toner cartridge box, and what's left of the briefcase is right beside it in a plastic bag. William is relieved, but he isn't sure how to interpret the data, which neither exonerates nor incriminates Lothrup.

Minutes later, two policemen arrive and introduce themselves as Officers Lewis and Klein. Klein is carrying a small aluminum suitcase, which he sets down in the living room, and Lewis, the officer in charge, is carrying an old laptop with a *Protect and Serve* decal on it.

Lewis gets right to the point. "Mr. Kessler, can you tell us where the burglar gained entrance? That's the first thing we need to know in order to process the crime scene."

"He came in through the service door to the garage," William says, "and from there he got into the kitchen."

"I'll take a look," Klein says. "Can you show me that part of the house, sir?"

William escorts him through the house to the kitchen, then returns to the living room, where Officer Lewis is typing on his laptop. "What's your full name, sir?" He types for a few more moments and then asks William several questions about the contents of the house, what time he and Amy got home from obedience class, and if they had seen anyone suspicious hanging around the neighborhood.

The dogs, who were upset from the moment they walked into the house, can now see Officer Klein in the kitchen, and they both start barking. Amy excuses herself and goes outside to quiet them down.

When Klein returns from the garage, he says, "Both locks were picked. Weird, huh?"

Lewis nods. "Very weird."

"I'm gonna see what shows up under UVL." Klein sets the aluminum suitcase on the coffee table, opens it and removes a camera and something that looks like a blue flashlight, which he attaches to the camera and turns on. "I'll start at the front," he says.

"Remember to check the light switches."

"Yep."

William has been waiting to ask a question. "So what's weird about the locks being picked?"

Lewis pulls a handkerchief from his pocket and wipes his glasses. "Maybe nothing. But picking locks is a lot harder than it looks on TV. Your average meth head wouldn't know how to do it."

Amy, who has just returned from placating the dogs, sits down next to William. "Is that who you think it was—meth addicts?"

"There's a lot of 'em around, ma'am," Lewis says, "but at this point, it's hard to say." He turns to William. "That reminds me—did you check your medicine cabinet?"

"Yes. Nothing was missing. Are you going to dust for fingerprints?"

Lewis shakes his head. "Probably not. We wouldn't call for a forensic team unless someone was injured or at least five thousand dollars' worth of property was stolen." Then he relents. "Of course … if we had really good fingerprints, that might change things." Lewis turns and hollers to his partner, who is in the front hallway. "Are you seeing any prints with the ultraviolet?"

"A few," Klein hollers back. "But I'm guessing they're the family's. Mostly what I'm seeing are a lot of smudges, like the bad guy was wearing gloves."

Lewis shakes his head. "I'm sorry, Mr. Kessler, but this probably won't end well. There are approximately eleven thousand homes in Chambliss proper, and we have about a hundred burglaries a year. So the odds of your home ending up on that list are less than one in a hundred, which is considerably better than the national average. But here's the problem—we only apprehend 14 percent of the perps, so ..."

And suddenly, William understands home burglary and the bleak arithmetic of justice in a whole new way—as a purely quantum phenomenon. Your average burglary wasn't the act of addicts with rotten teeth and nothing to live for. It was the logical outgrowth of arithmetical imperatives seeking to assert themselves. Being burglarized in Chambliss was approximately a hundred-year event because it had about a 1 percent chance of happening. As for the burglars themselves, roughly fourteen in a given year would be apprehended; eighty-six would not. So the odds ran seven to one in their favor. That was the universe at work—random but perfect.

Amy shakes his arm. "William, are you listening? Officer Lewis is talking to you."

"I'm sorry," William says. "I was just thinking about something."

"I understand," Lewis says. "A home invasion is quite a shock to the system. I was saying that the locks being picked and the likelihood that whoever did this was wearing gloves make the job look professional. But then ..."

"But then what?" William asks.

Lewis shrugs. "No professional would break in here."

"Why not?"

"This isn't exactly a target-rich environment, Mr. Kessler. You told me yourself that you have no guns, stereo equipment, cash or expensive electronics. That makes you the winner tonight. You were lucky."

At that moment there is commotion in the front hallway, and William can hear Kate's angry voice stepping all over Officer Klein's.

"I *told* you, Officer—I am Kate Benedict. This is my father's home, and I demand to see him."

"I understand, ma'am, but this is a crime scene. If you would just—"

"I'll thank you to get out of my way!"

William leaps to his feet. "Amy, you're about to meet my daughter. Strap in."

He heads to the front door with Lewis right behind him, and when Kate sees William, she runs to him and gives him a hug.

"Daddy, are you all right? Why are the police here?"

"I'm fine, sweetheart. There was a break-in, but everything's okay. Amy and I came here from obedience class, and this is what we walked into." He indicates the debris field with a wave of his hand. "Nice, huh?" William then turns to Klein and Lewis. "It's okay, officers—this is my daughter, Kate."

"Nice to meet you, ma'am," Lewis says. "We're gonna finish up and head back to the station, Mr. Kessler. We won't be long." And with that, both policemen head down the hallway toward the bedrooms.

"So ... Amy is here?" Kate asks.

"She's in the living room. I'll introduce you."

Kate smooths her hair. "I wasn't really expecting—"

"It'll be fine. C'mon."

Amy stands when the two of them walk in.

"Amy, this is my daughter, Kate. Kate, meet my friend Amy."

Amy smiles and extends her hand, which Kate shakes eagerly.

"I'm so glad to meet you," Kate says. "My father speaks of nothing but you."

"It's a pleasure to meet you too," Amy says. "What kinds of things does he say, your father?"

"Oh ... that you're smart, funny and ... and an excellent fisherman."

Amy laughs. "I think that last item might be the most important."

Kate looks around the room. "You've certainly had some excitement here tonight."

"Unfortunately, yes," Amy says.

Kate turns to her father. "Should we start putting this place back together? Are the police done?"

"I think they're done in this part of the house, but Amy and I can handle it. What brings you by? Is anything wrong?"

"No, I just wanted to stop after my class tonight and drop off that box with Baron's food and toys in it that Todd forgot to give you yesterday. But when I saw the police car in your driveway, I forgot all about it—it's still in the back seat."

"Thanks for bringing it over, sweetheart. That was very thoughtful. What class are you taking?"

"I'm not *taking* a class. I teach a class on Wednesdays—that's our church night. It's called 'How to Live a Christian Life through the Book of James.'"

"Love the title," William says. "And James—now there's a guy who could write a letter!"

Kate smiles and turns to Amy. "My father is a nonbeliever."

"Yes, I know," Amy says.

"And like most nonbelievers—let's just call them atheists—he thinks church and religion are a waste of time."

Amy nods. "I've sensed that."

"And yet, for an atheist, my father is a very moral person. That has always puzzled me."

"I prefer the term *rationalist*," William says. "And you know I can hear you, right?"

"Hearing and listening aren't the same, Daddy. Look, I'm going to call Todd and tell him where I am. Then I think we should get this place cleaned up." Kate begins singing "The Clean Up Song," and Amy laughs.

"That's one of the few songs I know the words to," Amy says.

"Well, when you have young children, you learn it in a hurry," Kate says. "I think if we split up we can get more accomplished."

William quickly discovers that "split up" means Kate and Amy will work together in one part of the house while he works alone in another. William knows that Kate is not about to miss an opportunity to wring everything she can from Amy about their relationship. But he doesn't mind. Amy can take care of herself. And perhaps this way Kate won't have to ask him so many questions.

Before the officers leave, Klein takes some photographs, and Lewis talks to William again.

"Mr. Kessler, we think whoever broke in here might have been looking for something. Does that make any sense to you?"

William plays dumb. "Not really. It's not like I have drugs or diamonds secreted away someplace. Maybe they got the wrong house."

"Could be. Or maybe something scared them off before they really got started. Of course, the only way we'll ever know is if we apprehend them." Lewis hands William his card. "We'll be in touch. Call this number if you have any questions. Good night, sir."

"Good night," William says.

By midnight, the house is back together and things are, for the most part, where they belong. There are a few broken items— mostly picture frames that were swept from shelves—but other than that, there is very little damage.

"I think that about does it," Kate says, looking around. "I'd say you were lucky."

"You and Officer Lewis," William says. "I sure don't feel lucky."

"I know, but it could have been worse."

"Spoken like a true Minnesotan," William says. "Thanks for helping with the clean-up. I really appreciate it."

"Glad to do it." Kate turns to Amy. "And in spite of the circumstances, I'm delighted we had the chance to meet."

"So am I," Amy says. "It was a pleasure working with you."

Kate laughs. "Okay, I'm going home. Amy, I parked behind you, but I'll be out of your way in a minute."

"It's not a problem," Amy says. "I'm staying, actually."

"Oh … yes, yes, of course," Kate says, clearly embarrassed. She hugs her father, shakes Amy's hand and leaves, only to return moments later with the box of dog toys. "Here's the stuff that I—"

"Yes," William says. "Thank you."

Kate leaves again, only this time she doesn't come back.

William and Amy look at each other.

"This has been one helluva night," Amy says. "We should let the dogs in."

William nods. "I'll get them. How about a drink?"

"I'd love one. Your daughter is very nice, very … take-charge."

"It's okay to say *bossy*. She gets that from her mother."

Amy laughs. "I really do like her, even though she didn't trust me with the vacuum cleaner."

"I like her too—most of the time."

William lets the dogs in and pours a brandy for Amy and another for himself, which they drink in the living room with the dogs stretched out at their feet. Amy wonders if they should spend the night at her house, but it's late, and they're both too tired to go anywhere, except to bed. But once they do, neither of them is able to sleep. Amy hears phantom burglars tiptoeing through the house all night long, and William is kept awake by the thought that his employer might be behind the break-in.

More than anything, he would like to barge into Sam's office and say, "Hey, buddy, what do you know about the burglary at my home?" And a few weeks ago, he might have done it. But in this instance, William feels that discretion is definitely the better part of valor. Besides, Sam would just deny everything. He'd give William the administrative stiff-arm and stare at him with that you-must-be-nuts look on his face. And Sam would have the high ground because there isn't a shred of evidence suggesting that Lothrop had anything to do with the break-in. In fact, on its face the idea is flatly ridiculous, totally unfounded. But even so ...

It's almost three in the morning before he and Amy fall asleep. William dreams about the shooting, something he hasn't done in a while, and his dream begins at the point where the student is running down the hallway, and the shooter—half man, half mirage—begins firing from the top of the stairs. The instant that happens, William stops dead in his tracks, and the student, blood spurting from his throat, struggles desperately to stay on his feet. After stumbling a few yards, past Jon and the janitors' closet, he grabs hold of the drinking fountain with both hands but can't hang on. As he goes down, he takes a little half step and collapses at William's feet. The boy is dead—half his throat and neck are gone—but William finds it hard not to look at his face—the astonished eyes, the mouth half open, as if he were about to ask what he has done that he should be brutally murdered on his way to class.

The shooter, who had lowered his weapon for a moment, resumes firing, and the bullets, skipping off the floor and walls, shriek down the hallway.

"Get out of there! Come to me!" Jon shouts.

William knows full well what he needs to do, but his body is no longer taking orders from his brain. William is immobilized so perfectly, so completely, it's as though he's frozen solid. And yet, strangely, he feels no panic or fear. His survival instinct gone, William dissociates, shuts down and prepares to die.

"What are you doing? Run, for Christ's sake!"

CHAPTER 22

A Parliament of Owls

SOON AFTER JON YELLS at him to run, the dream is over and William awakens. He can just make out the gray silhouettes of trees through the window and guesses it's a little before five, almost first light. It is suspiciously quiet on Amy's side of the bed.

"You awake?" he asks.

"Of course I'm awake. Burglaries are hardly conducive to sound sleep, William. Were you dreaming?"

"Yes, but it was more like … reliving. Did I say anything?"

"Nothing I could understand. Should we get up?"

"Might as well."

They go to the kitchen, put the dogs out and have coffee.

"I won't be able to see you tonight," Amy says. "Did I tell you that?"

"I don't think so. Is tonight the dinner meeting?"

"No, that's on the twenty-first. Tonight is Family Night at school. It's our last one of the year, and Wild & Free in Garrison is coming. They came two years ago and made an incredible presentation. Did you know that a bear's sense of smell is a hundred times better than ours?"

"No."

"I didn't think so. Anyway, I have to be at school tonight."

"Okay. Baron and I will just have to muddle along without you. More coffee?"

"Yes, thanks. For once we have time for a second cup."

William acknowledges that they have a little more time than usual, but in forty-five minutes, Amy is once again on her way home, and William is in the shower, wondering what the crazy quantum universe has in store for him today.

When he gets to the office, William looks at the *Beacon*, and sees that *Light It Up* has put its petition in the Opinion section: "We, the undersigned, urge Chancellor Gardner, the Board of Regents and the administration of Lothrup College to make our campus brighter and safer by installing LED lighting in the eleven locations indicated below." Beneath the letter is a small map of the college with eleven little light bulbs placed in the darkest areas of the campus, which are ranked from *dark* to *very dark*. *Light It Up* concludes by imploring students and staff to sign their petition before the June Board of Regents meeting. William wonders how many signatures they have and interprets the fact that they didn't say as a bad sign.

"You're not going to win a pissing contest with Herb Gardner," he says aloud.

Since there is nothing else in the paper that catches William's eye, he has little choice but to work on the book. He feels that he has satisfactorily established the interdependence of guilt, pain, love and redemption in Dostoevsky's work. But guilt is a difficult term in the study of Dostoevsky because there is more than one kind of it. Guilt is the feverish emotional turmoil of a character like Raskolnikov, but there is another kind of guilt, a less spectacular variety, that is the collective lot of humanity—the kind of guilt Father Zosima talks about in *The Brothers Karamazov*. We are all our brothers' keepers, he says. Everyone is guilty for everyone else, and this guilt lays the foundation for a special kind of brotherhood that transcends temporal relationships.

William recalls that Dostoevsky wrote something similar in *The Possessed*: "Each man sins against all, and each man is at least partly guilty for another's sin." This makes perfect sense to William, but he wonders why the idea resonated so well with Russians, who even had a name for it—*sobornost*, a cultural meme promoting unity and cooperation.

By any name, the idea of kinship and spiritual comity was attractive, but it certainly didn't take hold in New England when the Unitarians floated it, not even when heavy hitters like Ralph Waldo Emerson and Theodore Parker got on board. After a good deal of reading and thinking, William decides *the brotherhood of man* found such fertile ground in Russia because the idea of mankind as *family* is a habit of Russian thought, if not an actual archetype. This has never been the case in the United States.

"Okay," William says out loud. "I get it—I really do. But am I going to need advanced degrees in Russian philosophy, sociology and history just to figure this guy out?"

Baron, upon hearing both a question and the word *out*, stands up and stretches in anticipation of a walk.

"Hang on, Hürtgenvoss—that isn't what I said. I was talking about Dostoevsky."

The desk phone rings, and William picks up and says hello without even thinking about who might be on the other end of it—something unusual for him.

"Dr. Kessler? *William* Kessler?"

"Yes," William says. "What can I ... Bouchard, is that *you?*"

"Yes. I was just wondering if—"

"Christ, I thought I blocked all your phone numbers."

"You did. I'm on my wife's cell phone."

"What the hell do you want?"

"I just wondered how you were doing."

"Bullshit! You just wondered if there was anything left of my life that you could lay waste to."

"Dr. Kessler, did I ever write one word about you that wasn't true?"

"That's not the point," William says angrily. "You exploited my pain and misfortune because you thought it would sell newspapers. And your unstated goal was to make me look as crazy as possible."

"If that's the way you feel, Dr. Kessler, then this is your lucky day. I want to do a retrospective—a lookback at what's happened to you in the last two years, and it would be your opportunity to set the record straight, to say anything you want."

"Bouchard, don't you have anything better to do? I thought you were out in Williston covering the more lurid aspects of the North

Dakota oil boom. What was the name of that series—*Welcome to the Dark Side?*"

Bouchard laughs. "It was called *Dark Side of the Boom.* Did you read it?"

"No, but from what I hear, nobody is better than you when it comes to writing about sex, drugs and the seamy side of everything. I'll bet you did the same thing to Williston that you did to me."

"That isn't fair, Dr. Kessler. I thought Williston was a good story, just like I thought you were a good story. You were a national hero, and then ..."

"And then I had a breakdown that you feasted on for weeks."

Bouchard takes a deep breath. "I really didn't want to relitigate the past. I was hoping we might—"

"Look, Bouchard, there is no *we.* Please stop calling me—I've got nothing for you." William hangs up and looks at Baron. "Can you believe that guy?"

William leans back and puts his feet up on his desk, but this morning he doesn't think about the shooting or try to remember the locations of all the victims. Instead, he thinks about the strange break-in and continues to wonder if Lothrup has anything to do with it. But he doesn't get very far with his thoughts because there is a knock on the door, and a young man walks in. William is positive he knows him, and when the young man calls Baron by name, it all comes back to him.

"Jared Harding," William says, "the prelaw transfer student from Mankato State. How have you been?"

Jared smiles. "I've been good. And you?"

"Can't complain. Whatever happened with those transfer credits?"

"That's why I'm here, Dr. Kessler. All six credits were approved. I wanted to thank you for your help."

"Oh, that's great, Jared. Six credits is a lot of money."

"And time," Jared says. "I got an email from Dean Richter that said the two of you discussed the matter and made a recommendation to the registrar that the credits be approved. Fortunately, the TRC agreed with you, so—"

"Excuse me. Who is the TRC?"

"The Transcript Review Committee."

"Ah, yes, of course." William marvels at the level of bureaucracy that exists even within the comparatively benign Office of the Registrar. "I'm happy things worked out for you."

"Me too. Thanks again, Dr. Kessler."

After Jared leaves, William returns to the book and tries to explain how *sobornost*, like Dostoevsky's work and philosophy, can be both secular and Eastern Orthodox at the same time. The entire exercise is becoming intellectually light-footed and almost test-tubey, when William is saved from himself by another knock on the door. This time, it is a student in a motorized wheelchair. William has never seen him before.

"Dr. Kessler, I'm Adam Kozinski. You don't know me, and you're not my advisor or anything, but I'm graduating on Saturday because of you." Adam motors up to William's desk to shake hands, and Baron checks him out—hands, feet, wheelchair. Adam pets Baron and smiles. "Nice dog, Dr. Kessler."

"Yes ... thank you." William is puzzled. "Adam, if we don't know each other, why would you credit me with—"

"Oh, I know *you*, sir. You just don't know *me*. I was in the lecture hall two years ago when you killed the first shooter, the one who left and came back. I'm sure I'd be dead if you hadn't done what you did. I think a lot of us would."

William has heard this sort of thing a lot, but he's never been convinced. The way he sees it, what happened at Dewhurst had more to do with the second shooter than it did with him. That's because when William chased the first shooter back downstairs and into the lecture hall, his buddy had panicked and run out of the building. That's what stopped the slaughter at Dewhurst. At the time, William didn't know what happened to the second shooter, but he had jumped on his motorcycle and taken off for the far end of the campus, where he found Amanda Norris in front of the bookstore. After that, he made his way to Wellstone Hall, where he was killed by police in a gun battle after shooting the SWAT officer.

"Your last name is Kozinski?" William asks.

"Yes, sir."

"And you were one of Rupert Martin's students?"

Adam laughs. "Yes, I was a lucky student but not a very good one. I took a bullet in the spine that day and lost the use of my legs, but otherwise, I'm okay ... mostly." Adam clasps his hands in his lap. "You know, you hear a lot about the fifty-seven people who were killed, but there were forty-one others who were seriously injured and fourteen who spent more than a month in the hospital. They never got talked about much."

"You're right," William says, feeling guilty.

"And the worst part is that most of them were like me—trying to get better and fighting with their insurance companies at the same time. A lot of us had to open GoFundMe accounts, but that's no substitute for decent health insurance."

"But now that we have Obamacare ..."

"Yes, but Obamacare wasn't signed into law until a week *after* the shooting, and its provisions are still being phased in. That will go on until 2014, and it makes things impossible to figure out. And of course the insurance companies still get to decide what they're gonna cover and how much they're willing to pay—and it's never enough." Adam touches his thumb to his chest. "In my case, unless something changes, my parents and I will be paying off medical bills for the rest of our lives. And if you need a lot of PT or lifetime care, good luck getting it." Adam is frowning, and the sadness on his face seems all wrong, as if it doesn't belong there. "I'm sorry, Dr. Kessler. I didn't come here to talk about this stuff."

"It's okay. I just wish there was something I could do."

"There is," Adam says. "Be careful who you vote for." Adam is quiet for a moment, but soon his cheerful affect returns, and he's smiling again. "You want to hear a funny story? I was on academic probation in March of 2010. I was flunking Intro to Lit and Western Civ, and then ... the shooting changed everything."

"That's hardly surprising, Adam. A trauma like that can cause a person to reflect, to reexamine his goals."

Adam chuckles. "I'm sure you're right, Dr. Kessler, but that isn't what I mean. I was literally flunking out, and then my grades came when I was in the hospital, and somehow I got a B in Intro to Lit. That was completely insane, but it raised my GPA enough to get me another semester of probation. After that, I never looked back, and I've been an A-student ever since. I'll never know how I got that B, but it felt like it was supposed to happen."

"Maybe it was." William smiles, and for a moment he considers telling Adam that he was the one who had entered Rupert Martin's grades. But he likes the story the way it is—occult with a dash of quantum weirdness. Besides, if Adam Kozinski wants to believe there is a benevolent force in the universe that can sunder the linkage between academic performance and grades, then more power to him.

"In any case," Adam says, "things worked out well for me."

"It appears they did," William says. "What I enjoy about your story is the fact that when you got a second chance, you took advantage of it."

"That's true—I did. I've been accepted into the MBA program at Northwestern, and I have a fellowship that will pay for almost all of it."

"Go Wildcats!" William says. "I know you'll make us proud."

"I'll try, sir. Anyway … thanks for saving my life." They shake hands again, and Adam grasps the joystick on his wheelchair and heads for the door. Then he stops suddenly and spins the chair around. "I'm sorry about your son and all the things that happened to you."

William nods. "Me too, Adam. Thank you."

Adam leaves and William can hear his wheelchair whirring down the hallway in the direction of Sinclair Lewis and the elevator.

William thinks about what Adam had said, especially about health insurance. It was unconscionable that people had to fight for their lives while doing simultaneous battle with their insurance companies, but that was tragically commonplace these days. There are a great many things that William knows more about than health insurance—he barely understands his own policy. But when he hears problems like the ones Adam described, he can see the wisdom of universal coverage, which in the argot of American health care, usually translates as Medicare for all or, as it is sometimes called, single payer. For Adam Kozinski, it makes sense.

The problem with single payer is that it would end the health care system as we know it, which many people, including William, believe would be a bridge too far, at least right now. William would like to address all this in a letter, but he can't figure out who to send it to. Sending it to a Republican lawmaker like Mitch McConnell would be pointless, but sending it to someone like Chuck Schumer or Nancy Pelosi isn't the answer either—that would be a classic case of preaching to the choir. For a minute or two, William considers a collective audience, like the Senate Republican Caucus, but it's hard to write letters to groups. It's much better if he can see one face, a single visage on which to focus his thoughts. William is about to give up on the letter altogether, when he thinks of Marcia's half-brother, an ultra-conservative he and Marcia used to call "alt-right Dwight."

Dwight was a true believer and the bane of every family gathering he had ever attended. With the veins bulging in his neck, he would browbeat everyone around him, particularly the more liberal family members, with endless trickle-down bullshit gleaned from Breitbart News, Rush Limbaugh and the Drudge Report. Once, during an angry philippic against Obamacare, Dwight had told everyone at the table that people who couldn't afford health care didn't deserve to have it. William had been furious, and it is this remark that he remembers now, as he sits before his computer, thinking about Adam Kozinski.

"Congratulations, Dwight," William says. "You're exactly what I'm looking for."

William goes online for some facts and figures; then he writes the letter.

17 May 2012

Dear Dwight:

As of this writing, congressional Republicans have voted thirty-two times to repeal the Affordable Care Act. They will vote again in July, and should they succeed, as many as seventeen million Americans will lose their health insurance. Someone needs to explain to me how this outcome represents an ennobling goal for Republican lawmakers. And while they're at it, perhaps they could explain why the Party of Lincoln is so eager to return us to a time when insurance companies could deny coverage on the basis of preexisting conditions.

Dwight, I know you have all kinds of objections to the ACA, but you have to admit that our present system isn't getting the job done. The World Health Organization ranks the United States health care system 37th in the world. We are also 49th in life expectancy and 178th in infant mortality. What's worse, we spend 18 percent of our GDP to achieve these disappointing outcomes—nearly twice as much as the countries whose health care systems are consistently ranked above our own.

But despite all this, I agree with you that forcing 175 million Americans to give up their private health insurance (at an estimated cost to our government of three trillion dollars a year) is a bad idea. And like you, I'm not comfortable putting the two million Americans who work for our health insurance industry out of work. Plus, does anyone really understand the financial implications of destroying a $600 billion industry that accounts for almost 3 percent of the S&P Composite 1500? I think not.

So I'm wondering if perhaps we could meet in the middle and try a public option again—some kind of government-run health insurance plan that would compete with private health insurance companies and drive down costs.

Dwight, in the unlikely event that we find ourselves seated around the same table at Thanksgiving again, I would be interested to know what you think.

Sincerely,

William Kessler

William reads the letter over a couple of times and shakes his head. "I don't know, Baron. The thing is, the public option never really caught on. It *might* have, if Obama had gotten behind it back in 2010, but he never really did. And that's too bad because the public option could be the perfect stepping stone between private health insurance and Medicare for all—or Medicare for *more*, if that's the direction we decide to go." William thinks about what Dwight might say in response to the letter, and he can practically hear him inveighing against "socialized medicine" and a host of other bogeymen that run the gamut from George Soros to Planned Parenthood.

William sighs and looks down at Baron. "Hey, Hürtgenvoss—you up for a walk?"

Baron is absolutely up for a walk, so the two of them head over to the tennis courts by the education building, where they watch a very good doubles match for a few minutes. Then it's time to return to the office so William can tackle the concept of *sobornost* as it relates to *The Brothers Karamazov*. After an hour and a half of that, William packs up his books and heads home. But once he gets there, he's at a loss as to how he can kill the two hours until dinnertime.

After considering his options, William mows part of the lawn and then takes Baron down to the river, which is as low as William has ever seen it. As they come over the hill, three wood ducks get up from a little pool, but there are no fish to chase. Baron, ever hopeful, walks up and down the bank, double-checking every riffle, and William decides this is as good a time as any to have a Thoreauvian moment, to transcend his personal reality and forget about the supreme court, the jammer and the upcoming hearing. He sits down on his favorite log and does his best to apprehend the Benevolent Oversoul, but there are just enough mosquitos to make that impossible. So after Baron plays with a stick in the shallow water for a while, the two of them head back to the house, with William no more enlightened than before.

It is at times like this that William realizes he really doesn't know what to do with himself without Amy, even for an evening, and soon he's pacing the house in a funk, wandering from room to room like he does. Finally, he turns on the TV and scrolls the options until he finds someone with a plummy accent—but not David Attenborough—narrating a documentary about China's

Three Gorges Dam: *six hundred feet high ... twenty-seven million tons of cement ... ten times more steel than the Golden Gate Bridge.*

"I get it," William says happily. "It's a big sucker." He kicks off his shoes, stretches out on the sofa, and it isn't long before he drifts into a skitzy, dream-filled sleep. First he dreams about fishing; then about Marcia. Finally, he dreams that he's in bed and his alarm clock is ringing, but there's no way to turn it off—no button, no switch, no nothing—so it just keeps ringing.

William awakens with a start. *Five times the size of Hoover Dam ... more than 22,000 megawatts of electricity.* It takes William two or three seconds to clear the cobwebs, and when he does, he realizes it's his cell phone that's ringing, not a phantom alarm clock. He mutes the TV and pulls his phone from his pocket.

"Hello," he says.

"And did you know, my love, that a flock of owls is called a parliament?"

William laughs and tries to wake up. "Hi, Amy. I had no idea. Does that mean a flock of shitbirds is called a House of Representatives?"

"I'm afraid not, but it should. Were you sleeping?"

"Kind of ... Baron and I dozed off in front of the TV."

"We're taking a short break here, so I thought I'd call. I'm sorry I woke you."

"I'm glad you did. Please tell me we're going to do something tomorrow night. I miss you."

"I miss you too. Let's go out to dinner."

"Great," William says. "Where?"

"How about the Lonesome Pine?"

"The place by Bay Lake?"

"Yes—it's worth the drive. The Pine is famous for its pasta—it's *magnifico!*"

William laughs. "Okay, count me in. Where is it, exactly?"

"It's on Katrine Drive, about a mile and a half south of Hansen Sports."

"Oh, I know Hansen's—Jon bought a snowmobile there."

"So did I, way back when. I used to live near Bay Lake—my first teaching job was in Crosby."

"You never told me that. Okay, it's a date. I'll pick you up at six. Will that work?"

"Yes. I'm already looking forward to it."

"Me too," William says. "See you then."

"Wait, wait, don't hang up—did you know that bats are the only mammals that truly fly?"

"No, I didn't. All I know about bats is that the aluminum ones have more contact energy than the wooden ones."

"You're talking baseball, right?"

"I am. See you at six."

And just like that, William's loneliness is gone, his depression has lifted, and he feels whole again. All it took was a two-minute phone call from Amy. William knows he isn't much good without her, but he wonders if that's love or simply emotional dependence. Every day, William is more and more certain that he loves Amy. But the thing is, he's never once doubted that he loves Marcia, and that, of course, is troubling.

William and Baron have dinner, and then, unable to find another documentary, they go to bed early. By eight o'clock the next morning, they're over at the carriage house, setting up scaffolding and preparing to remove the cedar siding from the gable ends.

William, properly recognizing that dogs and falling boards full of nails are an awful combination, finds a piece of rope and ties Baron to an out-of-the-way sapling. Then he gets to work. The demolition—or deconstruction, as William calls it—goes better than he had anticipated, and by one o'clock William has removed all the lap siding from one gable end, which he must now prepare for shake panels.

William looks down at Baron. "Ready for lunch? Let's take a break."

William climbs down from the scaffolding, and the two of them walk over to the house, where Baron has two cups of kibble, and William makes a peanut butter sandwich with the last scrapings of peanut butter.

"You know, Hürtgenvoss, that went really well. I was afraid we might damage the soffit boards, but we never even scratched one.

Are you listening?"

Baron, who has finished his lunch, refuses to look at him, and William knows why.

"Hey, I'm sorry about tying you to a tree, but I didn't want you to get hit by a board. You can understand that, can't you?" Baron gives no indication either way, and William figures Baron will just have to pout until he gets over it.

When they return to the carriage house, the first thing William does is pull the nails out of the discarded cedar siding so that neither he nor Baron will get a nail through the foot. Then he stacks it up out of the way.

"You don't have to be tied up anymore, Baron, but stay attentive—this is still a construction site." William looks around at the various piles of discarded building material—siding, sheetrock and flooring. "And please remind me to call somebody about getting a roll-off out here. The detritus is piling up fast."

William studies the now-naked gable end and notices that the topmost piece of eight-inch siding extends a good three inches above the wall line. So using a cordless circular saw that Jon had given him for Christmas several years ago, he rips the top board to a width of five inches, which, as luck would have it, also eliminates the nail holes.

When he's finished with that, William nails a five-quarter cedar band board on top of the downsized piece of siding, adds a drip cap, and he's close to putting up the first shake panel. But before he does, he has to figure out how to cut the angle where the panels meet the soffit. The answer is a template, and after two failed attempts, he cuts a piece of plywood that fits perfectly, one he can use to transfer the soffit angle onto the shake panels. Because he knew he'd be working alone, William had ordered six-foot panels, as opposed to eight, and he's very glad he did. The panels fit together just as they're supposed to, and William didn't need to snap lines to keep things level, but he does it anyway, mostly out of habit.

At five William calls it quits, and he and Baron go home so that William can get ready for his date with Amy. It's been forty-eight hours since they were together, but to William it feels like a year, and he's surprised by how much he needs to see her, to hold her, to talk to her. He's confident that feelings this powerful are significant, but exactly what they mean is an open question.

Baron, who has finally come around, realizes that William is about to leave him for the evening and becomes sullen again.

"C'mon, Baron. You know I'll make it up to you. And if things go well, maybe Yoshi will come over tonight for a sleepover." At the mention of Yoshi, Baron's ears prick up but not for long.

At six o'clock William picks Amy up for dinner, and he has just opened the car door for her when his phone rings. He pulls it out of his pocket and points to the display. "It's Marv. I should take this." Amy nods, and William puts the phone to his ear. "What's up, Marv? I was just thinking we should—Oh, *oh*, I see. How are you, Daniel?" William looks at Amy and mouths the words, *It's Marv's son.* "I assume you got my message. Is your old man staying out of trouble?" Then Danny is talking, and almost immediately, William turns ashen and leans against the car. Amy, who has no idea what's going on, takes William's arm, and when William speaks again, his voice is shaky and tense. *You say the UPS driver found him? Yes, I sent it to him on Wednesday. I agree—very lucky. How long will he be in the hospital? You mean like Michael Jackson slept in? Yes, yes, I understand. Try not to hold it against him, Daniel.* William listens to Danny for another minute and then thanks him for calling. He puts his phone in his pocket and turns to Amy. "Marv tried to kill himself."

"But he's okay?"

"*Okay* is kind of a relative term, but I think so—Danny said the doctors expect him to make a full recovery. Can we ... sit down for a minute?"

"Of course." Amy points to her front porch.

"And could I please have some water?"

"Sure."

William sits down in an Adirondack rocker, and Amy brings him a bottle of water.

"Thank you." William unscrews the cap and takes a sip. "Here's what I know. When Marv was up here for the fishing opener last weekend, he left a very expensive leather jacket in the back seat of the Jeep. On Wednesday I sent it back to him via UPS, and this afternoon, a UPS driver attempting to deliver it heard a car running in Marv's garage. When he checked it out, he found Marv slumped over the wheel of his Beemer. The driver called 911, and an ambulance took Marv to Abbott Northwestern because they have hyperbaric chambers there."

"Hence, the Michael Jackson reference."

"Yeah, I read someplace that he slept in one. Anyway, Marv needs a full series of hyperbaric treatments to purge his system of carbon monoxide, but Danny didn't know how many treatments that is. He also didn't know how long Marv would be in the hospital, but he's in the psychiatric wing right now, and he isn't allowed visitors." William takes another sip of water and looks at Amy. "That's a good thing for me because I wouldn't know what the hell to say to him."

Amy shakes her head. "Do you realize that you saved Marv's life? If you hadn't sent that jacket back to him, the UPS driver wouldn't have been there to hear the car running, and no one would have found Marv or called 911."

This sort of abductive reasoning has become very familiar to William, although it usually involves his role in the shooting and speculation of the sort Adam Kozinski had made about what would or would not have happened if William hadn't done what he did.

The story of the jacket encourages a similar post hoc fallacy, and it's freighted with the same epistemic problems—specifically, creaky causal relationships and flawed premises. In truth, all William did was pay UPS to deliver Marv's jacket. That decision may have culminated in a happy accident, but William knows it didn't have much to do with him. In a way, it had more to do with whoever had given Marv the jacket. If they had given him, say, a set of golf clubs, the outcome would have been entirely different. The jacket episode was simply another instance of quantum chaos at work. It contained no more meaning than a football game, and it was dangerous to read too much into it.

William sighs. "I'm sorry, but I don't feel much like going out tonight. I think I'll just go home."

"I understand," Amy says. "But I'm going with you. I'll get Yoshi and follow you."

"Okay. Thanks."

When they get to William's house, they sit at the picnic table on the patio and talk about Marv while the dogs run around and play.

"Can you be shocked without being surprised?" William asks.

"Of course," Amy says.

"Then that's how I feel. I talked to Marv about taking his meds—at least I tried to. And I was worried about him enough to call his son, but deep down I didn't really think he was going to attempt suicide. Or maybe I did … Hell, I don't know. Marv has fought depression for years. I should have seen this coming."

Amy reaches across the table and touches William's hand. "It isn't your fault."

"I suppose not. It's just that I feel so …"

"Guilty?"

"I do, but I was going to say *scared*. What happened to Marv could happen to me at any moment. It's like Marv is the canary in the coal mine, and I've just been put on notice."

"You're not like him, William."

William makes a face. "I wish I could believe that, but in all the ways that matter, I'm *exactly* like him, and today he got behind the wheel of his car and went to a place it could take him years to return from. There will be inpatient recovery, medical and emotional stabilization and, for a repeat offender like Marv, outpatient maintenance like you can't imagine."

"Well, I wish he hadn't done it," Amy says. "But even more, I wish you wouldn't draw so many inferences from it. You guys may be friends, but Marv is a long way from being your doppelgänger."

"I hope you're right."

"Let's go inside," Amy says. "I'll make you something to eat."

Knowing that he hasn't been to the grocery store in a while, this strikes William as highly improbable. "Like what?"

Amy shrugs. "I don't know yet. It depends on how lucky I get."

They go in, and William sits at the kitchen table while Amy looks through the cupboards.

"I'm not finding much to work with," she says. "There's a jar of Ragu spaghetti sauce. Or I could whip you up an oatmeal sandwich … with olives. What do we have here?" Amy turns a small can around so she can read the label. "Sliced mushrooms—*fancy* sliced mushrooms, to be exact."

"I'll pass," William says. "I need to go to the store."

Amy goes over to the refrigerator. "Maybe I'll have better luck in here."

"I wouldn't bet on it."

Amy opens the refrigerator and looks around. "William, do you know what a use-by date is?"

"It's just one person's opinion, right?"

"Not exactly. Hey, here we go—a salami."

"Technically, that's *finocchiona.*"

"What's that?"

"Italian salami with lots of fennel. It's left over from the fishing opener."

"Okay, it's a start." Amy opens the freezer, digs around for a minute, and then turns to William with a single-serving Tupperware in each hand. "William, in my left hand is beef Stroganoff from October 2010. In my right is chicken cacciatore from …" Amy looks at the handwritten label. "December 2010." She holds them both up. "What's the story?"

William looks away.

"These labels are written in a woman's hand. Did Marcia make this stuff? Is that why you won't throw it away?"

William shakes his head. "I just forgot it was in there—honest! Let's get rid of it."

"Not a chance." Amy places the two containers back in the freezer and closes the door. "Listen, William … we've been over this before, and nothing has changed. If you want to carry a torch for a woman who doesn't love you anymore, be my guest. But don't lie to me."

"I'm not. I'm—I'm incapable of lying. You said so yourself."

Amy's voice softens. "Look, I realize that losing Marcia has been hard on you, and I accept that you loved her first. All I ask is that you love me *now.* If you can't do that, you need to tell me."

William looks at her. "Amy, I do love you, and I'm very sorry about this. I don't know why I kept that stuff. Please don't exaggerate its significance. I rarely know why I do things. I just … *do* them."

Amy nods. "Lame though it is, I will accept that explanation for the moment."

"Good. Thank you. Now, if you would please look in that tall glass container by the toaster—"

"You don't have a toaster. It was stolen, remember?"

"Then please look in the tall glass container that's not far from where the toaster used to be. There's something in it that you need."

Amy walks over to the counter and laughs. "Of course ... spaghetti. That's what I was looking for, and I didn't even know it. Do you have any red wine?"

"Yes, in the basement. I'll be right back."

William goes downstairs and quickly returns with a bottle of barbera. Amy cuts up the *finocchiona*, adding it, along with the olives and mushrooms, to the spaghetti sauce, and twenty minutes later, they're eating spaghetti and drinking a surprisingly good wine.

"This is terrific, Amy. It reminds me of that reality cooking show where the contestants have to make meals out of weird ingredients."

"Really? It reminds me of college."

William holds up his glass. "To Marv's better health."

"And to UPS," Amy says, touching her glass to his. "When do you think you'll be able to see him?"

"I don't know, but tomorrow morning I'm going to call Abbott and see if I can find out a little more about what's going on." William winds some spaghetti around his fork. "By the way, tomorrow is graduation, and I'm expected to be there. Would you like to go with me?"

"I would, William, but there's less food in my house than there is in yours, and I need a new suit for the dinner meeting on Monday. After that, I've got a million errands that—"

"Okay, okay—you're excused, but only if I can see you tomorrow night."

"We'll work something out. Are you feeling better now?"

William doesn't know how to answer. He's okay until he thinks about how much pain Marv must have been in to walk into his garage, start his car and close his eyes for what he clearly hoped was forever. And he's okay until he thinks about the probability that *he* will do something crazy and end up, once again, in the clutches of those perfidious forces he has fought so hard to escape.

"I don't know how I feel, Amy. I guess I feel like Michael Corleone—*just when I thought I was out, they pull me back in.*"

"You're going to be okay, William. I won't let anything happen to you."

William nods. Then he begins to cry, tears coursing down both cheeks.

Amy gets up and puts her arms around him. "Hey … I mean it. I'm here, and everything is going to be okay."

CHAPTER 23

Section 37

THAT NIGHT NEITHER William nor Amy sleeps much, and William gets up early.

"Where are you going?" Amy asks.

"I'm gonna call the hospital."

She looks at the clock. "At five o'clock in the morning?"

"A psych ward never sleeps, Amy. This is actually a good time."

"If you say so. Please come back and tell me what they said."

"I will."

William lets the dogs out, makes coffee and takes a cup to his office, where he calls the main number for Abbott Northwestern Hospital. "Gotta start someplace," he mumbles. When he asks the receptionist for the phone number of the psych ward, she points out, rather brusquely, that it's referred to as the Mental Health Unit—MHU for short.

"My apologies," William says. "Could you please connect me or give me the phone number?"

Without saying a word, she connects him to the charge nurse in the MHU, who is remarkably chipper for five in the morning, especially compared to the receptionist. She tells William that she is not permitted to discuss Marv's condition with anyone but family members, adding that it's all very frustrating because she has not yet been given a list of who they are. William sympathizes, explaining that he is Marv's brother from Seattle, and she immediately updates him on Marv's condition. William asks a couple of questions, thanks her for the information and returns to the bedroom.

"Are you asleep?"

Amy rolls over and looks at him. "No, what did you find out?"

"It's good news," William says. "Marv is stable and doing pretty well. He's talking and eating, but they're going to keep him five days for a full series of hyperbaric treatments. When I asked what a hyperbaric treatment is, the nurse said they put Marv in a big test tube—my word, not hers—and pump pressurized oxygen into it to get rid of the carbon monoxide in Marv's blood. Depending on his hemoglobin levels, he'll get one or two treatments a day for five days. Then, unless he has out-of-this-world insurance, I'm guessing they'll turf him out."

"You're right," Amy says. "It sounds encouraging."

"Yes, but that's his *physical* condition. I'm just as concerned about his head."

"I know, but for now, let's take good news where we find it. When can you see him?"

"Not for a while. I can call him on Monday, but he can't have visitors until Thursday—he's still under suicide watch."

Because it's Saturday, Amy is able to stay a little longer, but by eight o'clock, she's on her way home, and William has turned on the TV and is half listening to a news story about what actually happened on the night George Zimmerman shot Trayvon Martin— this according to Trayvon's girlfriend, who was on the phone with him at the time. Like everyone else in America, William has been supersaturated with coverage of the Trayvon Martin shooting. But what he can't understand is the media's tendency to reduce the event to a binary equation, a sort of morality play involving a good guy, a bad guy and a chorus of empaneled pundits. To William's mind, it isn't that simple—it is an impossibly sad story about a wannabe gangbanger who meets a wannabe cop in a quantum world of unforgiving probabilities.

"Baron, I think the whole kerfricken mess could have been avoided if Mr. Zimmerman had stayed in his car like he was told."

William's cell phone rings, and it's Kate.

"Hi," she says. "Have you heard anything from Lewis and Clark? Do they have any leads? Have they found any of your stuff?"

"It's Lewis and *Klein*, and no, I haven't heard anything. I'll give them a call next week." William clears his throat. "I got some bad news yesterday—Marv attempted suicide again."

"Oh, no! Is he ... okay?"

"I guess so." And William goes through the entire story, starting with Marv's leather jacket and ending with hyperbaric therapy. Kate is practically speechless—but not quite.

"If that isn't divine intervention, I don't know what is."

"What do you mean?" William asks, knowing he'll regret it.

"I mean the UPS driver didn't show up at Marv's house at that exact moment by accident. What we're witnessing is God's will, plain and simple."

"But Kate ... that hypothesis isn't really necessary. The sequence of events is the same with or without it. It's like Pierre-Simon Laplace said to Napoleon—"

"Daddy, please don't do that smug professor thing. If you can't see God's hand in this, then you're just not looking."

"Maybe not," William says, hoping to change the subject. "Are you going to graduation today?"

"Yes. At three o'clock. I sort of have to ... Hey, you want to go?"

"I can't. Todd and I will be at a soccer tournament in Detroit Lakes."

"Oh. Okay. Have fun."

"You too. Gotta go. We'll talk later."

The first thing on William's list is to replace the stolen toaster and TV, so he and Baron make a quick run to Walmart, where he purchases both items and is home again in an hour and a half. He could have made the trip even faster, but traffic is bad because it's the second Saturday of fishing season, in addition to being Lothrup's graduation day.

Lothrup's commencement activities haven't changed much over the years. It's a busy week filled with departmental receptions, teas and brunches that culminates with the commencement ceremony itself, which in fair weather, like today, is always held on the commons. The English Department's reception for graduates and their families had been from ten to one o'clock at Dewhurst, but William knows his department didn't really want him there. For one thing, he's still a distraction, and for another, he's not even teaching this semester. So William doesn't feel at all bad about skipping this event and using the time to pull the cedar siding off the other gable end of the carriage house. The job goes smoothly, except for a small tear in the Tyvek that happens when his pry bar slips. William doesn't have time to fix it and decides to let it go until he installs the cedar shake panels.

At two fifteen, William puts Baron in the backyard, apologizes, and heads for campus, which is a bit of a zoo, with drivers honking their horns and throngs of happy pedestrians making their way to the commons for commencement. Directly across the main aisle from Lothrup's 589 graduating seniors is a designated area for faculty, and William sits with two young professors he'd met in February when he was serving on the Student/Faculty Relations Committee, the group that had lowered parking fees.

The commencement addresses are lofty and filled with the usual palaver. William wishes that the speakers, instead of telling Lothrup's graduates to dream big and reach for the stars, would offer them more practical advice, such as contributing to their 401(k) right from the start, resisting the urge to run out and buy a new car, learning to cook five simple meals (spaghetti doesn't count), and perhaps most important, paying off their credit card balance every month. Of all the addresses, William thinks Gardner's is the worst, although it would've made an excellent drinking game, had the audience been required to take a sip every time he said *my friends—You are the future, my friends. Do not be afraid to fail, my friends. The world is yours, my friends.* Much to William's relief, and no doubt to everyone else's on the Commencement Committee, Clifford Wicks (*The News at Six*) delivers a good address—homespun and anecdotal, yet substantive enough to pass muster.

The three most interesting speeches, none of them more than five minutes long, are those given by parents of students who were killed in the shooting—students who, had they lived, would have received diplomas today. The best of these is given by a man named Gust Nelson, who happens to be the father of Leah Nelson, the *Wuthering Heights* enthusiast from William's Victorian novel class. Mr. Nelson's remarks are heartfelt and deeply moving, but as William listens, he wonders why Lothrup would allow one of the litigants who had sued them to speak at graduation. There had to be an angle, and William decides they probably liked the no-hard-feelings optics of it.

The valediction is short and sweet—one part inspiration and two parts playfulness. But the poor girl who delivers it never gets the microphone quite right, and it is often hard to hear her. She concludes her remarks by pointing out the inestimable value of persistence. Abraham Lincoln, she says, lost eight elections before becoming president. Michael Jordan failed to make his high school basketball team. And Oprah Winfrey struggled for years as a journalist before finding her niche as a talk show host. "So we must never give up," she proclaims, her tiny voice rising as best it can.

Once she takes her seat, the diplomas are awarded, and William is surprised by how everyone remembers the students who were wounded during the shooting. These graduates, Adam Kozinski among them, receive standing ovations, and Adam, to the delight of the crowd, pops a wheelie when his name is called, zipping over to Chancellor Gardner with his hand raised in a V-for-victory salute.

After the diplomas, Gardner delivers the closing remarks, and when he's finished, the air is instantly filled with mortarboards and the lively strains of Alfred Reed's "The Crowning Glory," which is performed with fierce determination by Lothrup's junior varsity brass ensemble. William thinks someone should have told them about the *ma*, because as he listens, it's painfully clear that the promissory intervals between the notes are filled with neither beauty nor potential. Instead, each one is a musical no-man's-land, a piece of contested terrain between unappeased, warring tones. But William gives the JV quintet high marks for effort, and Reed's piece, even imperfectly performed, is a fitting finale for the commencement ceremony.

William says goodbye to his seatmates and wanders into the crush of graduates and their families. He takes a few minutes to speak with former students who want hugs, handshakes and photographs, and in the middle of the madding crowd, William runs into Janice Grant and her husband, so he visits with them for a minute. He's about to head back to his car, which is parked behind Dewhurst, when he hears his name and turns around.

"Dr. Kessler, I'm Gust Nelson."

"Yes, of course," William says, shaking his hand. "Your remarks were very powerful, and … I'm sorry for your loss. Leah was a student of mine in 2009."

Mr. Nelson nods. "I know. And I also know about your son, Dr. Kessler. I wish it hadn't happened. I wish *none* of it had happened."

"You and me both, Mr. Nelson."

"Leah spoke so highly of you that I wanted to meet you." Mr. Nelson shifts his weight uneasily from one foot to the other. "I assume you heard about the supreme court, right?"

"Yes," William says. "I was very surprised."

"It seems like this business is gonna drag on forever. I know Leah wouldn't have wanted that."

William nods. "You should know that Leah was one of the finest students I ever had."

"That's what her teachers have said since she was a little girl, but her mother and I … we never got tired of hearing it."

"Are you heading over to the reception?"

Mr. Nelson shakes his head. "I don't think so, Dr. Kessler. I'm alone. My wife couldn't bear to come here, so …"

"Yes, I understand. I'm not going either." Then William has an idea. "Mr. Nelson, would you like to go somewhere and get a beer?"

Mr. Nelson smiles broadly. "I'd love to—but only if I can get you to call me Gust. Mr. Nelson is my cousin—he runs the funeral parlor back home."

"Tell you what—I'll call you Gust if you'll call me William."

Gust laughs. "Deal."

"Good. My car is right over there." William points toward Dewhurst.

When Gust gets into the Wagoneer, he settles into the seat and sighs. "I love these old monsters. What year is it?"

"1991."

"I thought so—360 V8, four-speed tranny, posi-traction. Am I right?"

"You are," William says. "You know your cars."

"I almost bought a Wagoneer years ago, but when you're a logger in Bigfork, Minnesota, a pickup makes a lot more sense."

"Bigfork … yes, I remember Leah mentioning that's where she was from."

"It isn't much of a place, but I make a living there." Gust laughs. "This is funny. We live in the middle of nowhere on a little class-5 road called Buck Scrape Lane. When Leah was a senior in high school, she applied for early admission to Lothrup, and after she filled out the application, she brought it to me and pointed to our address. 'How is a college supposed to take me seriously when I live on *Buck Scrape Lane?*' she said. 'I might as well write *jackpine savage* in the box where I'm supposed to describe myself.'" Gust laughs again. "Leah actually wanted to move for a while after that, but when Lothrup accepted her, she calmed back down."

"Lothrup has a weakness for high school valedictorians," William says, pulling onto the highway. "I think that and Leah's SAT scores trumped her address."

"Yeah, Leah was smart as a whip. By the time she was twelve, she was twice as smart as her mother and me, but she never let on like it and never once made us feel small. Jesus, she was a nice kid." Gust squints and lowers his visor. "How did you know Leah was valedictorian?"

William shrugs. "I'm not sure. Leah was one of my advisees. It was probably in her file."

"She was the valedictorian, all right," Gust says. "I dropped out of school in tenth grade to drive my daddy's skidder, so I didn't even know what a valedictorian was until Leah explained it to me. Of course … there were only twenty kids in her class, but we were still awful proud of her. In Bigfork we're talkin' nine-man football and a high school enrollment in the mid-fifties."

"There aren't many little schools like that left in Minnesota."

"We've been lucky—Bigfork is too far from everything to close. The nearest city is Grand Rapids, and it's an hour away."

"Bigfork sounds like a nice place to live," William says. "Have you always been a logger?"

"All my life. And my son—Leah's older brother—he's a logger too. I tried to talk him out of it, but he wouldn't listen. My grandfather worked in the iron mines for a few years, right after he came over from Norway, but basically, we're four generations of pulp cutters." Gust smiles. "Nelson Logging has been around a long time."

"Any company that survived the recession has something to be proud of."

"Yeah, but it's been tough. It costs a fortune to buy stumpage, most of the mills have closed, and the winters have been so warm that it's hard to get into the swamps, especially with a harvester." Gust looks over at William. "I hope we're not going to anyplace fancy."

"We aren't. We're going to a little bar just off campus called Otto's. It's one of my favorites." William has always liked Otto's. It's not exactly the Cheers bar, but it isn't Harry Hope's Saloon either. It's just a nice bar with good food.

When they get there, even though it's happy hour, the place is practically empty on account of graduation. They sit down at a small table.

"This is like goin' home," Gust says. "Otto's could be in Bigfork."

"Otto's could be anywhere," William says. "That's one of the things I like about it."

They order beers, and after a few minutes, Gust says, "What I was really looking forward to today wasn't graduation so much. It was going out to dinner afterward with my grown-up daughter, maybe meeting her latest boyfriend, hearing about her plans for the future. You know what I mean?"

"I sure do," William says. "You and I lost the big things, the little things and everything in between." William takes a long pull on his beer. "If you don't mind my asking, how did a man who sued the pants off Lothrup College get a speaking slot at commencement?"

Gust laughs. "It was easy. They asked all four families who sued them if any of us wanted to say a few words, but I was the only one who said yes."

"Good for you."

Gust doesn't say anything for a few moments. "Dr. Kessler—*William*—I want you to know something. I didn't sue Lothrup because I was angry or because I wanted to punish Lothrup for Leah's death. Hell, Leah loved it here. She loved her classes, her teachers, the campus—everything. Me and the other parents, we talked a lot about why we wanted to sue, and it always came down to the same thing—Lothrup didn't protect our children. We sent Lothrup the most precious thing in our lives, and when they couldn't get an active shooter alert to our kids in time, they dropped the ball. That's all there is to it, and they need to accept responsibility for what they did."

William thinks about Rupert Martin, the jammer, the shattered families. "I hear you, Gust. I do."

Gust loosens his tie. "You know, William, I'm not sure colleges understand something. Parents pay a fortune so a college can make their kids smarter and happier and give them a shot at a better life. But if they can't take care of our kids while they're doing it, then none of that matters. That's why I joined the lawsuit. It was never about money. Besides, if Lothrup wins its appeal, there won't be any money." Gust thinks of something and smiles. "On the other hand, if things go our way, my wife and I would like to start a scholarship in Leah's name."

"The Leah Nelson Memorial Scholarship—that's a wonderful idea, Gust."

"And we'd also like to help out the Bigfork library—Leah practically lived there when she was little."

"Another good idea. There's no better investment than a library."

"I'm telling you this so you don't get the wrong idea."

"I understand," William says. "Look, I may wear the other team's jersey, but I know exactly where you're coming from."

Gust puts his hands in the air. "In the end, probably none of it will matter. When our attorney called Tuesday to tell us about the supreme court, he said they don't reverse the lower courts very often—that's the good news. But he also said they wouldn't have agreed to hear the case if they were comfortable with the decision—that's the bad news." Gust looks at William and tries to smile. "Anyway … when it comes to a memorial scholarship and the Bigfork library, I'm probably cutting in section 37."

William makes a face. "You're doing *what*?"

"It's something loggers say, William. There are only thirty-six sections in a township, so if somebody's cutting in section 37, they're in a place that doesn't really exist, an imaginary place where all the trees are straight, and popple is worth seventy bucks a cord. In section 37 everything is perfect."

"Sort of like the Big Rock Candy Mountain?"

"Exactly."

"I don't think you're cutting in section 37, Gust."

"We're sure as hell gonna find out." Gust looks over William's shoulder toward the kitchen. "I'm kinda hungry. My wife packed me a lunch, but I was too nervous before my speech to eat it. What's good here?"

"Burgers and pizza."

So they order burgers and another beer, and William asks if Gust has been able to put Leah's death behind him and move on.

"I only ask," William says, "because I haven't been very successful in that department. I've tried, but ..."

Gust nods. "I know what you're saying. Six months ago, my wife and I hadn't figured out how to handle it. Now, we're doing better." Gust leans forward and rests his forearms on the table. "We just couldn't let go, William, so we hung on to Leah for all we were worth. I mean, we left her room exactly the way it was. We kept the same $128 in her checking account for a year and a half. We even renewed subscriptions to her magazines. I can see now that we didn't know how to grieve, and we got addicted to the pain. Hell, we would have been content to go on that way forever."

William thinks of the carriage house. "That's sort of where I am—stuck in the past."

"Then get the hell out of there," Gust says, his voice stern. "The past is a very dangerous place, William. It's cold and dark, and it smells like death. I know because I almost died there. I was drinking way too much last fall, and one night, just before Thanksgiving, I rolled my truck and wound up upside down in a peat bog. The cab was filling up with that stinking brown water, and as I struggled with my seat belt, I realized that I *chose* to be in that bog when I became a victim of my own pain. It was a real gut check, William. Anyway … I smashed the window with a felling wedge, climbed out, and the next day my wife and I signed up for grief counseling in Grand Rapids. What we learned is that holding on is about the past, and letting go is about the future. In a nutshell, nothing about the past is as important as leaving it behind."

William is moved by Gust's candor. "Thanks, Gust. I know that's not easy stuff to share."

After that, the waitress brings their food, and they shift the conversation to things that don't hurt so much. Later, when William drops Gust off at his truck, they shake hands, and Gust says, "It was nice to meet you, William. I'll always be glad you were my daughter's teacher."

William can feel his eyes filling up. "Me too, Gust. And I'm sorry."

"For what?"

"For not being able to save her."

Gust puts his hand on William's shoulder. "That's not your fault, William. Besides, you saved a lot of lives that day."

"But not my son's. And not your daughter's."

"No, but that wasn't up to you." Gust points to his truck. "I almost forgot—I brought something from home that I want you to have. Just a second." Gust walks around to the passenger door, opens it, and returns carrying a padded envelope, which he hands to William. "It's one of Leah's books. There are some notes in it that you might find interesting."

William looks at the envelope and nods. "Thank you, Gust. I'll cherish it."

"You're very welcome, William. I'd better be going—I'm sure at least three things have broke since I left home this morning."

As William watches Gust drive off, he has the feeling that something has changed, but he isn't sure what. He gets into the Jeep and looks at the envelope. "This one is gonna hurt," he says. He opens it, and inside is a worn copy of *Wuthering Heights* with a Post-it note on the cover. *This was Leah's favorite book. Gust Nelson.* William recognizes the edition immediately. It's the Penguin paperback that William had ordered for his Victorian literature class in 2009, and this one has been read to death. It's bound with a rubber band, which William removes carefully, lest the book fall apart in his hands. The pages, half of them loose, are a welter of highlighter, mostly yellow, and margin notes, mostly red: *How does Heathcliff know what's in Edgar's will? I love all the dogs. I will see the Yorkshire moors before I'm twenty-five.* The novel has three blank pages at the end, and Leah, clearly uncomfortable with white space, has filled them with an assortment of doodles, a map to a girlfriend's apartment, and a surprisingly good sketch of a man and woman, presumably Heathcliff and Catherine Earnshaw. There is also a question—*What is an ousel?*—the lettering jammed together and shaded like boxcar graffiti.

Written on the inside of the back cover are three more questions under the heading *Remember to ask Dr. Kessler:*

— Rooting for Heathcliff is like rooting for Hannibal Lector. Why do we do this?

— Why are there so many orphans in Victorian literature— Heathcliff, Jane Eyre, Becky Sharp, Oliver Twist, David Copperfield?

— Is WH about the claims of the individual or the reconstitution of the social order? I think I know the answer. Hope Dr. K agrees with me.

And then this note: "Dr. K wants us to ask why Heathcliff does the right thing in the end. But the reason doesn't matter to me—it's enough that he does it. 'Out of the strong came forth sweetness!'"

"You get high marks for quoting the only decent line in Judges," William says aloud. "But be careful seeing Heathcliff as a force for good, kiddo—he's no Noble Savage."

At first, William is happy that he remembers being asked the *Wuthering Heights* questions. But then he decides it doesn't mean much because no matter how much electricity was passed through his brain, he was unlikely to forget a student like Leah.

"I wish you had been able to see the moors," he says.

By the time William gets home, it's five thirty, and Baron is so excited to see him that he forgets to be angry about being left alone.

"Here, buddy—I brought you something from Otto's." William

unwraps the last bite of his hamburger and gives it to Baron, who devours it in a single pulsing gulp. "What have I told you about that? Chew your food at least five times."

William makes Baron's dinner, and before the mosquitoes get too bad, the two of them go for a walk. When they get back, he chases Baron around the backyard for a few minutes—one of Baron's favorite games—and when they go inside, his cell phone rings. It's Marcia.

"Hello," he says. "I'm so glad you—"

"You sound all out of breath, William—are you all right?"

"Yes, I'm fine. I was just playing with Baron."

"And who is Baron?"

"Baron is the German shepherd that Kate, Todd and the boys gave me for my birthday. He's really—"

"Oh, yes, Kate told me about him. So how have you been? Say, did you find the lawn mower?" Once again, Marcia's voice is like an old song that lights up the limbic regions of William's brain like a pinball machine.

"Yes, I found it. It was … it was at Holmgren's just like you said."

"Kate tells me you've had some excitement there."

William's nervousness, just as it had during their previous phone call, is getting worse by the second. "I'm sorry … what?"

"Work with me, William. Kate said the house was burglarized and that Marv had attempted suicide again. Thank God he's okay."

"Yes, yes," William says. "His doctors are optimistic."

"Where is he? Have you talked to him yet?"

"He's at Abbott, and no, we haven't talked. He isn't allowed any phone calls until Monday, and he can't have visitors until Thursday."

"And the burglary?"

William sighs. "I don't know what to say about that. It was a burglary in name only—almost nothing was taken."

"That's good. You were lucky." Marcia doesn't say anything for a moment; then she surprises him. "I've been homesick, William. Tell me about my flowerbeds. Are my mums and Shasta daisies up? What about the forget-me-nots?"

William isn't sure, so he wings it. "Yes, most of them. Of course …

I haven't been out there much."

"Oh, William, please tell me you aren't letting my perennials go to wrack and ruin."

"No, no—nothing like that. I'm on top of things."

"Good. Did you go to graduation today?"

"Yes, and I met a man who—"

"Did you take your friend Amy?"

That question puts William back on his heels. "How … how could you possibly know about—"

"Kate told me. She's an excellent resource person."

"And something of a busybody," William says. "No, I went alone."

"I apologize for asking, William. It's none of my business if you have a girlfriend. Look, I have to go."

"Not yet," William pleads. "There are so many things—"

"Another time, William. Bye-bye, honey. Be well."

"You too … thanks for calling."

William hangs up and thinks about the phone call. Yes, it had been a little shaky here and there—especially the part about Amy—but overall it was better than the one two weeks ago. Fortunately, this call was short, so there wasn't much chance of screwing it up. *Bye-bye, honey*? That came out of nowhere. Was it a slip of the tongue? An unquellable force of habit? William doesn't know, but he liked the sound of it. It's best not to think about things like that, though. He knows they don't mean anything, except maybe in section 37.

William goes into the living room and collapses on the sofa. He finds the remote—as usual, between the cushions—and channel surfs until he stumbles upon a movie. But when he does, he isn't sure what it is—there's a man in a blizzard, and everything is white, whirling, incomprehensible. Then he realizes it's *Dr. Zhivago*. How appropriate, he thinks. William gets to the part where Zhivago finds the key and a note from Lara behind the loose brick outside her flat in Yuriatin, and just as he does, William's phone rings again. This time it's Amy.

"So how was your day?" William asks, muting the TV. "Did you get all those things done that—"

"Yes, and I bought the most amazing Hugo Boss suit! And the best part is that I found it at Marshalls, marked down to two hundred dollars—that's over half off. I couldn't believe it. And it fits perfectly—no alterations." Amy takes a breath. "I tried to call you earlier and got your voicemail. Please tell me your phone wasn't off."

"It wasn't. I was talking to Marcia."

Amy doesn't say anything, and William knows he's in trouble.

"See … what happened was Marcia found out from Kate about Marv and the burglary, and she called just to see how I was doing. We didn't talk long."

Amy is slow to answer, and when she does, her voice is flat and emotionless. "She's going to make a move, William. She wants you back."

"Not a chance!" he says. "That would never happen." But then he realizes, like everything else in the universe, there is a mathematical possibility that it could. "What do you think she's going to do?"

"I really couldn't say. I'm more interested in what you're going to do when she does it."

William closes his eyes and sees Zhivago, plodding through the snow. "I'm sorry, Amy, but I don't accept your premise."

"Suit yourself. How was graduation?"

William is only too happy to change the subject. "Good. It was good. I met an interesting parent there." And William proceeds to tell Amy about Gust Nelson and Leah.

When he's finished, Amy says, "That's a nice story. Gust sounds like a great guy."

"He is," William says. "He sure gave me some things to think about."

"Oh? Like what?"

"Just … things. Hey, why don't you come over?"

"When I called, I was thinking I would. But now, to be honest, I'm not really in the mood."

"Because Marcia called?"

"No, because you're happy about it."

"But I'm not happy about it. I'm not *anything* about it."

"We'll talk tomorrow, William. A hot bath beckons."

Amy hangs up, and William is furious with himself for mentioning the Marcia call. *How could I be so stupid?*

William watches some more TV, then goes to bed early. But again he doesn't sleep well. Outside, the sulfurous air thickens, swirls, and begins to rise, creating gusts and eddies of wind that puff the curtains in and out. When William gets up to look out the window, he can see the distant flashes of heat lightning, and there is the feeling of a storm coming.

CHAPTER 24

Kishi Kaisei

IT BEGINS RAINING EARLY the next morning and continues to rain for a week. For the first twenty-four hours, the parched earth gulps down the moisture so quickly that puddles never form. But after forty-eight hours, the earth has drunk its fill, and the runoff becomes gushing freshets that rill the hillsides and pour into the creeks and streams, causing them to overflow their banks and turn low-lying fields into muddy lakes. On Sunday, at the first crack of thunder, everyone had unfurled their umbrellas and said, *Well, we need the rain,* as though whoever they were speaking to may have harbored secret doubts. But by Tuesday, sump pumps are overwhelmed, basements are flooding, and there is a two-foot-high circle of sandbags around many buildings on the east side of town, including the Yellow Horse Diner. At that point, *We need the rain* becomes *When is this shit gonna stop?*

William hears the rain and wind before he opens his eyes on Sunday morning, and when he gets up, he can see the gray trees swaying back and forth. He takes Baron out, and afterward the two of them sit at the kitchen table, wondering what to do.

"We need the rain, Hürtgenvoss, but it sure limits our options."

William's empty garbage can is still out at the curb, and when the wind blows it across the front yard, he decides it's time to walk over to the carriage house and make sure everything is all right.

He's glad he did because the little tear in the Tyvek has become considerably more than that, and now a sizable piece of house-wrap is snapping in the wind. Fortunately, the scaffolding is still in place, so all William has to do is climb up and secure it, but he gets soaking wet, and by the time he's finished, he's shivering.

But there is one more thing he wants to do. William goes inside, and on the back of a receipt from the lumberyard, he makes a list of all the jobs that still need to be done. When he's sure he hasn't missed anything, he places his list on the kitchen counter, and he and Baron go home, where he changes out of his wet clothes, wraps himself in a comforter and lies down on the sofa. When he finally gets warm, he falls asleep, but when he wakes up, his legs ache, and he has a sore throat.

"Goddammit, Hürtgenvoss—I think I'm getting sick."

He calls Amy to see if she's still angry about Marcia's phone call and is relieved when he detects no lingering rancor.

"I didn't want anything," he says. "I just haven't heard your voice today, and it was definitely time."

"I think you wanted to see if I was still mad."

William chuckles. "That too."

"William, you sound funny. Do you have a cold?"

"I don't know. I've got *something.*"

"I suppose you don't have anything in the house for dinner."

"No, I still haven't been to the store."

"I'll bring something over. What are you taking?"

"Taking?"

"For your cold—Tylenol? Advil?"

"I was about to take some aspirin."

"I guess that's as good as anything. I'll see you around six."

William returns to the sofa and falls asleep again, and at six Amy shows up with sloppy joe and buns.

"Hope you like this," she says. "It seemed like a good batch to me."

William doesn't have much appetite, but he eats half of a sloppy joe and feels better. "Right now, I think I just might make it. Can you stick around?"

Amy shakes her head. "I wish I could, but I have to go home and prepare for my dinner meeting tomorrow night."

"Right, right," William says. "How long do you have to speak?"

"Twelve to fifteen minutes. I will be delivering a scintillating disquisition on Media Literacy in the Constructivist Classroom. It's basically about how to make children critical consumers of online information, to teach them the difference between fact and opinion, news and propaganda—that sort of thing."

"Great idea! If it works on kids, we should try it on adults."

Amy laughs. "My goal tomorrow night is modest—I just don't want to look like a lightweight. I'm the only applicant who has never been a full-fledged elementary school principal."

"That could work in your favor—you're gonna do great."

"I sure hope so. Hey, I gotta go, but before I do, let's get you set up in the guest bedroom—sleeping on the floor isn't what you need." So Amy takes his phone, a glass of water and the bottle of aspirin down the hall to the guest bedroom and places them on the nightstand. Then she turns down the bed and motions to William. "You're all set. I think you'll like this better."

"Thanks, Amy. I appreciate your coming over."

"Hey, you're my boo. Call me if you need anything."

"I will, but I'm sure that won't be necessary. I'll be better by tomorrow."

But the next morning, William is the same or perhaps a little worse. Even so, he is determined that he and Baron will make it to school, which they finally do. William prefers to make all difficult phone calls from his office, and this is the first day he can call Marv. And after Marv, there is another call he has to make. Then, if he hasn't collapsed, he hopes to read Joyce Carol Oates' *Tragic and Comic Visions in The Brothers Karamazov.* He calls Marv and gets him right away.

"Marv, is that you? You don't sound like yourself."

"According to my doctors, I'm *not* myself. And I find that diagnosis puzzling, William. I mean, if I'm not *my* self, then whose self am I?"

"What I meant was—"

"I know what you meant—I'm hoarse from the hyperbaric treatments."

"How is that going?"

"Okay, I guess. I have earaches and nosebleeds, but other than that ..."

"The nurse I spoke with on Saturday said you're doing very well."

It's several seconds before Marv replies. "I tried to kill myself, William, and I botched the job. I obviously don't care whether I live or die, and my life, such as it is, has turned into a dumpster fire. If that's doing well, then I'm great."

"That's gonna pass. You'll see."

Marv takes a deep breath. "I understand that you, UPS and that damned jacket foiled my plans."

"We did," William says. "But at least we answered the big question."

"Yeah? What question?"

"What can Brown do for you?"

Marv laughs half-heartedly. "I'm not ready to thank you, by the way."

"I understand. Look, I know you have all kinds of confused and contradictory feelings right now, but I want to make mine perfectly clear. I love you, and I'm extremely glad you're still alive."

Marv clears his throat. "Thank you, William. As fucked up as I am, I appreciate that. By the way, you don't sound like yourself either."

"I'm a little under the weather. Do you know when you'll be released?"

"No. It depends on my hemoglobin tests."

"They say you can have visitors on Thursday. I'm coming to see you."

"William, it's not necessary for you to drive all—"

"I'll see you Thursday—get used to the idea."

"Okay. Thanks. How's Amy?"

"Wonderful—absolutely wonderful."

"Would you care to share any intimate details of your sex life?"

William laughs. "No, I don't think so."

"Then I'd better get back to counting the little holes in the ceiling tile."

"Hey, remember to watch the Twins tomorrow."

"Who do they play?"

William pretends to gasp. "A suicide attempt is no excuse for forgetting something like that. They play Chicago."

"Who's pitching for us?"

"That new kid ... Walters. They just called him up from the Red Wings two weeks ago—it should be interesting."

"I'll try to watch," Marv says.

"You do that. I'll see you Thursday."

After they hang up, William thinks about Marv for a while and then picks up his phone again. "I have another important call to make, Baron." William goes online and finds the website for Ferraro Brothers Construction, the outfit that built Kate and Todd's summer kitchen. He hesitates for a moment, and then calls them.

It's a short call, and after William hangs up, he fills Baron in on the details. "I was just talking to Chooch Ferraro—he's the older brother. He said the rain has set them back, but he's going to work us in. He said he might even take a look tomorrow." William shrugs. "It definitely feels funny, but I think I did the right thing. One call left."

William then calls Officer Lewis and has to leave a message, but inside of ten minutes, Lewis returns the call. Unfortunately, he doesn't know anything more about the burglary than he did on the night it happened, and when William gets off the phone, he knows he will never call about the burglary again.

After that, William turns his attention to *Tragic and Comic Visions in The Brothers Karamazov*, but it doesn't go well. Oates is a good writer, one whose words unspool in perfect paragraphs, but William is feeling worse by the minute and finds it impossible to concentrate. After reading the same page half a dozen times, he gives up.

"I'm gonna pull the pin, Hürtgenvoss. I need to go home."

When he gets there, William can't bear the thought of lying in bed, so he tries the sofa again and finds an excellent documentary about the 2011 Tōhoku earthquake-cum-tsunami that wreaked havoc at the Fukushima Nuclear Power Plant. But as hard as he tries to focus, William keeps drifting in and out in a feverish torpor. At one point, he wakes up and sees a young Japanese girl on her knees, rocking back and forth beside the motionless body of an apparent loved one. She is repeating a phrase that sounds like *kishay kytei,* but it's hard to make out against the sorrowful backdrop of Barber's "Adagio for Strings." The image is haunting, and William struggles to get it out of his head.

At four thirty, he drags himself from the sofa, feeds Baron and is about to call Amy when she calls him.

"How are ya doin'?" she asks. "Feeling any better?"

"Not really, but I made it into the office today. Listen, good luck tonight. Will you call me afterward?"

"Of course. This rain is almost biblical."

"Almost."

When Amy makes good on her promise and calls later that evening, William, who has grown weary of television, is in bed but awake.

"So how did it go?" he asks.

"I thought it went well," Amy says. "People laughed when they were supposed to, and they clapped really loud. Oh—Gardner and his wife were there. He said my presentation was 'compelling,' and she said I did 'a first-rate job.'"

"That's high praise, Amy—and from people who count."

"Yeah … I was pleased. Two more inquisitions to go. On the thirtieth, next Wednesday, I have the problem-solving Q-and-A with the regents and the school attorneys."

"What about obedience class? We have our final exam."

"It won't be a problem—my meeting is at ten o'clock in the morning." There is a pause, and William knows the conversation is about to revert to him. "Are you running a fever?"

"Off and on," he says. "I've pretty much concluded I have the flu."

"I think you're right. Do you need anything? What did you have for dinner?"

"Oatmeal."

Amy makes a sound of disapproval.

"I *like* oatmeal."

"That's fine, William. But tomorrow I'm going to the store for you—you need groceries."

"You don't have to do that."

"No, but I'm going to. I'll give you a call in the morning."

The next morning, Amy calls at ten, and William sounds so bad that it frightens her.

"You're getting worse," she says. "I wish you hadn't gone to school yesterday. I'm going to call Kate."

"What for?"

"Because I want her to know you're sick, and I'm going to ask her if she can check on you. I have meetings most of the day, but I'll stop by around four thirty or whenever I can get out of here. How's Baron? Are you able to take him out?"

"Yes, we're coping. I don't think he likes the new sleeping arrangements, though." William tries to turn his head so he can see Baron, but it hurts too much.

"Look," Amy says. "There's no way you're going to school tomorrow. Would you like me to call in for you?"

"Yes, I'd appreciate it. It's a lot of rigmarole, but I'm trying to be super-good about that stuff." He gives Amy his PIN and the phone number. "You'll hear this voice that sounds like Siri—just do what she tells you. You're requesting sick leave—the code is 008."

"I'll make the call as soon as I hang up."

"Oh, I almost forgot—would you please ask for Thursday too? I'm planning to visit Marv. That will be personal leave, not sick leave, and the code for that is—"

"I'll figure it out, William. Do you think you'll feel well enough?"

"Hard to say. I'll see you tonight. Thanks for doing this."

When Kate arrives an hour later, she lets herself in and finds William and Baron in the guest bedroom.

"What are you two doing in here?" she asks. "And what happened to the bed in *your* bedroom?"

"The frame is in pieces. It's in the garage."

Kate nods. "Promise you'll never tell me how that happened." She looks out the window. "Can you believe this rain? At first, The Weather Channel was calling it 'much-needed May showers.' Now it's 'an extreme rainfall event.'"

"Is there much flooding?"

"There's some—the underpasses and a few of the streets on the east side of town."

"Hey, before I forget—I called Officer Lewis."

"And?"

William shakes his head. "He didn't know any more than he did last Wednesday. I won't call again."

"I wouldn't let them off the hook that easy." Kate reaches down and picks up a magazine from the floor. "I need to straighten this place up a little." And with that, she becomes a whirlwind of solicitous efficiency—plumping pillows, refilling his water glass, creating a little chart so William knows when he last took aspirin.

"Oops," she says. "I almost forgot." She sits down and removes something from her purse that looks like a price gun and points it at William's forehead.

"I'll tell you everything I know," he says.

"Relax, I'm just taking your temperature. This is an infrared thermometer—all the cool moms use them." The thermometer beeps and Kate gasps. "102 degrees! That's a *kid* temperature, not an adult temperature. I'm taking you to the emergency room!"

"Like hell."

"Okay, then I'm taking you to urgent care."

"You're cutting in section 37."

"*What?*"

"Urgent care—it ain't gonna happen."

Kate's voice goes up half an octave. "Daddy, don't be so stubborn. You're sick!"

"I'm not *that* sick. I just have the flu."

"Well, that's a relief. In case you aren't aware, people with the flu get dehydrated, they get bronchitis, they get pneumonia, they *die*."

"You need to work on your bedside manner, Morticia—it's appalling. Would you mind letting Baron out before you go?"

Kate stands up with an exasperated sigh. "I give up, Daddy—you're impossible. C'mon, BearBear."

William sleeps the rest of the day with Baron on the floor next to his bed. At one point, he thinks he awakens with Amy's hand on his forehead, but he isn't sure, and he's pretty much out of it until Amy shows up after work with three bags of groceries, dinner and Yoshi.

"I'm going to spend the night," she says. "How are you feeling?"

"Not very well but … better. Were you here this afternoon, or did I dream it?"

"I sneaked out of school and checked on you at around two thirty. I thought you were asleep. What about fever?"

"I don't think I have one right now, but I've sure had some bizarre fever dreams. It seems that all the dead people in my life— Jon, my parents, our next-door neighbor when I was little—are alive and well, living in the land of 102 degrees."

Amy puts her hand on his shoulder. "I should put the groceries away—I got milk, eggs, bread, a small ham, and do you know what else?"

"No. What?"

"A phone call from Gardner—I was standing in the checkout line when he called to tell me that I'm one of the three finalists."

William takes her hand. "That's terrific, Amy! I'm so proud of you. I guess they liked your presentation."

"So it would seem." Amy sits down on the edge of the bed. "Kate was very upset with you this afternoon—she called me."

"You two are getting pretty chummy. Look out—she'll be asking you to attend her Bible class." William looks around. "Where's Baron?"

"In the backyard with Yoshi. I called in, by the way—you have tomorrow and Thursday off. I hope you feel well enough to make the trip to Crosswell."

"Me too."

"Oh—this is weird. When I was here this afternoon, there was a truck over at the carriage house. There was something written on the side, but I couldn't read it, and I didn't want to go over there."

"I'm sure it was Ferraro Brothers Construction. They're working up a bid."

"On what?"

William takes a ragged breath. "I want them to finish the carriage house ... It's time."

Amy's eyes open wide. "What? No more building, tearing down and rebuilding?"

William shakes his head. "No. I'm not sure the carriage house is good for me. I love the way the job kept me closer to Jon, but ..."

"But Jon is gone, and building a monument for the rest of your life won't bring him back?"

William nods. "Something like that."

Amy leans down and kisses him. "Now it's my turn to be proud of *you*—monstrously, terrifically, unbelievably proud."

"Thank you. The decision about the carriage house has a lot to do with us. It's taken years, but my life is finally turning around, and I'm afraid the past is going to crash the party and ruin everything." William throws off the blanket and sits up halfway. "So I didn't really have a choice, Amy. The carriage house is about letting go, and letting go is about the future. A wise man told me that."

"He was absolutely right, William. It's like I said at Ki's—you have to keep thinking forward. That's the only defense any of us has against the past." Amy points toward the kitchen. "Hey, I brought a surprise. I had to drop off my dry cleaning after school, which put me right across Dahlberg Road from Don & Angie's, so I picked up some chicken parm. How does that sound?"

"It sounds great, but I'm not really—"

"Do you feel well enough to eat in the kitchen?"

"I don't know, but I'm sure tired of being bedridden."

"Okay, I'll go deal with the groceries, put dinner in the microwave and be right back for you."

When she returns, William gets up, somewhat unsteadily, and with Amy's help, puts on his robe and heads for the kitchen. Although he doesn't have much appetite, William eats what he can. Halfway through the meal, he remembers something.

"Yesterday, I was half out of it, watching a documentary about the Tōhoku earthquake, and in the B-roll there was footage of a girl kneeling beside a body, repeating a phrase over and over in Japanese. I can't get it out of my head."

"What was the phrase?"

"Well … that's the thing. I'm not sure. To me it sounded like *kishay kytei* or *kinshay kytei*, but I couldn't hear it clearly."

Amy nods. "She was probably saying *kishi kaisei*. It means *wake from death and return to life*. It's a saying the Japanese reserve for desperate situations. The only reason I remember it is because we used to shout it at baseball games—you know, when our team was down by four in the bottom of the ninth." In rapid succession, Amy touches her chest, her opposite shoulder, and then thrusts her fist into the air. *"Kishi kaisei!"*

William smiles. "Yeah, I'll bet that's it ... Wake from death and return to life."

After that, William is quiet for a time, and eventually Amy touches his hand. "Where have you gone now?"

"Nowhere. I was just thinking."

"About what?"

"About how if I had one of those twenty-four-hour bugs, I would've been well at eleven fifteen yesterday morning. I sure hope you don't catch this."

"No worries, William. I'm around germy little kids all day long—I have an immune system to die for."

"Intriguing oxymoron," William says. "I need to go back to bed."

"Okay, Professor, let's go." Amy helps William to his feet, and together they make their way to the guest bedroom, where Amy remakes the bed and puts William in it.

"Try to get some sleep," she says.

"Not much chance of that."

"I saw NyQuil in your medicine cabinet. You want some?"

"Sure. What the hell."

Amy gets him the NyQuil, and William downs a capful, grimacing as though he were swallowing poison. "This stuff tastes like Jäegermeister—only worse."

Amy sets the NyQuil on the nightstand. "But it will help you sleep."

"Can I have another shot just to make sure?"

"No way. It says *one capful* right on the bottle."

William makes a face. "Then would you please bring me a glass of water so I can get the taste out of my mouth?"

"Of course."

While Amy is in the bathroom filling his glass, William grabs the NyQuil and takes a prodigious gulp, trying hard not to wretch.

The NyQuil does its job—and then some. William sleeps soundly through the night, and it's all Amy can do to wake him the next morning.

"C'mon, William. Rise and shine. I need to know how you're feeling."

"Ohhhhh," he moans. "Ohhhhh."

"What's wrong, William? Is your fever back?"

He points to the nightstand. "I took extra NyQuil last night."

Amy looks at him and laughs. "Feeling a little logy, are we?"

"I feel like I'm back at Cross, drugged out of my mind. What's *in* that stuff?" William takes the bottle of NyQuil off the nightstand and reads the back. "Doxylamine—I should have known."

"What's that?"

"An antihistamine that can knock you out cold." William rubs his eyes.

"I think the moral of the story is that one capful means *one capful*. I'll bring you some toast and—"

"I couldn't eat anything."

"All right, Dr. Leary—just coffee, then."

William's cell phone rings, and William puts his hands over his ears.

"You want me to get that?" Amy looks at the display. "It's Marv."

"Please."

Amy picks up the phone and taps ACCEPT. "Hi, Marv. This is Amy. Hey, all I'm gonna say is that you gave us quite a scare. Uh-huh, yeah. William's right here, but he's got the flu … I know, right?" Amy nods and listens for a few moments; then she makes a face. "Oh, no—what a shame! But to be honest, I'm not sure he could have made it anyway—he's pretty sick … Saturday and Sunday—I'll tell him. Yeah, it was nice to talk to you too. Okay, Marv. Bye."

Amy turns to William. "Marv says not to come tomorrow. He's being moved in the morning."

"Where to?"

"Crosswell."

William groans. "I was afraid you'd say that. I swore I'd never set foot in that place again."

"I'm sorry … I know how you feel about it. Marv said you could visit him there on Saturday or Sunday."

"Having to go to Cross is the second-worst thing in the world."

"Really? What's the worst?"

"Having to stay." Just then Baron arrives from somewhere. He puts his front feet up on the bed and stares.

"Good morning, Hürtgenvoss. I know you're worried about me." William looks at Amy. "Baron and I aren't going to make it to obedience class tonight."

"No, but a dog can miss one class and still graduate."

"The thing is, the next class is the final exam. Baron won't be ready."

"Sure he will," Amy says. "You'll just have to practice on your own."

William nods, unconvinced.

By the time Amy and Yoshi are ready to leave, William's head is beginning to clear, but he has a killer hangover.

"Will I see you later?" he asks.

Amy kisses his cheek. "Probably, but I'll look very blurry. I'll stop by at lunchtime."

CHAPTER 25

A Rainbow of Chaos

WILLIAM FALLS ASLEEP as soon as Amy leaves, and it isn't until he hears footsteps and rustling in the room that he halfway awakens. "Hello, Amy," he says, without opening his eyes. "Is it noon already? I'm still stoned."

"Stoned? We quit doing that when Kate was born. Wake up, William. It's me—*Marcia*."

William opens his eyes, but even so, he's sure he must be dreaming. Only when Marcia leans down and kisses him, enveloping him in Infusion d'Iris, is the dream usurped by reality.

"Marcia ... how did you—"

"You look like death warmed over, William."

"I have the flu."

"So I hear. Why are you in the guest bedroom? And what have you done to our bed? The box spring and mattress are on the floor!"

"It's a long story," William says, still breathing her in. "Have you met Baron? Where is he?"

"Yes, we've met. He's beautiful, William. He didn't want to leave your side, but I put him in the backyard so he could get a little fresh air. He wasn't happy about it—he made that clear."

William rubs his eyes. "My God ... is it really *you*?"

"Of course it's me. After the phone call I got from Kate, how could I stay away? Kate said you were being ... I believe the word she used was *pig-headed*."

"She wanted to take me to the hospital."

"Which is probably where you belong." Marcia sits down next to the bed and puts her hand on William's arm. "Any news about Marv?"

"Not much. I talked to him on Monday. They said he could have visitors tomorrow, and I was planning to go, but now they're moving him to Cross in the morning, so ... I don't know when I'll catch up with him."

"Whenever that is, I'm sure he'll be happy to see you."

William is doing his best to process everything, but his befuddled brain is working at half its normal speed. "What time is it? I have ... a friend coming at noon."

Marcia laughs. "Relax, William. It's a quarter to twelve, and if this 'friend' is Amy Mattson, that's good—I've been wanting to meet her."

"You have?"

"Of course. We're all adults, right?"

"Absolutely," William says, knowing that he's fucked. He's thrilled to see Marcia, but at the same time, he wishes he could hide her in the closet to avoid a scene with Amy. And he still doesn't understand why Marcia has come in the first place. "Did you fly in this morning?"

"I did," she says. "Phoenix to Minneapolis, and from Minneapolis I took a Delta shuttle to Chambliss, rented a car, and here I am."

"I've never been so surprised in my life," William says.

Marcia tries to smile. "Are you okay with it?"

"*Okay*? I'm thrilled. I couldn't be happier but ..."

"But what?"

"I'm wondering what Walter had to say."

Marcia nods. "Could we please defer that discussion for a little while? I'm going over some things I want to say to you in my head, and that's one of them."

"Yeah, sure," William says, even more confused than before. "Tell me about Phoenix. Do you like it there?"

"Yes and no," she says, explaining that she hasn't fallen in love

with Phoenix the way she'd hoped to—"It's just too damn hot"—
but on the whole, she likes it well enough. "I mean, if I were a
snowbird, I'd think it was heaven, but as a year-round resident, I
miss the changing seasons, the snow—that sort of thing." Marcia
hears something and looks out the window. "A red SUV just pulled
in the driveway."

"It's Amy," William says. "I don't know what to tell her."

"Tell her your ex is in town and stopped by to say hello." Marcia
stands up. "Excuse me for a minute—I have to go meet your girlfriend." She laughs softly. "Now *there's* something I never thought
I'd say to you."

Marcia leaves, and William tries to imagine what he can possibly say to Amy. He hears the front door open. Then he hears wom-
en's voices going back and forth like a badminton birdie, but he
can't make out any words. A minute later, Marcia and Amy walk
into the room together, but it's Marcia who does all the talking.

"William, you have company. It was very nice to meet you,
Amy. And so good of you to stop by."

Amy, who is holding a little paper bag, forces a smile.

"All right," Marcia says, "I'll leave you two alone. The rain
seems to have let up, so this is my chance to look at my perennial
beds. I hope to see you again, Amy."

As soon as Marcia is gone, Amy, her eyes blazing, jerks her
thumb in the direction of the doorway. "You got some 'splaining
to do!"

William puts his hands in the air. "Hey, I'm just as surprised as
you are."

"I seriously doubt it. *So good of you to stop by*? Did she really
say that?"

"She showed up out of the blue, Amy—I swear. She talked to
Kate and—"

"Let's cut to the chase, William—are you glad she's here?"

"What kind of question is that?"

"The kind you answer yes or no."

"It isn't that simple, Amy. When you're married to someone
for—"

"Actually, it *is* that simple, and you're taking the corner pretty wide. Are you glad she's here or not?"

William starts to speak, once, twice, then stops.

"Yeah ... that's what I thought. You never could lie." Amy sits down and gazes absently out the window. "You know, that woman isn't threatened by me at all. Notice how she left us alone together?" Amy shakes her head. "Talk about confidence!"

"When it comes to confidence, Marcia has always had—"

"I don't mean that she has confidence in herself, William. I mean she has confidence in *you*. That's why she isn't worried about me—I'm just a bump in the road."

"Amy, I know you think that Marcia and I—"

"Please don't tell me what I think, William." Amy shakes her head. "I've always known you were still in love with her, but I didn't worry much about it because you were like a dog chasing a bus. Now, it seems, you've caught the bus, so ... I'd like to know what you intend to do with it."

"Amy, you and I need to talk, but I don't think this is the best—"

"I couldn't agree more. I'm going back to school." Amy gets up, looks at the paper bag in her hand and tosses it on the bed. "I made you a sandwich. I hope you choke on it." She turns on her heel and leaves.

William closes his eyes and tries to absorb everything that's happened since he awoke to Marcia's perfume. How much of it is his fault? How much of it can be laid off on subatomic particles— on the mercurial quarks, neutrinos and bosons that help generate the tissue of events in our changing, unpredictable lives? Cézanne was right, William thinks. We live in a rainbow of chaos.

A few minutes after Amy leaves, Marcia returns with a cup of tea, which she hands to him. "I want you to drink this—it will make you feel better." She pulls the chair closer to the bed and sits down. "Amy is even prettier than her picture."

"What picture?"

"The one on the Hawthorne School website. Kate sent me the link."

"Our daughter needs a hobby."

Marcia smiles. "In addition to doing the Lord's work? Drink your tea."

"What kind is it?"

"Elderberry. I brought it with me—it's very popular in Phoenix." He takes a sip. "It's good. It tastes like blackberries."

Marcia doesn't say anything for a moment; then she asks the question William has been dreading. "So ... how are you doing?"

As William tries to formulate a response, he realizes the question is impossible to answer in under an hour. "I'm doing okay," he says, finally. "My immediate problem is that my fever's coming back. I need more aspirin."

Marcia puts her hand on his forehead. "You're right, but I have something I want you to take with them."

"What?"

"It's something my doctor in Phoenix gave me a while back." She takes a prescription bottle from her purse and hands it to him.

"Triazolam, 0.25 milligrams," he says, reading the label. "Triazolam is Halcion, and 0.25 milligrams is a big dose. What do you need this for?"

"I don't, not anymore, but I wasn't sleeping because ..." Marcia makes a face. "If it's all the same to you, I'd rather not get into this right now."

"Yeah. Sure." William gives the bottle back to her, and she removes a pill. Then she shakes two aspirin into her palm and hands the three pills to William, along with a glass of water. William swallows them and sets the glass on the nightstand.

"Attaboy," Marcia says. "You're going to be better in no time." She reaches over and takes his hand. "Are you writing? I know you're never happier than when you're working on a book."

William nods. "I'm working on a book about Dostoevsky—not him, one of his themes."

"For University of Minnesota Press?"

"For Norton."

"That's wonderful! What does Ruth say?"

"She says I need to wrap it up and write a book about the shooting. She wants us to make some money."

Marcia frowns. "Would you ever do that?"

"Not in a million years."

"Listen, when you fall asleep—and you will—I'm going to

make some soup. How does chicken noodle sound?"

"It sounds—"

"But first I need to go to the store, so on the off chance that you wake up and I'm not here, that's where I am."

"Okay," William says. "How fast do these pills work?"

"Pretty fast."

"Are you going to sleep in Kate's room?"

"Until you put our bed back together, I guess I'll have to. What's that all about, anyway?"

"Well ... I was afraid Baron might fall off the bed and get hurt—those antique beds are so high. By the way, would you please let him in? Baron has some anxiety issues, and we're not really used to being separated."

"It sounds like you have some anxiety issues of your own. Should I feed him?"

"Yeah, that would be great. His food is in the pantry ... Could these pills be kicking in already?"

Ten minutes later, William is asleep.

At seven o'clock that evening, he wakes up and has a cup of soup in the kitchen with Marcia.

"Good soup," he says. "Lots of chicken."

"Can you taste the lavender salt?" she asks. "There's nothing that finishes a chicken-based soup like lavender salt."

William takes another spoonful. "Yes, I think so ... it's very subtle. I like the big noodles."

"That reminds me ... I was over at the carriage house today. I thought the pasta maker might be in one of the boxes I took over there—that's what I use to make those pappardelle noodles."

"It's here—it's in the cupboard above the refrigerator."

"Yes, I finally found it. But tell me about the carriage house—it's practically finished!"

William nods. "It's close. I hired a contractor to wrap things up over there. It'll be done next month."

"A contractor? That doesn't sound like you."

"You're right, but I just don't have the time. I've got—"

"I wish Jon could see it." Marcia is quiet for a time; then she sets her spoon down and frowns. "Part of me hates to bring this up, but Kate told me you were in trouble at school. What's going on?"

William doesn't know where to begin. "I'm not really sure. Everything is sort of … up in the air. I'll give you the condensed version." So William tells her about the hearing, Gardner's decision to keep him in limbo, and how, if he's lucky, he'll be fully reinstated in the fall. "But of course Gardner wants to punish me first."

Marcia is furious. "I heard a little bit about that hearing from Kate. They can't treat you like that."

"But I'm guilty."

"Yes, but you were …"

"Crazy?"

"I didn't say that."

"No matter," William says. "I don't think they care about mitigating circumstances."

"Then we should make them care. We'll hire an attorney, file a grievance and go to arbitration. This isn't right, William."

William smiles. "From a purely legal standpoint, it would be hard to claim aggrieved status in arbitration when I've done exactly what they say I've done."

"It doesn't matter—you should fight back."

"I am fighting back. In fact, I have a secret weapon."

"What would that be?"

"I'll tell you when I feel better."

William returns to bed, and Marcia gives him another pill that knocks him out until morning. He doesn't stir until he hears her in the room again.

"How do we feel today?" she asks, opening the bedroom curtains.

"Like I'm under water," William says, trying to focus his eyes. "Those pills really do a number on me."

"I think that's the idea."

"Is Baron outside?"

"Yes, but he didn't want to go. I put a leash on him and sort of dragged him out the door. I don't think he likes me."

After breakfast, Marcia wants him to take a third pill. "Sit up, honey—you need to take this if you want to get better."

"I think I'll pass. I'm not sure—"

"No, William—I insist. You need to take it."

William shrugs. "Okay … if you really think they're helping." He puts the pill in his mouth and somewhat reluctantly raises his glass of water. "Here's to life among the lotus eaters."

That day is a huge blur with a bowl of chicken noodle soup in the middle of it, and that evening, when Marcia gives him another pill, William puts it under his pillow and slips into the REM sleep he's been missing.

He dreams for hours, and one of the dreams is so vivid that he remembers it when he wakes up: he's alone in a canoe on a river. The river resembles the Kawishiwi that flows through Minnesota's Boundary Waters, but it could be a lot of wilderness rivers. He paddles for hours through beautiful country and sees no one. Then, another canoe appears in front of him. There are two people in the canoe, and although William can hear them laughing and talking, he can't make out what they're saying. But the voices are familiar, and as he listens more closely, he realizes it's Jon and Leah Nelson. William hollers to get their attention, but they don't seem to hear him. He paddles furiously to catch up to them, and he's closing the distance when the river is suddenly enveloped in a clammy, low-hanging fog that hides everything from view. When the fog lifts, William is onshore, looking out on the river, and Amy is beside him. "*Kishi kaisei,*" she says. "Wake from death, William."

William sits up in bed with a start and gasps. "I'm awake! I'm awake!"

CHAPTER 26

Waiting for the Pain

PERHAPS IT WAS THE SOUP or the tea. Or Marcia's Halcion pills. Or maybe it was nothing more than William's lymphocytes answering the call to battle. Whatever the explanation, William feels much better on Friday morning, and he knows he's a man on the mend.

"You look good today," Marcia tells him at breakfast. "You've got your color back. I told you those pills would help."

William believes he's better in spite of the pills, not because of them, but all he says is, "Yes, I think I'm ready to rejoin the living."

"In that case, I'm going to tell Kate I can go with her. She took the day off today, hoping we could go shopping and have lunch. And I was thinking if she met me at the airport, I could drop off the rental car, and after that, we could swing by the cemetery, which reminds me—I have to cut some flowers. I told her I was pretty sure I could go, but I wanted to see how you were feeling this morning."

"I'm feeling good—go ahead. My plan is to play with Baron for a while, and I was thinking we'd go down to the river and see how high it is."

"Do me a favor. After you've done that—if you feel well enough—would you please put our bed back together?"

"Yeah, sure. I just lowered it for—"

"For the dog. Yes, I know. But can't he sleep on the floor?"

"I'll ask him."

"While you're at it, would you also ask him if he could pick up his toys once in a while?"

"I will, but I can't make any promises."

Marcia smiles. "What worries me is that you aren't kidding. I have to run out to the garden and then get ready to go."

While he's waiting for Marcia to leave, William gets an email from Ferraro Brothers Construction that contains a bid and a contract for finishing the carriage house. William looks the bid over carefully, and finding nothing amiss, he moves on to the contract, which is simple and straightforward.

A few minutes later, Marcia sticks her head in the door. "I'm leaving, honey."

"Okay. Have fun."

William prints the contract, which he signs, scans and emails back to Ferraro Brothers. He looks down at Baron. "The carriage house is now officially out of my hands, partner. And in case you're about to ask, it feels pretty good." William wonders what he will do to fill that void in his life, but it shouldn't be a problem—he can always remodel the house if he has to.

"Hürtgenvoss, this is going to be a very busy day for us, and I want to get everything done before I change my mind."

William doesn't know exactly when he made the decision to blow the whistle on Lothrup, but it had followed hard on the heels of the Minnesota Supreme Court's decision to hear Lothrup's appeal, the unexpected development that had backed him into a corner. And then, of course, he had met Gust Nelson, which was a game-changer.

William's initial impulse had been to contact the attorneys for the four families who brought the lawsuit, but the more he thought about it, the less he liked the idea. For one thing, William isn't sure how effective the jammer would be in a courtroom, where a team of good lawyers might reduce it to legal tatters and demonstrate that it had no probative value whatsoever. It wouldn't be hard to do. No one could prove that the jammer belonged to Rupert Martin, let alone that it was used in Dewhurst on the day of shooting. And equally

troubling, William cannot place the jammer within a chain of cus-
tody or prove that it was ever inside the waterlogged briefcase in his
basement. William knows he has a compelling story to tell, but so
did Marcia Clark and Christopher Darden—and yet O. J. Simpson
had walked. So William has spent a lot of time trying to figure out
how to turn the jammer into a drop-the-mic exhibit A.

But it wasn't until he quit trying to think like a lawyer that the
answer came to him: instead of worrying about how the jammer
would play in a court of law, William decided the real issue was
how it would play in the court of public opinion, where the circum-
stantial evidence would hold more sway. William knew he was
onto something, and it wasn't long before he decided to use Paul
Bouchard as a megaphone. Bouchard wouldn't be able to resist a
story like this, and he could hit Lothrup so hard and so fast that
they'd drop their appeal like a hot rock rather than risk the negative publicity. It wouldn't matter what was true and what wasn't.
Perception is reality, and Bouchard knew that as well as anyone.

William goes downstairs, removes the jammer from the toner
cartridge carton and looks around for a corrugated box more suit-
able for shipping. He finally finds one, but it has a Christmas can-
dle in it, so he swaps out the boxes and takes the new one, along
with the jammer, upstairs to his office.

Now what? he asks himself. "Right! I need a photo."

So William takes a picture of the jammer—something he'll
need later—and emails it to his computer. Then he types *Nelson
Logging Bigfork MN* into a search field, and moments later, he has
Gust's address. William laughs out loud when he sees it—*Buck
Scrape Lane*. He carefully prints the address on the box, and after
that, he writes Gust a letter explaining about the jammer, what it
means, and how he came to have it.

He also tells Gust that he will be contacted by a reporter named
Paul Bouchard, who will help him get the story out. "But be careful, Gust. Bouchard is about Bouchard—never say anything to him
that you don't want to read in the newspaper." William knows that
Bouchard will drag him into the story too—he would never miss
an opportunity to resurrect the Saint Patrick's Day hero. But that
doesn't matter. What matters are the fundamentals—the fact that

THE SAINT PATRICK'S DAY HERO

students died when a Lothrup professor broke the law and jammed their cell phones. If Bouchard is able to drive that point home, whatever else he might do en route to a Pulitzer can be forgiven.

William places the letter on top of the jammer and slides both of them into the box. But it's a sloppy fit, so he cuts some bubble wrap and stuffs it around the jammer, using an additional piece as a cushion on the top. Then he tapes the box shut.

"Baron, I want to get this part over with, so we're going to the UPS Store again. Let's boogie."

When he gets there, the same girl is behind the counter, and she remembers him. "Hi there! Was your friend happy to get his jacket back?"

"He was," William says. "And I was very glad I sent it to him." He sets the box on the counter.

She turns it around and looks at the address. "Bigfork?"

"That's right. Will it get there on Monday?"

She shakes her head. "Sorry—Monday is Memorial Day. It can be delivered on Wednesday before five. Is that okay?"

William sighs. "I forgot all about the holiday. Wednesday seems like forever."

"Well ... if you're willing to spend the money, you could overnight it and pay for Saturday delivery." She looks at the clock. "It can still go out today."

"How much?"

"Hang on." She weighs the package, measures it and enters the information in her computer. "To overnight your package and have it delivered tomorrow will cost fifty-three dollars. How does that sound?"

"Exorbitant but worth it," he says. "Thank you."

And just like before, William is back in his car in next to no time.

When he and Baron get home, they go straight to his office, and William writes a lengthy email to Paul Bouchard, care of the *Saint Paul Herald*. He explains everything, including how he has sent the jammer to Gust Nelson, who will receive it tomorrow. *Please help these people*, he tells Bouchard. *They deserve it.* He attaches the photo of the jammer, reads the message over and adds a PS—*Please do not contact me!* Then he places the cursor on SEND and rests his finger on the mouse.

"Moment of truth, Hürtgenvoss." William presses down, almost imperceptibly, and his job, Amy's aspirations and Lothrup's appeal all vanish in a mouse click. William thought doing the right thing would make him feel better, and he's surprised when it doesn't. But no matter, there's no turning back now: the battle is joined, the die cast, the fuse lit. All William has to do is wait for the bomb to go off. This is like hitting your thumb with a hammer, he thinks. There is the initial blow, then the stinging pressure that is followed a second and a half later by a surge of searing pain. And that's where he is—caught in that interstitial moment, waiting for the pain.

So William, having sown the wind, is prepared to reap a whirlwind, which he fully expects will be an EF5 tornado. But that's okay—he knows he can handle it. The real issue is Amy, who has been caught in the middle through no fault of her own. William feels as though he should give her a heads-up and let her know that she's never going to be director of the Lothrup Lab School. And worse, that he's the reason. Neither the regents nor Herb Gardner would ever tell her why she didn't get the job. If she were to press them, they might say that her public school background wasn't quite what they were looking for or that she didn't have enough executive experience. They might even take refuge in the explanation, much beloved of hiring committees everywhere, that she just didn't seem like *a good fit.*

William doesn't know when or where it will happen, but he supposes he will have to tell Amy the whole story at some point, maybe after things come to a head, which he figures will be Tuesday or Wednesday—whenever Bouchard can get the article written.

William turns his computer off and has just begun pacing when he remembers about the bed. *Oh shit! How did I forget that?* He quickly retrieves the frame from the garage and reassembles the bed, even putting fresh sheets on it. Minutes later, he walks into his office looking for his cell phone and steps on a discarded piece of bubble wrap that explodes like muffled gunfire. For an awful moment, William can taste the fear and smell the acrid odor of gunpowder, but he's able to talk himself down—*This isn't real. This isn't fucking real*—and what might have been a full-blown episode is, in the end, just a scare. Sometimes it's like that. Sometimes William's mind can gain the upper hand over the howling madness of his memories. But not often.

When he's sure he's okay, William and Baron make a run to the grocery store. "I need some limes, Hürtgenvoss. I should have stopped on the way home from UPS, but naturally, I didn't think of it."

They're back home in half an hour, and William tiptoes into the kitchen and puts the limes in the refrigerator before he realizes that Marcia isn't home yet. Good, he thinks. Couldn't be better.

Marcia walks in the door twenty minutes later, and they tell each other about their days. William's half of the exchange is pure invention, of course—Marcia has been out of the loop so long it would take a week to bring her up to speed on what he just did and why. But even so, William is struck by how rapidly the patterns of their old life are reconstituting themselves, and it pleases him.

"Where did you and Kate have lunch?" he asks.

"Alfie's. Did you work on the book?"

"Yes, but I'm afraid I did more thinking than writing."

Marcia heads for the bedroom. "Did you have a chance to fix our bed?"

"Yes, I even made it—no job too big or too small."

"Thank you," she says, turning around. "I thought I'd change my clothes and work outside for a while—it stays light so long now. Care to join me?"

"Yeah, sure," William says. "I'll cut some grass. All the rain has turned the yard into a jungle."

Ten minutes later, Marcia is working in one of her flower beds and William is trying to start the push mower.

"Why don't you use the rider?" Marcia asks.

"It's almost out of gas," William says, "and I need the exercise." But the real reason he's using the push mower is because there are times—and this is one of them—when he needs the brainless back and forth of it.

Very soon, that afternoon becomes like so many others. There is the same cornflower blue sky, the same lemony smell of the linden trees. But this time, there is something paradoxically new about the old scene, and it makes William feel as if he's trespassing in his own life.

After an hour, he shuts off the lawn mower and walks over to where Marcia is digging in the ground with a spade. "What are you doing?"

"Oh, hi," she says. "I'm dividing my hostas and moving some of this primrose out of here—it's taking over."

William lowers his voice. "Gerardo wants us to meet him on the patio."

"*Our* Gerardo? Seriously?"

"I found him in one of the boxes that you left at the carriage house. And I have to say … he was not amused."

Marcia laughs. "I hope he'll accept my apologies. I had a few other things on my mind." Marcia gets to her feet and stretches. "Can you help me gather up my stuff?"

The two of them put her tools and an open bag of potting soil in the wheelbarrow, which William pushes into the garden shed. Then they make their way to the kitchen, where William pulls Gerardo out of the cupboard.

"I don't even remember putting him in a box," Marcia says, "let alone banishing him to the carriage house … I'm sorry, Gerardo." She turns to William. "If you're wanting to make frozen daiquiris, we don't have any—"

"Yes, we do." William goes to the refrigerator and takes out the bag of limes. "Ta-da."

Marcia kisses him on the cheek. "You think of everything." She points to Gerardo's pitcher. "Let me wash that."

She cleans and dries the pitcher and gives it back to William, who twists it onto the blender's base and makes an elaborate show of filling it with ice, rum, triple sec, sugar syrup and lime juice. When he has everything in the pitcher, he plugs it in, puts the lid on and presses MIX. Gerardo springs to life and churns noisily through the ice cubes, gaining RPM as the contents of the pitcher become a beautiful silver-green slurry. For William, Gerardo isn't so much a blender as a time machine that has just dropped him and Marcia off in the middle of their old life together.

"*Es hora de un daiquiri,*" William says. "Time for a daiquiri."
He turns off the blender, fills two daiquiri glasses with the gelid
liquid, and he and Marcia go out on the patio, setting the pitcher
between them on the picnic table.

"I forgot how much I enjoy these after a long, hot day," Marcia
says.

"Same here," William says. "And I've really missed Havana."

Marcia laughs. "Many is the time old Gerardo has taken us there."

They talk mostly about the past but try to keep things imper-
sonal, which is difficult over the first pitcher of daiquiris and even
more difficult over the second. Baron, who has been lying patiently
beside the picnic table, finally gets up, walks over to William and
barks once.

"Another county heard from," Marcia says.

"He wants his dinner. I'll be right back." William goes inside
and comes back with a bowl of dog food that he sets down on the
flagstone. "Bon appétit, Hürtgenvoss. Sorry it's late."

"What about you?" Marcia asks. "Are you hungry?"

"Not really."

"I'm still full from lunch, but I could make you a grilled cheese
sandwich."

William doesn't answer right away. "A grilled cheese sandwich ...
no thanks. Did I tell you that I'm going to see Marv tomorrow?"

"No," Marcia says.

"I could have sworn I did."

"I'll bet you told Amy. I'm sure it's hard to keep track of things
like that."

William knows better than to respond, so he changes the subject. "Saturday and Sunday are the big visitor days at Crosswell."

"Yes, I know, William."

William is embarrassed. "Yeah ... of course you do. I have no
idea what I'm going to say to him."

"Did you make an appointment? You can't just show up there."

"Right ... I'll do that soon."

Marcia empties her glass. "I'm getting a little tipsy. And my lips
are getting numb—you know what that means."

William laughs. "I sure do—*cut her off.*"

Marcia looks down at her ankles. "The mosquitos are coming out."

"They've gotten a lot worse since the rain," William says. "Let's go inside. I'm gonna call Cross and get cleaned up. C'mon, Baron."

So the three of them go in, and William makes an appointment to see Marv at ten the next morning. Then he gets in the shower. He's about halfway finished when the shower door opens, and Marcia, completely nude, steps in and joins him.

"I thought you might like some company," she says.

"You were reading my mind," he whispers. He takes Marcia in his arms and kisses her. It's a long, deep kiss that obliterates the last two years in a heartbeat and leaves them in a place beyond the present, a place with no history and no memories. They kiss again, and their hands are everywhere—touching, caressing, remembering. They are nothing but their bodies, the hardness and softness, the heat and the bloodrush. They finish their lovemaking on the bed, and afterward William feels a delirious synthesis of joy and relief, as though he's found his way home after many days in the wilderness. Sex with Marcia is familiar and reassuring—the perfect synergy.

Marcia giggles. "We were always pretty good at that, weren't we?"

"Yes, and I see we haven't lost our touch. How long has it been?"

"A long time," Marcia says, "but I don't want to talk about the past. I'm more interested in the future."

"Are you suggesting we have one?"

"That will depend on you, but either way, it's time I told you some things." Marcia looks at him. "Let's start with this—it was a terrible mistake to leave you, William, and I'd give anything—I repeat, *anything*—if I hadn't done it."

William tries to say something, but Marcia stops him. "Please ... let me finish. You weren't the only one who went crazy when Jon was killed. I went a little crazy too, but by that time, you were too far gone to notice. I don't blame you for what happened to us, but when you built that wall around yourself, you shut me out, and I got frightened. I've never felt so alone, and I think that's one of the reasons why I made such an awful, stupid decision.

Honestly, William—when I look back on what I did, it's like a terrible dream." Marcia starts to cry, covering her face with her hands. "Walter is a great guy in so many ways, but … he isn't *you*."

William holds her close. "It's all right, honey. It's ancient history—water under the bridge."

She looks at him earnestly. "I want to be with you, William. I want things to be the way they were. Do you think you could ever forgive me?"

William kisses her hair, which smells like the forest after a rain. "I already have—except for the furniture."

"But … but my lawyer said if I didn't do that, it would look like—"

"Hey, I'm kidding. I don't care about the furniture. What matters is that we belong together. When you've been through what we have, you can't throw all that history away—it's *far* too precious. You and I made a life together, raised kids together, lost a child together. We shared all that, and if we don't have each other, we lose half of everything that ever happened to us."

"I know," Marcia says. "When I think about my life, you're a part of everything in it, and even if I wanted to, I couldn't change that. I can't just crop you out of the picture and pretend you were never there."

"Would you like to?"

"Not anymore. And I was foolish to try—I see that now. But I wish we could be part of each other's good memories and not the bad ones."

William smiles. "But that would alter the Gestalt. Our lives are a series of tensions formed by all the elements within them. If you could remove things—even bad things—it would change who we are."

Marcia rolls over on her side and faces William. "Do we need to talk about Amy? Do you love her? I'll understand if you do."

It's several seconds before William answers. "I think I do love her, but because I've always been in love with you, it was hard for me to tell. All I know is that I definitely don't love her in the way I love you."

"Do you need to talk to her? I mean, it's not like you're in high school—you can't just quit calling."

"I know. You're right."

But William couldn't have confronted Amy to save his life. And he can't decide if this is because he lacks courage or because he lacks moral fiber. But either way, a conversation with Amy isn't in the cards right now.

CHAPTER 27

The Hotel California

THE NEXT MORNING William is up early, getting dressed to leave for Crosswell, when he notices that Baron is running all over the house, obviously looking for something. After a couple of minutes, William realizes what it is and lends a hand.

"I'll check the kitchen and the living room," he tells him. "You take a look in my office."

Marcia is unloading the dishwasher but stops when William walks in and peers under the table.

"What are you looking for?" she asks.

"Baron's leather skate guard."

Marcia makes a face. "Is *that* what that was? I threw it away yesterday. No wonder he hates me."

"Baron doesn't hate you, but he found that skate guard by the boathouse at Lake Ellen. He gets very attached to things he finds."

"Just for the record," Marcia says, "how do you know that's the toy he's looking for? He has lots of toys."

"That's true, but the skate guard is his morning toy."

"Ah, of course. How did I not know that? Tell your alter ego not to despair. His skate guard is in the garbage can in the garage. I'm sure I can find—"

William puts his hand on her arm. "I've got this. C'mon, Baron." A few minutes later, William finds the skate guard, and Baron prances proudly through the house with it clenched in his teeth, hoping that William will try to take it from him.

"All's well that ends well," Marcia says, looking on. "I want to ask you something before you leave."

William looks at his watch. "I'm running a little late."

"This will just take a second. I was wondering how you'd feel about heading down to Minneapolis when you get home from Cross. I could make a reservation at the Marquette. We can have dinner someplace nice, and tomorrow we could go to the Conservatory. They've turned the pond and the sunken garden into Monet's garden at Giverny. They say it's unbelievable."

"But … I'd have to board Baron."

"Yes, but just for one night. I really want to do this, William."

William doesn't like the idea, but because he's in a hurry, he gives in. "Yeah … okay. Call Priscilla's Pampered Pet Palace and see if they have room."

"Thank you, sweetheart. I'll make all the reservations, and I'll have your carry-on packed by the time you get home."

"All right. I really have to get going. Cross is 120 miles from here and—"

"A hundred seventeen," Marcia says. "Say hi to Marv, and I'll see you this afternoon."

William takes Baron's head in his hands. "You be a good boy and don't cause any trouble. I won't be gone long."

William has never driven to Crosswell, but it's in Glenfield, and he knows where that is—halfway between Belvidere and Gunderson on Old Highway 57. For the first few miles, William is a wreck at the thought of returning to Cross, which he knows will feel like the scene of a crime. But after a while, he calms down and tries to concentrate on what he can say to Marv that won't sound hackneyed and insincere. It's hard to come up with much, especially since William can't decide the extent to which he's to blame for Marv's attempted suicide. He knew Marv was suffering. He should have done more than call his kid and tell Marv to take his pills.

By the time William gets to Belvidere, his nervousness has returned, and there's a knot in his stomach that tightens with every passing mile. At one point, he tells Baron it won't be much farther;

then he remembers that he left Baron at home with Marcia. It was the right decision. William dislikes leaving Baron in the car for indeterminate periods. A lot of things can happen to a dog in a car, and to a worrywart like William, they're all bad.

A few miles south of Belvidere, William sees a sign for Glenfield, then one for Crosswell, and for some reason seeing the name in print is much worse than just thinking about it. William crosses the Bowfin River, which he remembers—or perhaps it's the little K-truss bridge he remembers—and turns left on Old Highway 57. Ten minutes after that, he passes beneath a large stone archway and drives onto the campus of Mason Crosswell Hospital. From a distance—and by the way it catches the morning sun—William thinks the hospital looks like a cross between a fancy ski lodge and one of those swank *fin-de-siècle* sanatoriums, where rich Europeans went to recover from tuberculosis.

He follows a serpentine drive toward the hospital's main entrance, but before he gets there, he turns right and parks in the visitors' lot. William feels okay—or thought he did—but he takes no more than five steps from the Jeep when a wave of nausea washes over him and nearly brings him to his knees. He stops, wondering if he is going to vomit, but he doesn't, so he continues to the main entrance, which is overhung by a porte cochere big enough for a bus to pull under. Beneath it are two statues, one on either side of the sliding glass doors.

The statue to the left is mental health pioneer Mason Crosswell, a contemporary of Freud and Pavlov and close friend to William and Charles Mayo. The statue is bronze, covered with verdigris, and like so many Victorian-era statues, it depicts its subject in an Edwardian sack suit with a high collar and very short lapels. The statue on the right side of the door is Saint Dymphna, cast in concrete, holding a Bible and a small bouquet of lilies. The two statues appear to be staring at each other.

As soon as William enters the hospital, its institutional smell induces another wave of nausea, but this time he's ready for it. Two security guards are stationed just inside the front door, and one of them has William empty his pockets and pass through a metal detector, which he does without incident. An orderly that he recognizes makes sure William has an appointment; then he types something into a computer and tells William that Marv is currently in the main lounge. He hands William a visitor's badge on a lanyard, which William places around his neck, and tells him that patients are not allowed to have visitors in their rooms.

"I understand," William says.

"Please follow me, sir." A second orderly escorts William down a long hallway that leads to the lounge, and right away they pass two doctors wearing white coats over their blue scrubs. William recognizes both doctors, but he can't think of their names, and they don't even look at him.

William and the orderly get halfway down the hall when William hears someone playing "Pineapple Rag," *Tempo di marcia.*

"That's Marv Kreitzer, isn't it?"

"Yes, sir," the orderly says. "There are five pianos here at Crosswell, but Mr. Kreitzer, he likes that one best."

The main lounge is big—nearly the size of a basketball court—but it's supposed to be homey, so it's filled with groupings of furniture, each one a sort of ersatz living room. There are huge fieldstone fireplaces at both ends of the room and flat-screen TVs on the walls.

Because there are only a handful of people in the lounge, William and Marv spot each other immediately. William makes his way quickly across the room, and the two of them embrace.

"Thanks for coming, my brother," Marv says.

"You're a hard man to catch up with."

"I know. I'm sorry." Marv points to some tufted chairs in front of a wall of windows overlooking the manicured grounds. "This okay?"

"As good a spot as any," William says, looking around. "The lounge is about the same, except there's more furniture, and everybody's wearing street clothes."

"You have to in this lounge now—new rule."

William points to the center of the room. "Hey, the koi pond's gone!"

"Yeah, they took it out of here. I don't know why."

"That's too bad," William says. "I always enjoyed it. Remember when that kid—Bobby something—ripped off his clothes and peed in it?"

"Unfortunately, the image is seared into my brain."

William laughs. "Mine too. I remember it was the Fourth of July, and we were having sort of an ice cream social in here. All of a sudden, old Bobby walks over to the koi pond, and … What the hell was his last name?"

"Baldwin," Marv says. "Bobby Baldwin—I tend to remember piano names. Do you remember when Mad Max ripped a TV off the wall because they wouldn't let him watch Jerry Springer?"

"How could I forget? It took three orderlies to drag him out of here."

Marv nods toward the people in the lounge. "I think the biggest change from two years ago is that three-quarters of the patients today are heroin addicts. The psych ward, where I am, is practically empty, but the substance abuse wing is overflowing, and smack is the drug du jour."

"I hear fentanyl is a real up-and-comer too."

"It is—it's cheaper and more powerful than morphine."

William settles back in his chair. "So here we are again."

"Yes … here we are."

"How are you doing, buddy?"

Marv makes a so-so gesture with one hand.

"Was that a stupid question?"

"No," Marv says. "It's better than asking me about the food. That's what my kid does when he calls. He can't think of anything else to say."

"Give him time. At least he's calling."

Marv rubs his temples. "They take the bones out of my chicken, William."

"What are you talking about?"

"The kitchen does it. They take the bones out of my chicken because they think I might kill myself with a leg bone or something."

"They're just being careful," William says.

"I know, but it's humiliating."

"Is it time for you to tell me why you did it?"

Marv is slow to answer. "I don't know, William. I can try, but …"

"You weren't taking your meds."

"No, not with any regularity, but it isn't that simple."

William sighs. "And you didn't say one fucking word to me about what you had planned."

"But that's the thing—I didn't *plan* it."

"We're supposed to be friends."

"We *are* friends. You're angry."

"You're goddamn right I'm angry."

"Look, William, it's like I told you that night we went crappie fishing—this isn't about you. It's about *me*. You shouldn't take it personally."

"*Bullshit!* You can't possibly believe that."

Marv raises his eyebrows. "I don't think you're supposed to argue with me, my brother. Remember, I'm not well. If I get upset, I could scream and yell, break things, maybe even start a riot. There's no telling what—"

"Okay, okay—I'm sorry. I don't like what you did, and I'm a little out of sorts. Let's start over." William closes his eyes for two or three seconds and then opens them. "It's really good to see you, Marv. You scared the bejeebers out of me, and if it weren't for that leather jacket ..."

Marv smiles. "That was much better, William. Yes, the jacket changed everything, didn't it? But I don't care about that right now. You must tell me, earthling, what news you bring from the galaxy."

"Well ... here's a tidbit that will knock your socks off—Marcia and I are getting back together. She's in Chambliss."

Marv sits back in his chair. "Seriously?"

"Yeah, she's been here four days, and she wants to give it another try."

"What about Amy? I thought you two were—"

"Yes, but in my heart this is what I've hoped for. It's what I dreamed would happen. Amy is wonderful, but we're talking about my marriage here."

"I'm very happy for you ... if that's what you want."

William looks at him suspiciously. "Do I detect an undercurrent of disapproval?"

Marv shakes his head. "Not really. The past always wins. I know that. Life is like a concert—we pay to hear the old stuff, the stuff we know by heart. That's just the way it is."

"The fact that something happened in the past doesn't make it bad."

Marv throws his arms in the air. "Of course not. But the problem with the past is very simple—it's fucking *over.* Let me tell you something. Most of my time here is spent in group therapy—two different groups a day—and 99 percent of the problems eating at these people are caused by the past. Hell, if they aren't trying to *live* in the past, then they're trying to escape the past, bury the past, atone for the past or rewrite the past. And that includes me. I don't know anyone in this place whose past isn't fucking up their life somehow."

William leans forward. "Lower your voice, Marv. And quit waving your arms. There's an orderly over your left shoulder who's watching you pretty close."

"Fuck him."

"Just dial it down a little. I came a long way to see you, and I don't want you sent back to your room."

"Okay. Whatever. All I'm saying is that you don't end up in a place like this because you worry too much about something in the present moment, like the war in Syria, or about something in the future, like who the next president is going to be. You end up here because of bullshit in your past that hauls you down from behind—a parent who loved you too much or not enough. A spouse who ran off with someone else. A kid who rejected you because … because you made it easy."

"Or a kid who died."

"Of course," Marv says. "But I'm not talking about Jon or anything related—"

"Yeah, I know. I understand what you're saying."

"Then you agree with me—the past is the enemy?"

William makes a face. "I agree that's true for some people. But this all started because I told you Marcia and I are getting back together, and for me, being able to reconstruct that part of my past is a wonderful thing."

"Then congratulations, William. But when it comes to the big trifecta—the past, present and future—only one of them is real.

That's what hangs me up. Naturally, I wish you and Marcia the very best."

"You don't think people can repeat the past?"

Marv shrugs. "Put me down as skeptical. I read someplace that you can't step in the same river twice, and I understand that now. It means even if *you* could stay the same, the river will always be changing."

William nods thoughtfully. "You know, in quantum mechanics, the notion of time is completely different from the way we understand it. It can flow backward or forward, and the present can actually change what happened in the past. In fact, in some cases the future can actually *cause* the past. It's called retrocausality."

"Sounds like a load of crap to me."

"Maybe. But who says time has to be linear? What if it doesn't unfold like history in an A-B-C progression? What if everything is happening at once, like it does in our thoughts? Bobby Baldwin peed in the koi pond. He has *always* peed in the koi pond. And he will always *be* peeing in the koi pond, just as he was a few minutes ago when you brought him up."

"*You* brought him up," Marv says. "Don't hang that crazy bastard around my neck."

"Okay, but you know what I'm saying."

"Actually, I don't, but I know someone who does. There's a guy in my morning group who thinks he time travels whenever he has a seizure. I should introduce you."

"But what I'm talking about is perfectly sound theory. A lot of scientists believe in retrocausality."

Marv laughs. "A lot of scientists believed that Y2K would send us back to the Stone Age, but here we are."

"That's true," William says. "You've got me there. Hey, are you going to watch the Twins this afternoon? They play Detroit at home."

"Are they still in last place?"

"The Twins? Yeah, they're 15 and 31."

"Then I probably won't watch 'em. It's too depressing."

A young man with nerd glasses and a Vandyke goatee walks up behind Marv and puts his hand on Marv's shoulder. "Hi, Marvin—I knew you'd be here."

Marv smiles. "Hello, Avery. It's all about the piano."

"Yes, I know." The young man turns to William. "I could listen to this guy play all day. His touch is heavenly." He looks at Marv. "Aren't you going to introduce me to your friend?"

"Of course. Avery, this is William—he's an English professor. William, meet Avery. Avery is a psychiatric technician."

"It's nice to meet you, Avery," William says as they shake hands.

"The pleasure is mine. It's an honor to meet any friend of Marvin's, but the Saint Patrick's Day hero ... wow! That's really special!"

William looks at Marv, who averts his eyes. "I ... might have said something."

Avery puts his hand to his mouth. "I'm sorry. Was that supposed to be a secret?"

"No, not really," William says. "I just don't go around advertising it. It was all the Saint Patrick's Day hero crap that landed me in this place two years ago."

"Yes, I know," Avery says. "Marvin has told me all about you two desperadoes. I came here from Hazelden three months after Marvin was discharged."

"Yeah, I was gone too—I missed you by a month." William looks at Avery closely. "What is a psychiatric technician? It sounds important."

Avery laughs. "Don't I wish! We're sort of like orderlies, only we don't have to be as big, and nobody cares if we can bench press our body weight."

"Avery is the best friend I have in here," Marv says. "I was about to say I'd go crazy without him, but I'm already crazy, so ..."

Avery pats him on the shoulder. "We just hit it off. It was one of those things." He looks at William. "I didn't mean to interrupt your visit—well, actually, I guess I did. But I should be going. It was a pleasure meeting you, William."

"Nice to meet you too, Avery."

"Marv, I'll try to stop by later this afternoon. Be good." And with that Avery heads across the lounge toward the hallway.

"He seems nice," William says.

Marv smiles. "Avery is gayer than a handbag full of rainbows, but I like him, and he takes good care of me."

"Then I like him too."

William stays for almost two hours, and the two of them talk about the things they always talk about. Nothing is forced or awkward. When he senses that Marv is getting tired, William explains that he has to be going, that he and Marcia are heading down to Minneapolis when he gets home.

"That sounds like fun," Marv says.

"It better be. I have to board Baron, and I'm not happy about it." William sits up straight and puts his hands in his lap. "Look, Marv, there's something I have to tell you before I leave."

Marv looks uneasy. "How nervous should I be?"

"Not very, but next week you're going to hear a lot of things about me, and most of them will be true."

Marv slumps in his chair. "Good Christ! What are you about to do?"

"I've already done it. I blew the whistle on Lothrup, and in a few days everyone will know what I know—that the college screwed up two years ago and got some of its students killed."

"Should I assume this has something to do with the now famous three-minute delay in the active shooter alert?"

"It does, yeah."

"Are you kissing your job goodbye?"

"Yes, but I don't care anymore. I have to do this."

"Why?"

William laughs. "I'm not sure … Maybe it's because of a little girl with a crooked smile who thought *Wuthering Heights* was the greatest novel ever written."

Marv nods. "I'm gonna let that go for now, other than to point out there's a high likelihood the wrong one of us is a patient here."

"Speaking of which, when do you think you'll get out?"

"Who knows?" Marv says. "Maybe in a couple weeks, if I'm lucky. This place is like the Hotel California—'You can check out any time you like—'"

"'But you can never leave.' Yeah—I know what you mean."

Marv looks up at William. "When I do get out, can we go fishing?"

"Of course. We can even take a trip if you want. We could spend a week at Young's Bay on Lake of the Woods. Or if you wanted to try the English River, we could run up to Halley's—you'd love it there."

"Mille Lacs is fine, William. We don't have to go anywhere. I just need something to look forward to."

"Well, you got it. We can fish Mille Lacs, Otter Tail, the Whitefish Chain. Like I said, I'm gonna have lots of free time."

They both stand up and embrace.

"Thanks for coming. It means a lot."

"I'll be back soon. You're gonna have a lot of questions."

"This thing you did … it's gonna be in all the newspapers?"

"Yes, and on every TV station in the state."

"Good Lord, my brother—here we go again."

CHAPTER 28

Buzz and Neil

ON THE WAY HOME from Crosswell, William thinks about all the things he hasn't been able to get to lately, and high on the list is telling Marcia that, in a very short time, he isn't going to have a job anymore. That won't be a deal-breaker as far as getting back together goes, but William knows she won't approve of what he's done, especially when it comes to the economic consequences. That's because the way Marcia sees it, life is a ground acquisition game, like football, and the object is to keep moving the ball down the field without a lot of sacks and penalties that force you to pay for the same real estate twice. Living hand-to-mouth might be forgivable in one's youth, but if you find yourself clipping coupons twice in the same lifetime, it's a sure sign that you screwed up somewhere. William decides it's best to tell Marcia everything on the way down to the Cities. He wants to get it out of the way, and if it ruins the trip, so be it.

William doesn't pay much attention to the speed limit and gets home at ten minutes to three. Marcia and Baron both come out to greet him, and Baron acts as though he hasn't seen William for a month.

"I love you too, Baron," William says, "but please don't jump up on me."

"You're earlier than I expected," Marcia says, kissing him on the cheek. "How's Marv?"

"Better than I thought he'd be, but … it's hard to know for sure."

"Does he know how long they're going to keep him?"

"No, not really. He wants to go fishing when he gets out. I thought that was a good sign."

"I'm sure it is. Listen, I made the reservations at the Marquette Hotel and at Murray's for dinner tonight. And I've packed our bags."

"What about Baron?"

"He has a reservation too. We'll drop him at Priscilla's on the way out of town."

"Okay, I just have to gather up a few things."

Marcia looks at him. "Like what?"

"Oh, you know—Baron's vaccination history and a few of his toys. I don't want him to get lonely at the kennel."

"It's just one night, William."

"Yeah … I know."

"Since you just drove to Crosswell and back, would you like me to drive down to the Cities?"

"No thanks. I'm not tired."

At three fifteen, William, Marcia and Baron walk into Priscilla's Pampered Pet Palace, and in addition to Baron, William has brought along Baron's deer antler, Lamb Chop, Mr. Monk and the skate guard. Fortunately, Priscilla is used to pet owners like William, and she is very patient as he asks about everything from kennel cough to the fire code. Finally, and with perceptible reluctance, William hands Baron over, and he and Marcia head for Minneapolis.

After twenty minutes, Marcia asks William why he's so quiet. "Are you thinking about Baron or about Marv?"

William shakes his head. "Neither. I'm trying to figure out how to tell you something."

"Uh-oh … that doesn't sound good."

"Let's just say I've done something you aren't going to like."

Marcia tries to smile. "Don't worry about it. I owe you one."

"You don't owe me a thing," William says. "But this could take a while."

"Then you'd better get started."

So William explains everything, starting with the capricious cell phone signal strength in Old Dewhurst—something Marcia remembers—and ending with how he sent Rupert's jammer to Gust Nelson and how he told Paul Bouchard he'd done it.

Marcia is stunned, and it's hard for her to grasp all the pieces of the story. "And the jammer was in Rupert's briefcase the whole time?"

"Yes. But until recently, I had no idea."

Marcia shakes her head. "It's hard to believe. I mean, Rupert wasn't the type of person who would do a thing like that."

"To the contrary," William says. "Rupert was a frustrated, ineffectual professor who was humiliated every day by the students he was supposed to be teaching. He was *exactly* the type of person who would do a thing like that."

"And you say Joyce never knew about the jammer?"

"No one knew, and the people who had an inkling managed to talk themselves out of it."

Marcia points to a speed limit sign. "You can go seventy here. Look, I know that you think you're doing the right thing, William—and maybe you are—but it sounds like idealism gone to seed to me. I don't really understand why you did it."

William laughs. "Neither do I. Maybe it was just time."

"What does *that* mean?"

"I'm not sure." William moves over one lane to allow for merging traffic. "I saw a documentary last year about Death Valley, and it explained how the wildflowers there bloom only once a decade, if that. All the seeds just lie dormant in the soil until the proper conditions are met."

"What kind of conditions?"

"Well, it has to be an El Niño winter, for one thing. And there has to be a lot of rain in the fall, and we're talking about a place that gets maybe two inches a year. But if all the metaphoric planets align, Death Valley explodes in a mind-blowing profusion of wildflowers. It's called a superbloom."

"And your point is?"

"Maybe that's why I did it—maybe it was just time. I think my planets aligned, and I sort of … burst into blossom."

Marcia rolls her eyes. "My God, William."

"Yeah, I know, but *something* happened to me, and when it did, I found it impossible to sit on the sidelines and watch Lothrup cover up the fact that it was indirectly responsible for the deaths of its students. What should I have done?"

"I honestly don't know. But when Lothrup fires you, which of course it will, what are we going to do for money?"

"We'll be okay," William says. "I've saved enough that we can survive for a while. And you must have some of Jon's insurance money left."

"I do."

"Then we'll be all right. Eventually, I can get a job at a junior college."

Marcia laughs. "Yes, if you're willing to teach Freshman Comp and Intro to Everything."

"I'll do what I have to. If worse comes to worst, we can always move to Bulgaria. I hear you can live very well there on $1,500 a month."

"I've heard that too," Marcia says, "but there's a catch—you have to live like a Bulgarian."

William looks at her. "Maybe we're getting ahead of ourselves with all the gloom and doom."

"I'm sure we are," Marcia says. "Besides, what could we possibly have to worry about? You won't lose your job for at least ... two or three more days. You have a car in your blind spot over here."

"I see it. Where do I exit?"

"Twelfth Street. It's a ways yet. You'll take Twelfth five blocks to Seventh and Marquette—that's where the hotel is."

"It's coming back to me."

The Marquette is an elegant Minneapolis hotel tucked inside the IDS Center and connected to everything via the skyway. It's an excellent choice for a back-to-the-future *escapade romantique*, but William is having trouble getting into the swim of things. Having to put Baron in the kennel is part of the problem, but there's something else too, something vague and shadowy lurking just beyond the edge of his thoughts. William can't tell for sure what it is, and in his frustration, he feels like one of the blind men in the parable who touches an elephant yet is unable to describe what it looks like.

At the Marquette they check in, find their room and crank the air conditioning. William flops on the bed.

"Oh, yeah," he says, half groaning.

"Are you hungry?" Marcia asks. "We have a seven thirty dinner reservation at Murray's."

"Mostly, I'm just tired."

"Should we cancel? It's fine with me—we can order something from room service."

"Yeah, let's do that," William says. "All I want is a sandwich. There must be a menu around here someplace."

Marcia finds one by the phone, and after she cancels the reservation, she orders sandwiches and beer—a turkey sandwich for William and an avocado BLT for herself. Their food comes very quickly, and they eat sitting on the wrong side of the desk, looking across Seventh Street at the Wells Fargo Center.

"You've gotta try this," William says, offering Marcia a bite of his sandwich. "The turkey is smoked, and it has crushed blueberries on it."

Marcia shakes her head. "No thanks. I've got all I can handle right here." She lifts the BLT to her mouth with one hand, while trying to keep a slice of avocado where it belongs with the other.

They watch a little TV and go to bed early. William is tired and falls asleep right away, but he's awakened just before dawn by the ghostly whoosh of elevators that have already begun racing from floor to floor within the quiet building. Right after that, he hears muffled voices in the hallway, and he knows it's guests headed for the gym and hotel staff delivering newspapers and pots of coffee to the rooms. At eight o'clock Marcia wakes up, and by nine, the two of them are having breakfast on the balcony at Basil's, overlooking the IDS Crystal Court, a large indoor park covered by a canopy of skylights.

"It's prettier in the winter," Marcia says, "when the Christmas decorations are up."

William points to the fountain. "But that's beautiful any time of year. I'll bet it's over a hundred feet high." The water falls like rain, straight down from the top of the atrium, and splashes into a thirty-foot marble pool surrounded by olive trees in huge pots.

"We don't have to go home today." Marcia says. "I was hoping once I got you down here, you might agree to stay another day. We could go to a ball game."

William laughs. "You temptress—Detroit is in town." There are few places William loves more than Target Field, which to him embodies the very crosscurrents of Minnesota life. It's the intersection of Carhartt and Louis Vuitton, of country strong and urban chic. Or as Marv always says, it's where *Storage Wars* meets *Downton Abbey*. But William knows there will be no ball game on this trip. "The thing is … I don't want to leave Baron in the kennel any longer than I have to."

"I understand. I thought it was worth a try."

After breakfast they check out, take the elevator down to P2, where the car is, and begin making their way across town to the Saint Paul Conservatory.

"Naturally, I don't remember where it is," William says.

"It's over by the fairgrounds—take I-94 to Lexington Parkway."

"Right, right."

Traffic is light and it takes less than twenty minutes to get there. The Marjorie McNeely Conservatory is a half acre of beautiful gardens under glass in Saint Paul's Como Park. As always, the instant he steps inside, William is transported by the smell—a steamy, rain forest fecundity that seeps into every pore of his body and makes him feel as though he's been teleported into the Amazon basin.

Marcia touches her hair. "I'd forgotten how humid it is in here."

They spend almost two hours at the Conservatory, marveling at the homage to Monet's garden at Giverny, which has been created with amazing fealty to the paintings and has the same loose mélange of daisies, nasturtium, roses, hollyhocks, and, of course, irises and water lilies.

When they're getting ready to leave, Marcia says, "I'll never forget this. Talk about blurring the line between art and life—even the little bridge is perfect."

"They did a terrific job. I'm glad we saw it."

Before they go, Marcia asks if William would like to walk through the zoo, Como Park's other attraction. "I know you don't really like zoos, but as long as we're here …"

"Yeah, okay," William says. "It's been a long time."

They put twenty dollars in the donation box in the Visitor

Center, leave by the west exit and find themselves in front of the zoo's primate building.

"Nah," William says, hands in his pockets. "No monkeys."

"All right." Marcia points across the street to the bird building. "How about birds?"

"Birds are a go," he says.

So they check out the bird exhibit, and then walk through the "Africa" building and "Wolf Woods," but only one of the wolves is out.

"We should probably see how Buzz and Neil are doing," William says.

"You're right. It almost seems rude not to."

Buzz and Neil are two old polar bears that have been at the Como Park Zoo for what seems like forever. William and Marcia, unsure of where they are, consult a *You Are Here* guidepost and make their way north to "Polar Bear Odyssey," where they find Buzz and Neil lounging on the rocks in an expansive enclosure that resembles a Hudson Bay ecosystem, right down to its vegetation and pools.

"This is all new," Marcia says.

William is reading the sign in front of the exhibit. "That's a relief. I was afraid I didn't remember it."

Marcia pulls her phone from her purse and takes a picture. "They both look great. You know, we actually have photographs of the kids taken with Buzz and Neil—they're like big furry uncles. How have they been?"

William finishes reading and shrugs. "Good, I guess. It says they're seventeen years old now. They spent the last two years in Detroit while this new exhibit was being built." William shakes his head. "Detroit—I wouldn't wish that on anybody."

Marcia looks around at all the people watching the bears. "I'll bet these guys are the biggest attraction in the zoo."

"They probably are, but you know me—if I could press a button and return them to the Arctic, I'd do it." One of the bears slides into the pool and begins swimming around on his back.

Marcia takes another picture and walks over to William. "If you returned them to the wild, they'd hate you for it. This is the only life they know, William. Besides, the North Pole is melting. You can't go back to a life that doesn't exist anymore."

William looks at her but doesn't say anything.

On their way to the car, they pass a woman in the parking lot who is engaged in a contest of wills with her dog, a terrier of some kind. He has a Starbucks cup in his mouth, and the woman is trying to take it from him. But even though the dog is on a leash, every time she makes a move for the cup, the dog manages to get his mouth beyond her reach. The woman is becoming angry, and William is wondering if he should help her, when a man stops and holds the leash while she takes the cup away.

William has stopped walking at that point, and Marcia takes his arm. "Thinking about Baron?"

"No. Yes … I'm not sure." William looks at his watch. "But speaking of Baron, we need to rescue him from Priscilla's House of Alliteration by five o'clock, or we can't get him until tomorrow—that's what the sign said."

Marcia laughs. "We'll be there with time to spare. Trust me." She looks at William's hands. "Honey … you're shaking."

Embarrassed, William puts his hands in his pockets. "It still happens sometimes. It doesn't mean anything."

Marcia is right, and by four o'clock, they are standing at the counter of Priscilla's Pampered Pet Palace, waiting for Baron to be brought out. Suddenly, a door opens behind the counter, and there is the mad clatter of toenails on linoleum as Baron bursts into the room. He's pulling a kennel girl behind him, who is holding on to his leash with both hands, and Baron is doing everything in his power to get to the other side of the counter where William is.

"He heard your voice," the girl says, laughing. "He's really strong."

"But not especially obedient," William says, dropping to one knee. Baron is all over him, crying and whimpering with excitement. "It's all right, Baron. Everything is okay."

"Good heavens!" Marcia says. "Did he think you weren't coming back?"

William scratches him behind the ears as Baron licks his face. "I don't know, but he's kind of a worrier. Isn't that right, Hürtgenvoss?"

Baron calms down in the car but gets excited all over again when they pull in the driveway.

"He's really wild," Marcia says. "How are we going to live with him?"

"He just needs a little exercise. I'll take care of it."

William has no sooner unlocked the front door than Marcia is doing laundry and making a list for the grocery store. William would like to write a letter—in fact, he *needs* to write a letter—but Baron wants to play, to go outside where William can throw a ball for him. Or hide. Or chase him around the yard with his arms outstretched. Baron has twenty-four hours' worth of pent-up energy to deal with.

"William, I'm going to the store—we're out of *everything*."

Marcia sounds as though she's in the kitchen, and William hollers back, "Okay, see you later." He looks at Baron, so eager and hopeful. "Okay, buddy, you win—let's go play."

For twenty minutes William throws a ball for him, and after that, they go down to the river, which is still swollen with the rain and running fast. To Baron's delight there are suckers in the shallows, holding themselves in the current like trout, and he chases them for quite a while before giving up and joining William on shore.

"I know you get frustrated, Hürtgenvoss, and I sympathize. But you'll catch one eventually—it's all about practice." William rubs Baron behind one ear. "And speaking of practice, whaddya say we go home and brush up on the commands you're gonna get tested on next week? Thanks to me, we're one class behind."

So when Marcia pulls in the driveway a half hour later, William and Baron are in the front yard, working on the *long stay*.

Marcia gets out of the car and walks over to them. "What are you two doing? Are you practicing for obedience class?"

"Yes, did I tell you about that?"

"No. Kate did. Baron's all wet."

"He's been swimming. What else did she tell you?"

Marcia laughs. "Everything. She told me that you and Amy go to obedience class together on Wednesday nights. What kind of dog does she have?"

"An Akita."

"Oh, I love those. Did you see that movie with Richard Gere? He has an Akita, but then he dies."

"The Akita?"

"No, Richard Gere. He dies at work, and his dog meets the same train every day for the rest of its life, but of course ... Richard Gere isn't on it."

"Even a dog has to know when to stop meeting trains," William says.

CHAPTER 29

Memorial Day

THE NEXT MORNING, William, Marcia and Baron go to the Memorial Day parade, and after that, William and Baron go to Dewhurst to tidy up his office for the summer. Office cleanup is a Memorial Day ritual, but it seems silly this year because William knows he won't be back—except to remove his personal belongings after he gets fired. William stops on the first floor to pick up his mail, and because he hasn't been there for a week, he finds everything stuffed into his mailbox so tightly that he has trouble getting it out.

His partially shredded mail in hand, William follows Baron upstairs, and as soon as he unlocks his office and steps inside, William sees the voicemail light flashing on his desk phone. He sets the mail down and plays the message: *Hello, William. This is Gust Nelson. It's Saturday night ... The college gave me your office number. You're probably not there much in the summer, but I'm sure you'll get this eventually ...*

That's one helluva story about the jammer, William. UPS delivered it this afternoon, and I don't know what to say, except thank you. It's one of the nicest things anyone ever ... That reporter, Paul Bouchard, has called twice already, and he's coming up here tomorrow to meet us and take some pictures. He's an eager beaver, but he seems like a nice-enough person.

Oh—I almost forgot! We have a meeting with our attorney on Tuesday. I called him the minute I finished reading your letter, and he said the jammer could be a magic bullet for us, which is the kind of thing he never says. I've spoken with the other families too, and they really want to meet you. I hope we can work something out. Until then, thank you for this incredible thing that you've done. I'm sure glad that pipe in your basement sprung a leak. Take care, my friend.

There is dead air followed by a click, and Gust is gone. William smiles and gives an enormous sigh of relief. "Baron, this might actually work. Anyway, so far so good."

William goes through his mail, but despite its volume, there are only two things in it that interest him, and both of them are in last week's *Beacon*. One is a response from Gardner to *Light It Up*'s petition. His letter begins as a smarmy attempt to praise the members of *Light It Up* for their activism, but it soon becomes clear that his larger goal is to remind everyone that he is not only the boss but also the high court of appeals when it comes to deciding what the college will and won't spend money on. The other thing that catches William's eye is a short article on the selection process for a new lab school director. The article explains that there are now three finalists, and each one is briefly quoted. William reads Amy's statement several times: *I believe in the education of our children more than anything in the world, so to be the director of Lothrup's lab school would not only be a dream job, it would be a dream come true.*

"A dream come true," William says softly. "My feelings exactly."

He looks around his office and realizes that it won't take long to clean out, if only because it's too new for a lot of personal items to have accumulated there. Other than a couple of pictures and some stuff on the shelves, the place is nearly empty. William notices that his suitcase full of Dostoevsky books is sitting by the door. He'd forgotten to take them home last Monday when he was so sick and went home early.

"Baron, as long as I'm here and the books are here, maybe I should do a little work on *Regaining the Garden*—you know, to take my mind off things."

William has often taken refuge in the process of writing when his life became too difficult or too painful to face. And most of the time, it's a dodge that works. So William opens his suitcase and removes the three books he was studying before he got the flu. He begins to read, then to take notes, and it isn't long before he has written twelve hundred words about Saint Petersburg, Russia's window to Eastern Europe in the 1850s. In Dostoevsky's novels, European ideas are often represented as infectious diseases, and because of Saint Petersburg's proximity to Europe, Dostoevsky's morally debilitated characters often fall prey to these ailments, which attack their already inflamed feelings of guilt and moral dislocation.

William knows the idea of illness as metaphor, while hardly original, could work nicely in *Regaining the Garden,* and he works on it until late afternoon. But then, when he prints what he's written and reads it over, he isn't happy with it. "It's like Gertrude Stein once said, Hürtgenvoss—it looks like syrup, but it doesn't pour." He crumples up the pages and throws them in the wastebasket. "Fuck it!"

William closes his eyes and attempts to surrender to Dewhurst's ambient hum—a Zen-like syllable that is the conflation of fluorescent lights and rooftop air conditioning. He tries desperately to stop thinking, to annihilate the subject/object duality that fosters all pain and desire. But after ten minutes, he has failed to achieve anything like mindfulness, and he is no closer to apprehending nirvana, moksha or even satori than he ever was.

"This isn't working Hürtgenvoss. *Nothing* is working, and I guess I know why." William hangs his head. "I think it's time to go home." But before he leaves, he stands in the doorway, one hand on the light switch, and looks at his office. "Farewell," he whispers. "I hardly knew ye."

William can smell something cooking the moment he walks into the house, so he heads for the kitchen.

"I'm home," he says.

Marcia laughs. "You certainly are. Did you get your office cleaned up?"

"Not really. It seemed stupid to do that when I'm going to get fired."

"Yes, and when is that happening again? I want to get it on the calendar."

William smiles. "Your sarcasm is duly noted. Tomorrow or Wednesday would be my best guess. What do I smell?"

"I've got macaroni and cheese in the oven—the ultimate comfort food, wouldn't you agree?"

"Yes, unless single-malt Scotch is a food group."

"Which reminds me ... can I get you to make us a daiquiri? I've been thinking about one for the last hour."

"Of course." William takes Gerardo from the cupboard and fills the pitcher with the requisite ingredients. But this time, when he turns it on, nothing happens.

William stares at the blender, dumbfounded.

"Oh, no," Marcia says. "What's wrong with Gerardo?"

"I don't know. It could be a short. Or worst case, the motor's burned out."

"Maybe it's the outlet," Marcia says hopefully.

So William tries another outlet but to no avail. "I just can't believe it," he says, as though a close friend has just let him down.

"Can you use the Cuisinart?"

"I guess so, but ..."

The food processor gets the job done, and they tell each other the daiquiris are just as good, but somehow, they aren't the same at all.

After a daiquiri apiece, Marcia says it's time for dinner, and she makes them each a plate of food—ham, cornbread, macaroni and cheese.

William takes a few bites, but he isn't really hungry. He's nervous and fidgety, but either Marcia doesn't notice or she pretends not to.

"How do you like the mac and cheese?" she says. "Do you remember my secret ingredient?"

"No, I'm sorry. I don't usually remember things like—"

"It's a cup of buttermilk. That's what gives it that tang. Can you taste it?"

William shakes his head. "No, I can't, but ... I *never* taste it—not the buttermilk, not the lavender salt, not anything. I say I do, but I don't ... and I never will." They look at each other across the table, and in that moment, a dozen questions are asked and answered.

Marcia nods and picks absently at her food; then she sets her fork down. "Okay … so there it is. I've seen it coming since Minneapolis. Please say what you're going to say and get it over with."

"All right," William says. "I'm going back to Amy—that is, if she'll have me. I love you, Marcia, and I always will, but it feels as though you're part of something that I need to leave behind. It's not your fault, but I can't seem to separate you from everything that happened two years ago."

Marcia sits up very straight, her hands folded in her lap. "I actually understand that, William. I hate it, but I understand. That's what I meant when I said I wished I could be part of all your good memories and none of your bad ones. But like you said … it doesn't work that way."

"No," William says. "I guess it doesn't."

Marcia is close to crying, fighting back the tears. "I had to try to get you back, William. Please don't hate me for it."

"I could never hate you for anything. I'm glad you—"

"I shouldn't have intruded in your life the way I did. We had our time. I just … couldn't accept that it was over."

"Look, I'm glad you came back. I think we had some unfinished business to tend to."

"Yes," Marcia says, "and now we've tended to it." A single tear rolls down her cheek. "Some Memorial Day, huh?"

William nods. "Yeah."

"You really love her, don't you?"

"So much it hurts."

"It certainly does." Marcia dabs at her eyes with her napkin, folds it loosely and puts it beside her plate. "If you'll excuse me, I'm going someplace where I can cry for a while. I'd like to stay here tonight and go over to Kate and Todd's in the morning—if that's all right. I should spend a little time over there before I go back. Lord knows when I'll see them again."

"Sure … whatever you want."

Marcia gets up from the table and leaves the kitchen. Moments later, William hears her go into the bathroom and lock the door.

William doesn't know what to think. He had done what he had

to do, said what he needed to say, and it had gone neither well nor poorly. Perhaps that's the most he could have hoped for. William sleeps in the guest bedroom that night, and although he isn't sure where Marcia sleeps, he hears her in the master bedroom shortly before midnight.

When he wakes up the next morning, William assumes he'll be taking Marcia over to Kate's because she turned in her rental car on Friday. But when Kate arrives at eight thirty to pick Marcia up, it's clear to William that there's been some mother/daughter communication to which he wasn't privy, not that there's anything new about that. He carries Marcia's suitcase out to Kate's waiting minivan, and he and Marcia embrace. Kate says, *Hi, Daddy*, and that's it—no melodrama, no histrionics. As William watches the van disappear down River Road, he's struck by how much it feels like the end of something.

Part of him wants to go straight to Amy, to fall on his knees and beg her forgiveness, but he knows that would be a terrible mistake because he's unprepared. Getting Amy back will take more than an apology. It will require a strategy, a fail-safe plan with several moving parts. William is prepared to do whatever it takes—plead, grovel, cajole—but if he doesn't lay the groundwork properly, he knows he will fail. What will make winning Amy back so difficult is the fact that she was abandoned by a man once before, so she knows the emotional terrain. And because she survived the ordeal, it left her stronger and improved her defenses to the point where it will be difficult for William to reenter her life, let alone to rekindle a relationship.

William suddenly realizes what day it is and checks the *Herald* online to see if Bouchard's article is there. But it isn't. There is an explosion at the Sartell paper mill, a church fire in Isanti and some hail damage in Fergus Falls. But there is nothing about the campus shooting or the jammer.

"Very well, Horatio," William says, looking at Baron. "*If it be not now, yet it will come—the readiness is all.*"

Baron stares up at him so intently it makes William laugh.

"That's Shakespeare's way of saying the shit will hit the fan in its own good time, Hürtgenvoss. Our job is to be ready when it does."

William hears the distant back-up alarm of heavy equipment and goes into the guest bedroom, where he has a clear view of the carriage house. There are two pickups parked there, and the big flatbed truck from the lumberyard is backing up cautiously to off-load material. One of the workers in a yellow hard hat is motioning the driver to *c'mon back.*

"It looks like it's going to be a busy day over there, Baron. I'm glad that they're finishing the job. I just wish I didn't have to be here when they do it."

William holds out his hands, and they're trembling. No wonder, he thinks. In twenty-four hours, he will be part of a story that will dominate the news cycle for days—even longer if Bouchard is on top of his game. And William will be fifty-two and unemployed. What's worse, there's a good chance Amy will spit in his eye when he tries to fix everything he's fucked up. And if all that isn't bad enough, the carriage house is going to be completed by a bunch of men who have no idea what the job really means—and it was his idea to hire them.

William is about to write a letter but then decides on something else. "Baron, you'll have to stay in the car—dogs aren't really allowed—but ever since Marcia mentioned it, I've been thinking about going to the cemetery." William is not a cemetery person by nature, and he hasn't been there more than three or four times since Jon was killed—and only once with Marcia. The cemetery was another one of those things that he couldn't bring himself to share. But today is a good day to go. Yesterday, the cemetery would have been full of people paying their respects, but today it should be empty.

He and Baron head south out of town, over the Agate River, past the paper mill to St. Charles Road, which takes them to the north entrance of the cemetery. The cemetery looks like one would expect on the day after Memorial Day. The grass is trampled; there are tired bouquets and little American flags on many of the gravesites; and just inside the gate is a demountable dais, now in several pieces, waiting to be hauled back to wherever it came from. Other than a man operating a backhoe at the far end of the cemetery, there is no one around.

No matter where you're going in the Chambliss Cemetery, you have to drive by the fountain to get there—a three-tiered colossus that spills a thousand streams of water into a large stone basin. William turns right at the fountain, drives maybe seventy-five yards and parks near Jon's gravesite. He walks over to it and sees the flowers—a wilted bouquet of Shasta daisies and blue forget-me-nots by the headstone and a cross made of white amaryllis stuck into the ground next to it.

"I guess I know where these came from," William says. "I would have brought a sprig of rue if I'd known where to get one." Since there is no place to sit, William kneels like a penitent and tries to think of something to say. "Jon, words never come easy here, but ... I wish it had been me—I wish that more than any-thing." He remains at the gravesite for several minutes, listening to the birds and the wind in the trees. Then he heads back to the car. On the way he passes Rupert and Joyce Martin's headstone and stops for a moment.

"Rupert, I had no idea you were that young. You always seemed ... I don't know ... *older.*" As he stands there, William feels guilty about hanging Rupert out to dry, but there was no other way, at least none he could live with. "Don't you dare put this on me, Rupert," he mutters. "You were the one with the jammer."

When he gets to the Jeep, William drives back to the fountain, pulls off the little roadway and sits down on one of the marble benches with Baron at his feet.

"Like I said, Hürtgenvoss, you're not supposed to be here, so if anyone comes, plead ignorance." William points to the fountain. "Isn't that remarkable?"

The fountain is Italianate and grand, but its musicality is what William likes about it. People don't pay enough attention to the *sound* of a fountain, he thinks, but this one, with its soft minis-trations, is well worth listening to. Its soothing white noise could calm a crying baby or balance a man's chakras—maybe even his. In any case, it's a good place to think, and William does a lot of it. He thinks about the shooting, Rupert Martin, the jammer, the carriage house and Jon.

It had rained the morning of Jon's funeral, but by the time

they were in the cemetery, the rain had turned to snow, and the fountain, the headstones, the trees—everything was white. William had done his best that day to be strong for Marcia and Kate, who were good one minute and in tears the next. Unlike them, he did not allow himself the emotional luxury of peaks and valleys. Instead, he staked out a claim on the hard, flat plain of equanimity and did his best to stay there. But he nearly lost it during the three-volley salute, and Marcia had placed her hand on his arm and said, *It's okay, honey. You're safe now.*

There had been two buglers that day, one at the gravesite and another some distance away, and when they played "Taps," the beautiful silver echoes kept bouncing into each other, tangling and untangling the cold air. But there are no bugles now, only memories and confusion.

William and Baron stay for another twenty minutes or so and then leave. When they get home, William heads for his office. "I need to write a letter," he tells Baron. He sits down at his desk, opens a Word document and begins to type.

29 May 2012

Hi Jon—

I just got back from the cemetery, and I have some things to tell you that I can never seem to say there. For the thousandth time, I want to apologize for what happened at Dewhurst. I tried to tell you when you were hit, but I think you were already gone. Anyway, I'm sorry, and if I could trade my life for yours, I'd gladly do it. I know you're not a grudge-holder, Jon, and I can practically hear you saying, "Hey, don't worry about it, Dad. No bigs." But it's been an awful thing to live with, and it hasn't gotten any easier with time.

I need to tell you about your mother and me. We divorced a while back; then we tried to reconcile; and yesterday we gave up and went our separate ways again. Things with us have been messy and confused, and yet our relationship is still filled with love, along with an irreducible measure of pain and sorrow. I never told your mother what happened at Dewhurst, and I'm sure that played a role in driving us apart. But the thing is, I never told anybody. It was just too painful.

It's been a crazy couple years, Jon—as freaky as an Ambien dream. I was in a psychiatric hospital for several months, and when I got out, I met a woman so amazing that I'll never finish falling in love with her. But of course I made a mess of everything, and now I have to fix it somehow. What I'm trying to say is that a lot has happened to me, but in spite of it all, I've missed you every single day. And what hurts the most is knowing I'm the reason you aren't here.

That's pretty much all I have to say, except that I love you, kiddo.

Dad

PS: I think you'd be pleased with the carriage house. Most of your ideas—the ones we fought over—have now been incorporated into what is almost a finished product. Don't be angry, but I hired a contractor to wrap things up over there. There were a number of reasons for this, but I think the carriage house was becoming an unhealthy manifestation of my guilt. Or maybe it was my personal white whale. I'm not really sure, but what matters is that I've learned one of Life's Big Lessons: every time we choose our past over our present, we kill our future.

There are tears in William's eyes, and after he reads the message over, he looks down at Baron. "I've just written the ultimate dead letter, my friend."

But it felt good to write Jon, and William doesn't feel *too* crazy because he knows he'll never do it again.

CHAPTER 30

Regaining the Garden

THE NEXT MORNING William turns his computer on and checks the *Saint Paul Herald* with all the trepidation of a child peering through his fingers at a scary movie. What he sees is a picture of Gust Nelson holding the jammer and a picture of Leah, all dressed up, standing in front of a Christmas tree. Between the two pictures is Lothrup's logo. The headline, in a very large font, reads, *Lothrup Cover-up?* There is a second article—*Saint Patrick's Day Hero Turns Whistleblower*—accompanied by a two-year-old picture of William that was used a lot during his hero days. William doesn't read either piece—he knows he's accomplished what he set out to do.

When his phone rings, he assumes it's Sam, but it's Kate, calling from work.

"The newspaper—is it true?"

"I haven't read it yet," William says, "but I assume so."

"Wow! When I told Amy you were a very moral person, that wasn't the *half* of it."

William laughs. "Nothing about this feels moral, Kate. Stupid is more like it."

"Well, it may not be a good career move, but I think you did the right thing—it was very brave."

"Thank you."

Kate pauses for a moment. "Mom says you're going to get fired now."

"Yeah, I probably will. How's she doing?"

"Okay, considering. I just got a text from her, and she has a seven o'clock flight back to Phoenix tonight. Daddy, I want you to know ..." Kate stops, and William senses that she's close to tears.

"It's okay," he says gently. "What do you want me to know?"

"That I don't blame you for any of this stuff with Mom. It isn't your fault."

"It isn't anybody's fault, Kate. It's just ... life."

There is another pause, and when Kate speaks again, there's a slight edge to her voice. "How come Mom knows all about what happened, and I don't? She knows about Bouchard, the man in Bigfork, that thing in the briefcase. There isn't anything she—"

"I would've told you, Kate. But it's complicated, and I never really had a chance. I'll explain everything, but I'm expecting a call right now and—"

"From the college?"

"Yes."

"Okay. Get back to me when you can. I have a million questions."

"I'm sure you do."

After he gets off the phone with Kate, William takes a quick shower and awaits a summons from Sam or Gardner or whoever is going to fire him. When he doesn't hear anything by eleven o'clock, he wonders what the holdup is, but he knows it's only a matter of time.

And he's right. At eleven fifteen he receives a text from Sam: "My office thirty minutes."

"Be there," William replies, in the same laconic spirit. "C'mon, Baron. It's time to pay the piper."

When William walks into Sam's outer office, his secretary seems much busier than usual and nods toward the doorway of Sam's office without making eye contact. Sam, who looks exhausted, is sitting at his desk with the *Saint Paul Herald* in front of him. When he sees William, he presses a button on his phone and says, "Nicole, no calls please." He points to a chair, and William sits down.

"I'm sorry it came to this, Sam. I never wanted—"

"I thought we had a deal," Sam says, his eyes half hidden by dark circles.

William shakes his head. "No."

Sam makes an exclamation of disgust and turns the newspaper around so William can see it. "This was very clever, my friend. Now we can't even hit back without looking like a bunch of assholes who hate puppies, spring and Betty White." Sam picks up the newspaper and throws it into the wastebasket. "Hell, Jeffrey Dahmer's defense team was better positioned than we are."

"I'm sorry. I couldn't think of another way."

"Then you should have asked me," Sam says, his face reddening. "And if things aren't bad enough, AP has picked up the story, and we're getting calls from every news outlet in the country. You really outdid yourself this time, William. I just got off the phone with our lawyers, and they tell me this little development is 'dispositive.' That's legalese for *we're fucked.*"

"I know what it means, Sam. Look, if it helps, I waive my right to due process. You can just fire me."

Sam laughs bitterly. "Due process? Where do you think you are, William? This is a private college, not a state university. We can fire you any day of the week for *just cause*—what's more, we get to decide what that is."

William doesn't say anything.

"I just have one question. Why the hell did you do it?"

William has to think for a moment. "I did it because I couldn't bear the thought of *not* doing it."

"I never figured you for a crusader."

"I'm not," William says. "You made it personal when you used my silence to prop up a lie."

"I should remind you that Lothrup College hasn't broken a single law."

"I know you believe that," William says. "So let's get on with it—if you're going to fire me, *fire* me. I'm sure Gardner told you what to say."

"Gardner's gone, William."

"Gone as in … *not here today?*"

"Gone as in he got fired at three thirty this morning. We met all night—regents, administrators, Lothrup's attorneys, along with seventy-five members of *Light It Up* who were in the hallway, breathing fire."

William is incredulous. "Gardner got fired? What does *Light It Up* have to do with—"

"What I'm about to tell you stays between us." Sam's expression is grave.

"Yes, of course."

"The night before last, a young woman named Chloe Carmichael, a sophomore, was raped walking back to her dorm after a party. It happened between Hobart and the Student Union, which, as you may have heard, was identified by *Light It Up* as one of the most poorly lighted areas of our campus—and consequently, one of the most dangerous."

"Yes, I know. How is she?"

Sam picks up his coffee cup, looks into it and sets it back down. "I wouldn't presume to say. I guess she's gonna be okay physically, but beyond that ..."

"Yeah ... of course. I haven't heard anything about this."

"We've kept a pretty tight lid on it, and the newspapers have helped us out." Sam leans back in his chair. "When Gardner decided to go to war with *Light It Up*, he really stepped on his dick, William. And when *Light It Up* found out about Chloe Carmichael, it was Christmas come early for them." Sam chuckles. "Not to put too fine a point on it, but *Light It Up* went after Gardner with a full head of steam, and old Herb got wound around the axle. It was three thirty in the morning when he saw the writing on the wall and tried to resign."

"But you fired him instead?"

"It's not like we had a choice. Remember all the crazy things he said about buying flashlights and eating carrots? That kind of dumbfuckery is indefensible." Sam draws his finger across his throat. "Gardner was finished a month ago."

"So ... do we have a new chancellor?"

Sam nods. "We do, and you're looking at him. They were going to make me the *acting* chancellor, but then they decided there was enough instability around here without having an interim kahuna." Sam folds his hands and smiles. "I may have had something to do with that."

William whistles softly. "Congratulations, Sam. Well played! I guess you'll have to fire me yourself."

"I've told you this before, William—you never quite see the whole field. Right off the bat, I can think of two good reasons why firing you would be a stupid thing to do. First, Lothrup has enough PR problems right now without my picking a fight with the Saint Patrick's Day hero. Hell, it's just like last time. The media, the students, the parents—they all think you're the Second Coming of Christ for going to the *Herald* about Rupert's jammer. If you don't believe me, check the chat rooms, check Twitter—you'll love #lothrupcoverup."

William waits for a moment. "You said two reasons."

"Yes, I did. The second reason is … you're gonna owe me. I'm going to be chancellor, and Lothrup's celebrity professor is going to owe me a solid."

"Don't bet on it."

"Oh, c'mon, William. You're making over a hundred grand a year here. Do you really want to take a 40 percent cut in pay so you can teach technical writing in a junior college?"

William doesn't say anything, and Sam, now on a roll, keeps going.

"Here's what I mean when I say you're not seeing the whole field. Who do you think would make a good lab school director?"

"Amy Mattson."

"So do I, and I can make that happen."

"The selection process isn't over."

"No, but it *can* be—that's my point. Last night after Gardner was fired, and after I had been named chancellor, we were all dead on our feet, and the regents sent out an email canceling the Q-and-A interviews for lab school director that were scheduled for this morning. Bear in mind, this was *before* they'd read Bouchard's article. Once the paper came out, the regents' Executive Committee sent me an email containing a list of items they wanted off their plate immediately. They said they needed to focus on our current crisis, which is how to pay legal damages that amount to almost 7 percent of next year's operating budget."

"What does that have to do with—"

Sam holds up a finger. "Hang on. Along with recommendations that we address the campus lighting problem and quit obsessing over our credit rating, they also suggested that we end the lab school director search and just give the job to—wait for it—Amy Mattson."

"Excellent idea," William says. "But how can they be so peremptory as to terminate the interview process just because they're busy?"

"They're the regents, William—they can do whatever they want, especially in a crisis. And in case you haven't noticed, a crisis is what we're facing this morning. They said your girlfriend is the odds-on favorite to get the job anyway—she has the most points. But it's my call. All I have to do is sign off on it. Are you seeing the whole field now, William?"

William nods. "Every square inch. I assume you want something in return."

"You're goddamn right I do! I want you to stop talking to the media, especially Paul Bouchard. And I mean right fucking *now*! We can take our lumps, withdraw our appeal and hopefully put this mess behind us, but only if we cut off the oxygen to this story."

"What about the parents? A brand new lawsuit just fell into their lap."

"Yes, thanks to you. But our attorneys are confident that if we agree to pay the original award and not slow-walk it through the system, the parents will agree not to bring new lawsuits against us involving the jammer. We haven't approached them yet, but they'll take the deal. If they don't, three things will happen—their attorney will take a hike, we'll tie them up in court for the rest of their lives, and they'll never see a dime of their twelve million dollars. So there it is. It's over. What do you say?"

William looks at Sam and smiles. "I'd say I misjudged you, Sam. I used to think you didn't have what it takes to be an administrator, but I was wrong. You have exactly what it takes."

"Do we have a deal?"

"Yes."

Sam beams. "That's great! Just refuse to comment. Tell anyone who asks that your lawyer told you to keep quiet."

"Can I tell Amy that she has the job?"

"Sure. That's one less call I'll have to make. Give her my best, and tell her we'll meet next week."

"I will." William stands up and takes a step toward the door; then he turns around. "You know, if I don't ask you this now, I never will … Were you guys behind the break-in at my house two weeks ago?"

Sam looks everywhere but into William's eyes. "How can you even *think* a thing like that?"

Like every Wednesday, this one has come with the usual obedience class jitters, but today they're eclipsed by the gut-wrenching fear that Amy will tell him to get lost when he approaches her. William knows she's capable of it, but he has to get her back, and he's willing to pull out all the stops to make it happen.

When he gets home after his meeting with Sam, William looks up some information he needs for that evening and prints a few pages of it. Then he works with Baron on the Big Five, making sure he's ready for the final exam. Baron looks good overall, and William knows if he's going to have a problem, it will be with the *long stay.*

That afternoon passes with agonizing slowness, and William spends far too much of it imagining every scenario that could play out at obedience class that evening. Predictably, most of them end with him bollixing everything up and coming home alone. After a while, this defeatism takes a toll on his self-confidence, and by the time he leaves for class, William is a wreck.

When he gets to the armory, he sees Amy's car and parks as far away from it as he can—a chance encounter now could ruin everything. And even when he goes inside, William keeps his eyes straight ahead and waits on the sidelines for class to begin. A few people that know who he is walk over and thank him for coming forward about the jammer. William smiles and shakes their hands, saying as little as possible.

Amy and Yoshi are there, passing in and out of his field of vision like apparitions, but he doesn't really look at them. He just tries to keep it together and bide his time.

Two of the dogs have dropped out since the first class in April, so there are only thirteen remaining. Still, it will take some time to evaluate thirteen dogs on five commands, so Jackie gets the class started early, and she has two helpers with clipboards to write down the individual scores. Each of the five commands is worth twenty points, and it takes 50 percent to pass.

William reaches down and gives Baron a pat. "Okay, Hürtgenvoss. It's showtime."

After a couple of warm-up laps around the ring, Jackie begins the testing with the *sit* command. William is on the end of a row and unable to see much, but he has the feeling that all the dogs do what they're supposed to. The *come* command is next, and two dogs flatly refuse to do it. Several others receive point deductions because their owners have to give the command more than once.

The next test is the *heel* command, which is evaluated at three different speeds. It's a simple exercise, and success depends on maintaining a loose leash. If a dog moves ahead of its owner or lags behind, the slack goes out of the leash, and there is a sizeable point deduction. As the dogs and owners make their circuits around the ring, William sees a number of leashes tighten. Yoshi's is one of them. Evan Ball's is another. After the *heel* test, Jackie announces a short break, and William and Baron sit down outside the ring, not far from a man holding a little springer puppy.

"That dog of yours is really something," the man says. "He's totally dominating out there."

"Is he?" William has so many other things on his mind that he hasn't noticed.

"Oh, yeah—your shepherd will be hard to beat." He looks down at his puppy, half-asleep in his arms. "Bailey will be old enough for the next session, so we came tonight to see what it's like. Has it been a good experience?"

William looks at him. "A good experience? It changed my entire life."

The man smiles. "That's what I wanted to hear."

Jackie calls everyone back into the ring for the *down* command—one that only a few of the dogs are willing to obey. Owners are not allowed to touch their dogs at any time during a test, so their only option is to repeat the word *down*, and that's what they do, until the word fills the gym like an incantation. Point deductions mount so quickly that Jackie's helpers have trouble recording them all, but to William's relief, when Baron hears the command, he drops like a rock. *Four tests down, one to go.*

But the last test is also the hardest. For the *long stay*, each dog is required to sit at the end of a six-foot leash, where it must wait to be released from the *stay* for two minutes. If a dog stands up or barks, it loses ten points. If it comes to its owner, it loses all twenty. Jackie divides the class into two groups and sends William's group to the center of the ring. The owners tell their dogs to *sit* and *stay*; then they walk to the end of their dog's leash, turn around and hold their breath. Two of the dogs, tails wagging, run immediately to their owners. Another holds the *stay* for maybe ten seconds but finds the thought of being away from his owner any longer than that unbearable.

Because of Baron's tendency to lift his butt slightly on the *long stay*, William's eyes are riveted on his hindquarters. It isn't that Baron stands up exactly, but it would be a stretch to say that he's still sitting down. After about a minute, William sees Baron begin to lean forward, and suddenly there's three inches of daylight between his hindquarters and the floor. William could give Baron an additional *sit* command and suffer a point deduction. Or he could grit his teeth and communicate telepathically with Baron, establishing some sort of neural interface through which he can tell him to *sit the fuck down*. William goes with the latter option and is amazed to see Baron's rear end settle back to the floor. He isn't sure if anyone noticed Baron's little slip-up, but he thinks they probably didn't.

Of the seven dogs in William's group, only three survive the *long stay*, and Baron is one of them. The six dogs in Amy's group are up next, and Yoshi sits at the end of his leash like he's carved out of stone. But four other dogs in his group fail the *long stay* exercise, and after Amy's group is finished, the dogs and their owners are excused so that Jackie and her assistants can tally the scores.

William and Baron step out through a side door for a breath

of air, returning just in time to hear Jackie announce that every dog in beginners class has passed the obedience test. William is surprised by this and suspects that some of the point tallies may have been massaged a bit. But in William's view, there is nothing wrong with overthrowing the tyranny of mathematics if the cause is worthy—and he should know. There is a lot of excited cheering and clapping, and after everyone calms down, it's time for the award ceremony.

The advanced class is recognized first, and they receive their diplomas and bandannas from Cheryl Torgerson, the woman who had introduced Frau Hochstetler many weeks before. After that, Jackie Carroll does the honors for William's group, presenting each dog and its owner with an official-looking certificate that says they are now accredited graduates of "The Chambliss Kennel Club Beginners Class." There are some silly awards too. Yoshi gets one for being Most Improved. A golden retriever named Marabou is Biggest Flirt, and Evan Ball's Lab gets Class Clown.

"And Baron Kessler," Jackie announces, "who received a perfect score of one hundred, is named Most Likely to Succeed in the Intermediate Class." She hands William his award certificate to much applause, and William shows it to Baron, who has no idea what all the fuss is about.

After the beginners' bandannas are passed out, Cheryl Torgerson gets on the PA system and thanks everyone for their participation in the classes and asks that they take their dogs outside for a bathroom break. "But then come right back," she says, "because we're having a little party, courtesy of the Chambliss Kennel Club ladies. We even have some homemade doggie treats."

So William takes Baron outside and walks him around for a few minutes, being careful to keep his distance from Amy and Yoshi, who are out there too. When he takes Baron back in, there are a lot of people and dogs milling around, and William realizes this is the first time the "advanced" end of the gym has had anything to do with the "beginners" end. And, as if to underscore the fact, Marlene from Admissions walks by with her boxer. William tries to think of something to say to her, but she gives him a curt little nod and keeps going.

There are three folding tables pushed together with coffee and food on them—brownies, cookies, bars—but William is too nervous to eat. He picks out one of the special dog biscuits for Baron. It looks good, and a little sign says it's made of beef, bacon and flaxseed.

"Here you go, buddy," William says, handing it to him. "Two outta three ain't bad." Baron holds the biscuit in his mouth, as though he can't figure out what to do with it.

William visits with a few of his classmates, all the time trying to find Amy in the crowd. Finally, he sees her standing near the free-throw line at the far end of the gym, talking to a woman from the advanced class. He heads in that direction, and as soon as Amy is alone, William makes his move.

"Congratulations," he says, sidling up to her. "Most Improved—that's really something."

Amy is surprised but in control. "Thank you, William. And congratulations to you and Baron. I knew he'd win." Yoshi is very excited to see Baron, and Amy gives a little tug on the leash. "Settle down, buster." She turns to William. "It seems you're famous again. That was a nice thing that you did. A jammer ... wow! That makes much more sense than sunspots or ivy."

William nods. "It does."

"I recognized Gust Nelson's name. He's the man you met at graduation, right? His daughter was one of your students?"

"Leah, yes."

"Well ... did you get fired?"

William shakes his head. "No. I was certain I would, but then I was told I couldn't be terminated because it would generate too much negative publicity. Lothrup is very image-conscious since its credit rating was downgraded. The irony is that *I* didn't get fired, but Herb—"

"Were you ever planning to tell me any of this?"

"Yes," William says. "When it was over, which it finally is."

"Well, I'm glad things worked out for you, William." Amy turns to walk away, but he takes her arm.

"Please, Amy—don't go. There are some things—"

"I'm not sure I want to talk to you, William." She looks at his hand on her arm, and he quickly removes it.

"I just need a minute, Amy. Herb Gardner got fired early this morning. That's why your Q-and-A was cancelled—everyone was up all night trying to figure out what to do with him. That's what Sam Richter told me—he's the new chancellor."

Amy is struggling to keep up. "Gardner got fired? Why?"

"It's not important. What matters is—"

"Not important?" Amy looks at the floor. "With Gardner gone, my chances of getting the lab school job go way, way down."

"No, they don't. Please look at me—you have the job. The regents have ended the selection process, and the position will be offered to you. Sam told me that I could tell you. He said he'd meet with you next week."

Amy is in shock. "This isn't a joke? I really ... have the job?"

"Yes, you do. The regents needed to move on, and I guess you were ahead on points, so ... congratulations!"

"How can they just end the selection process like that? I don't ... I can't ..." Amy shakes her head in disbelief. After a few moments, she looks at William. "Is that why you came over here, to tell me I had the job?"

"That's part of the reason, but it's incidental to my purpose. I'm here to get you back."

Amy frowns. "I don't like your odds."

"I understand, but please give me a chance. On the day of the shooting—"

"Where is Marcia, by the way?"

William looks at his watch. "Probably somewhere over Colorado. She had a seven o'clock flight back to Phoenix tonight. Things ... didn't work out. On the day of the shooting—"

"Why not?"

"Because I didn't want them to. On the day—"

A man walks up to them, grabs William's hand and says, "The world would be a better place if there were more people like you in it. Thank you for stepping up."

"You're very kind," William says. When the man is gone, William asks Amy if they can go outside, and she agrees. They leave the armory and sit down on a bench halfway to the parking lot. The dogs, worn out from the evening's activities, collapse at their feet.

William tries for a fourth time. "On the day of the shooting, Jon had come to my office just before noon to take me to lunch, but we ended up getting trapped there. The gunfire from the first floor was steady, and we were sure we'd be killed if we stayed where we were, so we decided to take our chances on the rooftop observation deck, which very few people knew about. Jon went first, and he made it down the hall to the janitors' closet where the stairs to the roof are. Then it was my turn, and I was in the middle of the hallway when a student who had fled the first floor came running down the hall toward me. From the look on his face, I knew someone was after him, and not two seconds later, one of the shooters appeared on the second-floor landing and shot him. The kid was killed. He fell at my feet. And do you know what I did?"

Amy shakes her head.

"Nothing. I just … froze." William's voice cracks, and he tears up but keeps going. "Fear overtook me so completely that I couldn't so much as … wiggle my finger. The shooter was reloading, and Jon was yelling at me to run, but I couldn't do it. It was as though I was nailed to the floor." William is in trouble and wonders if he can get through the story.

So does Amy, who is close to tears herself. "Please stop. You don't have to tell me this."

"Yes, I do," William says. "If you think I haven't told you what happened at Dewhurst because I don't love you or because you don't matter enough to me, I need to fix that, and this may be my last chance to do it."

Amy wipes her eyes and tries to say something, but William goes on.

"So I'm in the middle of the hall, paralyzed with fear, and Jon has to come back and get me. But when he does, he gets shot under the left arm, and we both go down. He was alive for three or four seconds and died with his head in my lap. I was crying, begging him to stay with me, to open his eyes, but he was already gone. The guy at the end of the hall was still firing, and suddenly I felt like

... like I was on fire. For a second, I thought I'd been hit too, but a bullet had struck the drinking fountain, and cold water was spraying all over me. Everything changed after that. I don't remember getting up, but the next thing I knew, I was running toward the shooter in a blind rage, and it was all happening in slow motion. I could see the ejected casings, floating end-over-end through the air, all shiny in the sunlight. And the muzzle flashes were steady, but I couldn't hear them. The only sound was the bullets zipping past my head as I ran. When that stopped, I realized the guy's rifle had jammed. I could see him through the smoke, trying to clear the action, and I remember thinking, very calmly, that I might actually get to him before he could kill me. But then he dropped the rifle and ran back down the stairs, with me a half step behind him. He ran into the lecture hall, wheeled around and pulled a pistol from his belt, but I grabbed his arm before he could fire. What happened next was—"

"Please," Amy says. "I know what happened."

"No, you don't. It was the strangest thing ... The instant I put my hands on the guy, I knew I was stronger than he was, angrier than he was, and I knew I was going to kill him. I think he knew it too, because when I looked in his eyes, they were already dead. We were fighting over the gun when it went off under his chin. I didn't know this at the time, but when I came into the lecture hall and grabbed him, the second shooter, who was on the other side of the room, ran for his motorcycle and took off for the south side of the campus." William gazes up at the pink sky. "So that's the story, Amy—the story I've never told anyone. I got my son killed, and I've been living with it, not very successfully, for two years. I might have pulled it off if everyone hadn't insisted on turning me into a hero, but there was no talking them out of it. I was a lot of things that day, but *hero* isn't one of them."

Amy nods. "Thank you. I know that was hard."

"You're welcome," William says, wiping his eyes with the back of his hand. "Like I told you, I came here tonight to win you back, but I haven't even started. I wanted you to know about the day of the shooting, but that's just the first part of a three-part plan. Part two is to make you understand how much I love you. So let me begin by saying that I won't make it without you. Hell, I don't even *want* to make it without you. You're what makes me *me*—you're my secret ingredient."

Amy has given up fighting her tears by now, and they are running freely down her cheeks, taking her mascara with them. "William, I've never doubted that you loved me, but you really, *really* hurt me. Not only that, you made me feel like a fool. The problem was that you never stopped loving Marcia—and I *knew* that—but when she showed up here, it was clear that you loved her more than me."

William shakes his head. "Not more ... *different*. I'm so sorry, Amy. I know I don't deserve it, but I need a second chance more than I've ever needed anything, and I'm begging you to give me one. I wasn't seeing things clearly until a few days ago. I thought I wanted my old life back, but I was wrong. I'll settle for *any* life, as long as it's with you."

Amy is still crying but not as much. "May I ask what part three of your plan is?"

"Yes, and I'm glad you did." William pulls a document from his hip pocket, unfolds it and hands it to her. "This is part three."

Amy looks at the stapled pages, not quite understanding. *"Fifteen Canadian Vacations for You and Your Dog?"*

"Yes," William says. "It'll be much cooler up there, and I thought we could rent an RV and stay at some of the famous dog-friendly resorts in British Columbia."

"Okay."

"But if you'd prefer—and I like this idea too—we could go east, maybe rent a houseboat on Lac Seul, and then go on to Quebec and visit Montreal."

"Okay."

"Both of us have the summer off, so there's no reason we can't just—"

"William, I said okay. When you make the sale, stop selling."

He looks at her in amazement. "I'm not going to lose you?"

Amy is smiling and crying at the same time. "I love you, William, and I want us to be together. I don't care if it's in British Columbia or here in Chambliss."

"I love you too, Amy—so much it terrifies me." William pulls her close and they kiss, but this kiss is different, and they both feel it. This kiss is about tomorrow and the next day and the day after that. They hold each other a long time, and then William whispers in her ear, "I just have one question—and I really need to know— which part of my three-part plan won you over?"

Amy laughs, and with her lips brushing his cheek, she says. "I think it was a little bit of everything, but I especially like being your secret ingredient. That was good. Did you have a part four in case the first three parts didn't work?"

"No, but I was prepared to take hostages."

"William ... I just thought of something. Now that we've graduated, what will we do on Wednesday evenings? Everything is going to be so different."

"It already is, Amy ... We should go."

As they head for their cars, with Baron and Yoshi in the lead, the sun is beginning to set, and nighthawks are already swooping over the parking lot, hunting mosquitos near the lights. William is as happy as he's ever been, and he knows he has entered the quantum moment of his personal *ma*—a tiny interlude between love and redemption, between a painful past and a resplendent future. As he takes Amy's hand, the summer evening, which only moments before had been a formless jumble of sound, swells magically into music, and the notes are a million different colors that fall around him like rain. And then, quite suddenly and without even trying, William realizes he's also hearing the spaces between the notes, those beautiful little interstices filled with promise and brimming with profound, irrescindable grace.